Andy McDermott was born in Halifax, West Yorkshire and now lives in Bournemouth. As a journalist and magazine editor, amongst other titles he edited *DVD Review* and the iconoclastic film publication *Hotdog*. Andy is now a full-time writer. His debut novel, *The Hunt for Atlantis*, has been sold in twenty-two languages to date. His most recent novel, *The Covenant of Genesis*, has also been highly acclaimed. *The Cult of Osiris* is Andy's fifth novel.

By Andy McDermott and available from Headline

The Hunt for Atlantis
The Tomb of Hercules
The Secret of Excalibur
The Covenant of Genesis
The Cult of Osiris

ANDY McDERMOTT

THE CULT OF OSIRIS

headline

First published in 2009 by
HEADLINE PUBLISHING GROUP

First published in paperback in 2010 by
HEADLINE PUBLISHING GROUP

1

Cataloguing in Publication Data is available from the British Library.

ISBN 978 0 7553 5463 4

Typeset in Aldine 401BT by Avon DataSet Ltd,
Bidford-on-Avon, Warwickshire

Printed and bound in Great Britain by
Clays Ltd, St Ives plc

Headline's policy is to use papers that are natural, renewable and
recyclable products and made from wood grown in sustainable forests.
The logging and manufacturing processes are expected to conform to the
environmental regulations of the country of origin.

HEADLINE PUBLISHING GROUP
An Hachette UK Company
338 Euston Road
London NW1 3BH

www.headline.co.uk
www.hachette.co.uk

For my family and friends

Prologue

Giza, Egypt

The time-weathered face of the Great Sphinx regarded Macy Sharif impassively as she paced before its huge stone paws. She didn't give the ancient monument so much as a glance in return; in the two weeks she had been here, the Sphinx and the pyramids beyond had gone from awe-inspiring wonders to mere backdrops for a job that had fallen far short of her hopes. In the first week she had taken hundreds of digital photos and video clips, but now her camera was just a weight in one thigh pocket, untouched for days.

How had *Egypt*, of all places, turned into such a crushing disappointment? From an early age, she'd been entranced by her grandfather's stories of the land of his birth; tales of kings and queens and good and evil in a land of wonders, better than any fairy tale because they also happened to be true. It was an exotic, romantic world, as different from Miami's wealthy Key Biscayne as Macy could imagine, and even as a child she'd been determined that one day she would experience it for herself.

But the reality had not lived up to the dream.

She stopped pacing, checking the shelters beside the Sphinx's right paw. Still no sign of Berkeley.

A glance at her watch: approaching eight fifteen p.m. The expedition leader's daily videoconference with the International Heritage Agency in New York was due to start then, which gave her less time to catch him than she'd hoped. At eight thirty, the nightly sound and light show would begin, a gaudy display of coloured spotlights and lasers cast upon the pyramids and the Sphinx. Berkeley and the senior members of the archaeological team always departed soon after the opening chords boomed from the loudspeakers, leaving the juniors and the local hired hands with the scut work of securing and tidying the excavation.

Macy wasn't even sure if Berkeley considered her a junior team member, or a mere labourer. Okay, so she had another two years of study before she completed her degree, and maybe her grades didn't exactly put her at the top of the class, but she was still an archaeologist, kind of. Surely that granted her the right to do something more than make coffee and carry rubble?

She resumed her pacing, reflected light from the Sphinx's spotlit face casting an orange wash over her pale olive skin. Her surname might have been Egyptian, but her looks revealed her mother's Cuban heritage. She paused to straighten her ponytail, then at the sound of muffled voices hurriedly rounded the giant paw to see the team boss emerge from the dig. On their first meeting, she had initially thought Dr Logan Berkeley to be attractive, in an academic sort of way. Mid-thirties, a swoop of chestnut-brown hair across his forehead, refined features . . . then he'd opened his mouth and revealed himself as an arrogant jerk.

It was a description she could apply equally to the two men with him. TV producer Paul Metz was squat, barrel-shaped and bearded, with a lecherous gaze that to her distaste Macy often found aimed in her direction. She liked male attention, sure . . . but not from *all* males.

The other man was Egyptian. Dr Iabi Hamdi was a senior official with the Supreme Council of Antiquities, the government agency overseeing all Egypt's archaeological activities. The paunchy, thin-haired Hamdi was technically in charge of the dig, but seemed happy to let Berkeley do whatever he wanted, being more interested himself in getting his face in front of the TV cameras. Macy wouldn't be surprised if, at the moment the long-thought-mythical Hall of Records was finally revealed to the world, Hamdi popped up in front of the lens to boast of the crucial part he'd played in its discovery.

That broadcast was the current topic of discussion. 'So you're ab-so, pos-i-tively, one hundred per cent sure that you'll crack open the door right on time?' Metz asked, in a tone suggesting he thought otherwise.

'For the *last time*, we'll open the vault entrance exactly when I said,' Berkeley told him, his nasal, superior New England voice filled with frustration. 'I know what I'm doing. This isn't my first dig, you know.'

'It's the first one you'll have done live in front of fifty

million people, though. And the network won't be happy if their prime time special is two hours of you chipping at bricks. They wanna see something spectacular, and so does everyone else. People love this Egyptian crap.'

Torn between defending his heritage and keeping on good terms with the producer, Hamdi decided on the latter. 'Dr Berkeley, can you assure me that we will keep to the schedule?'

'Eight days from now,' Berkeley said through clenched teeth, 'we'll be showing the world something even more incredible than Atlantis, don't you worry.' He turned towards a nearby portable cabin with a satellite dish on its roof: the team's headquarters. 'And speaking of schedules, it's time I checked in.'

Maybe he wasn't in the most receptive mood, but Macy had to take the chance. 'Dr Berkeley, have you got a minute?'

'Only as long as it takes me to walk to the cabin,' he snapped, giving her a dismissive look. 'What is it?'

'It's about me,' said Macy as she kept pace. 'I was hoping I could get more involved with the actual archaeological work? I think I've proved that I'm up to the job.'

Berkeley stopped and turned to face the young woman. 'The *job*?' he said, letting out a sarcastic sigh. 'That says it all, doesn't it? Macy, archaeology is not a *job*. It's a *calling*, an *obsession*, something that drives your every waking thought. If all you want is a job, McDonald's and 7-Eleven are always hiring.'

'That's not what I meant—' Macy began, taken aback by his hostility.

'The reason you haven't been involved with the main

dig,' Berkeley interrupted, 'is precisely that: you haven't been *involved*. What, exactly, have you done to earn a place here? The other juniors all have multiple digs on their résumés, and they all graduated with the highest honours. You?' His mouth twisted with contempt. 'Charity fundraising connections. And good causes or not, I don't appreciate having unqualified undergraduates foisted on me because Renée Montavo at the UN owed your mom a favour. You ought to be damn grateful to be here at all. Now, go and finish the clean-up. I'm late for my videoconference with Professor Rothschild.' He strode into the cabin, slamming the door.

Macy stared after him in shock, then turned to find Hamdi and Metz watching her. Hamdi adjusted his little silk bow tie uncomfortably before going back into the shelter covering the main excavation, leaving her alone with Metz. 'Wanna career change?' he said, leering. 'I got the numbers of some modelling agencies.'

'Get bent!' She scowled and stormed off round the Sphinx. Ahead, one of the uniformed security contractors was heading up the ramp out of the excavated pit in which the Sphinx sat. Wanting to be alone, she turned and went into the ruined temple in front of the statue, dropping into the shadows within the broken walls.

She sat on a stone block, trying to hold her emotions in check. She was angry, but also upset. Egypt definitely hadn't matched up to her dreams – not so much wonder and romance as drudgery, smog, stomach bugs and hissing, pinching, cat-calling creeps accosting her on the streets. And now she'd just been completely insulted by her boss. *Asshole!*

The lighting changed, dropping the Temple of the Sphinx even deeper into darkness. The sound and light show was about to start; after two weeks, Macy practically knew the almost comically portentous narration by heart. Normally she would be packing away the team's gear during the display, but tonight . . .

'Screw that,' she muttered, lying back on the stone. Berkeley could pick up his own stupid tools.

Site security chief Sefu Gamal quickly traversed the walkway running between the Temple of the Sphinx and the smaller, marginally less ancient ruin to its northwest. At the walkway's end was a guarded gate. Since 2008, the once-open plain of the Giza plateau had been surrounded by over twelve miles of high steel and wire fence, partly to restrict the numbers of peddlers hawking trinkets and camel rides to visitors, and partly for security purposes: Egypt was unwilling to risk a repeat of the 1997 massacre of tourists at Luxor. Now, the plateau was observed by hundreds of security cameras and members of the Tourist Police, and all visitors were screened by metal detectors.

But there were more fences within, these not there to protect tourists from terrorists, but to protect Egypt's treasures from tourists. Access to the interiors of the pyramids was restricted to just a handful of visitors each day, while the Sphinx itself was almost entirely off-limits – and with a major archaeological excavation in progress, the Sphinx compound was even more closely guarded than usual. The sandstone pit containing the statue was bounded to the east by its temple, to the west and south by cliffs where it had been dug out of the desert, and to the north by a modern stone wall supporting a road across the plain. Only those with passes were normally allowed access.

But tonight there would be an exception.

Gamal reached the gate and waited as the *son et lumière* display began. A couple of hundred tourists sat in ranks of chairs beyond the Temple of the Sphinx, watching the spectacle. He would have preferred the meeting to take place much later, after the last display had finished and the tourists – and the IHA team – had gone, but the man he was expecting was impatient . . . and quick to anger.

Approaching headlights: a black Mercedes SUV. This must be his visitor – since the erection of the boundary fence, traffic through the site was restricted. The first person out was unfamiliar, a rangy, long-haired Caucasian in a jacket of what looked like snakeskin, his straggly goatee doing little to conceal the almost equally scaly roughness of his face. He rounded the vehicle to open the door for another man, like Gamal an Egyptian.

Gamal stepped through the gate to greet him. 'Mr Shaban,' he said. 'A great honour to meet you again.'

Sebak Shaban had no time to waste on pleasantries. 'The dig's behind schedule.'

'Dr Berkeley said—'

'Not *that* dig.'

Gamal concealed his discomfort as Shaban turned to look straight at him. An old burn scar ran across his right cheek from what remained of his ear to his top lip, the skin rippled and faintly glossy. The scarring had pulled down the outer corner of his lower eyelid, exposing glistening pink tissue within. From his previous encounters, the security chief was convinced that Shaban was well aware of the psychological impact of his injury upon others, favouring them with the unblemished, fairly handsome left side of his face until he wanted to express his disapproval in graphic form with a simple turn of the head. 'There was a slight delay – *very* slight,' he said quickly. 'Part of the ceiling collapsed. We've already shored it up.'

'Show me,' ordered Shaban, walking to the gate.

'Of course. Come with me.' Gamal glanced questioningly at the other man, who followed them through.

'My bodyguard,' said Shaban. 'And friend. Mr Diamondback.'

'Diamondback?' Gamal echoed uncertainly.

'Bobby Diamondback,' said the bodyguard, his accent a languid yet menacing American drawl. 'It's a Cherokee Indian name. Got a problem with that?'

'No, not at all,' Gamal replied, thinking he looked more like a cowboy than an Indian. He led them along the walkway. 'This way, please.'

Mocking the sound and light show's bombastic narration had slightly lifted Macy out of her black sulk when she spotted Gamal, from her position in the shadows only his upper body visible above the top of the temple's northern wall.

There were two other men with him, one an ugly guy with a greasy mullet and a snakeskin jacket, and the other someone she recognised. Mr Sharman, Shaban, something like that? She had seen the scar-faced man briefly at the start of the dig; he was connected with the religious organisation co-funding it with the IHA. Presumably he was here to meet Berkeley.

The trio made their way to the corner of the smaller temple, where Gamal paused and looked towards the Sphinx – almost furtively, Macy thought. The cold stare of the man in the snakeskin jacket swept over her as he surveyed the area, then unexpectedly flicked back. An involuntary shudder ran through her. She had no idea why – she had every right to be there, and wasn't doing anything wrong – but by the time the rational part of her mind told the rest of her body to relax, he had looked away again.

To Macy's surprise, rather than descending the ramp towards the Sphinx, Gamal hopped across the gap between it and the upper level of the Sphinx compound, disappearing from her view. The other men followed.

Weird. The upper temple was over a thousand years younger than its larger neighbour, a product of the New Kingdom from around 1400 BC, and while it was in relatively better condition than the Temple of the Sphinx it was much less important historically. Why was Gamal giving a private tour? In the dark, at that?

Standing, she saw the tops of the men's heads as they walked towards the temple entrance – and continued past it. Now she was *really* curious. There was nothing else up there. Where were they going?

Macy climbed out of the temple, seeing the trio rounding the ruin above. Some childhood Nancy Drew instinct kicked in, the urge to find out what they were doing rising, but she resisted it – until shouting came from the Sphinx. Berkeley, yelling at an Egyptian labourer who had just dropped a box.

Screw it, she thought. If Berkeley was still acting like a jerk, she didn't want to be anywhere near him. Instead, she ascended the ramp and jumped across to the upper temple.

Green laser lines flashed above her, projecting hieroglyphics on the pyramids as the narrator sang the praises of Osiris, the immortal god-king of Egyptian legend. 'Yeah, yeah, heard it all before,' Macy whispered as she peered round the temple wall.

Part of the plateau's north end had been cordoned off by orange plastic netting where repairs were under way on the high wall. A couple of small cabins and a tent-like structure stood amongst stacks of bricks and piles of rubble. It was such a mundane sight that while Macy had seen it every day as she entered the Sphinx compound, she had never actually *noticed* it before. Certainly nobody ever seemed to do any actual work there.

There was someone there now, though. As well as the men at the gate, other guards patrolled the compound to make sure no tourists tried to get up close and personal with the Sphinx. But the man waiting for Gamal and the others wasn't patrolling. He was guarding the construction site.

The lighting changed, more lasers and spotlights slashing the black sky. The guard watched the display, only turning away when the visitors reached him. Brief words were exchanged, then he let them through the netting.

Gamal reached the tent and pulled aside a flap, revealing lights within. The other two ducked through, and with another furtive backwards glance Gamal followed. Macy jerked back behind the temple wall, wondering if he'd seen her, before realising how dumb she was being. So what if he had?

She peeked out again. The guard was strolling along the

netting perimeter, looking bored. Through the gaps around the tent flap, she glimpsed activity within.

The movement stopped.

Macy kept watching, but it didn't resume. What were they doing in there? Unless all three men were squashed together at one end, the tent didn't seem big enough for them to keep out of sight. If anything, it now looked empty, but she couldn't see how that was possible. It was right against the high wall.

She noticed something else, though: a faint plume of smoke. No, not smoke – *fumes*, chugging up from the end of a hose. But there wasn't a generator in sight.

So where were the fumes coming from?

Interest now well and truly piqued, she rounded the corner, keeping low behind a pile of dirt. But she quickly realised her stealthiness was pointless; to reach the construction site, she would have to cross a wide, open space, and unless the guard was blind he couldn't miss her.

But in a few moments, maybe he *would* be blind . . .

She knew what came next in the sound and light show, having heard it every night. The narrator was about to begin his tale of Khufu, builder of the Great Pyramid – and the lights would briefly drop to black before illuminating Khufu's monument at full brightness.

Macy closed her eyes, waited . . .

The lights went out.

She opened her eyes again and raced for the tent. Only a few seconds before the Great Pyramid lit up like a beacon—

Dramatic music thundered from the loudspeakers, the Great Pyramid exploding into view to the northwest. Macy reached the gap in the netting and skidded to a halt behind one of the stacks of bricks. She glanced round it and saw the guard staring at the floodlit structure.

She let out a breath, feeling something she hadn't felt since first arriving in Egypt: excitement. No, that had been more like *anticipation*, but this was a genuine, almost child-like thrill. This was fun!

Holding in a nervous giggle, she looked at the tent. Now that she was closer, she could hear the chug of a generator – but only faintly, and with an odd echo. She checked again that the guard wasn't looking in her direction, then crept to the tent.

Nobody was inside.

'The *hell*?' Macy wondered aloud, slipping in. One end was taken up by a makeshift cubicle of cheap particle board. Since it was little more than three feet wide, she doubted Gamal and the others were huddled within.

But she lost interest in it when she saw what was at the tent's other end.

A trestle table had construction blueprints spread out across it; she recognised the topmost as a plan of the Sphinx compound. What had caught her attention, though, wasn't on the table, but hanging on the tent wall above it. Large colour photographs, blow-ups of ancient papyrus scrolls. The same scrolls that had brought her here in the first place.

The Hall of Records, a repository of ancient Egyptian knowledge beneath the Sphinx that was reputedly only surpassed by the Library of Alexandria, had long been considered nothing more than a myth. But a privately funded archaeological dig in Gaza had discovered papyrus pages that described not only the Hall itself, but also how to get into it – through a passage that had once descended between the Sphinx's paws. When the pages were scientifically confirmed to be over four thousand years old, the Hall suddenly became one of the hottest topics in archaeology, and the Egyptian government granted the International Heritage Agency's request to conduct the dig that would confirm whether or not what was said on the Scrolls was true.

The problem, Macy knew, was that the IHA had only been given three scrolls.

Yet here was a fourth.

She moved closer, silently mouthing the words as she translated the text. The ancient language had been taught to her by her grandfather along with Egyptian history and mythology, his hobby eventually influencing her choice of degree. The new scroll said more about the Hall of Records than the IHA had seen: not just its position, but its contents. Something about a map chamber, a zodiac, that revealed the location of . . .

'The Pyramid of Osiris?' Macy whispered in disbelief. That was nothing but another of her grandfather's myths, surely? Osiris was a legend pre-dating even the First Dynasty of almost five thousand years ago, and legends didn't have big-ass tombs built for them, only pharaohs.

But that was what the papyrus said. The Pyramid of Osiris, the tomb of the god-king. No suggestion that it was a myth; the text seemed as factually descriptive as it was about the Hall of Records. 'Whoa,' she said as she realised what that meant. If the Pyramid of Osiris was real, then so was the man buried inside it. Not a legendary god, but a flesh and blood ruler, until now lost in time. If his tomb could be found, it would be one of the greatest discoveries in history . . .

She looked at the plans on the table. The position of the east–west entrance tunnel to the Hall of Records and the IHA excavation were both clearly marked – as was another, longer tunnel from the north.

It crossed under what was now the modern road and ran, she realised, directly beneath the tent in which she was standing.

Macy turned to the wooden cubicle. The panel facing her was hinged, a roughly cut hole acting as a handle. She eased it open.

Now she knew where the three men had gone. *Down*. A ladder descended into a shaft, dim lights revealing the bottom over twenty feet below. The hose expelling the generator's exhaust fumes ran up one corner, the machine now clearly audible.

As were voices.

Getting closer.

Excitement fled Macy, replaced by fear. Someone was running their own secret dig, trying to beat the IHA team into the Hall of Records. Trying to find the Pyramid of Osiris for themselves.

Which meant that if she was caught in here . . . she was in trouble.

What should she do? Tell someone – Berkeley or Hamdi? But Gamal was obviously in on it, and they would believe him over her. She needed proof . . .

Weight in her thigh pocket. The camera.

She pulled it out and switched it on. The wait for the lens

to extend and the screen to light up had never seemed so long.

A rattling sound from the shaft. Someone climbing the ladder.

Throat tight with rising panic, Macy took a picture of the four papyrus pages, then tipped the camera down to capture the blueprint. *Click*—

'What the *fuck*?' The shout came from below, the accent American. The guy with the snakeskin jacket. He had seen the flash.

Another shout. The guard outside. Macy heard his footsteps thudding towards the tent. The clattering of the ladder was louder, faster, as the man hurried up it.

She ran—

The guard threw open the tent flap – just as Macy burst through, shoving him aside and sprinting for the temple. She was through the plastic netting before he regained his balance.

'Hey!' she shouted, hoping somebody from the IHA dig would hear her, but her voice was drowned out by the light show's narration. Behind, Shaban screamed orders to catch her.

Fright spurred her on. She rounded the ruin, the shadowed maze of the Temple of the Sphinx spread out below, ominously lit in shards of red and green. Someone was on the walkway—

'Dr Hamdi!' Macy cried. 'Dr Hamdi, help!'

Hamdi stopped, looking bewildered as she leapt over the gap to land in front of him. 'What is it, miss – Macy, isn't it?'

'Back there!' she gasped. 'They're digging, they're trying to rob the Hall of Records!'

'What? What are you talking about?'

Macy looked back as the guard ran round the side of the upper temple, slithering to an uncertain halt when he saw Hamdi. 'That guy with the scar, Shaban, he's in charge! He's got a fourth scroll – I took a picture!' She thumbed a button to bring up the image. 'Look!'

Hamdi's expression changed from confusion to shock. 'I see. Come with me.' He took her by the arm . . .

And gripped, painfully tightly.

'Hey, what—' Macy said, trying to pull free. He squeezed harder. 'Let go!'

He ignored her. The guy in the snakeskin jacket ran into view. 'Bring her up here!' he yelled.

Hamdi pulled Macy towards the gap. She thrashed at his face, but he deflected her blows with his free hand. The guard ran towards them—

She fired the camera in Hamdi's face. He flinched, dazzled by the flash – and Macy smashed the camera's hard edge against the bridge of his nose. Another strike to his forehead, and she wrenched herself from his grip.

The guard leapt across the gap, blocking the way to the Sphinx. Instead, she ran along the walkway – and saw the two guards from the compound gate rushing at her.

They were all in on it!

She changed direction, jumping on to the Temple of the Sphinx's northern wall and running along it. The ancient, weathered stone was uneven beneath her feet.

'Get after her!' the American shouted. The first guard followed her on to the wall. The two men ahead also changed direction, intending to leap over the ditch separating the temple from the compound's upper level and tackle her.

The wall was over twelve feet high, too far to jump down . . .

Instead she flung herself off the wall at an angle – just barely reaching the top of a ruined stone pillar five feet below, then springing off that, legs flailing, into the darkness beneath. Pain exploded in both feet as she hit the ground and fell, her phone and some loose coins flying from a pocket and skittering away.

The guard jumped off the wall after her—

The lighting changed, the red highlights on the lower block suddenly vanishing. The man's outstretched foot missed its top. His other shin cracked into the stone's edge, sending him spinning to the unyielding ground. He let out a keening wail as he clutched his injured leg.

Macy wasn't feeling much better, gasping in pain as she stood. She was not far from a passage leading to one of the temple's original entrances. Ankles throbbing, she limped into the deeper darkness behind the high eastern wall.

She turned the first corner, looking back. A guard was on the north wall, but his attention was on his wounded comrade. He hadn't seen her. Round the second turn—

And crashing to a stop against metal bars.

Shit! She'd known there was a gate to keep tourists out of the temple, but it was taller than she'd thought, too high for her to climb. Beyond it she saw the seated audience, but they were looking up at the brilliantly lit Sphinx, not the unimposing ruin in front of it, and wouldn't hear any shouts for help over the soundtrack's bombastic crescendo.

Macy could hear other shouts, though. Her pursuers were in the temple.

And she was in a dead end.

The shouts got closer.

The inner wall facing the gate was somewhat lower than the others – and in the light shining through the bars she could pick out footholds. She scrambled up. All the past hours of gym practice for the cheerleading squad no longer seemed such a chore.

She looked over the top of the wall – to see the guy in the snakeskin jacket only ten feet away on the other side, other men spreading out across the temple floor. One ran into the entrance to the passage.

Trapped—

She pulled herself up and lay flat along the wall's top, holding her breath as her heart pounded. The running man rounded the corner, reached the gate, looked through it. Nobody fleeing the temple, just tourists gawping at the display.

'Does anyone see her?' called the American, shining a tiny but bright LED flashlight between the ruined pillars. The shouted replies were all negative.

Hamdi and Shaban hurried to him. 'She can't have got out,' said Hamdi, one hand clutched to his nose. 'The entrances on this side are all blocked.'

'Who is she?' Shaban demanded angrily.

'One of the IHA team. Macy Sharif. She's just a student.'

'Student or not, she could ruin the entire plan if she gets out of here,' said Shaban.

'We gotta find her,' the American added. 'Fast.'

'What are you going to do with her, Mr Diamondback?' asked Hamdi.

'Whaddya think?' There was a metallic sound that froze Macy's blood. A gun's hammer being cocked.

'You're going to . . .' Hamdi tailed off, shocked.

'I'm sure as hell not spendin' the next twenty years in an Egyptian jail 'cause of some li'l whore of a *student*.'

'Dr Hamdi,' said Shaban, 'if she gets away, you and Gamal will have to handle Berkeley. Bobby, we need to send people to watch her hotel, the airport, anyone she might go to for help. She's American?' Hamdi nodded. 'Use our contacts there to find out where she lives – and where her family lives. Send people to watch their homes, tap their phones. We *have* to silence her.'

'Count on it,' said Diamondback. A second click – another gun.

Macy trembled, a terrified nausea churning within her. They were going to *kill* her! Every instinct told her to run, but she didn't dare move.

One of the guards called out from the temple's southern end, reporting that the other entrance passage was empty. Diamondback shone his light across the courtyard. 'What about those stones there, by the wall? Could she climb 'em?' He walked towards them, the heels of his cowboy boots clip-clopping on the stone flags.

'Go with him,' said Shaban. For a moment, Macy thought he was talking to Hamdi, before realising it was one of the guards.

The one who had come into the passage after her.

There was nobody between her and the east wall—

Adrenalin overcame her fear. She sprang up and ran along the wall, jumping up to a higher block.

'Hey!'

Diamondback had seen her.

Macy gasped in fright, expecting a gunshot – but it didn't

come. The sound and light show was ending, and a shot would be heard by hundreds of people. She climbed another block, finding herself at the edge of the east wall. The ground was over twenty feet below.

Diamondback scaled the wall on which she'd been hiding as effortlessly as a lizard. The guard ran back into the passage. Macy turned, crouched – and dropped. Fingers clutching the weathered stone, she slithered down the wall, toes rasping for purchase.

She let go—

More pain as she hit the ground and fell on her back, but she was too scared to let it stop her. She rolled and took off across the dusty expanse. The audience was dispersing, milling towards the nearby exit in the outer fence.

Behind her, the guard climbed the metal gate as Diamondback reached the highest part of the wall, eyes scanning for her, locking on – then losing her again as she shoved into the crowd. Someone hollered in protest, but Macy ignored him and ducked low, weaving between the clumps of tourists. If she could reach the exit, the edge of Cairo's urban sprawl was just yards beyond the fence . . .

The guard was over the gate. Diamondback landed beside him. More men ran along the walkway above the temple. Macy moved faster, knocking people aside in her desperation to reach the exit. There were two white-uniformed members of the Tourist Police at the gate, but they hadn't yet been alerted to the chase. *Come on, move—*

Diamondback and the guard were running. The guard shouted to the policemen, who looked round. Some of the tourists did too, stopping to see the cause of the commotion.

A gap opened up. Macy took it, rushing through the gate before either cop could react. By the time one started after her, she was already halfway to the dark alley between the nearest buildings. She raced into the shadows. A junction; she went right, deeper into the maze. Clattering footsteps echoed behind her. Left, right again. *Don't be a dead end, don't—*

A low, narrow gap in one wall just before an intersection. On some wild instinct she squeezed through it. She found herself in a small yard behind a house, faint light coming from a window above. The only other exit was a door into the house itself.

She pressed against the wall, eyes wide in fear as the footsteps drew closer – then passed, slowing at the intersection. More men ran up. *Clip-clop*. Diamondback. She held her breath. If one of them noticed the little gap . . .

They ran again, splitting up to follow each of the alleyways. The footsteps quickly faded into the night.

Macy slumped, panting.

She stayed in the yard for almost twenty minutes, waiting until she was absolutely certain nobody was nearby before creeping back through the hole. The alley was empty, silent. Getting her bearings, she headed deeper into the sprawl.

After ten nerve-racking minutes, she reached a small square. Muffled music came from a café on the far side, but all she cared about was the battered yellow box of a payphone on a pole nearby. Warily watching the street, she fumbled for her remaining change, then made a call.

'Macy? Is that you?' Berkeley sounded even angrier than before.

'Yes,' she said, voice low. 'They're going to rob the Hall of Records! There's another tunnel, they're digging—'

He wasn't listening. 'Macy, come back here and turn yourself in to the police *right now*.'

'What – what do you mean, turn myself in? I haven't—'

'Dr Hamdi has agreed not to press charges for assault, but only if you give yourself up and return the piece you took immediately.'

'What piece?' Macy protested, confused. 'I didn't take anything!'

'Macy, Dr Hamdi and Mr Gamal both saw you chip a piece off the Sphinx! Do you have any idea how serious that is? People have been sentenced to ten years in jail for less! Running away has just made it worse, but if you come back now, I'll do what I can to placate the authorities—'

'Look, *listen* to me!' she cried. 'Hamdi's part of it, and so's Gamal! Go and look for yourself, there's—'

'Macy!' barked Berkeley. 'Get back to the dig, *now*, and give yourself up. If you don't, there's nothing I can do to help you. Just—'

Macy slammed down the receiver, fear and panic back in full force. What the hell was she going to do? Shaban had sent people to stake out the hotel. She couldn't even collect her belongings. All she had were the clothes she was wearing and whatever she had in her pockets.

Which wasn't much. Her camera, a small wad of Egyptian pounds, about a hundred US dollars. At least she still had her passport and credit cards; there was no way she would have left them unattended in her hotel room.

She weighed up her options. Whether she turned herself in or the police caught her, Hamdi and no doubt a parade of others would be ready to testify against her. And if Shaban's people caught her . . .

The mere thought set her heart thudding again. They wanted her *dead*. And even if she got out of Egypt, they would be waiting for her to go home, watching her parents. She couldn't risk getting them involved.

Then there was Shaban's plan itself. If he got out with whatever he planned to steal before the IHA team opened the Hall of Records, nobody would even know they had done it, since Berkeley would be seen by millions as the first person to enter the chamber in thousands of years. She had to warn someone. But if Berkeley wouldn't listen, she had to find someone else – someone more likely to believe her, *and* convince others to take action.

Macy stepped away from the phone, unconsciously adjusting her ponytail . . . and that triggered a thought.

She reached back into her pocket. There was something else with her passport: folded pages from a magazine. When she opened them, the face of an attractive woman, red hair in a ponytail much like Macy's, smiled up at her.

Dr Nina Wilde. The discoverer of Atlantis, and more. Macy's inspiration, the woman who had given her the determination to get here in the first place.

And a woman whose claims had been utterly disbelieved . . . before being proved spectacularly right.

She regarded the picture. It was a long shot; Dr Wilde was no longer with the IHA after some controversy the previous year. Macy had been disappointed at not getting the chance to meet her. But surely she still had enough influence to help . . .

If she could reach her. As far as she knew, Dr Wilde was

in New York. And Macy was still less than a quarter of a mile from the Sphinx.

One step at a time, she decided, setting off for central Cairo.

1

New York City:

Three Days Later

Nina Wilde struggled to wakefulness, fighting simultaneously through the smothering sheets and the remnants of a cloying alcoholic fug to look at the bedside clock. It was well after ten a.m. 'Crap,' she mumbled, about to chastise herself for oversleeping . . . before remembering that she had nothing to get up for.

She almost pulled the sheets back up in the hope of returning to sleep, but even a brief glimpse of the small and ugly bedroom was enough to make her want to get out of it. Not that the rest of the apartment was much better, but it represented a least-worst option.

She put on a vest and a pair of sweatpants, ran her fingers

through her unkempt hair, then padded into the other room. 'Eddie?' she called, yawning. 'You here?'

No reply. Her husband was out, though he had left a note on the small counter separating the kitchen area from the rest of the cramped living room. As usual, it was as terse as a military communiqué. *Gone to work. Will call later. Probably out until late. Love Eddie x. PS We need more milk.*

'Great,' she sighed, picking up the small pile of mail beside the note. Credit card bill, probably large. Other credit card bill, almost certainly even larger. Junk, junk—

The last envelope had the name of a university printed in one corner.

Despite herself, she felt a flutter of hope, and hurriedly tore it open. Maybe *this* one was the way out of their miserable life of the past several months . . .

It wasn't. She only needed to see the words *We regret* to know it was another rejection. The academic world had turned its back on her. Once someone was labelled a crank, it was a tag that was almost impossible to remove – even if that person had been right all along.

Nina put down the letter, then slumped on the creaking couch and sighed again. A smear campaign by a powerful enemy had not only cost her her job, but also left her regarded as a nut, on the same level as those who claimed to have found Noah's Ark or El Dorado or Bigfoot. Her previous world-shaking finds – Atlantis, the tombs of Hercules and King Arthur – suddenly counted for nothing, academia as prone as any other field to having only a short-term memory: *what have you done for us lately?*

So now she was out of a job, out of prospects . . . and perilously close to being out of money. All she had was Eddie.

Except she didn't, because the demands of his work meant he was almost never there.

A baby started crying in one of the neighbouring apartments, the thin walls doing little to muffle the noise. 'God damn it,' she muttered, putting her hands over her face.

Eddie Chase emerged from the East Side brownstone building, glancing up and down the street before descending the steps.

'I saw that,' said a woman's voice behind him.

Eddie looked round at her. 'Saw what?'

'You, checking there wasn't anybody outside who might know you.' Amy Martin came down the steps, her dark bob bouncing, and squeezed the balding Englishman's waist. 'You're so cute.'

'It's not exactly something I want getting back to Nina, is it?' he told the younger woman. 'I'll tell her myself, when the timing's right. And I don't want anyone else to find out, either.'

Amy grinned. 'You enjoy it, though. Don't deny it.' She went to the kerb, looking for a cab. 'So, you wanna do this again tomorrow?'

'Yeah, if I can make it,' Eddie told her. 'Depends if Grant Thorn needs me or not.'

She grinned again, shaking her head. 'I still can't believe you get to hang out with a movie star.'

'I'm not exactly "hanging out" with him. I'm his bodyguard, not his best mate. And he's, well . . . kind of a prat.'

'But one with a Lamborghini, right? That's pretty cool.'

'Bit of a waste, though. He never drives it faster than ten miles an hour 'cause he wants everyone to see him inside it.'

'You guarding his body today?' A cab approached; Amy waved it down.

'Yeah, picking him up in a bit. He wants to buy a suit for some charity bash this evening, so I've got to keep an eye on him. 'Cause Fifth Avenue's such a dangerous place.'

The cab stopped as Eddie's phone rang. He looked at the screen: Nina. 'Well, have fun with your Hollywood buddies!' Amy said as she got in.

'I'll try,' he replied, answering the phone. 'Hi.'

'Hi,' said Nina. 'Where are you?' He had become all too familiar with her leaden tone over the past months, but this morning it had a little extra sprinkle of gloom.

'I'm . . . just at the gym with Grant Thorn.'

A pause. 'Oh. When will you be able to come home?'

'See you tomorrow!' Amy called as the cab pulled away.

He gave her a slightly annoyed wave. 'Not for ages, sorry. I'm with him all day.'

A second disappointed 'Oh'. Then: 'Who was that?'

He shot the departing taxi a guilty look. 'Someone in a cab.'

'I thought you were at a gym?'

'I'm waiting outside. What's wrong?'

She sighed. 'Nothing. It doesn't matter.'

'It matters to me. Look, I can call Charlie, see if someone can cover for me.'

'No, it's . . . it's okay. I mean, ha, we need the money, right?' The laugh came across as more desperate than amused.

'You sure? If you want, I can—'

'It's okay, Eddie. It's okay.' It sounded anything but.

His phone chirped, telling him someone else was calling. A glance at the screen told him it was his client. 'Sorry, but I've got to go. Oh, did you get my note about the milk?'

'Yeah, I did. I'll see you when you get back. I love you.'

'Love you too,' he said as she disconnected. Great. Now he felt even worse about lying to her.

He switched to the incoming call. 'Hello?'

'Hey, the Chase-ster!' came the laid-back voice of Grant Thorn. 'Where you been, man? Your phone was busy.'

'Yeah, my wife called.'

'The old ball and chain, huh? Just kidding, man. Not saying she's old at all. Hey, why don't I take you two out to dinner sometime? How about that?'

'Sounds like fun,' Eddie answered non-committally, secure in the knowledge that all memory of the offer would have vanished from the actor's mind by the time they met. 'You still want me to meet you at your apartment?'

'Yeah. There's this chick here, give me twenty minutes to get rid of her. Okay, two chicks. Make that thirty minutes. Oh, and can you pick me up a carton of OJ? Got a serious case of dry-mouth.'

'I'm your bodyguard, not your butler, Mr Thorn,' Eddie reminded him. His job might be to look after his clients, but that didn't include wiping their arses for them, and he always made sure they knew it. 'Maybe you could get one of your chicks to go out for it.'

'Oh, dude! I don't want them to come *back*! I mean, they're hot and all, but once the box is opened there's a no-return policy, right? Look, I got five hundred bucks in my wallet here. It's yours if you bring me a carton of OJ. Like a bonus. Huh?'

'I'll see what I can do,' Eddie told him before ending the call. Unlike the dinner, he was definitely going to remind Grant about *that* offer.

Nina sat morosely at the living room table, nursing a black coffee. Her laptop was open, awaiting her command, but so far she hadn't even checked her email.

She took an experimental sip from her mug. Without milk, the coffee had been too hot to drink immediately; now it had cooled, it was too bitter. She grimaced, wondering if she could drum up the energy to go to the store for milk. The more she considered it, the less likely it seemed.

Her phone rang, startling her. She picked it up. 'Hello?'

'Hello, Nina.' A familiar voice – Professor Roger Hogarth, an associate from her university days. They had been in occasional contact over the past months, but mostly by email.

'Roger, hi! What can I do for you?'

'Always business first with you, isn't it?' His chiding was delivered with amusement. 'I'll get to that in a minute. But how are you?'

'I'm . . . fine,' she said flatly.

'And the new apartment? Liking it any more than when you moved in?'

'The less said the better, I think.'

A small chuckle. 'I see. Don't worry, things will improve, I'm sure. Probably when you least expect it. And on the subject of unexpected things . . . first, you remember that I was trying to meet Maureen to complain about that ridiculous sideshow she's got going on at the Sphinx?'

'Yes?' said Nina, feeling a stab of anger at the mere mention of the name. She'd had plenty of reasons to dislike Professor Maureen Rothschild even before the woman became one of the principal architects of her fall from grace.

'Well, she finally agreed to see me. Tomorrow, in fact.'

'Really? That's great.'

'Took a lot of persuading, as you'd imagine. But unfortunately, the second unexpected thing is . . . I can't go.'

'Why not?'

'Slipped on the stairs, and now I'm sitting here with my foot bandaged up like a mummy.'

'Are you all right?' she asked, concerned.

'Just a sprain, thank God. The perils of old age are ridiculous, though – I did the pole vault and high jump when I was young, never so much as stubbed a toe. Now I drop six inches and I'm out of action for a week!' He tutted.

'So what are you going to do about Maureen?'

'Well, that's why I'm calling. I was hoping you might go in my place.'

'Are you serious?' Nina said, surprised. 'She's the person who *fired* me!'

'Okay, it could be . . . awkward. But what she's doing is a travesty of archaeology. It seems that every time I turn on the TV there's another commercial for this circus.'

'Yeah, I've seen them,' Nina muttered. The promos for the live opening of the Hall of Records had been omnipresent for the last couple of weeks, irritating her more with each repeat.

'It's shameless commercialism, not science. And if there's nothing in there, it'll make the entire archaeological profession look like utter fools by association. I doubt it'll make any difference, but somebody at least has to say these things to Maureen.'

'And you want *me* to do it? Sorry, Roger. Maureen Rothschild is one of the last people I want to see.'

'I understand,' Hogarth said after a pause. 'I thought you probably wouldn't, but I had to try. Someone of your standing would have more chance of getting the point across.'

Nina tried to hold in her bitterness. 'My standing's not very high with anyone right now.'

'Don't underestimate yourself, Nina.' This time, the chiding was more pointed. 'One setback doesn't end a career. I've had more than a few myself.'

'Not on my scale, though.'

'Oh, well,' sighed Hogarth, accepting defeat, 'we'll just have to pray this whole affair doesn't turn into a disaster.'

'Let's hope. Get well soon, Roger.'

'Thank you. And I'm sure things will get better for you too.'

She said goodbye, then hung up, blowing out a glum breath. The coffee had gone cold, but she was now even less enthusiastic about leaving the apartment than before.

True to his word, Grant Thorn really did present Eddie with five hundred dollars in exchange for a carton of juice. By the time he arrived at the Upper West Side apartment, both 'chicks' had gone, though either one had forgotten to retrieve her hot pink thong from Grant's lounge or the actor had a fetish he would prefer the tabloids didn't discover.

Whichever was the case, neither was Eddie's concern: his job was only to keep Grant from *physical* harm. After he and Nina had been fired from the IHA, he had called upon his extensive list of contacts from both his military career as a member of Britain's elite Special Air Service and his subsequent work as a freelance bodyguard and trouble-shooter to find new work. His reluctance to spend any length of time away from his new wife had limited his options, but eventually a friend had put him in contact with a man called Charlie Brooks, who ran a 'personal protection agency' for New York's wealthy and famous. The assignments meant unpredictable hours, but they at least paid enough – just – for Eddie to support himself and Nina.

Even if certain economies had been necessary.

Eddie suspected he would hear about the largest of them yet again when he got home, but for now his mind was on the job. Grant had just spent more on an Italian suit than Eddie used to earn in a month at the IHA, and the shopping expedition was far from over.

'Okay, that's my outfit for the mayor's event tonight,' said the actor, checking his reflection in a mirror and making a millimetric adjustment to his gelled hair before heading for the exit. Eddie opened the door for him, then smoothly moved past to check Fifth Avenue for potential trouble. No crazed fans or irate movie critics awaited them. 'So next, let's see . . . Harmann's.'

'Not your usual style,' Eddie remarked. Though every bit as far out of his price range as the store they had just left, he knew that the tailor's suits were considerably more conservative.

'I need something formal for tomorrow, dude,' Grant

explained. 'It's not every day I meet a religious leader.'

Eddie raised an eyebrow; nothing he had seen suggested his charge was the remotest bit spiritual. 'Didn't know the Pope was in town.'

'It's not the Pope, dude. Better than that! It's my man, Osir!'

'Who?'

'Khalid Osir! You know, the Osirian Temple?'

'You mean that cult?'

For the first time since Eddie had met him, Grant sounded offended. 'Dude, it's not a cult! It's a real religion, changed my life. You want to stay young for ever? They can help you do it.' He raised both hands to his tanned, blandly handsome face. 'I'm twenty-nine, right? But I haven't aged a day since I was twenty-*seven*. What more proof do you need, man?'

'Guess you're right,' said Eddie, straight-faced. Grant seemed mollified. 'So, this . . . religion. Expensive, is it?'

'No, no! It's not like some con job. You can donate whatever you like. And it's up to you if you want to buy their stuff.'

'Stuff?'

'You know, the stuff that tells you how to follow the path to eternal life. Books, DVDs, diet supplements, bottles of genuine Egyptian sand, these awesome little pyramid dealies that energise the air in a room . . .'

'Got you,' Eddie said, his suspicions about the cult's priorities confirmed.

'I'm going to a meeting tomorrow – got a personal VIP invite. Short notice, but no way was I going to miss it. Actually getting to meet Osir, it's like – like when an ordinary person meets me. Or Jesus! It'll be so cool.'

'Speaking of ordinary people . . .' said Eddie, suppressing his sarcasm as he spotted three wealthy-looking young women reacting with squeals of delight at the sight of the movie star. He moved in front of Grant to intercept them.

'I think I can handle this, dude,' Grant said, grinning. Eddie moved aside, but still kept a close watch as they clattered over on their Jimmy Choos. 'Hi, ladies! How are you?'

One woman seemed on the verge of hyperventilating, fanning herself with a small Gucci bag as the other two bombarded Grant with praise for his most recent movie – more specifically, the scene where he had worn nothing but a pair of Speedos. 'Can we get a picture?' one asked, digging an expensive phone from her handbag.

'Sure thing,' said Grant. 'Dude, can you do the honours?' Eddie took the phone and snapped a couple of photos as the trio crowded round the actor. They seemed thrilled with the results, thanking Grant before leaving, already forwarding the pictures to everyone in their address books.

The star watched them go, nodding approvingly as he checked them out. 'Damn. I shoulda got their numbers, see if they wanted to go clubbing—'

'Hey!' someone said. They both turned to see two men, one a beefy gel-haired twenty-something in a polo shirt with a popped collar, the other, smaller and nerdier, lurking behind him. 'You're Grant Thorn, right?'

Eddie knew what was about to happen purely from the bigger man's sneering smirk: his client was about to be insulted. The guy intended to impress his friend and provide them both with a boastful bar-room story for years to come. He moved forward as Grant answered. 'Yeah?'

'You *suck*, man.' The smirk widened. 'You really fucking suck. That last movie of yours, *Nitrous*? What a piece of shit. I watched a pirate download and I still wanted a refund.' Grant's expression was frozen in a clenched fake smile. 'And I'll tell you something else,' said the man, pleased to have provoked him. He raised a hand to jab Grant's chest.

Eddie stepped in. 'Put the hand down, mate,' he said in a calm but cold voice.

Polo-shirt was about to jab Eddie instead, but his finger stopped short under the Englishman's intimidating stare. 'What, you going to give me trouble?' he said.

'Only if you want it.'

Uncertainty crossed the young man's face, and he stepped back, his friend retreating with him. 'Whoa, big man, hiding behind a bodyguard,' he called as they walked away. 'You still suck, Thorn!'

'Fag!' added his friend, though not very loudly.

Eddie kept watching until they were a safe distance from his client, then turned to Grant. 'You want *their* numbers?'

Grant shook his head, rattled. 'Huh. Some people. No respect. Thanks, man.'

'It's what I do, Mr Thorn,' said Eddie, shrugging.

'Right.' They set off again. 'Course, I coulda handled him.' Eddie made a faintly dismissive noise. 'No, dude, seriously! Before I started shooting *Gale Force*, I went on a training course – like action movie school? A whole week of learning how to shoot guns and drive fast and do Krav Maga fighting. Pretty awesome.'

'A whole week?' said Eddie. 'I'm impressed.'

Grant was oblivious of his sarcasm. 'You gotta be good to

stay at the top.' They continued down Fifth Avenue, the actor attracting attention all the way to Harmann's. To Eddie's relief, it was only the star-struck kind.

'Ay up,' said Eddie as he entered the apartment. He raised his voice to counter the noise from the television. 'How's things?'

The sight of a three-quarters empty bottle of wine gave him his answer. 'Been better,' Nina replied.

'You're drinking too much,' he chided as he hung up his jacket. 'Why's the telly on so loud?'

'Because it's better than listening to crying babies or the Lockhorns next door arguing again or that monkey-faced asshole downstairs playing music at full blast. I hate this apartment.' She curled up, pressing her chin between her knees. 'I hate this building. I hate this neighbourhood. I hate this whole goddamn *borough*!' Blissville, Queens, was wedged between the Long Island Expressway, a cemetery and a miserable grey river lined with run-down industrial buildings, and could hardly have been more inappropriately named if it had tried.

Eddie found the remote and lowered the volume. 'Ah, come on, Queens isn't that bad. Maybe it's not Manhattan, but at least it's still New York.' He tried for some levity. 'Could have been worse; we might have had to move to New Jersey.'

It didn't work. 'It's not funny, Eddie,' Nina growled. 'My life completely, utterly *sucks*.' She looked over to the letter on the counter. 'I got another rejection this morning. To add to the five hundred and seventeen I already had. My career's over; Dalton and those other bastards took care of that. They turned me into a joke, Eddie, a fucking *joke*! Whenever I go out it's like people are looking at me and thinking, "Hey, it's that crazy bitch who thinks she found the Garden of Eden." Nobody takes me seriously.'

'Who gives a fuck what other people think?' Eddie hooted. 'You don't know 'em, you're never going to see them again, why should you care? Some wanker on Fifth Avenue gave Grant lip today, but he didn't let it ruin his day. Or his life.'

'There's a slight difference between him and me, Eddie,' said Nina. 'He's a millionaire movie star. I'm . . . I'm nothing.'

'Don't,' said Eddie firmly. 'Do *not* start all that again. You are *not* nothing, and you bloody well know it. And we took care of President Dalton. *He's* the fucking joke now. He had to resign, he can't do anything else to us.'

'He did enough.' A long sigh, the wet cloak of ennui settling over her once more. 'I'm never going to work in archaeology again.'

'Yeah, you will.'

'I *won't*, Eddie.'

'Jesus Christ, it's me who's supposed to be the bloody pessimist.' He opened the fridge, finding an empty space where he'd hoped to see a carton. 'Did you get any milk?'

'No, I forgot.'

'What?' He banged the door shut. 'How could you forget? I left you a note.'

'I didn't go out.'

'You didn't—' He threw up his hands. 'There's a shop round the corner, but you couldn't even be arsed to go that far because you were moping about all day watching TV?'

'I wasn't moping,' said Nina, a spike of anger poking through the cloak. 'You think I *enjoy* all this?'

'I know I sure as hell don't.'

She didn't like his tone. 'Meaning what?'

'Meaning I don't like seeing my wife being depressed!'

'What am I supposed to do about it?' she demanded, standing. 'Everything I do's been taken away from me!' She jabbed a hand at the TV as the face of the Great Sphinx appeared: yet another promo for the live opening. 'And then there's sensationalist bullshit like this rubbing my nose in it. It's not proper archaeology, it's a stunt! And I'm not the only person who thinks that – Roger Hogarth phoned. He was going to go to the UN to give Maureen Rothschild a piece of his mind, but couldn't make it, so he asked me to go instead.'

'So what did you say?'

'I said no, obviously.'

'What?' It was far from the first time Eddie had heard her grievances about the Egyptian dig, and he'd had enough of them. 'For fuck's sake, Nina! If it pisses you off so much, why don't you *do* something about it?'

'Like what?'

'Like telling Maureen Rothschild that she's full of shit! Don't just sit around feeling sorry for yourself and complaining to me every time that bloody advert comes on. Complain to *her*! You've got the chance, so go to the UN and tell that old bag exactly what you think of the whole bloody thing!'

'All right,' Nina snapped, wanting him to shut up and get off her back, 'I will! I'll call Roger and tell him I've changed my mind.'

'Good! Finally!' He dropped on to the couch, the springs creaking. After several seconds of silence, he looked up at her. 'Sorry. I didn't mean to get mad. I just hate seeing you like this.'

'I hate *being* like this,' she replied, sitting beside him. 'It's just . . .'

'I know.' He put an arm round her. 'But you know what? We're a pretty good team. We'll sort this out together. Somehow.'

'It'd be easier if you were here more. As if things aren't bad enough, I hardly ever get to spend an evening with my husband! It's just me and re-runs of *CSI: Miami*.' She gestured at the super-saturated scene on the TV screen. 'I see so little of you, I'm starting to feel, ah . . . *stirrings* for David Caruso.'

'What? Okay, I really *do* need to spend more time at home!' He huffed and stroked her neck. 'Look, I'll talk to Charlie. Maybe he's got some clients who like quiet nights in.'

'They won't have much use for a bodyguard, will they? And we need the money.'

'Bollocks to the money,' Eddie said firmly. 'You're more important. I've got another full day with Grant Thorn tomorrow, but I'll figure something out.'

'So it's just gonna be me and Caruso again? I'll need to buy some more batteries.'

Eddie's face twisted in mock disgust. 'Christ, your jokes are getting as gross as mine.'

'Well, they say married couples start to act more like each other, don't they?' She managed a sort-of smile, then glanced towards the bedroom door. 'Y'know, there's something else married couples are supposed to do. It's been a few days . . .'

'I'd love to,' he said, rubbing his eyes, 'but I'm really, really knackered. And if I've got to keep an eye on Grant until Christ knows when tomorrow, I'll need a decent night's sleep.'

'Oh.' She tried to conceal her disappointment. 'Well, maybe in the morning, hmm? Rev me up before I go to the UN.'

'I've . . . got to work.' He made a show of yawning to cover up his evasiveness. 'Grant wants to buy a suit for some religious thing tomorrow.'

'Considering how much he parties, I wouldn't have taken him for the religious type.'

'It's not a real religion, it's some daft cult thing. The Osirian Temple, it's called.'

Nina was surprised by the coincidence. 'Yeah? Huh. They're co-funding the dig at the Sphinx.'

'Must be doing all right for themselves, then. No shortage of idiots with money.'

'Some things never change.'

Eddie smiled, then got up. 'I want a shower before we go to bed. Are you okay?'

She slumped back on the couch. 'For now? Yeah. Long term? Not so sure.'

'Something'll come up,' he assured her. 'I'm sure of it.'

'*How* are you sure?'

He had no answer to that.

2

Nina gazed up at the dark glass slab of the United Nations' Secretariat Building with a glum sense of trepidation. It was over seven months since she had last set foot in the UN; seven months since she had been acrimoniously 'suspended' – more accurately, 'fired' – by the new director of the International Heritage Agency, and in truth a large part of her didn't want to return to the scene of her humiliation.

She touched the pendant hanging from her neck for luck, then, steeling herself, headed inside.

The elevator ride seemed to take longer than she remembered, the elevator itself somehow more confined, airless. Things were no better when she emerged and was buzzed through the security door. Even though she told herself that the reception area couldn't possibly have changed in seven months, there were enough subtle differences to render it disconcertingly unfamiliar.

One thing had not changed, though – the figure behind the reception desk. 'Dr Wilde!' cried Lola Gianetti, jumping up to greet her. 'Or is it Dr Chase now?'

'It's still Wilde,' Nina told the big-haired blonde as they embraced. 'I wanted to keep my professional name. Although it might have made it easier for me to find a new job if I'd changed it.'

'So how's Eddie?' Lola gestured at the ring on Nina's left hand. 'How was the wedding?'

'Spur of the moment. Which Eddie's grandmother still hasn't forgiven us for. She wanted a trip to New York.' Nina smiled, then her expression became more serious. 'How are you?'

'Recovered. More or less.' Lola glanced down at her abdomen, where she had been stabbed – in the very room where they were standing – seven months before.

'It must have been hard coming back to work.'

'It was . . . weird. For a while.' Lola shrugged, a little too casually. 'But I love the job, so . . .' She hesitated, glancing towards the offices, and lowered her voice. 'To be honest, I don't love it so much any more.'

'Rothschild?' Nina asked.

Lola nodded. 'You were a much better boss. Now it's all about who can suck up to her the most. And money.'

'That's part of why I'm here. Roger Hogarth couldn't make it, so he asked me to come in his place. And Eddie nagged me into it as well.'

'I see.' Lola returned to her computer. 'Professor Rothschild's in a videoconference with Dr Berkeley, but they don't usually take more than fifteen minutes. Her meeting with Professor Hogarth was scheduled for afterwards, so when she comes out I'll see if she'll talk to you.'

'Or even if she'll give me the time of day,' said Nina. The

thought of Rothschild was causing her long-simmering anger to rise again. She fought it back. The chances of her actually changing anything were slim to none, but now she was here she was determined to say her piece, and needed a clear mind to do so.

'I'll do what I can to convince her.' Lola glanced at a tray beside the monitor. 'Oh, that reminds me – there's a message for you.'

'For *me*?'

'Yes, from one of the interns . . .' She flicked through a small pile of papers. 'Here – Macy Sharif. She phoned yesterday, asking for your number. I didn't give it to her, of course, but I said I'd pass on the message. I tried calling your home number, actually, but it'd been disconnected.'

'We moved,' Nina said stiffly as Lola handed her the paper. 'What did she want?'

'She didn't say. It's funny, actually – people here have been wanting to talk to *her*. She was on Dr Berkeley's dig, but she left suddenly. Nobody's told me why, but I think she might have gotten into trouble with the Egyptian police. Hard to imagine – she seemed nice, but who knows?'

'I guess the IHA's hiring policies have gone downhill since I left,' said Nina with dark humour. She gave the paper a cursory glance – a brief transcript of the message in Lola's florid handwriting, and a phone number – then folded it.

'So where are you living now?' asked Lola.

Nina's expression soured. 'Blissville. It was about the only place we could afford that was still in the city and wasn't an actual war zone.'

'Oh,' said Lola sympathetically. 'Well, it's, er . . . convenient for the expressway, I guess.'

'Yeah. And the cemetery.'

They shared a smile, then Lola's look became slightly hesitant. 'Dr Wilde?'

'Nina, please. What is it?'

'I hope you don't think this is kinda presumptuous, but . . . I'm getting the feeling you're not having a great time right now.'

'Whatever gave you that idea?' They both smiled again.

'The thing is,' said Lola, 'I booked tomorrow afternoon off because I was supposed to be seeing an art gallery with a friend, and then we were going to have dinner. Only now he can't make it, so . . . I wondered if you might want to come?'

Nina almost turned down the offer out of hand before the part of her that had been stirred back into action by Eddie's prodding reminded her that all she had on the agenda otherwise was another evening with David Caruso. 'Where's the gallery?' she asked instead.

'Soho. And the restaurant's in Little Italy. It's a nice place, a friend of my cousin runs it.'

'I didn't know you were into art.'

Lola blushed faintly. 'Sculpture. It's a hobby; I make little birds and flowers and things out of metal and wire. I'm not very good at it, but I thought the gallery might give me some ideas.'

Nina considered the offer, then decided: *what the hell*. It might take her mind off her gloom, if only for a few hours. 'Okay. Yeah, why not?'

'Great! Let me give you the addresses.'

She looked for a notepad, but Nina handed her the sheet of paper with Macy's message. 'Here. Save a tree.'

'Thanks.' Lola wrote down the details, then returned the page. 'Three o'clock?'

'Two, if you want. The less time I spend in the apartment the better!'

A door up the corridor opened. Nina turned to see Maureen Rothschild emerge, and freeze as she saw Nina in the reception area. After a moment the professor walked towards her with a pinched, utterly insincere smile. 'Nina.'

Nina gave the older woman a response in kind. 'Maureen.'

'I didn't expect to see you here again. What do you want?'

'To talk to you, actually.'

Rothschild's eyes narrowed behind her glasses. 'I have a very busy schedule, Nina. In fact, I'm about to meet Roger Hogarth. I'm sure you remember him.'

'Oh, I do. As a matter of fact, he asked me to represent him. He's indisposed.'

'Oh.' Rothschild's face revealed no sympathy. 'Nothing serious, I hope.'

'No, but he'll be off his feet for a few days. Which is why he asked me to speak with you in his place.'

Nina could tell that Rothschild wanted nothing more than to give a flat refusal, but Hogarth was well regarded – and connected – in the academic community. Turning away his locum out of hand might be considered an insult . . . or a sign that she was afraid to defend her position.

'I suppose,' she said finally, with deep reluctance, 'I could spare a few minutes. As a favour to Roger.' She started back up the corridor, Nina giving Lola a brief smile before following her to her office.

Which had once been Nina's office. The view across Manhattan was instantly familiar, but everything else had changed. Nina's feeling of alienation returned full force.

Rothschild took a seat behind the large desk, gesturing impatiently for Nina to sit facing her. 'Well? What did Roger want to talk to me about?'

'About this, actually.' On the desk was a glossy brochure, promoting what it proclaimed as *The Live Television Event of the Decade!* The image on the cover was the Great Sphinx of Giza. Nina picked it up. 'It seems like every time I turn on the TV, I see a commercial for this. I'm just curious about when the IHA turned into a shill for prime-time television and wack-job cults.'

'The IHA is not a shill for *anyone*, Nina,' Rothschild said, voice oozing with condescension. 'Getting co-funding from organisations like the Osirian Temple reduces our operating costs, and our share of the advertising revenue will help fund numerous other projects, as well as boosting the IHA's profile worldwide. It's a win-win situation, and good business, pure and simple.'

'Funny, I didn't realise the IHA *was* a business.' She opened the brochure, seeing a picture of Logan Berkeley posing in a heroic stance with the pyramids behind him. 'And you put Logan in charge?'

'Logan was the best candidate for the job.'

'Logan's a self-promoting egotist. What about Kal Ahmet, or William Schofield? They've both got far more experience.'

'They were on the shortlist, if you must know,' said Rothschild coldly. 'But Logan was my personal choice. His presentation impressed me the most.'

You mean he kissed your ass the most, thought Nina, but she kept it to herself. 'And was Logan okay with totally perverting the principles of archaeology? Was that part of his presentation?'

'What do you mean?'

'I mean rushing everything and throwing out any notion of diligent scientific practice so the network can get big ratings during sweeps week.'

'You are the *last* person to lecture anyone about "diligent scientific practice", Nina,' snapped Rothschild. 'Your utter disregard for anything even approaching proper procedure is one of the main reasons why you were fired, if you remember!'

'This isn't about me,' said Nina, the simmering rising towards a boil. She waved the brochure. 'It's about the IHA selling out. It was established to *protect* these kinds of finds, not exploit them!'

'Ah, *now* I see why you're here,' Rothschild said, a sneering smile spreading on her thin lips. 'Some last desperate attempt at self-justification, is that it? You want to beat your fists against the temple walls of your oppressors so you can convince yourself that you're right and everyone else is wrong?' She stood, hands spread on the desk as she leaned forward. 'Get over yourself! Contrary to what you may think, you were *not* the indispensable heart of the IHA – the organisation runs perfectly well without you. In fact, it's *better* without you. Do you know how many employees have died since you left? None!'

Nina drew in a sharp breath. 'That was low, Maureen,' she said, tight-mouthed.

For a moment, Rothschild's expression suggested that even she thought she had gone too far. But the moment quickly passed. 'You've said what you came here to say, Nina. I think it would be best for everyone if you left now. And it would probably also be for the best if you didn't come back.'

Nina rose, clenching her fists to stop Rothschild from seeing that her hands were trembling with anger. 'What you're doing in Egypt is an embarrassment to the archaeological profession, and you know it.'

'We both know who the *real* embarrassment to the profession is,' Rothschild countered. Nina gave her a hateful look, threw open the door and left the office.

There was a park north of the United Nations; Nina strode round it, her anger barely lessened even twenty minutes later. In some perverse way, part of her actually wanted to keep stoking it – once it was gone, all she would be left with was misery, deeper than ever.

But she knew she couldn't keep it burning indefinitely.

Taking a long, slow breath, she took out her phone and called Eddie. To her surprise, his cell was switched off, rather than on voicemail. Odd. Eddie never switched off his phone.

Even that brief distraction took the edge off her anger, depression roiling back in like a wall of fog. Not in the mood to do anything but go home, she headed west along 42nd Street to the subway station at Grand Central. About halfway there, her phone rang. Thinking it was Eddie, she snapped it up, only to see an unfamiliar local number on the screen. She composed herself, then answered.

'Is that Nina?' said a Jersey-accented voice.

'Yes?'

'It's Charlie, Charlie Brooks.' Eddie's boss.

'Oh, hi,' she said. 'How are you?'

'Fine, thanks. Listen, I've been trying to get a hold of Eddie, but his phone's off. Is he with you? I need to talk to him about a new client.'

'No. I've been trying to call him myself.'

'Really? Huh. Not like him to be out of contact when he's not working.'

'Isn't he with Grant Thorn?'

'Nah, not till later. Well, if you talk to him in the next hour or so tell him I called, else I'll pass it on to one of my other guys.'

'I'll tell him.' She disconnected. If Eddie wasn't working, then what was he doing, and why was his phone switched off?

More to the point . . . why had he told her he would be with Grant Thorn all day?

In her current frame of mind, she couldn't help constructing scenarios. None of them were good. Was he doing something he didn't want her to know about? The past months had not been ideal for their relationship. What if he was seeing someone else?

She shook her head, refusing to countenance it. Eddie wouldn't do that to her.

Would he?

She reached Grand Central and rode the subway back to Queens, taking the gloomy walk south to Blissville. Along the way, her phone chimed – not a call, but a text message. Eddie. Terse as ever.

Sorry I missed call, in middle of something. Talk later. How did UN go? Eddie x

'Super fine,' Nina sighed.

The black Cadillac limousine cruised through midtown Manhattan. 'Almost there, Mr Thorn,' said the driver.

'Good, cool,' said Grant. He was wearing the formal suit he had bought the day before. He was also on edge, a far cry from his usual cocky self as he fingered his collar.

'You okay?' Eddie asked.

'Yeah, yeah, fine. Just, you know, this is a big thing. Even bigger than winning the People's Choice award.'

Eddie kept his opinions on that to himself as they arrived at their destination. The Osirian Temple's New York 'church' was actually an unimposing East Midtown building with a neon sign over its entrance, an Egyptian-style eye superimposed over a triangle, which he assumed was meant to be a pyramid. But while the building was nothing noteworthy, the crowd outside resembled the crush surrounding the red carpet on Oscar night.

'Lot of people,' he said. Several men in tailored dark green blazers cleared a space so the Cadillac could pull over.

'Fast-growing religion, man. I mean, who doesn't want to live for ever?'

'Depends who you're living with.' The limo stopped. 'You want me to wait with the car?'

'No, come in with me, check it out. Maybe you'll even want to join up.'

To his credit, Eddie just about managed to hold in a

sarcastic comment as he got out of the limo and opened the door for Grant. The crowd responded enthusiastically as the star emerged.

'Hi, everyone, hi! Great to see you,' said Grant, turning on the megawatt smile that had helped take him to ten million dollars a movie. The men in green acted as a human cordon as he headed for the entrance, shaking hands and posing for photos. As the limo pulled away, Eddie's experienced eyes swept the crowd for any hint of threat, but everyone seemed to be behaving. All the same, he subtly increased his pace, shepherding Grant towards the door.

It soon turned out, though, that the movie star wasn't the afternoon's top attraction. More men emerged from the building, a green-blazered phalanx driving through the crowd like a plough to clear a path across the sidewalk. Someone cried 'It's Osir!' – and as one, the throng turned to watch a longer limo arrive.

If Grant had been greeted with enthusiasm, this was nearer to hysteria. To Eddie's amusement, a hand that had been outstretched to Grant was snatched away just as he reached for it, leaving the actor with a brief expression of startled hurt. The minders flanked the limo's door.

Khalid Osir climbed out.

Even at first glance, Eddie could tell Osir had that special quality possessed only by a lucky few – a natural, powerful charisma, evident in the easy confidence with which he moved and the irrepressible sparkle in his eyes. Eddie guessed him to be in his mid-forties, though he somehow got the feeling that Osir was older than he appeared. And while Grant was a movie star, a man of the moment who had made it with the help of good looks, modest talent and a great agent, Osir looked more like a movie *legend*, someone who would outshine younger rivals generation after generation. He glanced at his client. Grant's face was a mix of awe and a hint of jealousy.

'Hello, my friends!' the cult leader boomed over the cheering. 'I'm so happy to see so many of you here today. May the light of the sun-god Ra bless you all!'

'May the spirit of Osiris protect and strengthen you!' people chanted in reply. Even Grant joined in, though he accidentally transposed 'protect' and 'strengthen'. Osir beamed and made his way to the building, talking to his followers along the way. Eddie couldn't help noticing that attractive women got the lion's share of his attention.

Another man had meanwhile stepped out of the limo, practically unnoticed by the crowd – though his scowl immediately stood out amongst the smiles, and the third man who followed him set off warning bells at the back of Eddie's mind. It was obvious from his features that the second man was closely related to Osir – a brother? – but it was equally plain that his sibling had been more favourably blessed both by the genetic lottery and by life itself, his own harder, thinner face scarred by a major burn across his right cheek. His wiry, greasy-haired companion in the snakeskin jacket, meanwhile, looked like a redneck, but from his alert stance and attitude Eddie could instantly tell he was ex-military.

Osir reached the door to find Grant waiting for him. 'Ah, Mr Thorn!' he said, clasping the actor's hand and shaking it firmly. Cameras flashed in the crowd; the two men instinctively turned to face them with their widest smiles. 'It's so good to finally meet you.'

'Same here, Mr Osir,' said Grant.

'Call me Khalid, please. I feel like I know you already from your movies.'

Grant grinned, pleased. 'Really? Cool! I've tried to watch all of yours, but they're kind of hard to get on Netflix. I saw *Osiris and Set*, though. You were awesome in that.'

Osir waved a hand modestly. 'You must visit the Osirian Temple's headquarters in Switzerland, and I will show you the others. Come whenever you like; my door is always open. But acting is behind me now – I have a new calling. And I am so very pleased that you,' he turned to address the crowd, 'that *all* of you have chosen to follow me on this incredible journey. There are already tens of thousands of us, all around the world, and our numbers will grow as more discover that only through the teachings of Osiris can true immortality be found. We shall all live for ever!' He raised his hands, the crowd cheering again.

His brother impatiently gave an order, and the minders pushed the crowd back. One opened the door, and with another wave Osir went inside with his companions, the man in snakeskin giving Eddie a disdainful look.

Grant went to the door, but hesitated when he realised Eddie wasn't following. 'What's up?'

'It's not really my kind of thing. You go in; I'll wait for you.'

'No, come on, man. You listen to what he's got to say – it'll change your life. You'll be able to reverse your ageing, look like you're in your thirties again.'

'I *am* in my thirties,' Eddie told him frostily.

'Really? Whoa. No offence, dude. You just look kinda . . .

battered.' Realising his words weren't thawing his bodyguard, Grant changed his mind. 'Okay, you . . . wait for me. Yeah.'

'Have fun, Mr Thorn,' Eddie said as Grant went inside. He shook his head, grinning faintly. His employer was living proof that some people would believe anything.

Still, at least the Osirian Temple appeared to be the harmless kind of crank cult.

Several hours later, Eddie returned home. 'So how did it go at the UN?' he asked as he entered the apartment – and saw that today's wine bottle was fully empty. 'Oh.'

'It was absolutely goddamn horrible,' said Nina, scowling. She had only felt up to calling Hogarth a few hours earlier, and the act of relating the argument had made her angry all over again. 'I didn't accomplish anything at all, and Maureen was an utter bitch who ended up making me feel *this* big.' She waved an unsteady hand at him, holding her thumb and forefinger less than an inch apart. 'I shouldn't have gone. I *wouldn't* have gone if you hadn't forced me.'

'I didn't force you,' Eddie objected.

'Yeah, you did! You might as well have carried me there in a sack!'

He shook his head. 'Jesus! Rothschild's the one who pissed you off, so why're you having a go at me?'

'Because you're *here*!' she cried. 'For a change.'

'Oh, for Christ's sake,' Eddie sighed. 'Not this again. I was working! I offered to try to work something out with Charlie yesterday, and you told me not to.'

The mention of Charlie reminded Nina of something.

'Where were you this morning? I tried calling you, but you didn't answer your phone.'

'Probably 'cause I was *working*. I'm not supposed to take personal calls when I'm on the clock. You know that.'

'But you weren't when I called you, though. Charlie phoned me – he couldn't get hold of you and asked if I knew where you were.'

He hesitated, uneasy. 'What time was this?'

'After I left the UN. About half past one.'

'Oh, right. Yeah, I was with Grant Thorn.'

'That's funny,' said Nina, amusement far from her face. 'Charlie told me you weren't working until later.'

The sound of wheels spinning in his head was almost audible. 'That's 'cause . . . I was doing Grant a favour. Off the books.'

'What *sort* of favour?'

'He wanted me to pick him up some orange juice.' Seeing her dubious look, he went on: 'Seriously! Lazy sod couldn't be bothered to walk a block to get it himself.'

'I thought you had a policy about not doing that sort of thing. Y'know, the whole bodyguard-not-butler principle.'

'Well, when he offers to pay me an extra five hundred bucks it's more like a guideline.'

'He paid you *five hundred dollars* to get orange juice?'

He retrieved yesterday's wad of notes from his jacket and tossed it on to the table. 'See? Bloke really does have more money than sense.'

Nina regarded the money suspiciously. She knew Eddie more than well enough to be aware that maintaining a poker face was not one of his talents, and he seemed to be inwardly congratulating himself on his quick thinking.

Maybe Grant Thorn really had been absurdly generous, but there was more to the story. 'So what were you doing for the rest of the day? It doesn't take that long to buy orange juice.'

'You didn't see the queue,' he said, with a half-laugh that faded under Nina's gaze. 'Yeah, I was doing something else too. I . . . met up with a friend.'

Her gaze intensified. 'A female friend?'

'A *cop* friend.'

To his concealed relief, Nina didn't point out that it was possible to be both female and a cop. Instead, she said, 'I didn't know you had any cop friends.'

'Sorry, *I* didn't know I was supposed to give you a complete list of all my mates everywhere in the world. I've got loads of friends.'

She wasn't sure if he'd meant to put emphasis on the *I've* part of his reply, but in her current mood she wasn't going to let it pass without comment. 'Unlike me, you mean?'

'Where did that bloody come from? I never said you don't have any friends.'

'Well, that's because I *do* have 'em. I've got . . .' She considered it, face falling over the seconds it took her to finish the sentence. 'There's Piper.'

'Who moved to San Francisco.'

'Matt! Matt Trulli's a friend.'

'Who you haven't spoken to for months.'

'He's still a friend! And there's Lola!' Nina added with a triumphant jab of her hand. 'Lola's a friend. And I'm having dinner with her tomorrow, actually. So, yeah, I've got friends.'

'I never said you didn't! Why're you getting all defensive about it?'

'Because . . . because that's something else that's been getting me down,' she admitted. 'Almost all of my friends are archaeologists or historians. And ever since I got screwed over by the media, they've been treating me like I'm radioactive.'

'Then maybe they weren't really friends to begin with,' Eddie told her. 'So why'd you instantly assume I was seeing a woman friend this morning? What, you – ha! – think I'm having an affair?'

'No, not really, just . . .' She sagged. 'It would have been the perfect capper to a really horrible day. The thought came to me, and it just wouldn't go away. You're out at all hours, and I . . . well, I haven't exactly been the best company recently. And we haven't, y'know, had sex for a while.'

'Five days is "a while"?'

'We only just got married – we're supposed to be having sex every five *minutes*!' She flopped back on the couch. 'God. After all the horrible crap that happened to us, I thought that at least our getting married would be one perfect thing that would see us through it. But . . .'

'You're not having second thoughts, are you?' Eddie asked, concerned.

'No, God, no. It's just . . . it hasn't been what I thought it would. What I *hoped* it would.'

'Marriage's like life, I suppose. Things always change, and you've got to adapt with 'em. There's a military saying – dunno who said it, Napoleon or someone – "No plan survives contact with the enemy." '

'It was Field Marshal Helmuth von Moltke,' corrected Nina, earning herself a double-take from her husband. 'But if marriage was the plan, who's the enemy?'

'Everyone and everything outside this room.'

'I hate this room.'

'Okay, off this couch.'

'Not a big fan of the couch, either.' They both managed half-hearted laughs.

'Well, look,' said Eddie, 'I'm not seeing anyone else, okay? I know what it's like to be on the other end of that from when I was married to Sophia. So don't worry about it. Or anything else, either. Have a nice girlie day out with Lola tomorrow, and take your mind off everything.' He gestured at the wad of money. 'If Grant asks me to pick up any more orange juice for him, maybe we'll even be able to afford a holiday.'

'That'd be nice. Somewhere exotic.'

'Egypt?' The TV was showing another promo for the opening of the Sphinx, the live event now only three days away.

Nina huffed. 'Yeah, right. I think it'd be a tad out of our price range.'

He kissed her cheek. 'Let's see what tomorrow brings, eh?'

3

Despite waking with another hangover, Nina felt better than she had for quite some time. Merely committing herself to doing something outside her depressed rut had acted like a spark; after Eddie left to babysit another client around town, she decided to follow his example and cross the river to spend time in her native Manhattan before meeting Lola.

She found the memo Lola had given her and double-checked the gallery's address. The message from Macy Sharif was written above it, forgotten until now. She didn't remember the name; the intern must have started at the IHA after she left.

Remembering what Lola had said about Macy's getting into trouble with the Egyptian police, she almost dismissed the note from her mind, but on a whim, prompted by her new-found urge to action, decided to follow up on it instead. It would take her the better part of fifteen minutes to walk to the nearest subway station, so making the call would at least pass the time. She left the apartment, dialling the number as she descended the narrow stairs.

'Hello?' A man's voice.

'Hi,' said Nina, thumb already hovering over the button to end the call. 'May I speak to Macy Sharif?'

Hesitation, then wariness: 'Who's calling?'

'My name's Nina Wilde. She left a message asking me to call.'

The ambient noise from the other end of the line became muffled as the man put his hand over the phone. There was a short exchange with someone else, then a cry of excitement. Nina raised her eyebrows. This Macy was *very* keen to speak to her.

A clunk and rattle as the phone was snatched from its owner. 'Hello? Hello! Dr Wilde, are you there? Is that you?' The woman's accent was upscale southern with a vaguely Hispanic lilt.

'Yeah, hi,' Nina replied as she reached the sidewalk, rounding a ridiculously large red pickup truck parked outside her building before crossing the street. 'Is this Macy?'

'Yes, it is, yeah! Dr Wilde, thanks for calling me back, it's such an honour to be talking to you. Really! I'm a big fan of yours.'

A *fan*? Nina wasn't quite sure how to take that. This wasn't some practical joke, was it? 'Uh . . . thanks. You left a message at the IHA that you wanted to talk to me?'

'Yes. Look, this'll probably sound weird and maybe a bit stalker-ish, but I really need to see you in person. I've got something I need to show you. You still live in New York, don't you?'

Nina eyed the streets around her. 'More or less.'

'I'm staying with a friend in the East Village. Is there any chance you could meet me?'

'I'm actually heading into Manhattan right now,' Nina volunteered without thinking, before realising that she'd just blown a chance to turn Macy down politely. 'But I don't know if I'll have the time today.'

'I can meet you whenever, wherever – I just need ten minutes of your time.'

'For what?'

'It's about Dr Berkeley's dig in Egypt, at the Sphinx.'

The mention of Berkeley brought back the previous day's humiliating meeting with Rothschild, which didn't do Macy's request any favours. 'That dig's nothing to do with me,' Nina told her. 'If you want to talk to somebody about it, you'd be better off finding someone at the IHA.'

'No, I really need to show this to *you*. In person. You'll understand why once you've seen it. Please, Dr Wilde? Just ten minutes. Five minutes, even. It's really important.'

The pleading in her voice seemed completely genuine. 'Look,' Nina finally said, 'I'm meeting a friend, and we're going to dinner later. But I might be able to see you after that.' The East Village was her old neighbourhood, not too far from where she and Lola would be having dinner. She tried to think of somewhere fairly close to a subway station, so she could return home afterwards with the minimum of fuss. 'There's a coffee shop called 52 Perk-Up on 7th Street, near Second Avenue. If I've got time, I'll call you and we can meet there. I can't promise anything, though.'

'That'd be awesome,' said Macy with evident relief. 'Thank you, Dr Wilde. Thanks for talking to me.'

'No problem. Bye.' Nina disconnected, already

wondering if she could come up with an excuse to let Macy down gently. Whatever she had to say about Berkeley's dig, it wasn't her problem.

Still, ten minutes of her time wouldn't kill her.

Eddie spotted the long queue of people outside the nightclub from the far end of the block. Even relatively early in the evening, people were lined up four abreast in the hope of getting into one of the Upper West Side's hottest new venues.

'Looks pretty cool, huh?' said Grant as his bright orange Lamborghini Murciélago cruised slowly along the street. For day-to-day travel round New York the actor relied on the ostentatious anonymity of the limo service, but when he wanted to be noticed he employed a vastly more eyecatching vehicle. 'Check out that crowd – hell, check out those legs!' He lowered his window for a better look at the miniskirted women waiting to enter. The car had already attracted attention, and when people realised a Hollywood star was at the wheel the reaction was almost a riot. Grant grinned his expensive grin and waved, blipping the throttle to let a tiny fraction of the supercar's 631 horsepower howl through its exhaust pipes.

A section of sidewalk at the club entrance was cordoned off by velvet ropes: the VIP area. Grant pulled over, a valet swooping in to collect the keys in exchange for a token as he got out and stood before a galaxy of flashing phone cameras. Nobody needed to check that his name was on the VIP list, though Eddie didn't receive the same star treatment. 'Whoa, guys, he's with me,' said Grant as two bouncers closed ranks in front of Eddie like meaty sliding doors. 'It's cool, he's my bodyguard.'

'This little guy?' rumbled the larger of the two hulks, smirking. Eddie gave him a scathing look. A brief stand-off, then the bouncers moved apart and he followed Grant inside. Behind, a snarl announced the Lamborghini's departure for the parking structure down the street.

The club's interior was on three levels, the lowest an almost pit-like dance floor with a higher area containing the long, neon-lit bar surrounding it. Overlooking both was a glass-walled balcony: the VIP lounge. The pounding music was as trendy and contemporary as the overdone hairstyles of the clubbers, and Eddie didn't have the slightest idea of the band's name.

'Christ, I feel old,' he muttered as he followed Grant up to the balcony.

Nina almost didn't call Macy after her pleasant afternoon and dinner with Lola; in fact, until she opened her bag to check her phone for messages and saw the note, she had completely forgotten her earlier conversation. She could have simply shrugged and gone home, but the twin proddings of politeness and minor guilt swayed her otherwise.

She had no messages, so entered Macy's number again. The same man answered, with the same suspicious air, before she heard Macy say in the background, 'Is that her? Joey, give me the phone!' One brief scuffle for possession later, and she was on the line. 'Hi? Dr Wilde? Is that you?'

'It's me,' Nina assured her.

She sounded relieved. 'Thanks for calling back. Can you still meet me?'

'Do you remember where I said?'

'The coffee place? Yeah, Joey knows where it is. Can you meet me right now?'

'Yeah, I guess,' said Nina, still not sure if she should go through with it. 'I can be there in . . . fifteen minutes?'

'That's great! I'll be waiting for you. Dr Wilde, thank you so much for doing this. I'll see you soon.' She hung up.

Nina made a faint noise of exasperation, then set off. She might as well get it over with.

The area hadn't altered much in the two and a half years since she'd moved out of the East Village; some stores and restaurants had changed hands and a few buildings had been renovated, but 52 Perk-Up looked much the same as the last time she'd been there. The paintings on the back wall were by different local artists, and new faces were serving, but beyond that it was as self-consciously bohemian as ever.

It was also small; she would have deduced which customer was Macy within moments even if she hadn't sprung up to greet her. 'Dr Wilde! Hi!'

'You're Macy, I take it,' said Nina, coming to her table. Macy Sharif was not what she had expected; she had assumed that anyone involved with a dig as major as the Sphinx would be at least a post-grad. But the extremely attractive young girl before her, black hair tied back in a ponytail, was too young even to be a graduate, maybe still in her teens. She was also dressed more for spring break than study – as well as an extremely short denim skirt, she wore a very tight designer top emphasising her breasts. The slightly malicious thought crossed Nina's mind that Berkeley might have chosen her for his team for reasons other than her academic qualifications, before she decided that was unfair. She didn't know anything about the girl; she should at least give her the benefit of the doubt.

'Yeah, that's me! Hi.' Macy seemed genuinely pleased at the meeting; maybe she really *was* a fan. 'I'm really glad Lola managed to get hold of you – I tried calling your number in the phone book, but it wasn't working. So I went there in person, but the building super said you'd moved out.'

'Yeah, a few months ago.' Now Nina was faintly unsettled; perhaps Macy was a fan in the original sense of the word, derived from 'fanatic'. But she appeared normal and polite enough.

'Do you want a coffee?'

'No thanks, I'm fine.' The table had another occupant, a man of Macy's age with a fake tan, a necklace of chunky wooden beads and a spiky hairstyle that resembled something from a Japanese cartoon. He briefly looked Nina up and down, then turned his gaze back to Macy's chest. 'Hi,' Nina said. The young man grunted.

'You sure?' Macy said. Nina nodded. 'I could use something. Joey, go get me a cappuccino, will you? I want to talk to Dr Wilde in private.'

Joey grunted again and got up. 'I'll sit over there, keep an eye on the door.'

Nina gave Macy a curious look. 'Something I should know about?'

'I'll tell you soon. Please, sit down.' Nina sat opposite her. 'Joey's just watching out for me. He's a friend from college – well, a friend with benefits.' She grinned, making Nina a little uncomfortable about her openness. 'He's about the only person I know in New York. I'm from Miami.'

'Right,' said Nina, not particularly interested. 'So, what did you want to talk to me about?'

Macy sat straighter. 'First thing – can I just say it's *so* great that you were willing to see me? I've wanted to meet you for ages. You're like my hero!'

'Really?' Nina felt a little glow inside her; it was a long time since she'd had any kind of professional flattery.

'Oh, totally! It's because of you that I picked archaeology for my major. I didn't really know what I wanted to do, but then I read this and thought: wow, that is *so* cool.' She took out several slightly tattered magazine pages from her bag, laying them out flat on the table. Nina immediately recognised them as an article from around a year and a half earlier, about her discovery of Atlantis. One of the pictures was a photograph of herself, beaming proudly. Her younger self had her hair in the ponytail she had favoured at the time, prompting her to glance up at Macy's very similar style.

'Er, yeah,' said Macy bashfully as she fingered her own tied-back hair. 'I, ah, kinda borrowed your look. I thought if it worked for you . . . Hope you don't mind.'

'No, not at all,' Nina said, the glow moving to her cheeks in slight embarrassment.

Joey returned and delivered a cappuccino, then sat at a table near the door. 'See, when I read this,' Macy continued, 'it made me realise that wow, there really is all this amazing stuff still out there to discover.' She tapped Nina's picture.

'And when I saw it was you who'd found it, it was like, oh my God! I mean, most archaeologists are guys, right, and they're usually pretty old, but you? You were like a real-life Lara Croft. I thought, well, if *you* could do this, I could do it too!'

Nina knew the younger woman had meant it as a compliment, but wasn't thrilled by her phrasing. 'So . . . you weren't sure what you wanted to do until then? You weren't serious about archaeology?'

Macy shrugged. 'The big, exciting stuff, sure. And I was already into Egyptology 'cause of my grandparents – they were from Egypt originally. My grandpa used to be a teacher, and he taught me to read hieroglyphics when I was a kid, which was pretty cool. But most of my first year, I kind of goofed off. I was in a sorority, I was a cheerleader, every night was party night – you know what it's like!'

'Hmm,' said Nina, who at university had been anything but a party animal.

'But then I almost flunked out, and that was when I realised I needed to pull myself together. Part of it was because I didn't want to let down my mom and dad – I mean, they were paying for it! So I started working harder, and picked up my grades. But then when I heard about the IHA dig at the Sphinx, I realised it would be such a huge boost for me if I could be a part of it. So I managed to get on the team—'

'There must have been a lot of competition.'

'Oh, totally. But my mom does a lot of fundraising for international charities and she's got friends at the UN, so that helped!' She smiled brightly.

'I'm sure it did,' said Nina, unimpressed that nepotism,

not hard work, had won her a place on the dig. While she didn't consider herself the kind of person who made snap judgements, she was forced to admit that her initial appraisal of Macy – a party girl who relied on her looks and money to coast through life – seemed accurate. 'Well, look, it's been nice meeting you, and I'm glad I was such an inspiration, but I need to get moving.'

Macy's face fell. 'Oh, no, wait! Please, wait – I need to show you this.' She hurriedly stuffed the pages back in her bag, her hand returning with a digital camera. 'You know about the scrolls that told us how to find the Hall of Records, right?'

'The ones that were found in Gaza? Yeah. I still keep up with the news.'

Macy didn't register the sarcasm. 'Okay, well, the Osirian Temple gave three pages to the IHA, right? Turns out they didn't give us *all* of them.'

An image appeared on the screen. Nina looked more closely, seeing what appeared to be ancient Egyptian papyruses, though the hieroglyphics were too small to read on the LCD display. 'Are these the pages?'

Macy pointed at the three leftmost pages. 'These three are. But *this* one,' she tapped the one on the right, 'is something nobody's seen before. Not at the IHA, anyway. The first three pages talk about what the Hall of Records is and how to find it. This one says what's actually in it.'

Nina regarded her dubiously. 'And what *is* in it?'

'A map that tells you how to find the Pyramid of Osiris.'

'What?' Only the memory of having been at the other end of a similar discussion, trying to convince others of the truth of a legend, stopped Nina from letting out a dismissive laugh. 'The Pyramid of Osiris? That's barely even a myth – it's more like a fairy tale. You could count all the references to it in known ancient Egyptian texts on one hand, and even then it's only mentioned in connection with the mythology of their gods. It's not real.'

'Well, I didn't think so either,' said Macy, bristling, 'but *somebody* does. Somebody who's going to dig into the Hall of Records before the IHA and steal the map.'

Now Nina did laugh. 'You've got to be kidding me. Someone's digging under the Sphinx at the same time as the IHA? In the middle of the busiest tourist attraction in the entire country, and nobody notices?'

'It's true!' Macy protested. 'They've dug a shaft at the north end of the Sphinx compound – I saw it!' She flicked through the images on the camera. 'I took a picture of the plans, look!'

Nina gave it only a cursory glance. 'There's no way they could do that without attracting attention. They'd be arrested the moment they stuck their shovel into the ground.'

'No, the people in charge, they're in on it! Gamal, the head of security, and Dr Hamdi – look, see?' Another picture, this one a blown-out closeup of a man's startled face. 'They're both working for a guy from the Osirian Temple!'

Nina kneaded her forehead. 'Why are you telling *me* this? If you really did uncover some conspiracy to rob the site, why didn't you just tell Dr Berkeley? Or the Egyptian police?'

'I didn't know who I could trust. Dr Berkeley might have been in on it too.'

'Logan Berkeley's many things,' said Nina drily, 'but I don't think he's a crook.'

'He didn't believe me, anyway. He already had some problem with me, I don't know why. He's kind of a jerk.'

Nina couldn't help a sardonic smile; that was certainly one of the 'many things'. 'The police, then. The Egyptians take artefact theft very seriously.'

'I couldn't go to the police.'

'Why not?'

'They kinda . . . wanted to arrest me. They think I stole a piece of the Sphinx and hit Dr Hamdi.'

'*What?*'

'I didn't!' Macy reconsidered that. 'Okay, I did hit Dr Hamdi . . .'

Nina stood. 'I think I've heard enough.'

'No, wait, please!' Macy jumped up; across the room, Joey half rose, watching Nina suspiciously. 'Look, they chased me, they were going to kill me! I had to get out of Egypt.'

'So why come to me? Why didn't you tell the IHA?'

'Because they wouldn't listen; they thought I was a thief. I came to you because . . .' Her expression crumbled to downcast disappointment. 'Because I really thought you'd believe me.'

Despite herself, Nina felt a pang of sympathy for the young woman. Whether she was paranoid or just the victim of a hyperactive imagination, Macy had still gone through a lot to meet her 'hero' – only for the meeting to fall short of her hopes. 'Look,' she said, more quietly, 'right now I don't exactly have the highest opinion of the IHA, but that doesn't mean they won't listen to you. Okay? There aren't bad guys hiding round every corner – you can go to them and tell them your side of the story.'

'I . . . suppose,' said Macy unhappily.

'You don't have to do anything right now.' Nina glanced at Joey, who had relaxed. 'Go home with your friend, sleep on it, then call the IHA in the morning. I promise, it'll be okay.'

Macy didn't appear convinced, but she nodded reluctantly, then moved to meet Joey near the door.

Nina sat again, deciding to wait for them to go before leaving herself. The meeting certainly hadn't been what she expected, but at least it had been different, a break from blankly vegging out in front of the TV.

Though that was all she had to look forward to when she got back to the apartment. Eddie probably wouldn't finish work for hours. She sighed.

Macy and Joey turned to go. The door opened before they reached it.

And Macy shrieked.

Nina looked up in surprise. In the doorway was a greasy-looking man in a snakeskin jacket, his straggly goatee twisting as he leered at the young woman.

Macy jerked back. 'That's him! He's one of them!'

'Hi again, li'l girl,' said the man, his grin widening unpleasantly as he advanced. Jaw set, Joey stepped in front of him—

And crumpled to the floor, doubled over as the man smashed a punch – and a set of brass knuckles – into his stomach.

The other customers reacted in shock. The man stepped over Joey as Macy fled past Nina to the back of the room.

He followed—

'Hey!'

He turned towards Nina's shout – and she flung Macy's untouched cappuccino into his face. The cup hit his jaw, foaming coffee splashing everywhere.

She kicked a chair at him as he lurched back. 'Macy! *Run!*'

4

Macy shoved past a waitress to a door behind the counter, hesitating as she looked back at the moaning Joey.

'Don't stop!' Nina ordered as she ran after her. Macy went through the door. Nina followed. The manager moved to bar her way, but flinched back at her shout of, 'Not me, *him*! Call the cops!'

The man in the snakeskin jacket hurled the chair aside. She slammed the door, seeing several large boxes full of bags of coffee beans on shelves. A pull, and a box slammed to the floor.

Macy reached a fire door, barging through it into an alley—

A thick arm lashed out, clotheslining her to the ground.

Snakeskin had set a trap, an associate lying in wait outside.

Another shelf held several hefty Pyrex coffee pots. Nina snatched one up and ran for the fire exit. The door behind her was kicked open. The box crumpled – but the beans inside it absorbed the impact, stopping the door from opening wide enough to get through.

Nina reached the fire exit. Macy lay dazed on her back outside, a doughy, shaven-headed man bending down to grab her—

The coffee pot hit the top of his head with a flat clonk. He let out a surprised grunt of pain, stumbling back. Nina swung the pot again. This time it shattered against his skull, chunky fragments bursting outwards like hailstones. The man fell against a dumpster. Nina reached out to Macy. 'Come on, get up!'

Pain and fear momentarily replaced by wide-eyed wonder, Macy gazed up at her before grasping her hands. 'Oh – oh, my God! That was *amazing*!'

'You should see me with a teapot. Come on!' Nina pulled her up, jumping over the bald guy as they ran down the alley.

'How did he find me?' Macy cried. 'I didn't tell anyone where I was, not even my parents! How'd they know I was in New York?'

'You told Lola,' Nina realised. 'She must have told someone at the IHA, they told Berkeley, he told – whoever those guys work for.' They reached the street.

'But how did they know I was meeting you?'

'What am I, a detective?' Nina saw a cab up the street. She waved furiously as they ran after it. 'Taxi!'

'We're getting a *cab*?' said Macy in disbelief.

'Unless you've got a helicopter, then yeah!' The cab stopped – but not, Nina realised, for them. A well-dressed couple stood on the opposite sidewalk, the man's hand outstretched. 'Hey, that's our cab!'

The man grabbed the door handle. 'He was stopping for us.'

'This is an emergency, we need it!' Nina reached the vehicle and yanked open the other rear door. 'Macy, get in!'

'What the hell are you doing?' the woman shrilled. 'Driver, don't take them!'

'I don't want no trouble,' said the driver, a skinny man with a strong Brazilian accent, as he leaned out of his open window to address Nina. 'I stop for this gen'leman and lady, okay? You wait for next—'

The window of Nina's door exploded. The driver screeched in agony as a bullet ripped into his left shoulder, speckling the windscreen with blood. Nina whipped round, seeing Snakeskin at the end of the alley with a gun in one hand.

Aiming—

'Get down!' she yelled. Macy shrieked and dived headlong into the cab as the rear windscreen blew apart.

Nina threw herself to the asphalt. A bullet hole erupted in the cab's flank just above her with a plunk of cratered metal. Another window shattered, the woman screaming hysterically. Other pedestrians ran for cover.

The onslaught stopped.

The gunman's weapon was a revolver, a six-shooter. He needed to reload.

Nina jumped up and threw open the driver's door. The Brazilian was hunched in his seat, right hand squeezing his wounded shoulder. 'Move over, move!'

He gasped something in Portuguese before reverting to English. 'You crazy? I been shot!'

Nina stabbed at his seat belt release, then tried to shove him into the other seat. 'I'll get you to a hospital – just move over!'

'You can have the cab!' the well-dressed man gabbled as he ran off, his screaming companion clacking after him as fast as her high heels would allow.

Macy peered over the top of the back seat. 'Oh, oh oh!' she cried, pointing.

' "Oh!" what?' Nina demanded, finally forcing the weakly protesting Brazilian out of the driver's seat and jumping in to take his place. She looked back and saw the reason for Macy's panic. The gunman had drawn a *second* pistol. 'Oh, shit!'

She slammed the gear selector to Drive and stamped on the gas pedal.

The balding tyres screeched before finally finding purchase, the taxi lurching away. It was one of the city's remaining Ford Crown Victorias, the former mainstay of New York's taxi fleet being phased out in favour of less-polluting hybrids. To Nina, it seemed as though it should have been retired itself a long time ago, the transmission clunking and whining.

Whatever its state of repair, it could easily outpace a man on foot.

But not his bullets.

'Duck!' shouted Nina. Macy dropped flat again as more shots clanged against the taxi's bodywork. One whipped over her and struck the bulletproof partition between the front and back seats with a crack, leaving a jagged scar across the Plexiglas.

'My cab!' the driver moaned, financial pain briefly overcoming physical. Teeth gritted, he forced himself upright, took his hand from his wound . . . and started the meter.

Nina looked at him. 'Are you *kidding* me?'

'No free rides,' he gasped. 'Now get me to hospital!'

More noise from behind – not gunfire, but the shriek of tyres as a massive, bright red Dodge Ram pickup truck skidded to a standstill. The bald man lumbered from the alley and climbed in, the snakeskinned gunman glaring after the retreating taxi before holstering his empty weapons and running to the cabin's rear door. With a V8 roar almost as loud as the gunshots, the Ram snarled into pursuit.

Nina now remembered seeing the distinctive vehicle earlier that day – outside her apartment. They had found out that Macy was trying to contact her . . . and staked her out in the hope that she would lead them to their prey.

'Forget the hospital,' Macy said. 'We need the police! Where's the nearest precinct?'

'I don't know,' said the driver. Both women shot him looks of disbelief. 'I only live here three weeks!'

'Do you know where it is?' Macy asked Nina.

'Ah . . . no.'

'You said you used to live around here!'

'I never needed to go there – New York's not *that* dangerous! Well, normally.' Nina swerved round a couple of cars waiting at a red light and made a wallowing turn to head north. 'I think there's one on 21st Street.'

Macy looked up at the street signs. 'That's over ten blocks! Have you got a phone? I'll call 911!'

'Yes,' said the driver, nodding. 'Yes, call an ambulance, good idea!'

The road ahead was still busy. Pounding the horn, Nina

swung out into the opposite lane to get past a crawling garbage truck, barely missing an oncoming car as she darted back in front of it. Macy slithered across the back seat, broken safety glass tinkling with her. 'Not an ambulance, the police – whoa!' Nina gasped as another cab braked sharply ahead of them. She spun the wheel as fast as she could, but clipped its rear quarter and ripped off the end of its bumper. Enraged horns blared. 'Shit! Sorry,' she added to the mortified driver.

She fumbled in her bag for her phone, fighting to keep control of the cab with one hand. Behind, a skirl of rubber and a flare of spotlights in the mirror warned her that the Dodge had made it through the intersection as well. She found the phone, shoving it through the partition's money slot. 'Here!'

Macy dialled 911, giving a hurried, panicky description of their situation to the operator as Nina swerved through traffic to keep out of their pursuers' line of fire. 'The cops said to head for 21st Street,' Macy said, ending the call. 'They're going to try to meet us.'

'If these assholes don't catch up first.' Despite Nina's best efforts, the Dodge was gaining. Macy tried to push the phone back through the slot, but she held up a hand. 'No! Go to the contacts, call "Eddie".'

'Who's Eddie?'

'My husband.'

'This isn't the best time to tell him you'll be late for dinner!'

'Just dial it, smartass! He'll know how to get us out of this!' She shared a worried look with the driver as the cab shot through the next intersection. 'I hope.'

★

Eddie had taken an immediate dislike to Grant's buddies, a pair of overgrown fratboys who were taking full advantage of the extra pulling power granted by association with a movie star. But he kept his opinions to himself as they pawed at the skimpily dressed girls who had been easily persuaded to join them in the VIP lounge. Instead he lurked discreetly nearby, concentrating on his job, which was to get rid of the arseholes and nutters his client didn't want near him. The arseholes and nutters he *did* want near him weren't his problem.

His phone rang. Nina. He wasn't supposed to take personal calls when he was working. But Grant wouldn't notice while trying to count his latest ladyfriend's teeth with his tongue. 'Hey, love. What's up?'

'Someone's trying to kill me!'

He could tell she wasn't joking. It sounded as if she was in a car. 'Where are you?'

'The East Village, round 12th Street.'

Shit! That was almost half the length of Manhattan away, a hundred blocks – the better part of five miles. 'How many bad guys? Are they armed?'

'At least three, and yeah!' An *urk* of overstressed tyres came from the other end of the line, followed by a high-pitched shriek and angry car horns.

The shriek wasn't Nina. 'Who's with you?'

'Someone from the IHA, and the cab driver – he's been shot!'

'Why aren't you calling an ambulance?' demanded a pained but angry male voice.

Eddie's fists tightened in frustration. He was too far away

to help directly – all he could offer was advice. 'Have you called the cops?'

'Yeah – we're trying to get to a precinct.'

His eyes locked on to Grant, an idea forming. 'I'll call you right back,' he said. 'Just keep ahead of 'em!'

He ended the call and strode to Grant's table. 'And I do my own stunts, too,' the actor was boasting to the wide-eyed young woman. 'In *Nitrous*, when I ran along the top of that tanker truck as it blew up? That was really me.'

He was neglecting to mention the computer-enhanced fireballs and all the safety gear that had been digitally painted out of the shot, but Eddie decided not to enlighten her. Instead, he held out his hand. 'Mr Thorn. I need your valet parking token.'

Grant looked up, confused. 'What?'

'The parking token. Give it to me.'

The actor stared at him uncomprehendingly. One of his friends rose with a drunken smirk. 'Hey, Mr Bodyguard, how about you chill the fuck out and give us some priva—'

An instant later, his arm was twisted up behind his back and his face slammed against the table. Grant flinched. 'Token!' Eddie snapped. 'Now!'

'Uh, what are you doing?' Grant asked as he fumbled for it.

Eddie shoved his friend to the floor and snatched it from him. 'I need your car,' he said as he hurried for the stairs, the VIP lounge's other occupants not sure how to react to the lightning-fast burst of violence.

'Dude, you are *so* fired!' Grant shouted, jumping up and following. 'And there's no way you are taking my car. No way!'

'Way,' Eddie replied. He raced down the stairs and pushed through the crowd. Shouts rose behind him as the clubgoers realised there was a Hollywood star in their midst and closed in as if drawn magnetically.

He reached the street and thrust the token into the head valet's hand, together with a fifty dollar bill. 'Mr Thorn's car. Quick.' The valet pocketed the money and issued instructions into a walkie-talkie. Eddie impatiently tapped a foot. It wouldn't take Grant long to force his way through the mob.

His phone rang again. 'Nina! What's happening?'

'Still being chased!'

'I'll be there as quick as I can.'

'How quick will *that* be?'

He heard the high snarl of the Lamborghini's engine from the parking garage. 'Very.'

He moved to the kerb, glaring at the parking structure. The Lamborghini's engine note echoed as the valet gingerly manoeuvred the supercar down the ramp. *Come on, get a bloody move on!* Grant would reach the doors at any moment.

The Murciélago emerged from the garage, street lights gleaming from its polished orange skin. It pulled up in front of the VIP entrance, driver's door scissoring upwards. Eddie held up another fifty to entice the valet out—

'Hey!' Grant rushed on to the sidewalk, shrugging off his fans. 'Stop him! That's my car!'

The valet was still unfolding himself from the low-slung driver's seat. The bouncer who had mocked Eddie's height earlier advanced. 'Okay, hold it—'

Eddie kneed him in the groin, then smashed a powerful punch up into his face as he doubled over, knocking him backwards into his companion. Both men tumbled, pulling down the velvet rope. Clubbers saw their chance and rushed for the doors, the queue suddenly degenerating into anarchy.

Eddie yanked the gawping valet from the Lamborghini, tossing him on to the bouncers, then swung himself into the car and pulled down the door. He put the Murciélago into gear and was about to take off when Grant leapt in front of it, banging his hands down on the bonnet. 'You're not taking my car, man!'

Eddie revved the engine, jolting the car forward a few inches. Grant's face flashed with fear, but he held his ground. Changing tack, Eddie looked through the narrow rear window to make sure he wasn't about to squash anybody, then snicked the gearstick into reverse and sharply pulled back.

Grant almost fell flat on his face before regaining his balance. He caught up as Eddie stopped, flinging open the passenger door. 'What the hell are you doing?'

'Someone's trying to kill my wife!' Eddie shouted. 'I need to get to her, fast – either get in or get out of the way!'

Grant chose the former, his bewildered expression returning. 'Dude? Seriously?'

'Seriously!'

'Shit, dude, no way! Well, come on, let's go save her!' The half-smile on Grant's face suggested that he was already picturing himself as a real-life action hero. 'What are you waiting for? Let's roll!'

Eddie held back a sarcastic comment. Instead, he blasted the Murciélago away from the nightclub with an ear-splitting V12 howl.

*

Nina looked back. The Ram was still behind them, closing as both vehicles weaved through the traffic along Third Avenue. The pickup truck was much larger than the cab, not a vehicle at home on the streets of New York, but it was also more powerful – and better maintained. The Crown Victoria now sounded as though several important parts were rattling around loose in the gearbox.

The driver was making just as much noise. 'For the love of God,' he cried, 'stop! You can keep the cab, just let me out!'

'Look – what's your name?'

'Ricardo!'

'Ricardo,' said Nina, 'we're almost at the police precinct. Okay? Just one more block!' She pounded on the horn and swung the cab into the wrong lane to avoid cars stopped at the 20th Street intersection, cringing as she saw headlights rushing at her from the left – then the taxi was through. She hauled it back into the right-hand lanes.

The Ram also swerved, smashing into a car and sending it spinning on to the sidewalk. But the truck was barely slowed, the heavy bullbar across its radiator grille taking the brunt of the impact.

Macy stared back at the crash. 'Jesus!'

'Just hang on!' The next intersection was just ahead . . .

Which way was the precinct? Left or right?

21st Street was one-way, traffic running westbound across Manhattan – and the road to the right was blocked by waiting cars.

No choice—

Nina turned hard left, the cab tipping on its suspension.

A Porsche was parked just beyond the crosswalk, the Crown Vic skidding right at it.

'Shit, shit, *shit*!' She wrestled with the controls, feeling the back end sliding. If she braked, the cab would spin out and hit the other car—

Instead, she spun the wheel back and stepped on the gas.

The rear wheels writhed and squealed, kicking the taxi out of its skid – but not quickly enough to stop its tail from bashing against the Porsche. There was a horrible crunch as the cab's rear bumper was ripped off.

Nina straightened out. 'Sorry,' she told Ricardo. He made a disgusted sound.

Rising sirens. Flashing lights, the red and white strobes of police cars—

In the mirror.

'Damn it!' The precinct had been in the other direction, and now they were heading away from it, away from help.

Macy, looking back, was happier. 'Yes!' she crowed as the cars at the lights pulled out of the way to let the cops through. An NYPD patrol car accelerated across the intersection—

And was hit by the Ram as it ploughed round the corner, the police cruiser smashing into the Porsche and folding it like wet cardboard. The pickup tore away the police car's front wheel as it wrenched free of the wreckage and continued the pursuit, twisted debris dangling from its bullbar like streamers.

Macy's relief vanished in an instant. 'No!'

'Have you still got the phone?' Nina shouted.

'Yeah, but—'

'Call Eddie again!'

Macy thumbed through Nina's contact list. 'What can he do?'

'You'd be surprised. Just call him!'

Macy frowned, but found the number and selected it. 'It's busy!'

'What? Who the hell's he talking to?'

The Lamborghini powered out of 108th Street and turned sharply south, its broad tyres and four-wheel drive keeping it clamped firmly to the road. The lateral G-force of the turn, on the other hand, threw Eddie against the door. Ahead, the long straight of Central Park West stretched to infinity, the park itself a swathe of darkness to their left.

Streetlights and windows streaked into hyperspace as the Murciélago accelerated. Eddie leaned back upright, Grant holding the phone to his ear. 'So can you help us?'

'I'll do what I can,' said Amy – now in her official role as Officer Martin of the New York Police Department. 'But it'll take a while to get the word out to every unit – if you get stopped before then, you'll get a ticket.'

That was the least of Eddie's worries. 'I'll just not have to get stopped, then.'

'Or you could not break the speed limit . . .' Amy's tone became dubious. 'You're speeding right now, aren't you?'

'A bit,' he admitted as the speedometer needle flashed past eighty.

'Where are you?'

'105th Street . . . 104th . . . 103rd . . .'

'God *damn* it, Eddie! Don't you know how dangerous that is?'

'Just make sure all your guys know that Nina's the good

guy and the fuckwits chasing her are the bad guys, okay? Bye!'

'So . . .' Grant said cautiously as he withdrew the phone, free hand tightening round the leather armrest, 'you've driven fast cars before, yeah?'

'Yeah,' said Eddie, focusing on the road. The Lamborghini's grip and handling made weaving through the traffic a precise, almost game-like experience, but the slightest mistake would not only total the Murciélago, but probably injure or even kill innocent people as well.

'Like what?'

'Last thing I drove this fast was a Ferrari 430.'

Grant nodded approvingly. 'Cool car. Yours?'

'You think I'd be working as a bodyguard if I could afford a Ferrari?'

'Good point, man. Whoa, bus, bus!'

'I see it.' The oncoming lanes were almost empty for at least two blocks. Eddie whipped round the bus and accelerated, the Lamborghini surging effortlessly past a hundred miles per hour.

Grant let a relieved breath escape. 'So this Ferrari – you took good care of it, right?'

'Nope,' said Eddie with a small smile. 'Smashed it to fuck.' The gulp from the other seat sounded as though Grant was trying to suck the breath back in. 'Don't worry, I'll look after your Lambo.'

'Not a scratch, okay?'

'If it gets anything bigger than a scratch, you probably won't be in any state to worry about it.' He let the actor figure that out for himself as the phone rang again. 'Get that, will you?'

*

'Eddie!' Nina shouted as Macy poked the phone through the slot. 'What are you doing?'

'I'm on my way,' came the Yorkshireman's voice. 'I've told a mate in the NYPD what's going on, and I'm coming south – head uptown, I'll meet you. Where are you?'

'Going north up Park.' She had turned off the narrow 21st Street on to the much broader Park Avenue.

'The bad guys?'

'Right behind us!' yelled Macy.

She wasn't kidding. The lights in the mirror flared brighter, the Ram's engine roar like a charging beast. Figures leaned from its windows, the bald man in the front passenger seat, Snakeskin behind the driver.

Both had guns raised—

Macy dropped flat, the phone snagging in the slot and falling to the dirty floor. Gunfire crackled, the flat boom of the revolver and the rapid chatter of a TEC-9 machine pistol. More shots struck the cab. The bulletproof screen took another two rounds, a fist-sized section crazing just behind Nina's head. Another hit and it would shatter . . .

She made a savage left turn, the Crown Victoria crashing heavily over the central divider between two trees. Ricardo yelled in pain.

The Ram was too big to fit through the gap after them. She straightened and headed into the oncoming traffic, a car swerving on to the sidewalk to avoid a head-on collision, then turned again to swing the cab westwards.

The Dodge had to take the turn at a sharper angle. Its back end slewed wide, throwing Snakeskin back inside – and almost pitching the bald guy out on to the street. The oversized vehicle screeched to a halt to give the gunman time to pull himself back in.

The stop had opened up the gap between the two vehicles. But not by much. Nina scoured her mental map of Manhattan for anything that might widen it further, at the same time working out the quickest way to meet Eddie. Across Fifth and Broadway, then north on Sixth Avenue . . .

The Ram re-joined the pursuit, gaining fast.

The Lamborghini screamed southwards, eating up the three-mile straight of Central Park West. It was now near the bottom of the long avenue, approaching Columbus Circle. Eddie danced through the gaps in the traffic, accelerating.

'Er, dude,' Grant pointed out, 'you're gonna have to slow down for the turn – it's one-way.' Southbound vehicles on Central Park West were forced to turn on to 62nd Street, the southernmost two blocks being northbound only.

'It's *my* way,' Eddie corrected. There wasn't time to take a detour. Instead he fixed his gaze on the lanes ahead. Was there a space?

There would have to be.

'Dude,' said Grant, voice rising in urgency as they neared 62nd Street. He jabbed a finger ahead – at the approaching headlights filling every lane. 'Dude, dude, *dude*!'

Grimacing, Eddie turned—

Not right on to 62nd, but *left* – up the sloping kerb at a crosswalk and on to the broad sidewalk along the park's walled edge. A long line of parked cars flicked past to their right, hemming them in.

'You're doing seventy on the *sidewalk*!' Grant choked.

'Yeah, I noticed!' He batted the horn, people leaping aside as the Lamborghini swept past.

'If the cops stop us, I'm totally gonna say this was a kidnapping!'

Eddie ignored him. They were at Columbus Circle, a large multi-lane roundabout.

And they were about to go round it the wrong way . . .

Grant let out a stifled gasp as Eddie whipped the Murciélago between two parked bicycle rickshaws and off the kerb, landing with a bang. Teeth clenched in a rictus grimace, he swung the Lamborghini between the disbelieving drivers rushing at him. Horns blared, tyres squealed, headlights streaked past on either side as he swung the supercar from left to right and back again, each barely missed vehicle making a sharp *swip!* of displaced air as it whipped by.

Central Park South—

He turned, foot down to blast through a gap before a truck closed it – and was clear.

For a moment. A siren wailed, a police car on Columbus Circle entering pursuit.

Grant looked back. 'Oh, man! Cops!'

'Just like in *Nitrous*, eh?' Eddie said. He powered along Central Park South, swerving through traffic to make a screeching turn on to Seventh Avenue. The road down to Times Square was relatively clear; relieved, he accelerated again. Over the rising song of the engine he heard a voice. Nina.

'The phone!' he said. Grant held it up.

'Eddie, Eddie!' said Nina. 'Are you there?'

'Yeah, I'm here. Are you okay?'

'They're still after us! Where are you?'

He ducked across the lanes to avoid a knot of traffic. 'Seventh.'

'*Seventh?*' He knew the scathing tone; that of every single New Yorker, convinced they alone knew the best way to navigate their city. 'Why the hell are you on Seventh? Take Broadway!'

'I know where I'm going!'

'Dude, not the time for a domestic,' Grant warned, pointing ahead. The neon glare of Times Square was approaching fast, the traffic getting thicker.

'Where are you now?' Eddie asked Nina.

'On Sixth, coming up to 30th.'

He remembered that if he got on Broadway south of Times Square, it intersected Sixth Avenue at Herald Square, around 34th Street. 'Keep going – I'll meet you!'

'And then what are you gonna do?'

'I dunno – something violent! Just stay ahead of them!'

He ignored the sarcastic '*No!*' from the phone, fixing on the road as the Lamborghini wailed through Times Square. Grant's face, two storeys high, watched it pass from a billboard advertising his latest movie. Cars streamed across their path on 44th Street – and beyond, he saw more flashing lights as cops from the small police station at the square's south end started their vehicles.

He speeded up, angling for a gap—

'Shit!' gasped Grant as the Murciélago shot through the crosstraffic, one car's front bumper passing so close that it brushed the Lamborghini's rear corner. 'You said not a scratch, man, not a scratch!'

'It'll buff out,' Chase replied, the joke a cover for the

shudder that ran through him as he realised just how near he had come to a crash. He shot past the little police station, then turned hard, cutting across a short section of 42nd Street to join Broadway.

Strobe lights flashed across the buildings behind as more police cars joined the chase. He swore under his breath, looking down Broadway.

Where was Nina?

Where was Eddie?

The cab reached the lower end of Herald Square. Nina risked a glance up Broadway as she crossed the intersection and continued up Sixth Avenue, seeing police lights in the distance, before looking back at the nearer and much more menacing lights in the mirror. The pursuing police cars had also drawn closer, but were unable to overtake the powerful truck.

'Hey, there's my store!' said Macy. Nina looked back, wondering what the hell she was talking about. 'You know, Macy's.' She pointed as the giant store rolled past to their left.

'Just hold up the phone,' Nina snapped. 'Eddie, where are you now?'

'I'm almost there. Where are you?'

The taxi reached the 36th Street intersection, Nina checking for traffic coming from the left – to see a bright orange sports car zoom down Broadway. 'Eddie, are you in an orange car?'

'Yeah, why?'

'I just missed you! I'm going north on Sixth!'

Eddie said something, but it was drowned out by Macy's

cry of, 'They're catching up!' The pickup's driver had put the hammer down, the great chromed whale-mouth of its grille looming large.

And Snakeskin was leaning out of the window again, revolver raised—

Nina hurled the cab into a desperate left turn on to 37th Street as a bullet punched through the door just above her thigh.

Eddie heard the unmistakable sound of a bullet impact over the phone. 'Shit!'

He had to double back – but two NYPD cruisers were moving to block Broadway ahead, despatchers alerting them to the second high-speed chase.

And there were more police cars behind him . . .

'Hang on!' he shouted to Grant as he stabbed a button to deactivate the traction control – then dipped the clutch as he spun the wheel with one hand and yanked hard on the handbrake with the other.

Even with four-wheel drive the Lamborghini couldn't keep its hold on the road, slithering round in a 180-degree spin as Eddie mashed the accelerator to the floor. The engine roar was accompanied by an earsplitting scream from the smoking wheels as the Murciélago lunged forward again, the tortured tyres laying thick black lines of rubber on the tarmac.

Ahead, the other police cars moved to box him in – then hurriedly swerved aside as the cops realised he wasn't going to stop. He shot between them, the two cruisers behind him pulling into single file to follow the writhing Murciélago through the gap.

The tyres found grip again, the sudden jolt of acceleration like a kick to the back as the oncoming traffic peeled off to either side, headlights flashing, horns blaring. 37th Street was coming up fast. Eddie eased off, about to turn right to catch up with Nina—

A battered yellow cab hurtled across the intersection right in front of him.

Time slowed to a crawl as Eddie recognised the red-haired figure at the wheel, Nina looking round at him open-mouthed as the Lamborghini thundered straight towards her—

Eddie twitched the wheel – and *accelerated*. The world snapped back to full speed as the Lamborghini crossed just in front of the cab. He thought he heard Nina's scream behind him, but it was probably his imagination: it would have been lost in his own.

Adrenalin surging from the almost-collision, Nina looked in the mirror – to see the Ram smash square on into a police car that had been chasing Eddie. The cruiser cartwheeled along the street in a storm of flying glass.

The impact had affected even the Dodge, the bullbar buckled back through the radiator grille and the hood crumpled upwards. Behind it, another police car skidded to a halt, cops breaking off their pursuit of the Lamborghini to help their colleagues.

'Did you see that?' Macy said breathlessly.

'Kinda hard to miss,' said Nina. 'Eddie!'

'You okay?' Eddie asked her as Grant held out the phone in his shaking hand.

'Yeah! Jesus, I nearly hit you!'

He turned west on to 39th Street. 'Head for Times Square – I'll get behind you and block them.'

'Eddie, one of them's got a machine gun!'

'I'll worry about the machine gun – you just put your foot down!'

Grant blinked. 'Worry about the *what*?'

But Eddie had something else to worry about. Ahead, a truck was reversing into a loading dock, blocking the street. He braked hard and blasted the horn in frustration. 'For fuck's sake! What next, two guys carrying a sheet of glass?'

The truck was clear; he veered round it, powering towards the Seventh Avenue intersection.

Nina's cab shot across the junction, heading north. If he could get ahead of the pickup—

The dented Ram roared past just before he made the turn. 'Shit!' He swung in behind it, vision filled by the broad red tailgate. Headlights blurred past on both sides. Like Broadway, Seventh was a one-way street, southbound only.

Grant cringed as an SUV passed uncomfortably close to the Murciélago. 'We'll never get past!'

'What're you talking about?' Eddie countered. 'We're in a fucking *Lamborghini*!' He dropped down a gear—

And floored the accelerator.

There was a gap in the traffic to the left – only short, but it was all he needed.

He hoped . . .

The Lamborghini surged forward, rocketing past the Ram with a triumphant howl and darting back in front of it. Eddie braked. Startled, the pickup's driver also slowed, his vehicle weaving, before realising he had the clear weight advantage and could just barge the supercar aside.

Eddie accelerated again, just enough to keep ahead of the truck. He saw Nina's cab pulling away as it headed for Times Square, its tail lights the only red points in the sea of headlights parting before it.

And directly ahead of it, a bus.

Ricardo gestured feebly. 'A bus, there is a bus.'

'I see it,' Nina told him. It was a red British-style double-decker, an open-topped tour vehicle for sightseers.

Coming straight at them.

'There is a bus!'

'I *see* it!' She flashed the headlights and pounded on the horn, keeping her foot down.

'What are you doing?' demanded Ricardo.

Macy stared in disbelief through the cracked partition. 'We're gonna hit it!'

'He'll stop, he'll stop . . .' Nina poised her other foot over the brake, ready to jam it down—

The bus driver chickened out first, the safety of the few passengers on the last tour of the night his top priority. He braked hard, the bus's wheels locking . . .

It skidded.

'Oh, that's bad,' Nina gasped. The bus slewed round through almost ninety degrees, a metal and glass roadblock.

But a driver in the lane to the right saw the danger and accelerated away just before the bus hit his car from behind – clearing a space.

Nina took it.

The Crown Victoria hit the kerb with a bang. A huge

NYPD logo on the wall of the Times Square station house filled Nina's vision; she screamed and spun the wheel, the front bumper rasping against the sign as the car careered along the sidewalk. People dived out of the way, but there was an obstacle dead ahead—

'Shit!' Nina wailed as she hit a hot dog cart. The vendor had already sprinted away, his stall spinning like a top in a spray of boiling water and flying frankfurters as the cab bowled it into the intersection.

Then she was clear, powersliding on to Broadway. She looked back . . .

The bus swayed to a standstill – blocking three lanes right in front of the Lamborghini.

'*Shiiiiit!*' Eddie and Grant cried. The only way to avoid a collision was to follow Nina—

A spine-jarring thump as they mounted the sidewalk, then Eddie turned hard left to round the bus, barely missing the whirling hot dog cart.

He too looked back—

The skidding Dodge Ram hit the bus.

It ploughed straight through it, the lower deck bursting apart in an explosion of shredded metal and flying seats. Most of the passengers were on the upper deck, those few downstairs fleeing for each end of the vehicle as the pickup rolled through its middle. It crashed down in Times Square, screeching to a stop on its side.

The Lamborghini also shrieked to a halt. Eddie opened the scissor door and jumped out, landing in a crouch to look over the supercar's bonnet. The overturned Ram was dribbling fuel from a ruptured line, its driver slumped bloodily through the smashed windscreen. Another of its occupants, a chunky bald man, had been thrown clear and lay near the hot dog cart. He still had a weapon clutched in one hand, a compact TEC-9 sub-machine gun.

The Lamborghini's other door swung up. Grant emerged – and to Eddie's dismay ran straight for the bald guy. 'Wait, get back!' he shouted.

The actor ignored him, reaching the weakly moving gunman – and kicking the TEC-9 out of his hand, sending it skittering away to clank against the wrecked Dodge. 'This is a citizen's arrest!' he proclaimed, putting a foot on the man's back and striking a pose. He grinned at Eddie. 'Just like in *Citizen's Arrest*, huh?'

'Idiot,' Eddie muttered, hurrying round the Murciélago. He passed the steaming hot dog cart, a blue flame from a squat gas cylinder still burning under its water tank. 'You okay?'

'Yeah, man. That was . . . intense. Wow!' A flash came from the top deck of the ruptured bus as someone took his photograph. 'So, did we save your—'

A cop ran round the bus, pistol raised. 'Freeze!' he bellowed. 'Put your hands up and get down on the ground, *now*!'

Eddie immediately raised his hands. Grant, meanwhile, faced the cop, unconcerned. 'It's okay, man. We're the good guys.' He nodded towards his billboard. 'See? It's me!'

The cop twisted his arm behind his back. 'Shut up! Get on your—'

The Ram's rear door flew open and Diamondback burst out like a Jack-in-the-box. He saw the three men and aimed his revolver—

Eddie tackled Grant, wrenching him from the cop's grip

as Diamondback fired. The bullet caught the cop in the chest. Blood spurted out as he crashed to the ground, his gun bouncing away and sliding under a stalled taxi. Its driver ran for cover.

Hauling Grant with him, Eddie dived over the cab's bonnet as Diamondback fired again, the taxi's windscreen exploding. He shoved Grant against the front wheel, spotting the cop's gun near the back.

Diamondback jumped down from the Ram. He fired another two shots at the cab, blowing out windows, then snatched up the TEC-9.

Eddie threw himself into a forward roll to the rear wheel and grabbed the gun, a Glock-19 automatic. He pressed his back against the wheel and checked on his charge.

Grant was shuffling towards him—

'Back!' Eddie yelled, diving at the actor as Diamondback opened fire on full auto. A string of ragged bullet holes blew open in the doors just behind him as he knocked Grant back. More bullets ripped into the front of the cab, piercing the thin steel bodywork – before clanging ineffectually against the solid metal of the engine block.

'Cars are *concealment*, not *cover*!' Eddie shouted at the shaken Grant as the onslaught stopped. 'Didn't they teach you *that* at action movie school?' He popped his head up. The snakeskin-jacketed gunman was out of ammo, dropping the TEC-9 and switching back to his revolvers. Nearby, the bald man, face a patchwork mess of cuts and grazes, staggered to his feet.

'Eddie!' a woman shouted. He looked round and saw the uniformed Amy approaching in a rapid crouch, her partner behind her.

Diamondback fired again, forcing everyone down. His companion drew a pistol as they retreated. 'What the hell's going on?' Amy demanded.

'Ask them!' he replied, gesturing towards the gunmen. 'They're the twats who just tried to kill my wife!'

Another shot punched through the cab, spitting shrapnel. Grant yelped, and Amy flinched. 'NYPD!' she shouted. 'Drop your weapons!'

More bullet hits on the cab, the sharp crack of an automatic joining the revolvers' louder blasts. The two men weren't receptive to orders. Eddie looked under the taxi's front bumper to see them hurriedly backing away as other cops returned fire. With an officer already down and civilians at risk, they were shooting to kill – but he needed at least one of the gunmen alive to learn why they wanted Nina dead.

He hefted the Glock – and fired it under the car, the bullet tearing a bloody hole in the bald man's right ankle. He fell, screaming. Eyes narrowed to agonised slits, he looked up at Diamondback. 'Help me!'

Diamondback returned his gaze . . . then without even changing expression shot him in the head. A sunburst of blood sprayed the street beneath him.

'Jesus!' Amy gasped as Diamondback took refuge behind the overturned Ram. Then she realised what Eddie was about to do. 'No, wait!'

But Eddie had already sprung out from behind the taxi, running at the pickup with the gun raised. His target was behind the Dodge . . . and it was no more bulletproof than the cab. He aimed low, hoping for a leg shot as he blew a line of holes from the back of the truck to the cabin—

Diamondback dived out from the front of the truck – and fired.

But he wasn't aiming at Eddie.

The shot hit the hot dog cart's gas cylinder – which detonated like a bomb.

The concussion knocked Eddie off his feet. By the time the roiling explosion dissipated and the cops recovered from the shock of the blast, Diamondback had sprinted away down 43rd Street, shoving through the fleeing crowd.

Eddie swatted away a burning hot dog bun and stood painfully. Amy hurried to him, other cops running past them – some to help the injured officer, the rest in fruitless pursuit of the killer. 'You okay?'

'I'll live,' he grunted, looking at the bald man. 'Unlike him.'

Amy shook her head, still stunned by what she had just witnessed. 'Cold-blooded murder, right in front of a bunch of cops? That guy's insane.'

'Maybe, but he's good at what he does. I don't think your guys'll catch him.'

'We'll see,' Amy said with wounded professional pride – but also a certain resignation.

Grant came over, face white. 'Whoa. Man. You, you . . .' He pumped Eddie's hand vigorously. Amy's eyebrows shot up as she recognised him. 'You saved my life, man! I'd be dead now if you hadn't been there!'

Eddie decided not to mention that it was Grant's own fault he'd become a target. 'All part of the job.'

'No, man, seriously. Anything you want, anything you ever need, just let me know. It's yours.'

'How about your Lamborghini? Kidding,' he clarified,

seeing from Grant's face that 'anything' didn't literally mean *anything*.

'Man!' said Grant, gazing at the Murciélago. 'I can't believe it. You said not a scratch, and damn, you did it!'

Even with the scrapes it had taken the Lamborghini appeared unscathed, reflected firelight gleaming off its paintwork. 'Yeah. Normally anything I drive gets totalled. Must have got lucky this time . . .'

The trickle of gasoline from the wrecked Ram reached one of the burning buns.

'Buggeration—' Eddie began, throwing Grant and Amy down as a line of flame scurried back to the pickup's fuel tank—

The Ram exploded, somersaulting end over end through the air – to smash down on top of the Murciélago, crushing it flat.

Eddie sat up. 'And fuckery.'

Grant gasped plaintively at the sight of three hundred thousand dollars of scrap metal. Somebody on the bus took another photo. 'Oh, *man*!'

'You had insurance, right?' said Amy.

His expression gradually relaxed. 'Yeah. Huh. Good point. And I wasn't sure about the colour anyway.'

'Eddie!' Eddie got up as Nina ran to him. 'Oh my God, you're okay!'

'Forget me, it's you I was worried about.'

They embraced, then she looked back at her battered cab. Macy had done as Nina told her and run off, but there was still someone in the vehicle. She turned to Amy. 'You've got to get an ambulance. The cab driver got shot.'

'I think we'll need more than one,' Amy told her, radio

already in her hand. 'Eddie, I don't know what just happened here, but you are sure as hell going to tell me.' She regarded Nina, then Grant. 'And so are you, and you . . . hell, I should arrest everyone in a five block radius!'

'You know her?' Nina asked Eddie.

'Yeah, she's a friend.'

Her expression became more suspicious as she looked the attractive police officer up and down. 'Wait . . . your *cop* friend? The one you were with the other morning?'

'Ah . . . yeah,' he admitted. 'That one.'

'You're Eddie's wife?' Amy asked. Nina nodded. 'Okay, tell you what – how 'bout we make all the introductions down at the precinct?'

5

'Well,' said Eddie, slumping on to the couch the following morning, 'when I said "Let's see what tomorrow brings" . . . that was more than I had in mind.'

'Getting chased and shot at?' Nina replied. 'It was just like old times – in exactly the way I *didn't* want. I'm amazed we didn't end up in jail.'

'You can thank Grant for some of that. You know who he rang with his phone call? His manager. Who rang his publicist, who rang the mayor . . .'

'The mayor?' said Nina, surprised.

'Yeah. That charity thing the other night? They met each other there. And since the mayor was fawning over the hot Hollywood star and having loads of photos taken with him, it would've been a massive embarrassment if his new best mate got locked up a couple of days later.' He grinned humourlessly. 'Which is why Grant's in today's papers as a real-life action hero instead of as a mugshot. But it's Amy we really owe.'

Nina's lips tightened. 'Why her?'

'She vouched for us, basically. That twat in the snakeskin

jacket blowing someone's head off in front of half the NYPD made it pretty obvious who the bad guys were, but we'd still have been in trouble if she hadn't stood up for us.'

'Stood up for *you*, you mean.'

Eddie knew the tone. 'Oh, God. What?'

'You *know* what, Eddie. That woman, Amy – you were with *her* the other day when you said you were with Grant Thorn!'

He held out his hands in exasperation. 'Yes, I admit it! But there's nothing funny going on – she's just a friend. I've got loads of other female friends all over the world, and you've never had any problems with them.'

'That's because you didn't lie to me about them! How many other times did you tell me you were working while you were seeing her?'

'For fuck's sake,' he sighed, 'I'm not *seeing* her, okay? We're not meeting up in secret to bang each other's brains out, if that's what you think.'

'Then what *should* I think?' Nina demanded, but before she could get an answer the door buzzer rasped. She went to the speaker. 'Yes?'

'Dr Wilde? It's Macy.'

'Come on up.' She pushed the button to unlock the outer door, then turned back to Eddie. 'We'll discuss this later.'

'There's nothing *to* bloody discuss,' he said. 'She's just helping me with something, all right?'

'So why didn't you ask me to help you? That's what husbands and wives are supposed to do – y'know, help each other.'

'It's not that kind of thing.'

Nina was about to ask what kind of thing it actually was

when there was a knock at the door. She opened it to find Macy, still in her skimpy clothes from the previous night. Eddie automatically checked her out, earning a scowl from his wife. 'Macy, come in,' she said.

'Thanks, Dr Wilde,' she replied, entering the apartment. 'I'm glad you're okay.'

'Yeah, me too. Are you okay? Is your friend all right?'

'Joey? He's fine, just a bit banged up. I called him after I found a hotel for the night. Oh, here's your phone.' She handed it back to Nina. 'What about you?'

'We spent most of the night being questioned by the police, which was fun. This is my husband, by the way,' Nina said, indicating Eddie. 'Eddie. Chase. Who lives up to his surname when it comes to skirts, apparently.'

Eddie made an irritated noise, then went to Macy. 'Hi. Yeah, I'm Nina's husband – and part-time bodyguard. For all the thanks I get.'

'Hi.' Macy gave his hand a perfunctory shake, giving him a look-over that was equally brief. Nina could tell what she was thinking – *too old, too bald* – and smirked.

'So,' he said, sitting down, 'now you're here, maybe someone can finally tell me what the hell's going on? Like why something in Egypt meant I had to nick Grant Thorn's Lamborghini and chase you halfway across town?'

'You know Grant Thorn?' Macy asked. 'He is *so* hot. Wow. That's cool.'

'Grant Thorn's not who we should be talking about,' said Nina, seeing that Macy's opinion of Eddie had just been revised upwards. 'It's those guys who were after you. Were they the same ones who chased you in Egypt?'

'Only the guy with the bad hair and the terrible jacket.'

'Thought his jacket was pretty cool, myself,' said Eddie. He frowned, a memory tickling his mind.

'What?' Nina asked.

'I saw someone with the same jacket, just recently . . .' His frown deepened as he tried to recall the image. 'Shit! It wasn't just the same jacket – it was the same guy! He was at that cult thing Grant dragged me to.'

'The Osirian Temple?'

'Yeah, that's it. He was in a limo with the head guy, some ex-actor. There was another bloke too, this miserable-looking sod with a big burn scar—'

'Oh, my God!' Macy interrupted. She tapped her right cheek. 'The scar, was it here?'

'Yeah, right across his face.'

'He was there too!' she told Nina excitedly. 'He was at the Sphinx – he was in charge of the whole thing!'

'What *is* this thing at the Sphinx?' asked Eddie. 'What are they after?'

'You know those TV commercials that get me so mad?' said Nina. He nodded. 'They're after that.'

'They're trying to dig in before the IHA so that they can steal what's inside,' Macy elaborated.

'Which is?' Eddie said.

Macy took out her camera. 'I'll show you.' She saw Nina's laptop. 'Can I connect it to that?'

Nina rummaged in a drawer for a connecting cable, then plugged the camera into her MacBook Pro so Macy could copy over the relevant files. A minute later, she was able to take a proper, detailed look at the images she had seen in miniature on the camera's screen. 'So those are the three scrolls that were given to the IHA . . .'

'And that's the one that wasn't,' said Macy, pointing at the fourth of the ancient pages. She zoomed in. 'This part here describes the north entrance to the Hall of Records – it would've been reserved for the pharaohs' use, 'cause the Egyptians had a big thing about the Pole Star symbolising royalty and the gods.' She flicked through to the next picture, showing the blueprints of the Sphinx compound, and pointed out the two tunnels. 'Everyone else would have used the eastern entrance.'

'The one Logan's excavating,' Nina said, nodding. 'What else does it say?'

Macy returned to the first picture and scrolled down it. 'Something about a map chamber . . . here! There's a zodiac in it, which if you know the secret tells you how to find the Pyramid of Osiris.'

Nina's scepticism returned. 'Are you *sure* that's what it says?'

Macy sounded almost peevish, before remembering to whom she was talking. 'Yes, I'm sure, Dr Wilde. I thought it was weird too, but that's what it says. The zodiac's some kind of map.'

Nina regarded the screen. The first three scrolls about the Hall of Records had proved accurate, and if the fourth were as reliable . . . 'This could be huge. If the Pyramid of Osiris really existed, it'd change everything we thought we knew about Egyptian history.' She looked at Macy. 'And the guys after you obviously believed it's real enough to kill for.' Her gaze returned to the papyrus. 'What else does it say?'

Macy read on. 'The tomb of Osiris, the immortal god-king, keeper of . . . of the sacred bread of life.'

'Not much of an immortal if he's in a tomb,' Eddie pointed out.

'It's complicated,' said Macy. 'He was murdered by being trapped in a coffin, resurrected, murdered again, became immortal but could never come back to the living world . . . kind of an ancient daytime soap opera.'

'It's a *bit* more than that,' Nina said tartly. 'The Osiris mythology is the foundation of the entire Egyptian religion. But does this text tell us how to find the pyramid using the zodiac?'

Macy scanned through the rest of the papyrus. 'No. I guess that's a need-to-know thing for the priests or whoever. But it definitely says the zodiac's the map to the tomb.'

Eddie leaned closer to the screen. 'So if this pyramid's real, what's inside it that's worth blowing up half of Times Square for? Are we talking Tutankhamun's treasure?'

'More than that,' Macy told him. 'Osiris is who all the other pharaohs aspired to be – the greatest Egyptian king *ever*. Even though they thought they were going to become gods themselves when they died, none of them would ever have dared try to out-bling him, because he's the guy who actually judges if they deserve to go into the next life or not.'

'So all the pharaohs' treasures that have ever been found,' said Nina thoughtfully, 'would still be less valuable than whatever's in Osiris's tomb. And considering how incredible some of the finds from other tombs have been . . .'

Eddie stood back. 'There's your motive, then. Money. Lots and lots of money.' He indicated the screen. 'Go on the

Internet – I think we should have a gander at this Osirian Temple thing.'

Macy opened the browser, typing in the address of the Qexia search engine. 'Not using Google?' Eddie asked.

'This is cooler,' she said, entering a search string for the Osirian Temple. A 'cloud' of results appeared, the largest at the centre. She clicked it, taking them to the cult's home page. A heavily airbrushed portrait of Khalid Osir, standing before what appeared to be a large pyramid of black glass, smiled at them.

'That's the guy I saw the other day,' said Eddie. 'Used to be a big movie star in Egypt.'

Nina read his potted biography. 'And then he got religion. Though I guess his ego was too big for him to just join someone else's – he had to start his own.' According to the bio, Osir had founded the Osirian Temple fifteen years previously, the organisation now headquartered in Switzerland and established in over fifty countries.

'Looks like it's a nice little earner,' Eddie said as Macy clicked through to other pages. As much of the site seemed to be devoted to selling merchandise as to explaining the cult's beliefs.

Macy snorted sarcastically at one section of the latter. 'What? That's not even right! Osiris wasn't immortal while he was still alive – that didn't happen until he entered the Underworld.'

Nina scanned the rest of the text. 'Huh. For a cult that's based round the myths of Osiris, it doesn't seem too interested in the accepted versions of those myths. It's like this guy Osir's deliberately ignoring anything that conflicts with what he's trying to say.'

'Trying to *sell*, you mean,' Eddie corrected as another page opened, more catalogue than catechism. 'Look at all this stuff. Diets, exercise plans, vitamins . . . it'll all help you live longer, yeah, but he slaps a picture of a pyramid on it and charges five times more than you'd pay at the supermarket, *and* makes you listen to a load of religious twaddle while you're doing it.'

'It's not just "twaddle", Eddie,' Nina chided. 'People might not believe in it now, but it was the basis of a civilisation that lasted for almost three thousand years.'

'Maybe, but this Osir bloke's making it up as he goes. So, typical cult, really.'

Macy had meanwhile found another page: the Osirian Temple's leaders. Osir took pride of place at the top, but below his entry was a smaller, black and white picture of another man with similar features.

'Sebak Shaban,' Nina read. 'They look a lot alike – maybe they're brothers.'

'Yeah, I thought that,' Eddie said, remembering seeing them together two days earlier. 'How come they've got different surnames?'

'Duh,' Macy said off-handedly. 'Osiris, Osir? It's like a stage name.' Eddie glared at her, but she didn't notice. 'And yeah, total Photoshop.' The picture of Shaban very much favoured the left side of his face, but the part of his upper lip that in real life was scarred here appeared completely normal.

Nina leaned back. 'And you're absolutely sure he was in charge of whatever was going on at the Sphinx?'

'Totally. It was him.'

'And the guy from last night works for him?' Macy nodded. 'Okay, so they really, *really* want to make sure you don't tell anyone about it.'

'So what do we do?' Macy asked.

'We tell someone about it,' said Eddie. '*Duh.*'

She pouted. 'I tried. Nobody in Egypt would listen to me. When I phoned Dr Berkeley, he just told me to turn myself in to the police.'

'How did you get out of Egypt if the police were looking for you?' asked Nina.

'Through Jordan. I heard him,' she indicated Shaban, 'say to watch the airports, so I couldn't get out that way. But I had my passport and some money with me, so once I got back into Cairo I took a bus to this little town out on the east coast, and persuaded some guy to take me across to Jordan in his boat. Then I got another bus to Amman, flew back to America, and here I am!'

Macy was more resourceful than she seemed, Nina decided. Even Eddie appeared mildly impressed that she had evaded the authorities. 'And then, out of everybody you could have turned to, you came to me.'

'Because I knew you could help. And you did. If you hadn't saved me, that guy would have killed me. So, thanks!'

'Not a problem,' Nina replied. Eddie grunted sarcastically. 'But now you're safe—'

'I hope,' Macy cut in, glancing warily at the door.

'I think that after last night's little debacle, the bad guys will be trying to get as far away from New York as possible. But since you're *hopefully* safe, and we've got the pictures, we can tell the IHA what's happened.' She gave Eddie an uncertain look. 'That's assuming Maureen Rothschild will even speak to me.'

Persuading Lola to ask Rothschild if she would take a call from Nina was easy. Actually getting Rothschild to answer proved harder. It took three attempts, Nina telling Lola to relay increasingly hyperbolic pleas before the older woman finally, and resentfully, picked up.

'Well, this should be interesting, Nina,' she snapped. 'After last night, I'm surprised you're not calling me from prison. From what I saw on the news, there were two dead, several injured, a colossal amount of property damage and half the city thrown into chaos. Just another day for you, isn't it?'

Nina held back an acidic reply, forcing herself to remain diplomatic. 'Maureen, this is very important. It's about the dig at the Sphinx.'

'What about it?'

'Someone's trying to rob the Hall of Records before Logan can open it.'

There was a brief silence before Rothschild's disbelieving, explosive, '*What?*'

'The Osirian Temple – they're behind it. They used a *fourth* page of the Gaza scrolls that they didn't give to the IHA to locate a second entrance. They're digging into it right now.'

Another pause. Then, to Nina's anger, a mocking laugh. 'Thank you, Nina, for confirming my theory – you *have* gone completely insane. I thought claiming to discover the Garden of Eden was outrageous enough, but this? Why would the Osirian Temple carry out a second dig when they're already helping pay for the first one?'

'Maybe you should ask them,' Nina growled. 'But I've got a picture right here of the fourth scroll, as well as a plan of the tunnel.'

'And where did you get these pictures? One of those websites that claims there are flying saucers recorded in Egyptian hieroglyphics?'

'No, from Macy Sharif.'

'Macy Sharif? You mean the intern?'

'That's right.'

'The intern who's wanted by the Egyptian police for assault and antiquities theft?'

Nina glanced at Macy, who was watching anxiously. 'I think she was framed. Everything that happened last night was because they were trying to kill her, so she couldn't tell anyone what she'd discovered.'

Rothschild's voice turned cold. 'Nina, I really do not have the time to listen to paranoid conspiracy theories. Don't call me again.'

'At least look at the pictures. I'll send them to you—'

'Don't bother.' She hung up.

'God damn it,' Nina muttered. She emailed the pictures anyway, then called Lola once more.

'I'm guessing it didn't go well,' said Lola. 'Professor Rothschild just told me never to put you through to her again.'

'Yeah, I thought she might. Listen, I just sent her an email with some photos attached – she'll probably delete it without even looking, but I'm going to send it to you as well. Can you print them out and put them in her in-tray or something? It's *really* important that she at least looks at them.'

'I'll see what I can do. Hey, did you see what happened in Times Square last night?'

'I might have heard something,' said Nina, deadpan. 'Bye, Lola.' She sent a second copy of the email to Lola, then slumped in her chair. 'God, this is so frustrating! If I'd still been at the IHA I could have had someone check it out in five minutes.'

'There's got to be something else you can do,' Macy protested. 'If these guys get their hands on the zodiac, they'll work out how to find the Pyramid of Osiris and go rob it – and nobody else will ever know that they've done it. The whole place'll be lost for ever! Is that what you want?'

'Of course it's not what I want,' Nina snapped. 'But there's not really much I can do about it, is there? Unless we actually go to Egypt and catch them red-handed . . .' She tailed off.

Eddie recognised her look. 'No,' he said in a warning tone.

'We *could* go to Egypt.'

'No, we couldn't.'

'Yes, we could.'

'We don't have visas.'

'Our UN visas are still valid.'

'We've got no bloody money!'

'We've got credit cards.'

'That are almost maxed out!'

'*I've* got a credit card,' offered Macy. 'I'll pay.'

Nina gave the nineteen year old an incredulous look. 'Are you serious?'

'Sure! I've got tons of credit.'

'Must be nice,' Eddie muttered.

Nina was still dubious. 'I don't know how much it costs to fly to Egypt, but I'm pretty sure it's not cheap. We can cover it ourselves.'

He made a face. 'If we sell a kidney or two.'

'It's not a problem, I can afford it,' said Macy. 'Well, my mom and dad can, but same diff. My dad's a plastic surgeon and my mom's a psychiatrist, they're really rich. They pay for all my stuff anyway.'

'Wait a minute,' said Nina. 'Macy, have you actually *told* your parents about any of this?'

She looked sheepish. 'Ah, that would be *no*. They don't even know I'm back in the country.'

Nina was horrified. 'Oh, my God! How could you not tell them?'

'I was trying to protect them! That scar-faced guy said he was going to send people to watch our house and tap the phones, so they could find me. If Mom and Dad didn't know anything was wrong, they wouldn't get worried, and they couldn't give me away.'

'Well, they'll know something's wrong now,' Nina told her. 'Even if the IHA didn't contact them after you got in trouble – which I'm pretty sure they would have done – I had to tell the police about meeting you last night. They'll have got your parents' details from the IHA, and called them.'

Macy went pale. 'Oh. I . . . didn't think of that.'

Nina indicated the phone. 'Call them, right now. Let them know you're okay.'

She picked it up and dialled. 'Mom, hi! Mom? Mom, calm down – I'm okay, I'm fine. Yes, I'm okay, really! Oh, the IHA called, huh?' She grimaced. 'No, that's not what happened at all, they're totally lying!' She huffed impatiently. 'Mom! No, I can't come home, not just yet. I'll come back as soon as I can, but there's something I need to do first, it's really important. I'll tell you and Dad all about it afterwards. Oh, and if you think anyone's watching the house, call the police, 'kay?'

That prompted a near-hysterical response loud enough for her hosts to overhear. 'Jeez, Mom! Look, really, I'm okay. I'll talk to you soon, okay? Give my love to everyone. Mom. Mom! I said I'll *call* you. Okay, hanging up now. Bye. Bye.'

Macy lowered the phone, looking flustered and frustrated. 'Parents! God! They can be such a pain sometimes.' Then she looked at Nina, suddenly apologetic. 'Oh! Sorry.'

Nina was confused. 'For what?'

'I read in the *Time* article that your parents died when you were about my age, so I didn't want you to think I was saying that about *all* parents. I'm sure yours were great. Sorry.' She went back to the laptop.

'Er . . . okay,' said Nina, taken aback.

'Subtle, ain't she?' Eddie whispered.

'Yeah. I think you two'll get along fine.'

'Tchah!'

'Okay,' said Macy, looking round at them, 'so, flights to Egypt. Do you guys want regular or vegetarian meals?'

6

Giza

'Hey,' joked Eddie, 'didn't they get smashed up by the Transformers?'

'I am *so* never letting you choose the movie again,' muttered Nina as she gazed in awe at the three enormous monuments before them. The Great Pyramid of Giza was the only survivor of the Seven Wonders of the ancient world, the others lost to time and conflict millennia ago. Part of the reason for its endurance was sheer size; though Khufu's pyramid and its companions, the slightly lower Pyramid of Khafre and the markedly smaller – but still massive – Pyramid of Menkaure, had long since lost almost all of their white limestone outer casings, their colossal cores of sandstone and granite remained intact after more than four and a half thousand years.

Macy was less impressed. Her hair hidden beneath a

baseball cap and her face partly covered by a pair of oversized sunglasses, she ground an impatient foot into the gritty sand. 'I've already seen the pyramids. Like, every day I was here. Why aren't you talking to Dr Berkeley?'

'Partly because he's not here yet.' Afraid of being recognised, Macy had not gone with Nina and Eddie to the Sphinx compound, where they unsuccessfully tried to persuade the IHA team to grant them access. 'He's doing some TV show in Cairo, talking about the dig. He won't be back for a couple of hours. And partly because . . . well, I'm not coming all the way to Egypt and *not* visiting the pyramids!'

They set off up the road along the compound's northern side. Eddie peered over the wall at the construction site below. 'This shaft, it's down there?'

Macy joined him. 'Yeah. In that tent.' She pointed it out.

He made a mental note of its position, also taking in that it was better guarded than Macy had described. Two men in uniform – though not that of the Tourist Police, suggesting they were private security contractors – were on watch.

Macy looked towards the Sphinx. 'There are more guards than before.'

'Making sure nobody else cocks up their dig,' Eddie said. 'Might be a good thing, though.'

'How?'

'If they've brought in new guys, there's less chance of someone recognising you.' He ran his fingers along the underside of the stone slab topping the wall as if testing its weight.

'Something?' Nina asked.

'Just planning ahead. So, we going to get some pyramid power?'

The Great Pyramid's base was only about a quarter of a mile from the Sphinx, though the massive area it covered, the bottom of each face over 750 feet long, meant the walk needed to reach the entrance on the northern side was close to twice that. The entrance itself, where several dozen people were already waiting, was gated and watched by the Tourist Police and official guides. Access to the pyramids' interiors was only allowed twice a day to small numbers. Even exhausted by the eleven-hour flight from New York, Nina had insisted they be there the moment the ticket office opened.

When the gate opened, some discreet but firm blocking by Eddie allowed Nina and Macy to be the first to scale the stone tiers and enter. 'It's steeper than it looks in pictures,' Nina commented. The narrow, smooth-walled passage descended into the heart of the pyramid at almost a thirty-degree angle, and the ceiling was uncomfortably low.

Eddie caught up, squeezing past an annoyed tourist at the entrance. 'Christ, it's cramped,' he complained. 'Guess the pharaohs were all short-arses. So, where does this go?'

'There're two routes,' said Macy. 'If you keep going down you end up in the original burial chamber, but it's kinda boring, there's nothing there. They decided to use a different chamber while the pyramid was being built.'

'Must've pissed off the architects,' Eddie said, grinning. 'I can just imagine it. "He wants to do *what*? But we're already halfway finished. Fucking clients!" '

After sixty feet the passage split, one leg continuing down while the other, its ceiling even lower, headed upwards at an equally steep angle. Though she wanted to explore the entire place, Nina opted to take Macy's words to heart and follow the latter route. Even this early in the morning, the air in the tunnels was hot and stifling. Leg muscles protesting at the floor's steepness, she headed up the passage, bent low.

'So did this place have any booby traps?' Eddie asked.

'Booby traps? Shyeah,' said Macy sarcastically. 'You only get those in *Tomb Raider* games.'

'Oh, ya think?' Nina said, prompting a surprised look from the other woman. 'You should try reading the *International Journal of Archaeology* rather than just magazine articles sometime.'

'I *do* read the *IJA*!' Macy insisted. 'Well, the interesting bits.'

'It's *all* interesting,' said Nina, affronted.

'Right, like finding sixteenth-century Mongolian toothpicks compares to discovering Atlantis.' Behind Macy, Eddie laughed, annoying Nina even more.

But her irritation vanished as she arrived at another section of the pyramid's interior. A horizontal passage branched off the one she was ascending, but it was the continuation of the climb that caught her attention. Though little wider than the tunnel from which she had just emerged, it was far taller, almost thirty feet high. The Great Gallery was a long vaulted chamber constructed from massive limestone blocks.

'Now this is more like it,' said Eddie, stretching as he emerged from the passage. 'What was it for?'

'There's a theory that it was part of a counterweight system to lift blocks up to the top, but . . . nobody really knows,' Nina admitted. Like so many aspects of the pyramids, the Great Gallery's exact purpose was a mystery. She looked down the horizontal passage. 'That's the Queen's Chamber down there, right?'

'Yeah,' said Macy as more tourists entered, most of them opting to take a break from the climb by going along the flat corridor. 'Although there was never a queen in there – her pyramid's a little one outside. It's just another boring unfinished burial chamber.'

'Another one?' said Eddie. 'Christ, the architects must have been throwing down their papyruses by now.'

'Even if it's empty, it's hardly boring,' Nina objected as she continued up the steps that had been added to the Gallery. 'The workmanship – of all of this – is amazing even by today's standards, and they did it all with just simple tools.'

'And loads of slaves.'

'Nuh-uh,' Macy countered. 'The builders were actually all skilled craftsmen. They got paid. The slave thing's just a lie that the pharaohs who came after Khufu, or Cheops, whatever you want to call him, spread to make themselves sound better. "Sure, *we* could have built an enormous pyramid too if *we'd* used loads of slaves," kind of thing. Khufu wasn't any worse than any other pharaoh.'

'So why'd they decide to build pyramids in the first place?' Eddie asked. 'What's so special about that shape?'

'Nobody knows,' said Nina.

'I'm going to hear that a lot, aren't I?'

'It's probably symbolic, something of religious significance, but nobody's come to any agreement on exactly what. But it's a shape they spent a lot of time and effort trying to perfect, even in the earliest dynasties. The pyramids back then were stepped like ziggurats, one layer on top of another, but as their engineering skills improved they started building them with smooth sides. A pharaoh called . . . Sneferu, I think?' Nina glanced back at Macy, who nodded, pleased to be asked. 'He built the Red Pyramid at Dahshur, which was the first "true" pyramid. It was pretty big – but the pyramid built by his son was a lot bigger. And we're in it.' She swept out her hands to take in the vast structure surrounding them. 'As for *why* they were so determined to build pyramids . . . like I said, nobody knows.'

They reached the top of the incline, Nina pausing to recover her breath. To her mild irritation, Macy appeared completely unfazed by the climb. Another low horizontal passage led deeper into the tomb, opening into a taller chamber after just a few feet. Eddie peered inside, seeing deep grooves running up the far wall. 'What's this?'

'Anti-theft device,' said Macy.

'Thought you said there weren't any booby traps?'

'It's not really a trap. More like a vault door. They built it with three huge stone blocks hanging from the ceiling. Once Khufu was buried, they dropped the stones so tomb raiders couldn't get in.'

They entered; the room was completely empty. 'So where are the stones?'

'Tomb raiders got in,' Macy chirped. 'They smashed the stones, then walked right into the burial chamber. It's just through here.' Another hunched traversal of a short stone tunnel, then . . .

The King's Chamber. The burial vault of the pharaoh

Khufu, sealed over four and a half thousand years before.

'This is it?' asked Eddie, disappointed. The rectangular room was almost forty feet by twenty, dominated by the remains of a large granite sarcophagus – but apart from the lidless coffin it was completely empty. Not even the walls bore any decoration. 'I was expecting something a bit more flash.'

'It *did* get Lara Crofted,' Macy pointed out, a little condescendingly. 'If it was like Tutankhamun's tomb, the whole room would have been full of treasure.' Her eyes lit up at the thought.

'It wouldn't all be treasure,' Nina reminded her. 'A lot of it would have been items for Khufu's journey through the Underworld to be judged by Osiris – food and drink, things like that. But yeah, there would still have been plenty of treasure.'

Eddie stood aside as other tourists entered, leaning against the granite wall. He watched as Nina examined the sarcophagus, after a minute saying, 'I don't think he's in there.'

'I *know* that. I just don't get many chances to see things like this in person any more, do I?'

'You should have asked the Egyptians when you were at the IHA,' Macy suggested. 'They'd have probably given you a private tour.'

Nina's mouth compressed into a sour line. 'Yeah, thanks for reminding me.'

'So when will Dr Berkeley be back at the dig? We should get back there – the sooner you talk to him, the sooner you'll be able to check out the construction site.'

'She's got a point,' said Eddie.

'All right,' Nina muttered, reluctantly leaving the sarcophagus. 'I'm going to be pissed if you've dragged me out of here and he still hasn't arrived when we get there, though.'

To Nina's annoyance, Berkeley indeed had not yet returned from his TV appearance when they got back to the Sphinx compound. He was expected in thirty minutes – thirty minutes Nina could have spent exploring the Great Pyramid.

When he eventually did arrive, it was closer to fifty than thirty minutes later, which did not improve Nina's mood. But she put on a pleasant face, knowing she would need to charm him into allowing her access to the dig. Berkeley got out of a white-painted government car, its driver emerging as well. 'Hey,' Eddie whispered.

'What?'

'The other bloke, he's the one from Macy's photos. The one she clocked with her camera.'

'Crap, you're right.' Berkeley's companion was Dr Hamdi. She glanced past the Temple of the Sphinx at the more intact Valley Temple to the south. Macy, still in her baseball hat and sunglasses, was lurking amongst the milling tourists, as close as she dared come to the dig site. 'If Macy's right, then he's not going to want anyone to go near that tent.'

'Bit late to start wondering *if* she's right, innit?'

'Maybe we'll find out now – we'll see how this Dr Hamdi responds.' She approached Berkeley, Eddie behind her. 'Hey, Logan! Logan! Hi!'

Berkeley reacted with first surprise, then wary

uncertainty when he realised who was calling to him. 'Nina? What are you doing here?'

'Oh, just on vacation,' she replied airily. 'We wanted to drop by and say hello, seeing as it's your big event tonight.'

'Tomorrow morning, technically – the live broadcast starts at four a.m., local time.' Berkeley's wariness was creeping towards outright suspicion, not believing for a moment that their presence was a holiday-related coincidence.

Hamdi had an odd look of half-recognition. 'Friends of yours, Dr Berkeley?'

'Colleagues,' Berkeley said firmly. '*Ex*-colleagues. Nina, Eddie, this is the SCA's representative at the excavation, Dr Iabi Hamdi. Dr Hamdi, Nina Wilde and Eddie Chase, formerly of the IHA.'

Nina noted that Berkeley had omitted her title from his introduction, but had no time to make a sarcastic correction before Hamdi spoke. 'Dr Wilde! But of course! How could I not have known?'

'Well, I did change my hairstyle.'

He smiled. 'A great pleasure to meet you.'

'Likewise.' She shook the Egyptian's hand. 'And this is Eddie, my husband.'

'Husband?' said Berkeley, taken aback. 'You got married?'

'Don't worry, we weren't expecting a present off you,' Eddie said.

Nina looked over the ruins to the Sphinx. 'I was wondering . . . would it be possible for us to see the actual excavation site?'

'Sorry,' said Berkeley, tight-lipped. 'Authorised personnel only.'

Again, Nina restrained herself from remarking on his dismissive attitude. Instead, she addressed Hamdi. 'That's a shame. Couldn't the SCA make an exception, Dr Hamdi?'

The Egyptian was more polite, but just as unhelpful. 'I'm afraid not, Dr Wilde. Once the Hall of Records has been opened and everything properly catalogued, then perhaps, but for now we have to maintain strict security.' He nodded towards the guards at the nearby gate. 'We had some trouble on the site recently.'

'So I heard.'

Berkeley frowned. 'You did?'

'Yeah. A girl called . . . Macy Sharif, wasn't it?' She watched their responses closely. Berkeley seemed stung that word had got out about something so potentially embarrassing – but Hamdi physically flinched, as though he had just received a real sting. 'Something about her stealing a piece of the Sphinx, wasn't it?'

'And – and assaulting me, yes,' said the flustered Hamdi, rubbing his nose.

Berkeley's expression darkened. 'Where did you hear about that?' he snapped. 'It was Lola, wasn't it?'

'No, it wasn't, actually,' she said, defending her friend. 'It was Macy.'

Whatever had stung Hamdi was now draining the blood from his face. 'You've spoken to her? Where?'

'In New York,' she said casually. 'She told me an interesting story about what was going on here.' Her gaze hardened, fixing on Hamdi. 'And after what happened when I met her, I'm inclined to believe her.'

'What *did* happen?' Berkeley asked.

'Things went a bit Michael Bay,' said Eddie. 'Gunfights, car chases, explosions – the usual.'

'Whatever she told you is a lie,' Hamdi said, a little too quickly.

Nina indicated the wall below the road. 'There's an easy way to find out. Logan, there's a tent over there. If you take a look inside, I think you'll find something interesting.'

'Like what?'

'Like a shaft that leads to a second entrance to the Hall of Records. Somebody's trying to beat you to it.'

Berkeley stared at her. 'Absolute horseshit,' he finally said.

'Excuse me?' said Nina, affronted.

'This is pathetic, quite frankly. Maureen told me you'd been to see her with some holier-than-thou protest about the opening of the Hall being televised – as if you've never taken advantage of the media when it suited you! The cover of *Time*? Appearing on *The Tonight Show*?' His face curled into a sneer. 'Well, now it's someone else's turn in the spotlight, and you just can't take that, can you?'

'It's nothing to do with me,' she growled. 'It's about protecting an archaeological treasure – and maybe even saving you and the IHA from a huge embarrassment.'

Berkeley rolled his eyes. 'Oh, please. The only embarrassment to the IHA is *you*, Nina. I suppose after that Garden of Eden garbage you were spouting last year, whatever nonsense Macy came up with to cover her ass was probably right up your street.'

Nina could tell that Eddie was on the verge of punching Berkeley, and moved to block him, though she was sorely tempted to take a swing herself. 'I wasn't "spouting" anything – that was a smear job. Not that I expect you to believe me. But you don't have to believe me about this either. Just look in that tent. I'll even wait right here, so if I'm wrong and there's nothing there you can call me an idiot to my face! How about it?'

'This is ridiculous,' blustered Hamdi. 'There is no shaft, there is no robbery.'

'Well, you would say that,' said Eddie. 'Seeing as you're on the take.'

The Egyptian's eyes bulged in outrage. 'That – that is slander!'

'Easy way to prove it, isn't there? Look in the tent.'

Hamdi scurried for the security gate. 'Dr Berkeley, I refuse to stand here and be insulted. I will see you at the excavation – and I am very tempted to have these two removed from the plateau!' One of the guards raised a hand to stop him, apparently unaware who he was, but the other said something and he stood back.

Berkeley shook his head. 'You know, it's really sad that you've come down to this level, Nina. I don't know whether I should pity you or laugh at you.'

'One of 'em'll hurt you a lot more than the other,' Eddie rumbled.

Berkeley looked decidedly uncomfortable at the not-so-veiled threat. 'I always thought you were too close to the edge,' he sniffed as he followed Hamdi. 'Guess I was right.'

'Yeah? And I always thought you were an asshole, and guess what – I was right too!' Nina called after him. This time, both guards stepped forward, not letting him into the Sphinx compound until he presented his ID. With a final glare back at Nina, he headed after Hamdi.

'That went okay, I think,' said Eddie with a half-smile.

Nina was more aggravated. 'God damn it! All he has to do is look in the tent, and this whole thing'll be over!'

'Well, he can't say you didn't warn him. And Rothschild too. They'll be the ones who'll look like tools if the place really does get robbed.'

'But if these guys are smart and connected enough to organise something like this, they'll be able to clean the place up and cover their tracks before Logan opens the entrance. Nobody'll even know there was anything there to rob. Oh, God.' She looked tiredly towards the Valley Temple to see Macy waving impatiently at them. 'Great, and now we're being summoned.'

'What happened?' Macy demanded when they reached her. 'Is he going to look?'

'Take a guess,' said Eddie.

'He's going to look?'

'Guess again.'

'Oh.'

'And also, he hates us,' added Nina.

From Macy's expression, the possibility of failure hadn't occurred to her. 'But . . . No, no way! Now what do we do?'

'What *can* we do?' Nina asked rhetorically. 'Logan won't listen to us, Hamdi's involved in it, and we can't get inside the compound to find the thing ourselves.'

Macy delved into a pocket. 'I've still got my ID,' she said, producing a card. 'If the guys at the gate are new, they won't recognise me, so I could get in.'

'And then what? If Shaban's guys see you, they'll try to kill you. And even if you get proof, Logan'll have you arrested if you try to give it to him.'

'But we've got to do something! The IHA is going

to open the Hall of Records in less than eighteen hours, which means whatever the bad guys are doing, they're doing it right now! This is the only chance we'll have to stop them!'

'I don't want them to rob the Hall of Records either,' said Nina, 'but unless we have solid proof we can take to the Egyptian authorities, we can't do anything to stop them.'

'So you're just giving up?' Macy said in disbelief. She pulled out the magazine pages and flapped them at Nina. 'Did you just give up when someone said you wouldn't find Atlantis? Did you give up when nobody believed the Tomb of Hercules was real?'

Nina irritably snatched the papers from her hand. 'Did you get your motivational speeches from fortune cookies?' she retorted. 'I'm being practical here. We can't do anything unless we can get inside the compound, which we can't do without IDs – and even if we do, there are fifteen archaeologists and a whole TV crew plus God knows how many guards wandering about the place!'

'They can't all be there the whole time,' said Eddie. 'They're doing this thing at the crack of sparrowfart tomorrow morning, right? So the IHA and telly guys have to get some sleep beforehand.' He looked over at the high wall. 'Do they still do that light show that was in *The Spy Who Loved Me*?' Macy nodded. 'So everyone'll be looking at the Sphinx, not anything else . . .'

'Something in mind?' Nina asked.

'I might have a way to get us all in.' He turned to Macy. 'It means you'll have to risk getting caught, though. You up for that?'

Nina gave him a warning look, but Macy was already

responding with an enthusiastic affirmative. 'What do I have to do?'

'Get through that gate without being arrested, for starters.' He glanced back towards Cairo. 'But first, we need to do a bit of shopping.'

The sound and light show was under way by the time they returned to Giza.

Eddie regarded the spotlit Sphinx, then followed the direction of its gaze over the seated audience. 'Huh,' he said, spotting a particular illuminated sign on a building beyond the perimeter. 'The Sphinx is looking right at a Pizza Hut.'

'Whoever built it'd completely freak out,' Macy said. 'The whole point of it looking in that direction was so it would see the sunrise. Now? Start the day with a Pepperoni Feast.'

'You don't know who built it?'

'I thought it was Khafre,' said Nina.

Macy shook her head. 'Doubt it. Haven't you heard of the Inventory Stele?'

'The what?' asked Eddie.

'This ancient text a guy discovered in 1857. According to that, the Sphinx was already there when Khafre was building his pyramid. That's why the causeway to the pyramid doesn't point due east – they had to work round the Sphinx.'

'Actually, I *have* heard of the Inventory Stele,' Nina said frostily. 'And I don't think the argument about what it says has been definitively settled.'

'But finding the Hall of Records makes it look a lot more likely to be true, huh? None of the Third Dynasty pharaohs ever mentioned the Hall. Maybe they didn't know it was there. And if the Sphinx is a lot older than Khafre, that might explain why its head's so small compared to the rest of its body. One of the pharaohs had the original head re-carved to look like himself.'

Eddie chuckled. 'I think,' he said, leaning closer to speak quietly into Nina's ear, 'you just got owned.'

'Shut up.'

They stopped not far from the gate, and Macy looked at the two uniformed men. 'I don't recognise either of them.'

'You're sure?' Nina asked.

'Built, good-looking young guys? Yeah, I would have remembered them.'

'And are you sure you want to do this?'

'I'm ready,' Macy insisted. She took out her ID card, about to head for the gate – then paused and opened a couple of extra shirt buttons.

Nina raised an eyebrow. 'What're you doing?'

'Cloaking device. Trust me.' Her décolletage adjusted for maximum effect, prompting a faintly lecherous grin from Eddie quickly followed by a swat from his wife, Macy crossed to the security gate. She held up her ID, but even from Nina and Eddie's vantage point it was obvious that both guards were less interested in her face than in what was on display below it. The gate was opened, Macy giving the two men a cheery smile as she sashayed through.

'Better get moving,' said Eddie, starting for the road.

Nina frowned. 'Unbelievable. She does something that sets women back about thirty years . . . and it works!'

'Jealous, are you?' Eddie teased.

'*No*. And you can stop leering at her, as well. They're fake.'

'What?' He shook his head. 'You sure?'

'Eddie, she looks like a broomstick with two watermelons taped to it! And her father's a plastic surgeon. Do the math. Also, she's young enough to be your daughter.'

'Thanks for depressing me.'

'I thought it was someone else's turn.' They both smiled.

They reached the section of road directly above the construction site and looked down. There was still a pair of guards standing watch – but two other men instantly caught their attention. Neither was familiar, but Nina had a horrible idea what was inside the large case they were carrying out of the tent.

'Damn it!' she said. 'They're already cleaning the place out!'

'You think the zodiac's in that box?'

'Maybe. Or part of it. They might have had to cut it up to get it through the tunnel. God, what if we're already too late?'

However, both men soon returned, now empty-handed. They entered the tent.

'I guess they haven't finished yet,' said Eddie.

'Good – maybe we can still stop them. Have you seen Macy?'

Eddie spotted her peering over a wall inside the upper temple, where she had been hiding from the men carrying the case. 'Yeah, in there.' He pointed, then gestured for her to leave cover and approach the construction site. 'Okay, let's hope the twins work as well on those two down there.'

He reached under his leather jacket and T-shirt, drawing

out the twenty-foot length of nylon line bought in a Cairo store that he had wound round his waist; carrying it openly would have roused the suspicions of even the sleepiest Tourist Police officer. Once he had gathered it up, he fumbled with his belt. 'Steady,' he said to the grinning Nina. 'You'll get what's in my pants later.'

'About damn time!'

He smiled back as he pulled out a metal hook from behind the buckle, where he had wedged it to trick the metal detectors. By the time the line was tied to it, Macy had emerged from the upper temple and was approaching the construction site – attracting the guards' attention.

Nina regarded the hook nervously as Eddie wedged it under the slab topping the wall. 'Will it take your weight?'

'You saying I've got a fat arse?' He looked down again. The guards were moving to meet Macy before she reached the perimeter of orange netting. A quick check to make sure nobody was coming along the darkened road, then he dropped the rope over the wall – and followed it, rapidly lowering himself down the stone face. The hook scraped and creaked.

He glanced over his shoulder as he descended. The guards had almost reached Macy. Twelve feet to the ground ten, eight . . .

She stopped, making the two men come to her. Eddie let go and dropped the last six feet, landing almost soundlessly in a crouch and immediately moving into cover behind one of the piles of bricks. Macy was holding up her camera, gesturing at the Sphinx. He couldn't hear her over the booming voice of the light show's narrator, but guessed she was asking them to take her photo with the monument behind her.

They didn't seem cooperative, one holding out a hand for her ID. Eddie silently advanced on the trio as Macy shrugged, showing off her impressive cleavage once more. These guards were less distracted, the man impatiently snapping his fingers.

She had seen Eddie by now, and made a show of checking her pockets before finally producing her ID. The guard snatched it from her, holding it up to his torch.

Eddie slipped through the plastic netting. Both men had their hands near their guns.

If they heard his footsteps or caught him in their peripheral vision . . .

The guard looked back at Macy, shining his light in her face. He frowned.

About to remember her—

'Holy crap!' Macy cried, suddenly whirling and pointing excitedly to the west. 'Look! *Pyramids!*'

The guards instinctively turned to see – as Eddie rushed up behind them and slammed their heads together with a dull crack of bone against bone. The two men collapsed nervelessly.

Macy jumped back, startled. 'Oh my God! Did – did you *kill* them?'

'Only if they've got fucking Humpty Dumpty heads,' he said. 'Give me a hand.'

'But that was like something out of a movie! How did you do that?'

'Take head, hit hard. Pretty simple.' He lifted one of the limp guards by the shoulders. With reluctance, not sure if he really was still alive, Macy helped Eddie drag him behind a dirt mound.

The first man out of sight, Eddie returned for his companion, looking up at the wall to see Nina hesitantly climbing down the rope. By the time the second guard was concealed, she was close to the ground.

She looked round as Eddie came to her, Macy following. 'Check it out!' she gasped, straining at the rope. 'Pretty good for someone who hasn't exercised in months—'

There was a faint ping of metal from above as the overstressed hook broke, and Nina dropped the last three feet to the sand. 'Ow, dammit!' she yelped.

Eddie helped her up. 'Wasn't my fat arse we had to worry about, was it?' Macy giggled.

'Shut up,' Nina grumbled, brushing dust from her butt as Eddie coiled the rope and moved off to hide it. 'And what the hell was that?' She flapped a hand at Macy's chest. 'Put them away, for God's sake.'

Annoyed, Macy refastened her shirt. 'What? It worked.'

'Eddie wouldn't have fallen for it.'

'Why, 'cause he's old?'

'No,' Nina said, offended, 'because he's ex-special forces and they're trained not to fall for things like that.'

Macy was surprised. 'He was in the army? I thought he was just some archaeology guy. You mean he wasn't joking when he said about being your bodyguard?'

'No, he wasn't. That's how we met – he saved my life. More than once, actually. Although I've saved *his* life a few times now, so we call it square.'

'Cool,' said Macy, now even more impressed by Nina's

husband. 'So . . . does he have a younger brother or something?'

Eddie came back. 'Don't know how long they'll be knocked out,' he said, 'but I think we need to do this pretty sharpish anyway.'

'Definitely,' Nina agreed. She went to the tent, listening for any indication of life inside before opening the flap. It was empty – but as Macy had described, there was a wooden cubicle occupying one end.

'Crap,' Macy muttered, finding only an empty table at the other. 'This is where the plans were, but they've taken them!' She looked back. 'One of those guys carrying that box was Gamal, the security chief. Maybe they've almost finished – what if we're too late?'

'Let's find out.' Nina opened the cubicle door.

Macy had been right: there was indeed a shaft descending into the plateau. The sound of a generator came from somewhere below . . . as did another, more distant noise, the screech of a power tool. She went to the ladder, but before climbing on to it she tied her hair into a ponytail.

'She's back, baby, yeah!' said Eddie, grinning. Macy smiled too, touching her own matching hairstyle as Nina started down the ladder.

7

The shaft descended over twenty feet to a gently sloping, stone-walled tunnel. Nina checked that nobody was waiting at the bottom before dropping down. The way north was blocked by compacted sand, but to the south had been dug out to re-open a passage not used for thousands of years. Light bulbs were hung from the ceiling every fifteen feet, stretching off into the distance.

Towards the Sphinx.

The blueprint Macy had shown her was accurate. The Hall of Records had two entrances – the one on the east side that the IHA team would shortly open, and another to the north, reserved for royalty. Only the conspirators of the Osirian Temple knew about the latter . . . and Berkeley hadn't looked for any other ways in. With a deadline to meet and his eyes filled with stars, he had rushed straight for the obvious target, not even considering that there might be another.

It was a mistake that could cost dearly.

Eddie jumped down beside her. He sniffed. 'Smells like they're cutting stone.'

Nina picked up a faint burning odour. 'That's what that is?'

'Yeah. I had a summer job at a monumental mason's once – they used power saws to cut the gravestones. Smelled like that.'

'You used to make gravestones? I learn something new about you every day.'

He smiled. 'Man of mystery, love.'

Macy hopped from the ladder, looking round in wonder. 'Oh, my God. This is awesome!' She rubbed the sand coating one wall to reveal darker stone beneath. 'Pink granite – probably from Aswan. This is definitely a royals-only way in. It was too expensive for anyone else.'

'You know your stuff,' said Eddie.

'Of course I do!' Then, more self-conscious: 'The Egyptian stuff, anyway. I'm not as hot on the rest . . . Can we get going now?'

'Behind me,' Eddie said firmly, moving in front of her. 'We don't know what's down here.'

They discovered one thing about two-thirds of the way down the tunnel – a petrol-powered generator, its exhaust hose leading back to the surface. Just past it, the passage showed signs of major damage: the ceiling was propped up by hefty wooden beams.

'Looks about to cave in,' said Eddie, passing warily beneath them.

Nina looked more closely. 'Maybe it already did – looks like they had to rebuild the roof to get through. They must have been working here for weeks – what are you doing?'

Macy raised her camera. 'Getting proof of everything.'

'You can't use the flash in here, they might see it!'

'I know that, duh! I'm recording a video.' She fiddled with the controls, then filmed the ceiling. Eddie and Nina moved on. 'Hey, wait!'

Eddie approached the end of the passage. Sand-crusted pillars, ornate carvings discernible beneath the grit, marked the entrance to a chamber. The echoing grind of the power tool was louder here.

He peered into the room. The ceiling bulbs were replaced by banks of brilliant lights mounted on heavy-duty tripods, illuminating the western half of a large rectangular chamber. There was nobody in sight, but the noise was coming from beyond an opening in the west wall, where more lights were visible. He entered, signalling for Nina and Macy to follow.

Nina could barely contain her amazement. 'My God,' she whispered, taking in the two rows of hieroglyph-covered cylindrical pillars running along the room's length, the further symbols on the walls, the ranks of niches containing lidded clay containers to protect the papyrus scrolls inside . . .

The Hall of Records. Until recently, believed to be nothing more than a myth – but now very real. And she was one of the first people to enter it in millennia.

Not *the* first, though. The modern artefacts amongst the ancient were proof enough of that. A large block was propped up on wheeled jacks by the entrance – the stone that had once sealed it, ready to be moved back into place once the robbers were done. The floor was covered in dust, numerous bootprints passing to and fro through the room.

'Ay up,' said Eddie, spotting a familiar item of clothing

draped over a workbench near the entrance. 'I recognise that.'

'So do I,' said Nina, seeing the snakeskin jacket. She looked past it into the shadows of the chamber's eastern end. On the far wall, more pillars marked another entrance: the one through which Berkeley and his team would enter.

Macy, meanwhile, went to the other end of the room, passing a chugging compressor and an electrical junction box. Power cables and a hose ran from them into the short passage to the next chamber. She was about to go through when Eddie waved her back. 'Over here.' He went to a darkened opening directly opposite the royal entrance.

Nina joined him, noticing that there were almost no footprints outside the area between the entrance and the next illuminated chamber. The robbers were only interested in one specific part of the Hall of Records, completely ignoring the rest. 'What's in there?'

'Egyptian stuff.' She made a sarcastic face. 'But I think it goes round and joins back up. I can see some light at the far end.' He took out a small penlight and swept its beam across the new room. Though smaller than the chamber in which they stood, it contained just as much ancient knowledge. This room had sustained damage, however, possibly from an earthquake; one pillar had partly collapsed, leaving large chunks lying on the floor.

Eddie moved inside. Nina followed, Macy behind her, camera in hand. A rectangle of dim light in the west wall marked the entrance to a fourth chamber; crossing to it, they saw the back of another lighting rig in the exit at its northwestern corner. They entered the new chamber and crept along the wall to the lights, which illuminated a flight of steps.

Nina looked round the tripod. The broad stone stairs led upwards – into, she realised with a thrill, the body of the Sphinx itself. The room at the top had been carved directly out of the heart of the great statue.

And over the sound of the power tools she heard voices.

'What're you doing?' Eddie demanded as she tried to push past him.

'I want to see what's up there.'

'Yeah, and they'll see you!'

'No, they won't – there'll be too much glare from these lights.' He frowned, but backed up.

The chamber Macy had almost entered earlier was across the bottom of the stairs, more light stands within. The trail of dusty footprints ran from it up the steps. Nina leaned out to see what was at the top – and felt another adrenalin shot of discovery.

Mixed with fear.

Several figures were visible in the upper chamber, and even without his snakeskin jacket she recognised the man from New York, who Macy had said was called Diamondback. She also spotted Hamdi, talking to someone outside her narrow field of view. But it was the object of their attention that had also grabbed hers.

It was on the ceiling – a zodiac, a star map about six feet in diameter, the constellations carved into the stone in the form of the ancient Egyptian gods. Nina knew of others – there was one in the Louvre in Paris – but unlike them this was still painted, as its creators had intended.

But it was no longer complete. It had been dismantled,

desecrated. Only one part remained on the ceiling, a roughly triangular section running from its southern edge to just past the centre. She could see the circular outline of where the rest had been clearly enough; power tools had carved away the surrounding stone, then pieces had been carefully and precisely cut from the ceiling. A man wearing goggles, a facemask and ear protectors was using a circular saw to free the final piece.

Another masked man was also working on the ceiling, but with much less sophisticated tools – a hammer and chisel. Nina was puzzled, before realising what he was doing: knocking dents into the perfectly flat swathes cut by the saw. All he had to do to remove any evidence that the zodiac had ever been there was roughen the newly exposed circle to match the limestone ceiling. With so many other treasures in the Hall of Records, nobody would pay any attention to a discolouration of the roof. She appreciated the ingenuity of the operation . . . even as she was utterly appalled by it.

The man Hamdi was addressing stepped into Nina's view. She recognised him from his picture.

Sebak Shaban.

She also saw that Macy hadn't been exaggerating about his facial scar, which dominated the right side of his face from the top lip to the nub of the ear. She couldn't help cringing at the thought of the pain he must have endured.

But that didn't earn him her sympathy. He was still a thief, stealing one of the world's greatest archaeological treasures.

The saw's screech died down, its user gesturing to a third man – Gamal, who had helped to carry the case from the tent. Now she was sure what it had contained: a piece of the zodiac. The cramped vertical shaft made it impossible to remove the map intact, so it had been cut into more manageable sections.

That, and the care being taken not to damage the last piece, suggested the thieves intended to reassemble it. Maybe it could still be restored.

But for that to happen, the conspirators would have to be caught.

'Give me your camera,' she whispered to Macy, who passed it to her. 'How does it record?'

'Just press the button, then press it again when you want to stop.'

'Okay.' Nina held the camera out past the lighting rig and started recording, watching the image on the LCD screen. To her annoyance, Shaban and Hamdi had turned to regard the zodiac, only the backs of their heads visible. 'Turn round, dammit,' she hissed. If she could get a clear shot of their faces, they would be heading to prison for a very long time.

Eddie crept alongside her, straining to hear what they were saying. The discussion was in Arabic; he could make out some words, but not enough to understand the entire conversation. 'Is that the zodiac?'

'What's left of it.' And the last section would soon be gone. Gamal moved a piece of equipment into position beneath it – a support frame, padded bars mounted on a pneumatic jack. He operated a control, and a piercing hiss of compressed air echoed round the chamber as the jack slowly extended. Hamdi put his fingers to his ears and backed out of the camera's view.

Shaban remained focused on the jack. The frame rose until it was just below the zodiac, then slowed, advancing step by tiny step until the pads touched the ancient carving.

The jack's hiss stopped – but was quickly replaced by the whine of the circular saw as the masked man cut into the stone once more. With the jack supporting it, the last piece of the zodiac could be safely cut free of the ceiling.

Diamondback said something to Shaban, and both men moved out of sight. Nina cursed. But at least the camera now had a clear view of the zodiac as it was being stolen. That would hopefully be enough to convince the Egyptian authorities—

Movement forced her to duck back into the darkened room. A muscular Caucasian man with close-cropped grey hair started down the stairs. He was carrying what looked like a chainsaw, though its heavy teeth set it apart from the average lumberjack's tool: a piece of specialised stone-cutting equipment. As he descended, he coiled up the saw's power cable, following it into the illuminated chamber.

'Looks like they're about to sod off,' Eddie whispered once he was out of sight.

'We probably should too,' said Nina. She stopped the recording, and they retreated through the two dark chambers – only to stop at the entrance to the first room.

'Buggeration,' Eddie muttered. The man was checking the jacks supporting the stone slab.

'We could just run past him,' Macy suggested.

'Yeah, but if he's got a gun, he'll have an easy shot at us in that tunnel. We need to get out without anyone seeing us.'

But that soon became even less likely. Diamondback swaggered into the entrance chamber, wiping dust from his beard. The saw's noise died away, replaced by the hiss of the jack lowering. Before long, Gamal and the other man brought another case into the room, Shaban and Hamdi close behind them.

'That everything?' asked Diamondback. 'So what now?'

'Now,' said Shaban, 'we clean up.' He looked at his watch, then indicated the eastern entrance. 'We have just over five hours before the IHA open that door. Lorenz, how long will it take to seal the royal entrance?'

The grey-haired man looked up from the jacks. 'Once we've got everything out of here, about an hour to move the block back into position,' he said, his accent Dutch.

'There can't be so much as a footprint left behind,' Hamdi said, nervously regarding the tracks on the dusty floor.

'There won't be.' Shaban indicated some gas cylinders beside the compressor. 'We'll use compressed air to clear the floors – by the time the IHA get in, the dust will have settled.' A nod to the man standing with Gamal. 'Broma, get started.'

'Shit,' Eddie whispered. 'We'll have to make a run for it after all. Soon as they go back upstairs for their gear, we'll leg it.'

They waited in the darkness as Broma began erasing stray footprints with blasts of compressed air. The other men moved away from the swirling dust clouds.

'Should we risk it?' said Nina.

'There's still that bloke by the door,' Eddie said, watching Lorenz check the jacks. 'When he moves away . . .'

Broma suddenly stopped working, peering with a puzzled expression at the floor near the entrance to the dark chamber. Eddie immediately knew why.

He had seen their footprints, freshly made in the dust.

'Back, back, back!' Eddie hissed. Broma followed the new tracks to the entrance. He squinted into the shadows.

Eddie and Nina ducked down behind a section of the ruined pillar. Macy crouched beside a smaller hunk of broken stone as Broma swept a torch beam across the floor. He fixed the circle of light on one set of tracks and followed them.

To Macy's hiding place.

Frightened, she hunched lower – and crunched a small piece of debris under her sole. It was only a faint scrape, but it was enough to make Broma twitch. The torch beam locked on to the fallen pillar. He put down the air cylinder . . . and drew a knife.

Macy froze. The beam exposed more of the pillar as he approached . . . then found the young woman hiding behind it.

The knife snapped up—

Crack!

A five-thousand-year-old piece of pottery exploded into fragments as Eddie smashed it over Broma's head. The man fell to his knees against Macy's hiding place – and Eddie kicked the back of his head, cracking him face first against the stone. Broma slumped unconscious to the floor.

In the entrance chamber, Shaban looked round sharply at the noise. 'Broma?' he called. No reply. He gestured to Lorenz. 'Check it.' Lorenz grabbed a pickaxe and hurried to investigate.

Nina jumped up. 'Come on,' said Eddie, grabbing Macy's hand and quickly following Nina to the other doorway.

Lorenz entered the room, seeing Broma's fallen torch –

and the body slumped beside it. He looked round in alarm, spotting fleeing silhouettes in the faint rectangle of light across the room. 'Hey!'

'Shit!' Nina gasped. She raced through the next darkened room, passing the light stand and glancing up the stairs. Nobody in the zodiac chamber, but there was no way out either. Instead she ran into the last room, a smaller repository of records with four supporting pillars lit by two more light stands. An opening in the east wall led back into the entrance chamber.

Through it, she saw Gamal running towards her with a hammer in one hand. Backing up, she almost collided with Eddie at the bottom of the stairs. 'This way's blocked!'

'So's that way!' Macy cried, pointing behind her as Lorenz charged after them.

'Up!' Eddie yelled, taking the steps three at a time. Nina and Macy dashed after him.

Gamal and Lorenz reached the bottom of the stairs simultaneously, rushing up them to catch their cornered prey . . .

Only to run back down even faster as a screaming Eddie pursued *them*, the circular saw shrilling in his hands. 'Come on, you fuck-sticks!' he bellowed as he chased them into the illuminated room. 'Who wants some?'

Gamal clearly didn't, sprinting back into the entrance chamber, but Lorenz turned to face him. He swung the pickaxe, trying to smash the saw from Eddie's grip. Eddie jerked back – and another swipe brought the sharp point alarmingly close to his head. 'Whoa!'

The spinning blade was producing a gyroscopic effect, making the bulky and heavy saw even more awkward to wield. Sweeping its trailing power cable out from under his feet, Eddie hefted it, watching Lorenz's movements closely as the two men circled. He would have to be fast.

Lorenz lunged—

Eddie twisted away from the metal spike – and jerked the saw upwards. There was a brief *skzzt!* as the blade sliced effortlessly through the pickaxe handle, the head flying across the room. He grunted, annoyed. He'd been aiming for Lorenz's hands.

It had the desired effect, though. Lorenz dropped the handle's stump and rapidly retreated into the entrance chamber. Eddie glanced back at Macy and Nina. 'Think I've got this under control!' he shouted over the noise of the whirling saw. 'You two get ready to run, I'll – oh, shit!'

Through the passage he saw Diamondback at the workbench, donning his snakeskin jacket and drawing a revolver from inside it – but the more immediate danger was Gamal, running back past Lorenz with the chainsaw in his hands!

8

Eddie scuttled backwards as Gamal ran into the room, his weapon's cable whipping behind him. The chainsaw was smaller and lighter than the circular saw – and its blade was much longer. 'Go round the other way!' he shouted to the women, only to realise they had separated. Nina was at the doorway to the stairs, but Macy had jumped the gun and was halfway round the room before she froze as she saw the new threat. Eddie was now between them – and with Gamal coming straight for him, Macy was cut off.

Gamal thrust the chainsaw at Eddie's stomach. He swung his clumsy weapon downwards to protect himself, and the two blades clashed against each other. The circular saw was almost wrenched from Eddie's hands as the edge of his blade momentarily caught in the chainsaw's teeth, spinning metal coming perilously close to his leg. With a strained roar, he hauled the saw back up – as Gamal stabbed at him again.

Sparks sprayed as Eddie's weapon rasped along the chainsaw's flat blade before snagging in its teeth once more.

The jarring impact knocked him backwards, and he almost tripped over the jack's air hose. Gamal advanced.

Lorenz re-entered the chamber. He saw Macy trapped in the corner and moved towards her, fists raised. 'Uh, little help?' she cried.

Nina was about to try to reach her when she saw Diamondback running towards the room, gun raised. She dived back to the foot of the stairs as a bullet shattered a scroll container.

Macy backed towards the light stand as Lorenz closed in. Eddie moved to interpose himself, but if he tried to attack Lorenz, Gamal would be able to get a clear strike with the chainsaw.

The hose—

He swung the saw – not at Lorenz, but at the floor, slicing through the air line. There was a ringing shrill as his blade carved a groove into the stone, but it was nothing compared to the ear-splitting hiss as compressed air surged from the hose's severed end, sending it whipping insanely about the chamber.

It lashed Lorenz, opening a deep cut in his cheek as it struck him and blasted gritty air into his eyes. He screamed, staggering blindly away from Macy – to smack head first into a pillar. He dropped to his knees, groaning.

Gamal backed away from the demented hose – blocking Diamondback's aim. 'Turn off the compressor!' the Egyptian shouted.

'Go round, get out!' Eddie told Nina, gesturing for her to escape through the darkened chambers.

'Not without you!'

'I'll catch up, just go!'

The writhing hose abruptly died, slapping lifelessly to the floor. Diamondback had shut down the compressor. Nina saw him dart back to the doorway, gun at the ready. She turned and ran as another Magnum round smacked into the wall.

Gamal went back on the attack. Eddie swung his saw defensively, the blades grinding with another shower of sparks. Macy shrieked and took cover behind a pillar as the two men passed, Gamal driving his opponent into a corner.

Something brushed her foot. She looked down, seeing the saws' power cables shifting as their wielders moved. A memory from the entrance chamber flashed through her mind – the junction box, equipment plugged into it.

Including the chainsaw . . .

Both cables were orange – but the chainsaw's seemed a deeper shade. She grabbed the darker of the two lines at her feet and reeled it in.

Diamondback was about to pursue Nina when his attention was caught by the saw fight. He took aim at the Englishman – but Gamal, back to him, unwittingly obscured his sight as he lunged at Eddie once more. The American released the trigger, impatiently waiting for another opportunity to fire.

Eddie tried to slash at Gamal's arm, but the uniformed man easily countered, the chainsaw bitting a chunk out of the circular saw's casing. Eddie flinched as plastic fragments spat into his face. The sheer mass of the machine was rapidly wearing him down – and behind his adversary he saw Diamondback, revolver tracking him. Gamal jabbed the chainsaw, forcing him back. He could feel the heat of the lamps on the back of his head.

Cornered—

Macy felt the cord pull taut. She yanked it as hard as she could.

In the next chamber, the plug popped out of the junction box . . .

And Eddie's saw fell silent.

The chainsaw's electrical flex wasn't darker. It was just *dirty* – and she had taken hold of a similarly grubby section of the circular saw's power cable.

'What the *fuck*?' Eddie yelped. He looked at Macy, crouched with the cable in her hands and a guilty expression. '*Macy!*'

The blade was still spinning, but slowing – and Gamal had already seen his opportunity, stabbing the chainsaw at him. He jerked up the dead power tool like a shield—

The chainsaw's teeth ripped through its casing and smashed the blade's axle assembly. The steel disc shot across the room like a lethal Frisbee. It clanged off a pillar, whipping at the passage – and forcing Diamondback to dive backwards to avoid being decapitated. The blade shot over him and bounced off another pillar in the entrance chamber. Shaban ducked and Hamdi screamed as it flew between them.

Eddie hurled his useless weapon at Gamal. He hoped the other man would make the mistake of trying to deflect the heavy piece of machinery with the chainsaw and knock his own blade back into his face, but the security chief spun out of the missile's way and faced his target again.

His *defenceless* target.

The chainsaw swung, forcing Eddie back against the light

stand. Gamal grinned, driving the saw straight for his chest—

Macy pulled the other cable.

The unexpected tug was just hard enough to throw off Gamal's aim. The blade's tip slashed through the shoulder of Eddie's leather jacket, drawing blood – but the wound wasn't enough to stop Eddie from grabbing his unbalanced enemy and flinging him round—

Into the light stand.

The chainsaw carved through the high-powered bulbs – and their power lines. Glass exploded and crackling blue flashes arced as Gamal took the full force of the electricity through his body. Muscles paralysed, unable even to scream, he crashed on to the tripod. Smoke coiled from his nostrils and eye sockets as he was cooked from the inside out.

Eddie jumped clear. 'Bright spark,' he said as he pulled the horrified Macy upright. 'Come on!'

Nina ran through the dark rooms. In the glow from his dropped flashlight she saw Broma woozily pushing himself up – and stomped on his back as she vaulted the fallen pillar, slamming him back down.

She reached the short passage. Shaban was by the royal entrance across from her, Hamdi leaning breathlessly against a nearer pillar, ghost-pale. He saw her, and reacted in shock. 'Dr Wilde?'

'Dr Hamdi,' she replied. 'I think you've got some explaining to do.'

He came towards her. 'If you think you can—'

She punched him in the face and continued towards

Shaban, leaving the Egyptian official squealing and holding his nose. A crowbar was propped against a pillar; she picked it up, holding it like a sword. Shaban seemed unconcerned, a slight smirk twisting his scarred lip. 'Dunno what you're grinning at,' she said, indicating the case. 'You're not taking that out of here.'

He didn't answer, but his brief glance to one side warned Nina that something was wrong. She turned her head towards the western exit – and saw Diamondback returning.

Aiming—

A bullet blew a chunk from a pillar as she leapt past a light stand to take cover behind the ornate column. 'Kill her,' Shaban ordered.

In the second dark chamber, Eddie heard the shot. 'Hide in here,' he told Macy before running into the first unlit room. Broma was struggling to rise again, so he trampled him back down, then saw his knife glinting in the spill of torchlight and snatched it up.

Nina kicked the light stand. Top-heavy, it crashed to the floor, the bulbs shattering and plunging the room's eastern end into darkness. She ran to another pillar near the sealed entrance. Diamondback jogged towards her. Behind him, Lorenz stumbled into the room, blood on his face. The shadows wouldn't hide her for long . . .

Eddie ran in, guessing Nina's position from where Diamondback was pointing his gun. 'Oi!' he yelled. Diamondback saw him, spun, fired – as Eddie ducked behind a column, the wall cratering just behind him.

'Get the zodiac out of here!' Shaban ordered, waving Lorenz over. Hamdi scurried to join him.

Diamondback closed in. Back pressed against the column, Eddie raised the knife. The American's revolver fetish meant he only had two shots remaining in his Colt Python. Even with a speedloader, it would take him several seconds to re-arm once they were gone, leaving him open to a counter-attack.

But he had to use up the remaining bullets first.

A sound from the nearby doorway. Broma had recovered, face gnarled with anger. He lumbered towards Eddie. Shit! That left only one direction he could retreat – and Diamondback was waiting—

From the shadows, Nina saw Diamondback's face light up with the anticipation of a kill. 'Eddie!' she cried, flinging the crowbar as hard as she could at the gunman.

It hit his shoulder. The .357 Magnum boomed as his finger flinched on the trigger. Broma jumped back from the bullet impact on the column – and Eddie ran into the darkness to Nina.

'Broma! Lorenz! Take the zodiac!' Shaban shouted, angry impatience rising. Broma hesitated, then crossed the chamber to pick up one end of the case. Lorenz took the other. Hamdi turned and fled up the tunnel, holding his nose. The two men carried the case after him.

'Dammit!' Nina said as she watched the zodiac disappear, before looking at Eddie. 'What, you brought a knife to a gunfight?'

'He's only got one more shot,' Eddie countered. 'Then he'll have brought fists to a knife fight!'

Diamondback was closing on them, but Shaban shouted to him. 'Bobby! Come on!'

'What about these two?'

'The zodiac is all that matters – go! We'll collapse the tunnel and seal them in!'

Nina and Eddie shared an anxious look. 'Buggeration and fuckery!' they said as one.

Shaban entered the tunnel. Diamondback followed him as far as the entrance, holding position beside the stone block with his gun raised, daring the couple to show their faces.

'Give me one of those pots,' Eddie said.

Nina grimaced at the thought of another priceless artefact's destruction, but handed him a container. He hefted it.

Shaban's voice echoed down the tunnel. 'Bobby, move!' Diamondback's gaze flicked towards to the sound, just for a moment—

Eddie sprang out and hurled the pot.

He was already rolling for the cover of the next pillar as Diamondback fired – and hit the container in mid-air. It exploded like a clay pigeon. Some of the pieces struck Eddie, but he ignored them, only one thought in his mind.

Six shots.

He jumped up, hoping he hadn't misidentified the revolver and that Diamondback wasn't carrying a *seven*-shooter . . .

He wasn't. The American turned and sprinted up the tunnel.

Eddie pursued him, light bulbs flashing past.

Too late, he realised Diamondback was carrying a *second* revolver. He tugged it out of his jacket, slowed, turned—

Eddie tackled him. Both men hit the floor beside the chugging generator. Diamondback raised his gun, but

Eddie swiped it from his hand. The lank-haired gunman tried to scramble after it, only for Eddie to slam a sledgehammer punch into his kidney, dropping him flat.

But Diamondback wasn't out of the fight, wrenching himself round and smashing an elbow into Eddie's chest. Eddie gasped at a stab of resurgent pain where his rib had been broken seven months earlier.

Diamondback saw the weakness and lashed at the spot again. Eddie thumped back against a support beam.

The American pulled free, trying to get up, but Eddie kicked him hard on the backside. Diamondback stumbled before falling again . . .

At Shaban's feet.

Eddie looked up. Shaban had retrieved the revolver.

And was pointing it at him—

He rolled behind the generator as Shaban fired. The first shot smacked off the floor and ricocheted down the tunnel – but the next hit the generator. The machine jolted, mechanism grinding. The lights flickered. Another shot – and the fuel tank burst open, petrol gushing out.

'Get back,' Shaban told his henchman, a cruel smile forming. Diamondback stood with a sadistic half-laugh. Both men retreated.

'Oh, shit,' Eddie whispered. He had a choice of death by bullet – or death by incineration.

Shaban fired. Hot lead ignited the fuel vapour, flashing it into fire.

Eddie leapt up and ran—

The generator exploded. The lights instantly went out, but Eddie could see all too well as a bright orange fireball erupted behind him, singeing his skin and hair as he dived.

A greasy wave of flame roiled over him, clinging to the ceiling.

The echo of the blast faded – but that wasn't the noise he was concerned with. Instead it was the sinister crackle of flames consuming wood, the deeper crunch of stone as the damaged ceiling gave way . . .

Eddie sprang up and raced into the darkness – as the roof caved in with a huge boom behind him. He tumbled across the entrance chamber in a swelling, choking cloud of sand.

'Eddie!' Nina shouted between coughs. 'Are you all right? Eddie!'

'I'm – I'm okay,' he spluttered, pulling his T-shirt up over his mouth and nose. The noise of the collapse had stopped, only the hiss of falling sand audible from the tunnel.

'What the hell happened?'

'The generator blew up, took out the props. Ceiling fell down.'

'You mean we're *trapped*?' A ball of ghost light resolved itself into Macy holding Broma's dropped torch. 'Oh, my God! We'll run out of air!'

'This place is pretty big, so we'll be okay as long as nobody starts running laps,' Eddie assured her. 'Or starts panicking.'

'I–I'm not panicking! I mean, we're only trapped under the Sphinx, what's to panic about?'

Nina helped Eddie up. 'You okay?'

'I'll live – although I owe that mulleted twat a good kicking. Macy, give me the torch.' He aimed it down the tunnel. Though the swirling dust was still thick, it was plain that the passage was completely blocked. 'Huh. We'll have a job digging through that.'

'We don't need to. Remember?' Nina turned his hand to illuminate the chamber's eastern end. The beam fell on the carved pillars of the second entrance. 'We just have to wait for prime time . . .'

Berkeley composed himself before taking hold of the final broken stone and, with deliberate theatricality, moving it aside. 'This . . . is it,' he said to the camera behind him. Though the tunnel's confines meant there was only room for half a dozen people to witness the opening of the Hall of Records first-hand, the cyclopean glass eye was an avatar for millions all round the globe. His words in the next few minutes could be as well remembered as those of Neil Armstrong when he made the first footfall on the moon.

As he passed the stone back to another team member, he briefly glanced at his watch – 4.46 a.m., 9.46 p.m. in New York, exactly on schedule – before picking up a crowbar and facing the camera again. 'The last piece of rubble has been cleared from the entrance,' he said, with as great a tone of expectant gravity as he could manage. 'The only thing now standing between us and our first sight of the legendary Hall of Records beneath the Sphinx is this stone slab. Once it's opened, we will be the first people to enter for over five thousand years. Nobody knows exactly what treasures are within . . . but there's one thing we can be sure about. Whatever we see beyond this door will be remembered for a very long time.'

Behind the cameraman, he saw Metz making a 'hurry up' gesture. Concealing his annoyance at being rushed, Berkeley inserted his crowbar into the gap at one side of the block, then turned back to camera. 'Here we go.'

He pulled at the crowbar. For a moment the only sound was the scrape of metal on stone, then with a low grumble the slab moved. Berkeley could hardly contain his excitement as the stone inched outwards from the wall. It was finally happening! The Hall of Records, revealed at last . . . and *he* was the one the world was watching. Not any of the other archaeologists who had been so desperate to win the IHA assignment, and certainly not Nina Wilde . . .

The slab turned slightly, revealing a line of blackness. A puff of dust billowed out. Berkeley's heart raced. He pulled harder. The slab came free. He pushed it aside, then looked through the opening. The cameraman moved forward, the camera's light shining on what lay within . . .

It found the grubby, dust-covered face of Nina Wilde.

'Hey, Logan,' she said, as Berkeley's heart plunged down through his chest cavity and fell deep into the ground below. 'Welcome to the Hall of Records. What kept you?'

9

'These people are nothing more than vandals and thieves. They should be thrown in prison for twenty years!'

There was anger in Hamdi's voice, but also an undertone of fear. Which was hardly surprising, Nina thought; if the Egyptian authorities saw proof of his involvement in the zodiac's theft, *he* would be the one facing twenty years in prison.

Unfortunately, she didn't have such proof – certainly not enough to stand up in court. After she, Eddie and Macy emerged from the Sphinx – and were arrested, the default action when those in charge had no idea what was going on but had to be seen to be doing *something* – they were eventually taken to the Ministry of Culture to explain themselves, with Hamdi and Berkeley acting as an impromptu and rather strident prosecution.

What they did have, though, was enough evidence to prove that *someone* had indeed beaten the IHA to the Hall of Records. The recording from Macy's camera had been copied to a computer, and was now displayed on a large TV in the minister's office. The image was frozen, the last section of the zodiac revealed on the ceiling, with Shaban and Hamdi standing before it. Unfortunately, the glare from the lights in the zodiac chamber rendered them barely more than silhouettes.

'We weren't the ones who robbed the place,' said Nina. 'Eddie and I only arrived in the country yesterday morning. But the work needed to dig out the tunnel must have been going on for weeks. Since it was happening right there in the Sphinx compound, it had to have been done with the collusion of someone at Giza.' She eyed Hamdi. 'Wouldn't you say?'

The minister, an elderly, long-faced man called Malakani Siddig, examined a photograph. 'The dead man, this Gamal, was in charge of site security. I think it's a safe assumption that he was working with the robbers.'

'It was a mistake to use private security contractors,' mused Dr Ismail Assad, the Secretary General of the Supreme Council of Antiquities. 'We should have brought in the army – maybe even the Antiquities Special Protection Squad.'

Eddie worked out the acronym. 'ASPS? Cool name.'

'It's more likely that Gamal was following Dr Wilde and her gang and was murdered when he tried to arrest them,' said Hamdi. Even Berkeley regarded his suggestion with disbelief.

Assad leafed through more photos of the equipment the thieves had been forced to abandon. 'This was a much larger operation than just one man, one woman and a girl could have carried out.'

'I'm not a "girl",' Macy protested.

Nina batted her arm with a 'Shush!' then continued: 'There were at least ten people involved – the six men on the video, plus the guards at the construction site and the ones at the compound gate. Probably more. If you're going to investigate everyone at Giza who might have been involved, I'd suggest starting at the top.' She stared at Hamdi.

'This is outrageous!' Hamdi blustered. 'They are trying to implicate me to deflect attention from themselves.'

'You sound a bit bunged-up, mate,' said Eddie.

'Looks like someone hit your nose,' Nina noted. 'Wonder where that happened?' She examined her knuckles. 'Funny, I've got kind of a nose-shaped bruise here . . .'

'Minister,' growled Berkeley, 'at the very least Dr Wilde and her husband should be charged with trespass and damage to an archaeological site.' He glared at Nina. 'You couldn't let me have my moment, could you? No, you had to ruin everything so you could be the centre of attention and take all the credit.'

'Oh, grow up, Logan,' Nina snapped.

Assad leaned back in his chair. 'Dr Berkeley, there are more important crimes to be investigated first.' He pointed at the image of the zodiac. 'A priceless national treasure has been stolen – from under your nose! People will want to know how you could have possibly not known about a second tunnel being dug right in front of you.'

'They might even wonder if you *did* know,' said Siddig with veiled menace.

Berkeley looked shocked. 'But – of course I didn't! Why would I wreck my own career and risk going to prison?'

'People risk all kinds of things for the right amount of

money,' said Nina. She was certain that he hadn't been involved, but still took a little pleasure in watching him squirm.

Siddig seemed uncomfortable at the mention of money. 'Dr Wilde, you believe the Osirian Temple is involved?'

'That's right.' She crossed to the television. 'This man on the left is Sebak Shaban.'

'It could be anyone,' snapped Hamdi.

'So could his buddy on the right, huh, Dr Hamdi?'

'Dr Hamdi has a point, though,' said Assad. 'The video never shows their faces. And there's too much noise from the saw to identify their voices.'

'It's Shaban,' Nina insisted. 'The Osirian Temple is behind this.'

'It's certainly not a religion I believe in, or even approve of,' said Siddig, 'but the Osirian Temple is a major charitable contributor in Egypt. Khalid Osir doesn't just help fund archaeological projects – he also donates money to health and agricultural causes. He's a popular man.' A small frown. 'Even if he chooses to live in a Swiss tax haven rather than his own country.'

Hamdi made a theatrical shrug of disgust. 'Now she is accusing Khalid Osir of being a thief. Who next, the president?'

Assad had his own questions. 'Why would they only take the zodiac? The Hall's other contents would be worth hundreds of millions of dollars on the black market.'

'They don't just want the zodiac for its monetary value,' said Nina. She switched programs on the laptop connected to the television, bringing up the picture Macy had taken of the fourth papyrus. 'This scroll – the one the Osirian

Temple kept from the IHA – says the zodiac is the key to finding the Pyramid of Osiris. *That's* their real objective – the pyramid's treasures.'

Hamdi laughed sarcastically. 'The Pyramid of Osiris? Minister, Ismail, why are you even listening to this woman? It's a myth, a fantasy, no more real than the Garden of Eden.' He shot Nina a malevolent smirk. 'Anyone who believes it is real is obviously deranged.'

'Well, I did think the guy you're taking bribes from seemed a bit nuts,' Nina fired back.

Hamdi rose to his full height. 'False, baseless, slanderous accusations! In front of unimpeachable witnesses, no less. Dr Wilde, I will see you in court.'

'Oh, sit down, Iabi,' grumbled Assad. Hamdi looked offended, but obeyed his boss. 'Dr Wilde, I would recommend that you don't make any more accusations without proof. We will investigate this outrage, and those responsible will be punished, you can be sure of that. But we will not jump to any conclusions without evidence.'

'But while you're getting it, they'll have nicked everything in the Pyramid of Osiris that's not nailed down, then come back for the nails,' Eddie said.

Siddig put both hands firmly on his desk. 'Everyone involved in this robbery will be found and brought to justice.' His stern gaze passed over everybody before him, finishing on Nina – though, she was pleased to notice, pausing for a moment on Hamdi. 'Everyone. Now, go. Dr Assad, we have a lot of work to do.'

Hamdi waved an angry hand at Nina, Eddie and Macy. 'You aren't going to keep them in custody?'

'If I had everybody arrested who might possibly have been involved in this,' the minister snapped, 'I would be arresting a lot of people. Including you! As Dr Wilde pointed out, she has only been in Egypt since yesterday, but digging this tunnel would have taken weeks. Now get out, all of you.'

He waved a dismissive hand towards the door. Everyone filed for the exit – except Macy, who instead approached the desk, hands held demurely in front of her. 'Excuse me? Minister?'

Siddig glared up at her, but his face quickly softened at the sight of her wide-eyed and hopeful expression. 'What can I do for you, young lady?'

She looked across at the laptop, next to various items from the Hall of Records – and her camera. 'I was wondering if it would be possible for me to have my camera back?'

'I'm afraid it's evidence,' he said. 'I'm sorry.'

'Oh.' Her lips quivered into a small, sad pout. 'It's just that it's got all the pictures and videos that I took for my grandparents. They were from Egypt originally, and they wanted to see what the country was like today . . .'

'I'm sorry,' Siddig repeated, 'but I can't return it until the investigation has finished.' He thought for a moment. 'But I suppose we could make a copy of the memory card. For your grandparents.'

Macy gave him a delighted smile. 'Oh, that would be awesome! Thank you, Mr Siddig, thank you so much!'

'I'll have somebody get the copy to you, Miss Sharif. Now, if you'll excuse us?'

'Thank you,' Macy said again, beaming as she backed

away. 'You're a really cool guy.' Siddig's reaction suggested it was not a compliment he generally heard, but he took it with good grace.

'What was *that* about?' Nina hissed as Macy caught up with her and Eddie outside.

Macy smiled smugly. 'We've still got the zo-di-aaaac,' she sang. 'Well, on video, anyway.'

'So we have,' Nina realised. A straight copy of the camera's memory would duplicate all its contents – including the video of the zodiac's last piece. 'But how did you know he'd go for it?'

'Didn't you see the photos of the kids on his desk? He's way too old for them to be his. So I figured he was a grandpa – and I played the "grandkid doing something nice for her grandparents" card. Although it didn't totally work, because I really did want my camera back! But at least we've got *something*.'

'I don't know how much it'll help, though,' said Nina. 'The zodiac's probably out of the country by now. And we've only seen one piece of it – they've got the whole thing. If it really is a way to find the Pyramid of Osiris, they're the only ones who'll be able to use it.'

'Hey, hey,' Eddie chided. 'I thought you were going to pack it in with the pessimism? Look at it this way – you found the Hall of Records, and we just walked out of there without getting thrown in jail. Plus, you visited the pyramids. This is like a holiday for you!'

She smiled a little. 'Maybe. But I don't know what we can do next, even with a video of the zodiac.'

'They were talking – maybe they said where they were taking it,' Macy suggested.

'Talking in Arabic,' Nina reminded her. 'And anyway, we couldn't hear them over the saw.'

Eddie looked thoughtful. 'I know someone who might be able to help with that.'

'Nina!' said Karima Farran, hugging her. 'It's wonderful to see you again. Though I did see you not long ago – on the news.'

Nina returned the Jordanian woman's embrace. 'Yeah, that wasn't exactly planned. I've had some bad experiences with the media lately.'

Karima was one of what Nina had jokingly come to call Eddie's 'international girlfriends', contacts from his time as a soldier and freelance contractor who always seemed to share certain characteristics: a great loyalty to Eddie . . . and equally great physical beauty. This last had in the past caused her the occasional pang of jealousy, but she had trusted him enough to accept that his friends were indeed *just* friends – whatever he might suggest otherwise with his cheeky innuendoes.

His recent dissembling about Amy in New York had made the joke considerably less amusing, but though Karima was even by 'international girlfriend' standards quite stunningly attractive, Nina saw that she had no cause to suspect Eddie of any improprieties, as she had made the short flight from Amman to Cairo accompanied by a man of her own. 'This is my boyf— my *fiancé*, Radi Bashir. Rad for short,' Karima said, ushering forward a tall, strikingly handsome Arab man with a mane of glossy black hair. Eddie and Nina shook his hand. 'I finally got him to make a commitment – by using you two as an example.'

'She wore me down,' said Rad in mock complaint, an Oxbridge tinge to his accent. ' "Eddie and Nina" this, "Eddie and Nina" that. Although it was your trip into Syria with her that really forced me to pop the question – it was the only way I could think of to keep her out of trouble!'

Eddie laughed. 'Trust me, mate – it doesn't work.'

'Although you seem to have got ahead of us again,' said Karima, regarding Eddie's wedding ring before grinning mischievously at him. 'And for some reason, I missed the ceremony. Invitation lost in the mail, perhaps?'

'It was . . . kinda short notice,' Nina admitted.

'*No* notice,' said Eddie, nodding.

'So you eloped?' Karima said. 'How romantic.'

Nina snorted. 'Yeah, nothing says romance like a cab ride to the Justice of the Peace in Greenwich, Connecticut. But congratulations on getting engaged, anyway.'

'And congratulations on your marriage. Even if they're a little late.' Karima looked at Macy. 'But I take it there's more going on than just you turning up inside a five-thousand-year-old chamber under the Sphinx?' She arched an eyebrow. 'Strange. With anyone else, that would sound bizarre. With you, it's almost normal.'

Nina completed the introductions. 'Macy's why we're here,' she told Karima and Rad. 'She found out about the attempt to rob the Hall of Records.' She held up a DVD-R; Siddig had, true to his word, provided a copy of the memory card's contents. 'There's a video on here of the actual robbery.'

Rad's eyes lit up, but Karima sternly said something in Arabic that immediately dampened his enthusiasm. 'He works for a news network,' she told Nina, giving Rad a look that was both teasing and warning. 'I just told him that no, he can't have it as an exclusive.'

'Great. So, Rad, what can you do to help us?'

Rad reached into his messenger bag, taking out a travel-scuffed Apple laptop. He opened it, revealing a keyboard covered with sticky labels in different colours: shortcuts for professional video-editing software. He grinned. 'The question is: what *can't* I do?'

Rad set up shop in a quiet corner of the hotel bar, the others peering over his shoulders as he worked. 'I know my cologne is irresistible,' he said, 'but could I have a *little* more space?'

'Sorry,' Nina said, retreating slightly, but still anxious to discover what hidden secrets the recording might hold. So far, Rad's efforts to enhance the image had met with limited success; the video mode on Macy's camera had been designed with small Internet-friendly clips in mind, not high definition footage. Shaban and Hamdi were visible only from behind or with glare obscuring their features – and, as Eddie remarked, real life wasn't like an episode of *CSI: Miami*. No matter how powerful the software and how clever its user, digital information couldn't be extracted if it was never there in the first place.

Rad was having more luck with the audio, though. Wearing earphones, he looped the recording, adjusting filters with each pass. 'The saw's making a fairly constant sound,' he explained, pointing at a jittering waveform display in one window. 'I won't be able to get rid of it completely, but I can tone it down enough to hear the dialogue.'

Karima leaned closer. 'Let me listen.'

Rad removed one of the earphones and passed it to her. She ran her thumb round its edge before putting it in her own ear. 'I saw that,' Rad said.

'What?'

'You just wiped my earbud.'

'I don't want your wax in my ear.'

'I do *not* have waxy ears!'

'You sound married already,' Eddie said, sharing a grin with Nina. 'So what are they saying?'

Karima translated what was being said by the two men as Rad replayed the filtered recording. 'The one on the right, Hamdi, is worried about how long it will take to clean up the Hall of Records. If there's any suspicion, it might fall on him . . . He's just complaining.' The playback continued for several more seconds without further commentary.

'What's he saying now?' Eddie asked.

'Still complaining!' Another pause, then: 'Oh, now they're talking about the Pyramid of Osiris. The other man, Shaban – he says it will definitely lead them to it. They . . . I can't hear properly,' she said, the waveform display jumping as the noise of the machinery spiked. 'Rad, wind it back. It's . . . something about planets and constellations, but it's very hard to make out. He wants to compare them to something.'

Rad rewound the recording again. Karima frowned, frustrated. 'There's too much noise, but I think he wants to compare the zodiac to the constellation of . . . Dendera?'

'There's no constellation called Dendera,' said Eddie. 'Least not that I've heard of.'

'Dendera's not a constellation,' Macy said. 'It's a place – it used to be a provincial capital of Upper Egypt. The Temple of Hathor's there . . .'

She tailed off, realisation dawning, but Nina was a step ahead. 'He's not talking about Dendera the place – he means the Dendera zodiac!'

'What's the Dendera zodiac?' Eddie asked.

Macy darted in before Nina could answer. 'It's a star map on the ceiling of the Temple of Hathor.'

'At least, it *was* on the temple ceiling,' Nina added. 'There's a replica there now; the original was taken – well, stolen – by Napoleon in the 1790s.'

Rad paused the recording. 'So they're going to Dendera? You might still be able to catch them.'

Nina shook her head. 'No. The replica's a close copy, but it's not exact. They'll want to compare the Sphinx zodiac to the original.'

'Where's that?' said Eddie.

She smiled. 'You want to see some art?'

10

Paris

'Been a while since we were here last,' said Eddie as he, Nina and Macy crossed the Cour Napoléon, the central courtyard of the Louvre. 'Must be, what? Three and a half years?'

'God, where did the time go?' Nina sighed.

They passed the 72-foot-high glass and aluminium pyramid at the courtyard's heart and continued to the ornate Sully Wing beyond. There were more security guards than on her previous visit; a spate of high-profile art thefts around the world in recent months had prompted the Louvre to pre-emptively deter the robbers from trying anything in Paris. 'Okay, so we want room 12a in the Egyptian bit,' Eddie said, unfolding a tourist guide. 'Typical. It's right round the far bloody side. So let's see, right *there*, then left *there*, then straight on through . . .'

'Eddie, we are not just going to charge through the Louvre, look at one thing and then walk out again,' Nina insisted.

'Yeah, but you've already seen the Mona Lisa, so it's not like you'll be missing anything.' He winked at Macy to show he was just winding up his wife – and succeeding. 'Anyway, Shaban and his mates are probably halfway to the Pyramid of Osiris. We don't have time to play art critics.'

'Philistine,' Nina sniffed, but saw his point. The great museum's treasures would still be here the next time she visited Paris, but those inside the Pyramid of Osiris would be gone for ever if the Osirian Temple reached it first.

But she was still able to take in some of the exhibits along the way, the halls lined with splendid displays of Egyptian antiquities ranging from simple papyrus scrolls to full-sized statues and carved temple columns. She took small revenge on Eddie by stopping to examine various items, forcing him to come back for her with increasing impatience each time.

Eventually, though, her curiosity about the importance of the Dendera zodiac drew her to it like a magnet. Room 12a was a small antechamber off one of the main halls. At one end of the room was a sandstone relief from the Temple of Amun at Karnak, but it was what waited at the other end – or rather, *above* it – that caught their attention.

'That's a fancier decoration than anything at Home Depot,' said Eddie.

Nina tipped her head back to take in the sight. The Dendera zodiac was a slab of pale brown stone behind glass some nine feet above them, lit to pick out the detail carved into it. It was larger than the zodiac in the Hall of Records, but the stylised figures of the constellations were arranged in the same way around the central pole of the sky.

'Well, I can see Leo and Scorpio,' Eddie said, indicating the forms of a lion and a scorpion, 'but I don't recognise a lot of 'em. I can't even see the Plough.'

'It's there,' said Macy, pointing at a shape slightly off the centre.

'What, the leg of lamb?'

'That's what the ancient Egyptians thought it looked like,' Nina said. 'But pretty much all the major constellations – Libra, Taurus, Aries – are there, just in slightly different forms. The modern western zodiac was taken more or less directly from the Egyptian one, with a few name changes.' She pointed up at a particular figure. 'Orion, for one. The Egyptians knew him as someone else, a major figure from their mythology. See if you can guess who.'

Eddie took a stab. 'Osiris?'

'Ding! Ten points.'

Macy took out a colour printout of the section of the zodiac Nina had captured on video. Rad had enhanced it as best he could, providing two versions – a straight blow-up of the video frame, and a copy in which he had adjusted the perspective in Photoshop to make it look as it would viewed from directly below. The low quality of the original image meant that both pictures lacked detail, but the Sphinx zodiac's painted figures made picking them out an easier task.

She compared the printout to the zodiac overhead. 'They're pretty close, but there are some differences. This red circle here, it's not on the one from Dendera.'

'If it's red, it's probably meant to represent Mars,' Nina

realised. 'I don't know how much the positions of the constellations would change over a few thousand years, but the planets would be in different places after just a few weeks. It's how you can work out the date when a particular zodiac was made – if Mars is in Aquarius, Venus is in Capricorn and so on, you can use a computer to list all the times when the planets were in that exact configuration.'

Eddie looked at the printout, then back up at the ceiling, a thoughtful expression forming. Nina was about to ask what he'd noticed when Macy snapped her fingers. 'Oh, oh! This is different.'

She tapped a figure on the printout, offset from the lighter sweep of the Milky Way against the dark background. 'This guy – I think it's Osiris again. Same colour as his other constellation – green.'

'Osiris was green?' said Eddie. 'Was he a Vulcan or something?'

'Green was the colour the Egyptians associated with new life,' said Macy. 'But this guy,' she pointed at the figure again, 'he's not on the big zodiac.'

Nina looked more closely. 'Is that something next to him?' Beside the second, smaller Osiris was a little yellow-orange shape.

'Another planet?'

'I dunno . . .' Even in low resolution the symbol of Mars was clearly circular, whereas this was distinctly angular.

Three angles. A triangle.

A pyramid.

'No way,' gasped Macy, coming to the same conclusion as Nina. 'No. Fu—' She gave Nina an embarrassed look.

'It's okay,' Eddie said, grinning. 'You can swear.'

'King. *Way!*' Macy finished. '*That's* the Pyramid of Osiris!'

'It must be,' said Nina, looking to the ceiling for confirmation. Though the paint on the Dendera zodiac had long since flaked away, the carvings remained in perfect clarity . . . and there was no trace of either the additional figure of Osiris or the small triangle on the relief above. 'When the position of the stars overhead exactly matches what's shown on the Sphinx zodiac, you're at the location of the Pyramid of Osiris!' She noticed Eddie shaking his head. 'What?'

'Doesn't work like that,' he said. 'Yeah, you can use the stars to navigate. But you can't just look up, compare what you're looking at to a star map, and know if you're in the right spot or not – not without a sextant and an almanac with all the star positions on that day of the year.'

Nina's excitement evaporated. 'Oh.'

'But that's not the only thing. The zodiac they nicked from the Sphinx, they think it's a map, right?'

'Right . . .' Nina said, unsure where he was heading.

'But like I said, it can't be just a star map, so it's got to be some other kind of map.' He looked up at the ceiling. 'Problem is, this ain't exactly portable, is it? So when you go out to find the pyramid, you'll need to make a copy. Only when you do . . .' He grinned lopsidedly. 'This'll freak you out. Got a pen and paper?'

Macy produced a ballpoint and notepad and held them out to him, but he shook his head again. 'No, Nina, you try this. I want to see your face when you work it out.'

More puzzled than ever, Nina took the proffered items. 'Okay,' said Eddie, 'now hold it upside down, right above your head, and draw the shape of the room.'

Tilting back, Nina drew a rectangle on the page above her. 'All right, now what?'

He went to the room's empty end. 'Say this is the north wall. Write *north* on your map – but keep it held upside down.'

She did so, on her drawing marking the wall he was facing with an N. 'If that's north, then obviously the opposite end's south,' he said. 'So write that too. Now,' he raised his right arm and pointed at the wall to that side, 'that means this wall's east, and the last one's west. Okay?'

'Yeah, got that,' said Nina, adding the appropriate letters.

Eddie turned back to her with an expectant smile. He turned clockwise, pointing at each wall in turn. 'North, east, south, west – "Never Eat Shredded Wheat". Matches what you've just drawn, right?'

'Yes, and can I look down now? My neck's starting to crick.'

'Yeah, sure.' With relief, she brought down the notebook. 'Okay, this is the freaky part. Turn your map so that your north's pointing at the north wall.' She did. 'Now, what's wrong with your picture?'

Nina stared at her drawing, just a rectangle with a letter against each side, not sure what she was meant to be seeing . . . until it struck her like a slap to the forehead. 'Hey!' North was north, and south was south – but on her crude map, east and west had reversed positions from reality, east on the left of the page and west on the right. 'That's . . . that's just weird.'

'Told you it was freaky,' said Eddie. 'Mac showed me that when I was doing navigation training. It's one of those things that's so obvious, you never even think about it until somebody points it out.'

Macy looked at Nina's drawing. 'I don't get it.'

He passed the notebook and pen to her. 'Go on, try it for yourself.'

'So how does that help us find the Pyramid of Osiris?' Nina asked as Macy bent backwards and started drawing.

'To be honest, love? Not a fucking clue.' They both smiled. 'It just means that the zodiac they nicked isn't a straightforward map. Shaban and his lot might have a job figuring it out even with the whole thing to look at.'

'Let's hope so.'

Macy lowered the notebook, looking between it and the walls with dawning comprehension. 'So east and west swap round when you look up or down . . . That is *so* wild.'

'Yeah, see?' Eddie said. 'Not such a boring old fart now, am I?'

'I never said you were *boring*!' she objected.

He grunted, but any further comment was cut off as an officious man in a tweedy suit came to the doorway, speaking in rapid-fire, supercilious French.

'Sorry, mate,' said Eddie, even though he and Nina were fluent enough to get the gist of what he was saying. 'English. Well, I am. They're American.'

'English and American. I see. I hope you are enjoying your visit to the Louvre,' the man said, manifestly not caring whether they were or not. 'But I am afraid I must ask you to leave this room. A VIP has requested to view the Dendera zodiac in private.'

'Oh, a VIP!' said Eddie with exaggerated brightness. 'Well,

of course we'll shift out! Don't want a VIP to have to share the room with any *common* people, do we?'

'Good God, no,' Nina added, adopting a haughty tone. 'We shall most certainly take our leave before we sully the nasal passages of our betters with our noxious emanations!' She linked arms with Eddie, and as one they pivoted to face the exit.

The museum official was unamused, even less so by Macy's fit of the giggles. 'I apologise for the inconvenience,' he said, mouth a narrow line, before addressing someone outside.

Still arm in arm, unable to contain their smiles, Nina and Eddie went into the main hall.

The smiles vanished instantly as they found themselves facing Sebak Shaban and Bobby Diamondback.

11

'Ay up,' said Eddie, first to recover from the foursome's mutual shock. 'Fancy meeting you 'ere.'

Diamondback's hand whipped into his snakeskin jacket, but a sharp look from Shaban froze it.

'Right, smart move,' Nina said, trying to mask her nervousness. 'This isn't *The Da Vinci Code*. You can't just do, y'know, *stuff* in the middle of the Louvre – in broad daylight in front of witnesses, no less.'

The official looked dubiously back and forth between the two groups. 'Do you know each other?'

'We haven't been formally introduced,' Nina said with cold sarcasm. 'But yeah, we know each other. Mr Shaban, I believe. And your charming friend.'

'Bobby Diamondback,' drawled Shaban's companion. 'Sorry I missed y'all earlier. If you catch my drift.'

'Diamondback?' said Eddie mockingly. 'Bollocks! There's no way that's your real name.'

Diamondback's eyes creased into slits. 'I'm Cherokee Indian, asshole.'

'What, one sixty-fourth? You're whiter than I am! And Puff Adder'd suit you better.'

'Y'know,' said Diamondback, shaking his head, 'you oughta watch your mouth when you're talkin' to a Marine. It might get shut. Permanent, like.'

'No proper Marine'd let their hair get into that state,' Eddie replied, unimpressed by either the American's threat or his greasy mullet. 'Dishonourable discharge, was it?'

'Eddie, honey,' said Nina through a strained grin, 'can you please stop provoking the man?'

'I know you, of course, Dr Wilde,' said Shaban. 'In fact, after your little stunt at the Sphinx, I think a good part of the world knows you.' The official blinked, recognising her. 'And Miss Sharif too,' the Egyptian added as Macy peered out of the antechamber. 'All of you here together. How convenient.'

'Why are we still here?' Macy asked Nina in a fearful whisper.

Shaban's eyes narrowed intently. 'Why *are* you here, Dr Wilde?'

'The same reason as you, I'm guessing.' Her gaze flicked down; under one arm, he carried a leather-bound folder that she imagined contained photos of the reassembled zodiac. 'A keen interest in ancient astrology.'

His eyes tightened still further. 'Very keen.'

'I'm sure. But we really should be going. See you – well, not soon at all, I hope.'

'Tell you what,' said Diamondback, his hand once again edging into his jacket, 'how 'bout I show you the way out?'

'Tell *you* what,' Eddie replied, doing the same and hoping

Diamondback couldn't tell that he wasn't armed, 'how about you *don't*?'

'It's all right, Bobby,' said Shaban, touching his arm. 'Stay with me. I'm sure we'll meet them again. Hopefully,' a small smile, genuine but nasty, 'in less formal surroundings.'

'Can't wait,' said Eddie, still holding his hand near his non-existent gun. He and Nina backed away, Macy scurrying into cover behind them. Shaban and Diamondback stood like statues, watching as they reached a short flight of stairs leading down to the next room. 'Okay, leg it!'

They ran through the underground room – somewhat ironically, a display of items relating to Osiris – then clattered back up more stairs into a chamber full of mummies, attracting surprised looks from the other visitors. Eddie looked back. 'He's not following, but I bet he's already calling for a goon squad.' He flapped open the tourist map. 'Where's the nearest bloody exit?'

They found the way out, emerging on the Place du Louvre to the museum's east. 'Christ, I really need to buy a new gun,' Eddie complained.

Nina, meanwhile, was more interested in a car parked in a restricted zone nearby – a large black Mercedes SUV with tinted windows. 'Think that's Shaban's car?'

'Maybe,' Eddie said as he led the two women across the street. 'Why? Want to key it?'

'No, but I was thinking we should follow it.'

'We just got away from the guy, and now you want to meet him again?' Macy asked.

'We can't find the Pyramid of Osiris without seeing the

complete zodiac,' said Nina. 'And Shaban's got it.'

They took cover round a corner. Nina looked back. No sign of anyone coming after them.

'It might not even be his car,' Eddie pointed out.

'Well, then we're screwed. But parking on the lines is kind of a VIPy thing to do, so let's wait and see.'

As it turned out, it *was* Shaban's car. About ten minutes later, the scar-faced Egyptian emerged from the Louvre. He and Diamondback entered the Mercedes.

'You think he figured out how to find the pyramid?' Macy wondered.

'Only one way to find out,' Nina said. The SUV pulled away. She hurried to the kerb and raised a hand. 'Taxi!'

'Bloody hell,' said Eddie, peering along the narrow street. 'Didn't realise this thing was big in France as well.'

Nina, Eddie and Macy had followed Shaban's SUV across Paris in a taxi – after first convincing its driver that their request to '*Suivez cette voiture!*' wasn't *une blague*. The Mercedes pulled up outside a building bearing the logo of the Osirian Temple – which, like its counterpart in New York when Eddie had visited it with Grant Thorn, had a sizeable and excited crowd outside.

'All these people are here just to see this guy Osir?' Macy asked in disbelief. 'I know he used to be a movie star, but come on!'

Nina told the taxi driver to pull over. 'Maybe you should make up your own religion too and see what happens.'

Macy considered it. 'Could all my followers be, like, buff shirtless firefighters? Young ones, obviously.'

'Y'know, I think that's a religion *I'd* like to start.'

'Oi,' Eddie growled.

They got out and watched as Shaban and Diamondback left their vehicle, green-blazered men clearing a path to the building's entrance. Once they were inside, Nina led the way to the fringe of the crowd.

'So now what?' Eddie asked. 'Wait for them to come out again?'

'I don't know,' Nina admitted. 'I think we should stick close to them, though.' She regarded the crowd. 'And I have to admit, I'm kinda curious about this whole Osirian Temple thing – and why Osir's going to such lengths to find the Pyramid of Osiris. We should try to get inside.'

'You do remember that they know what we look like?'

'So we'll sit at the back. There must be three hundred people here – if we keep our heads down, Shaban and his pal won't see us. And nobody else knows who we are.'

'Er, Dr Wilde,' Macy pointed out, 'you were just on TV in front of millions of people. And you were already kinda famous before that.'

Nina looked at the nearby shops. 'Okay, maybe if we had disguises . . .'

'These are crap disguises,' whispered Eddie as he and Nina found seats on the very back row of the Egyptian-styled hall, watched over by two large statues of Osiris flanking the entrance.

'Well, I'm sorry that we weren't in Paris's fancy dress quarter,' Nina hissed back. All they had been able to find to hide their faces were baseball caps with *J'aime Paris* written above the bill.

The buzz of excitement around them rose to a roar. The

crowd stood and applauded as Khalid Osir strode on to the stage at the far end of the hall, basking in the adulation of his followers. Behind him, other senior members of the Osirian Temple lined up, Shaban and Diamondback among them. Eddie tugged his hat lower. 'Macy had the right idea staying outside . . .'

'*Merci, merci*,' Osir said at last. '*Bonjour, et bienvenue! Malheureusement, mon français est terrible*,' his deliberately stilted pronunciation raised a laugh from the crowd, 'so I will have to speak through an interpreter!' He nodded to a man on the stage, who stepped forward and repeated his words in French, to more laughter.

He gestured, and the audience sat. The others on the stage, with the exception of the interpreter, did the same. 'Thank you all for coming,' said Osir. 'May the light of the sun-god Ra bless you all!'

'May the spirit of Osiris protect and strengthen you!' the crowd replied, some in English, others in French.

'It is truly a great pleasure to see so many people here today. Our church gains strength with each new follower – and the world will be made a better place by the wisdom of Osiris!'

The audience kept cheering as he continued his oratory. Nina had to admit that while she thought his 'church' was utter nonsense, Osir himself was a magnetic performer – had he chosen to remain an actor, she didn't doubt that he could easily have made a big name for himself in Hollywood.

On the other hand, she thought, by having the Osirian Temple officially recognised as a religion, he had achieved something that even Hollywood's A-list could not – tax exemption. Maybe there was method to his madness after all.

'We praise you, O Osiris!' cried Osir, raising his hands. The congregation startled Nina by unexpectedly also chanting 'Osiris!' 'Osiris, the lord of eternity, the judge of all souls, the great one who awaits us in the land of the dead beyond Abydos! O Osiris!'

'Osiris!' the crowd chanted again. This time, Nina and Eddie got the idea and half-heartedly joined in.

'The gods of the sky sing your praises, and the gods of the Underworld bow down before you. You are the provider of the divine bread that will grant immortality to all your followers in this life and the next. You are the protector against the evil of Set, the destroyer. O Osiris!'

'Osiris!'

'Greatest of all men and all gods, show us the path to life everlasting! Guide us safely through the perils of the Underworld to your judgement! We praise you, O Osiris!'

The crowd chanted the god's name, each repetition growing in volume and passion. On the stage, Osir's eyes were closed; whether or not he really believed in what he was saying Nina couldn't tell, but he had the look of a theatre actor receiving the greatest ovation of his life.

The same couldn't be said of his brother, though. Shaban's face was cold, tight, clenched with suppressed anger. Eddie had noticed too. 'What's his problem?'

'Dunno,' Nina replied, 'but there's definitely a problem with that prayer.'

'How come?'

'It's like a simplified – *really* simplified – version of a real

Egyptian prayer, dumbed down. And the mythology's wrong, too. Set wasn't a nice guy, but he wasn't the ancient Egyptian equivalent of Satan either.'

Osir lowered his hands. The tumult died down. 'Who's Set?' Eddie asked.

'Osiris's brother – and murderer. He was jealous of him, and wanted to take his kingdom. But he was also the champion of Ra, the sun-god, just as important a part of the Egyptian pantheon as Osiris – and in some parts of the country he was actually worshipped *over* Osiris.' The middle-aged woman to Eddie's other side irritably shushed her.

Osir spoke again, no longer with the voice of a preacher, but more like a salesman. 'My friends, following the guidance of Osiris will bring you life everlasting. And I am here today to tell you that as the voice of the spirit of Osiris, I have channelled his wisdom once more. His words are my words, and now they shall be your words too. The twelfth volume of the Book of Osiris is now finished, and all his followers must now take it to their homes, and to their hearts.'

'Is this a sermon or an infomercial?' Nina asked quietly as Osir continued what was rapidly turning into a sales pitch. But the audience was lapping it up, all but holding out their credit cards. She wasn't sure what she found more appalling – Osir's almost transparent hucksterism, or that everyone seemed to be falling for it.

'All the books, and more, will be available to you before you leave the temple today,' said Osir. He smiled. 'And now, it is time for something I know you have been waiting for – the chance to ask me personally any questions you have about the teachings of Osiris!' A good proportion of the congregation responded by thrusting their hands into the air. Osir laughed. 'I wish I had the time to answer each and every one of you,' he said. 'But unfortunately, I soon have to return to the Osirian Temple's headquarters to take care of matters there, then after that I will be travelling on to Monaco to spread the word at the grand prix – and I hope you will all be cheering Team Osiris to a win!'

Those cultists who were apparently also motor racing fans cheered. Shaban looked irritated, but he remained silent as Osir waved them down. 'Thank you, thank you. So now, I will send Gerard among you,' he nodded to the translator, 'for your questions.'

Gerard moved down the central aisle, scanning the field of waving hands before extending a microphone to a young and pretty dark-haired woman. She seemed almost overcome, stuttering out a question in French. The translator delivered it to Osir: 'The thought of the journey through the Underworld frightens me. What happens if I fall to the guardians before I reach Osiris?'

Osir gave her a reassuring smile. 'There is nothing to fear in the Underworld for those who truly follow the words of Osiris. The guardians can only harm the unprepared or the unworthy.' The smile widened, his dark eyes gleaming. 'If you come to Switzerland for my personal teachings, I will show you everything you need to reach Osiris, and more besides.'

'Did he just try to chat her up?' Eddie whispered as the young woman gave her heartfelt thanks.

'I think he did,' said Nina. ' "Personal teachings", my ass.'

'*Shhhh!*' the woman next to Eddie hissed.

The translator picked the next questioner, another young, attractive woman, though this time a blonde. The next was also a blonde, followed by a brunette. 'I think I'm seeing a pattern,' Nina said.

Eddie shook his head in a mixture of disbelief and admiration. 'Jesus. He's figured out the ultimate bloke fantasy – how to get rich *and* have hot women worship you like a god.' His grin froze as Nina raised her hand. 'What're you doing?'

'I've got a question.' Osir's mangling of Egyptian mythology for personal gain had made her increasingly annoyed on a professional level – but she was also curious about how seriously his followers took their religion. Was it just some transitory New Age nonsense to fill a void in their lives for a time before they moved on to the next new thing . . . or did they genuinely, deeply believe it?

The translator had almost reached the back of the room, still focused on finding one particular kind of questioner – and Nina fit the bill. He held out the microphone to her.

'We're supposed to be inconspic— oh, for Christ's sake,' Eddie muttered, hiding his face beneath his baseball cap.

'I, ah, I have a question?' Nina said, raising the pitch of her voice to bimbo level. She regarded Osir on the stage – but also watched Shaban and Diamondback for any signs of recognition. 'I was wondering how we can have eternal life in both this world and the next, when to get into the next life we kinda have to die in this one?' Faces turned to her, the crowd's disdain almost physical.

From Osir's condescending smile and the ease with which he replied, it was a question to which he had long since devised a stock answer. 'Both lives are the same life,' he said. 'As one ends, another begins, as long as Osiris has judged you worthy of life everlasting. The next life follows on from this one without interruption.' His salesman voice returned. 'These things are taught in the first volume of the Book of Osiris. If you have not yet read it, then copies are available outside.' There was a ripple of mocking laughter – aimed not at the cult leader, but at Nina. The church clearly had little patience for those who weren't up to speed on its scripture.

Gerard was about to back away when Nina spoke again. 'And I have a question about mythology,' she said in her normal voice, edged with irritation at being patronised. 'How do you reconcile your interpretation of the Osiris story with the accepted Egyptian myths? You know, the part where Osiris wasn't actually granted immortality until *after* he died and was briefly resurrected by Isis only for Set to cut him into fourteen pieces, and then had his severed penis eaten by a fish?'

Hostile murmurs ran through the crowd. On stage, Shaban's eyes suddenly bugged as he realised who was speaking. 'Time to go,' Eddie muttered.

Osir was ready to deliver another canned reply, but looked round as Shaban said something. He raised his eyebrows. 'We have a surprise guest: Dr Nina Wilde. I'm sure you all saw her unexpected television appearance a few nights ago.'

'Hello, hi,' said Nina with a sarcastic wave as she and Eddie pushed their way to the aisle. Behind Osir, Diamondback quickly made his way from the stage. 'Okay, so if you don't want to talk about the penis thing, how about the Osirian Temple's connection with the theft of the zodiac from under the Sphinx, and why you're looking for the Pyramid of Osiris?'

'I have no idea what you mean, Dr Wilde,' said Osir, though his acting skills couldn't conceal his surprise at her use of the term.

Behind him, Shaban stood, signalling to the green-blazered men at the rear of the room before calling out to the congregation. 'Our temple has been defiled by unbelievers! Are you all going to take this insult?'

Some of the cultists began to boo, several standing with enraged faces. Osir looked concerned. 'Wait, there is no need for anger,' he began, but the men ignored him, shoving towards the aisle in response to Shaban.

'Definitely time to go,' said Eddie. He turned to the exit, seeing the greenjackets closing ranks. 'Bollocks! You *would* have to get mouthy, wouldn't you?'

'Okay, not my smartest idea ever,' Nina admitted. She now had the answer to her question of how seriously Osir's followers took their religion – *very*.

Eddie looked towards the stage. Diamondback, marching down the aisle, was almost certainly armed – but there were now several people between him and them. If they could get outside before he had a clear aim . . .

One of the green-blazered men reached out to grab him—

'Go!' Eddie shouted, smashing a fist into his jaw.

Nina jumped the falling man and ran for the door. Another man clawed at her – but caught only her hat, pulling it from her head. She lashed out, hitting him hard on one cheek, and kicked open the door. The room outside was set up with display tables, loaded with books and DVDs and pyramidal geegaws. The people at the stalls jumped back in surprise as she burst in. 'Eddie, come on!'

The man Nina had hit started after her – only to take a savage kick to the groin from Eddie's booted foot. He collapsed with an animalistic squeal.

Someone clutched at Eddie's leather jacket, pulling him back. He punched the man's face, red blood squirting on to his green blazer. The man tumbled, hitting the statue of Osiris beside the door – and falling through it with a splintering crack, what looked like stone turning out to be nothing more than fibreglass and plaster. The statue rocked.

Osir's shouts for order went unheard as the cultists in the aisle reacted with fury to the desecration of the statue, running at Eddie. Diamondback charged after them.

Eddie jumped and grabbed the statue's arm, kicking back off the door frame to pull it over. He threw himself through the open door as the nine-foot sculpture crashed down behind him and exploded into sharp-edged fragments.

The shocked cult members stopped. Diamondback barged through them, drawing his revolvers.

Nina was at the exit to the street. Eddie slammed the temple door and tipped over a table, stacks of DVDs clattering across the floor. The next stall was still being set up, a cardboard box of books half-unpacked upon it. The flat plastic tie that held it closed in transit had been cut; he grabbed it and sprinted after Nina.

The temple door crashed open. One of the men in green ploughed through it, Diamondback right behind him, guns raised—

The goon stepped on the scattered DVD cases – and fell, plastic gliding over plastic like ice beneath his foot. Diamondback couldn't stop in time and tripped over him. One of his guns went off as he hit the ground. The stall-workers fled screaming.

Eddie ran through the wooden double doors after Nina and slammed them shut. The handles were heavy knobs of time-worn brass; he looped the plastic tie repeatedly round them and knotted it, pulling it as tight as he could.

Macy ran to them. 'Dr Wilde! What happened?'

'They didn't like having their beliefs challenged,' Nina said. She looked for the fastest escape route.

Eddie had already seen it. He whistled sharply to signal the women, hurrying to Osir's parked limousine. The startled chauffeur took the impacts of Eddie's fist and the road surface to his face in rapid succession as he was thrown out on to the street. 'Come on!'

'We're stealing his *limo*?' Macy cried.

Nina opened the rear door and shoved her inside. 'It's better than a cab!' She dived in after her. 'Eddie, go!'

Eddie floored the accelerator. The limo leapt away from the kerb, clipping the car parked in front of it as he swerved. Then they were clear.

Nina looked back, seeing the wooden doors shaking violently before the plastic tie finally broke. Diamondback ran on to the street, shouting after them – but with enough presence of mind not to open fire right outside his employer's building on a busy thoroughfare.

Eddie powered through the Parisian streets for barely more than a minute before skidding to a stop near the entrance to an underground Métro station. 'All out!' he called. They abandoned the vehicle – though Macy was surprised that they ran past the station rather than into it. 'They'll think that's where we went,' he explained. 'If *les flics* are all busy checking the subway stations, they won't be looking for us in a Starbucks round the corner.'

'You're pretty good at this stuff, aren't you?' said Macy with a certain amount of admiration.

'Not bad,' he said, smiling as they rounded a corner to see an Internet café ahead. 'There we go. Not a Starbucks, but near enough.' They went inside.

A police car sped past the café a few minutes later, siren wailing, but that was the only sign of pursuit they saw. The authorities and the Osirian Temple appeared to have fallen for Eddie's ruse. All the same, he remained tense, looking out through the front window until the noise faded. 'I think they've gone,' he finally said, turning back to Nina and Macy. They had booked time on a computer, initially so as not to attract any attention, before looking up the cult on the Internet again. 'So, what now?'

Nina had been giving that exact question some thought. 'Osir's definitely got the zodiac, and he really is after the Pyramid of Osiris. You saw how he reacted when I mentioned them.'

'Yeah, and we were bloody lucky to get out of there. I think we ought to tell the Egyptians what we've found out and let them handle it. It's their zodiac, they can get it back themselves.'

'We don't have any proof yet,' Nina objected. 'It's probably at his headquarters in Switzerland,' she indicated the Osirian Temple's web page on the PC's screen, 'but we'll need more than that to convince the minister or Dr Assad to take any action.'

'Whatever we do, we'll have to do it fast,' said Macy. 'Otherwise they'll find the pyramid and take everything inside it.'

'There's not a lot we can do to stop them, is there?' Eddie said irritably. 'They're not just going to let us stroll into their HQ and take a gander at the thing.'

'Well, *obviously* not,' Macy replied, annoyed, 'but – but you could break in!' she went on, suddenly enthusiastic again. 'You were like some special forces guy, weren't you? Dr Wilde and I could cause some sort of distraction, and you could sneak in and do your ninja thing to find the zodiac—'

Nina put her fingertips to her temples. 'Oh, shut up, Macy,' she growled.

Macy was startled, and hurt. 'No, really, we could—'

'This isn't a movie, and Eddie sure as hell isn't a ninja. It's a stupid idea.' She frowned, rubbing her forehead. 'Let me think.'

'Speaking of stupid ideas,' said Eddie as Macy sat back tight-lipped, 'going into that temple and telling those nutters about the time their god had his knob chopped off was pretty fucking dim.'

Nina glared at him. 'Right, like getting into a macho pissing contest with an armed murderer was a smart move. Way to keep out of trouble there, Eddie.'

'Excuse bloody *me*,' he cried sarcastically. 'I'm not the one who's looking for trouble. I didn't decide to blow up Times Square or wreck the Sphinx or pick a fight with a load of fucking looney-tunes cultists! Quick, tell the shrinks – you've found a new way of getting out of a depression!'

'They don't like being called shrinks,' Macy snapped.

Nina ignored her. 'Yes, of course! Why didn't I see it before? *Obviously* what I need to get me past the worst time of my life since my parents died is being chased and shot at!'

Eddie snorted in a mix of anger and dismay. 'Oh, good to know our marriage got off to such a great start.'

'I didn't think you'd noticed!' she shot back. 'Since you'd apparently found other ways to occupy your time.'

He looked up at the ceiling, rolling his eyes. 'For fuck's sake! Not this again.'

'What am I supposed to think?' Nina demanded. 'I find out that not only are you spending time with another woman, but you're also lying to me about it!'

'And I told you there's nothing going on between me and Amy.'

'Then why won't you tell me what you were doing?'

He threw up his hands. 'You know what? I was going to, even though I wanted to keep it a secret until the right time, but I'm not going to bother. It's not like you've paid any attention to anyone but yourself for the past seven months, no reason you'd start now.'

'What the hell does *that* mean?' Nina demanded.

He made a sarcastic sound. 'You're not the only one who got fired, remember? I lost my job too. And look at all the crap I've had to do to support us both, working all bloody hours buying orange juice for a bunch of paranoid rich tossers while all you do is sit around and moan about moving out of your precious bloody Manhattan!'

'I didn't just lose a *job*,' Nina snarled. 'I lost my career, my reputation – everything! And if you can't see why I might be a bit goddamn depressed about that, maybe you don't know me at all!'

'Maybe I don't,' he shot back. 'I didn't think the woman I married would be such a bloody whiner, for a start.'

'*What?*'

'You didn't hear me going on and on about how crap everything was, did you? No, I got off my arse and actually did something about it!'

'Oh, so the five hundred letters I wrote trying to find work didn't count?' she cried. 'Maybe you think I should have gotten a job at McDonald's!'

Macy slapped a palm on the table. 'Okay, look! This isn't helping. We need to find—'

'Shut up!' they both shouted. Macy stared at Nina, then, lips quivering, jumped up and hurried out.

'Shit,' said Eddie, after a moment. 'I'd better go after her, make sure she doesn't run straight into Diamondback or someone.'

'You do that,' Nina replied coldly. Eddie shook his head and followed Macy. 'God damn it.' She looked at the screen. Osir's portrait beamed back at her. Nina regarded him, silently thinking.

And making a decision.

After a few minutes, Eddie and Macy returned. She still looked upset, and his expression didn't appear to have lightened either. Nina was sure what she was about to say wouldn't improve their moods. 'I've decided what I'm going to do,' she announced.

'Oh, you have, have you?' Eddie replied suspiciously.

'That's right. Macy's plan wasn't entirely stupid.'

'Glad you think so,' Macy said, unimpressed.

'I'm going to Osir's headquarters in Switzerland, like she suggested. But there won't be any sneaking around. I'm going to give him what he needs to find the Pyramid of Osiris.' She stood. 'And you know something? I'm going in alone.'

12

Switzerland

Nina walked along the short road to the edge of the lake, tension churning in her stomach. A gatehouse on the shore marked the entrance to the headquarters of the Osirian Temple . . . which were not what she had imagined.

Some forty feet out from the lake's edge was a rocky island, bordered by a sheer wall of grey stone battlements with men patrolling them. Circular towers stood higher at the corners, topped by conical roofs of bright red slate; another, larger rectangular roof above the far wall marked the castle's Gothic keep. A drawbridge, its two halves currently raised, linked the castle to the mainland.

The whole scene, backed by a range of Alpine peaks beyond the blue lake, was almost ridiculously picturesque – with the exception of one thing that stood out as utterly incongruous. Inside the castle's expansive courtyard, rising above the walls, was a pyramid of black glass. It was the same structure Nina had seen behind Osir in his photo on the Osirian Temple's website.

The drawbridge's heavy dark wood beams rose like a wall through the gatehouse archway, blocking her view of the castle beyond. To one side was an intercom, a camera regarding her glassily.

The knot in her stomach tightened. She was taking a huge risk in coming here. But she still reached up and pushed the intercom button.

'Yes?' said a voice from the panel's speaker.

'My name is Dr Nina Wilde,' Nina said as she stared directly at the camera to make sure the guard got a good view of her face. 'Tell Khalid Osir . . . I want to make a deal.'

'I must admit, Dr Wilde,' said Osir ten minutes later, 'I'm surprised to see you again. Certainly here.'

'I'm still a little surprised myself,' she said, as she was escorted into a large room inside the keep. It was a museum, dedicated to a singular subject.

Osiris.

'Why are you even talking to her?' snapped Shaban. He had met her at the main gate, leading a squad of green-blazered men, and Nina was sure that if he had been in charge rather than Osir, he would have had her killed on the spot. 'This is obviously a trick. Bobby can dispose of her somewhere she will never be found.'

'You must excuse my brother,' Osir said, giving Shaban a dismissive wave that only increased his anger. 'He has never been one for social pleasantries.'

'Yeah, I got that impression,' said Nina, taking a closer

look at one of the display cases. It contained an ancient papyrus scroll, carefully preserved between two sheets of glass.

Osir saw her interest. 'I think you know what that is.'

'The fourth page of the scrolls that led to the discovery of the Hall of Records, I'm guessing.'

'Yes. The Osirian Temple funded an archaeological dig just beyond the Egyptian border in Gaza, which my experts – who are also my followers – thought might uncover something interesting. They were more right than I could have imagined.'

'So you kept the final page for yourself.'

'I had no problem with the Egyptian government taking possession of the Hall of Records. It's a national treasure. But once I found out what was inside it,' he gestured at the papyrus, 'I knew it was something I *had* to keep for myself. Whatever the price.' He indicated the other exhibits, which ranged from carved figurines of the ancient god to large sections of stone, seemingly cut from walls, bearing more hieroglyphs. 'This is the greatest private collection of Osirian artefacts in the world. I've been collecting them for years – but I hope the collection will soon become much larger.'

'Once you find the Pyramid of Osiris,' said Nina.

'Indeed. And apparently you are willing to help me do that.'

'If she can be trusted,' Shaban growled.

'We'll see. This way, Dr Wilde.' Osir guided her towards a door. They passed a space amongst the exhibits which to Nina seemed the perfect size to accommodate the zodiac, but she had no time to remark upon it as Osir led her into the next room.

Despite the Egyptian theme to the decor, the luxurious lounge was decidedly playboyish in style, all chrome and pale wood and black leather. 'Please, sit down,' said Osir. Nina took a place on a plump leather couch with white sheepskin cushions and drapes. She expected Osir to sit in the chair facing her, but instead he joined her on the couch. Shaban remained standing. 'So,' said Osir with a smile, 'can I get you anything?'

'No, thank you.'

'Then I hope you don't mind if I have something myself.' There was a stylish speakerphone on a glass coffee table; he pushed a button and said, 'Fiona? My usual coffee, please.' A glance at Shaban, who scowled and shook his head. 'Just the one, thank you.' He leaned back and rested an arm along the top of the couch, fingertips almost touching Nina's shoulder. 'Well then, Dr Wilde . . . or may I call you Nina?'

'Sure, I guess,' she said uncertainly.

'Call me Khalid, if you like. Whatever makes you most comfortable.'

'Okay . . . Khalid.' She managed a faint smile, which Osir returned with added magnitude.

'So, Nina. You want to offer me a deal.' The smile was still there, but it was now businesslike. 'I am very interested to hear it.'

'So am I,' Shaban said coldly.

'Let's put all our cards on the table,' Nina said. 'You've got the zodiac from inside the Sphinx – you know it, and I know it.'

Osir looked to Shaban. 'We scanned her,' Shaban told him. 'No bugs, no wires – just a phone.'

'I don't want anyone knowing about this any more than you do,' Nina told them. 'So, the zodiac. You have it?'

'Yes, I have it,' said Osir.

'Ha, you admitted it! Busted!' She jabbed an accusing finger at him – then withdrew it, grinning at the angry Shaban. 'Psych.'

Osir chuckled. 'I think I am going to like you, Nina. But yes, I have the zodiac.'

'Which you intend to use to locate the Pyramid of Osiris, right?'

'Again, you are correct.'

'I usually am.'

'Except about the Garden of Eden,' Shaban said scathingly.

Nina shot him a nasty glance. 'No, even about that. Except that I got utterly screwed over by people who wanted to keep its existence a secret.' She looked back at Osir. 'Which is one of the reasons why I came to you. I can help you find the Pyramid of Osiris . . . but I want my cut.'

One eyebrow twitched quizzically. 'I hadn't expected the famous Nina Wilde to be quite so . . . mercenary.'

'It's new. I'm trying it on for size.'

'I don't believe her,' said Shaban.

'Yeah, nobody has, lately.' Nina's voice was cutting. 'You know why I came to you? Because those bastards at the IHA ruined my life. They destroyed my career and took away everything that mattered to me.'

'What about your husband?' asked Osir.

She smiled sarcastically. 'Eddie and I are . . . on a break. We had a fight – over this, over coming to see you. He said he wouldn't go along with it, and I knew he wasn't going to change his mind. He never does. So I came on my own.'

'And what made you decide to come?'

'Everything,' she said, then more bitterly: 'Everything! They made me into a joke, a goddamn *joke*! And I'm sick of it. The IHA can go *fuck* themselves!' Osir, and even Shaban, seemed surprised by the vehemence of her outburst. 'You want to know the truth? I *enjoyed* making the IHA look like a bunch of incompetent assholes in front of millions of people. Screw them. I already took the Hall of Records away from them – so now I want to finish the job with the Pyramid of Osiris too. So long as I get well paid, I don't care any more.'

'Money will not be a problem,' said Osir in a concerned yet soothing voice. He lightly touched her shoulder; she didn't pull away. 'But are you sure about leaving your husband?' His tone suggested that he approved of the decision.

'My husband,' said Nina, almost growling. 'My husband makes me so goddamn *mad* sometimes. He's inflexible and sanctimonious and – and an idealist. He's an idealist in a pragmatic world. Well, this is me being pragmatic. I've had enough of sitting around and hoping the world takes pity on me. If everyone else is getting ahead by playing the system, then screw it, I want my share.' Her gaze dropped to her hands, her voice lowering. 'If Eddie doesn't like it, then to hell with him.' She was breathing heavily and her cheeks were flushed, realising she was genuinely angry as pent-up grievances boiled to the surface.

After a moment of silence, she looked back up at Osir to find his dark eyes regarding her intently – he was reading her, as one actor scans another. Judging her performance.

If he thought she was faking, he would turn her over to his brother—

Osir's face broke into a broad smile. 'I think we can make a deal, Nina. *If* you have something to offer me.'

'I do,' she said, relieved. 'I've made some deductions about the pyramid's location.'

'How?' demanded Shaban. 'You never even saw the entire zodiac!'

'I saw enough. Let me guess – you're trying to work out how to read the zodiac as a map.'

Shaban sneered. 'You hardly need to be Sherlock Holmes to deduce that.'

'Maybe not – but how about if I also deduce that you've had no luck relating what you see on your star map to anything in the real world?'

It was clear from the tightness of Shaban's mouth that she was right. Osir nodded. 'But you have?'

'Like I said, it's one of my deductions. And I'll give you this first one for free. Just to prove I'm serious about helping you. Everything after this'll cost you.'

Another small smile from Osir. 'I'm intrigued what you could have discovered without even seeing the full zodiac.'

'Pretty simple, really.' She explained what Eddie had shown her at the Louvre: that a map intended to be viewed on the ceiling would have to be mirrored left to right when viewed more conventionally. 'I'm taking a guess here, but I'm fairly sure you haven't stuck the zodiac to the ceiling.'

'Another correct deduction,' said Osir. He looked at Shaban, shaking his head. 'You were in the army. Weren't you paying attention in map-reading class?'

'Our maps were not on the ceiling,' Shaban replied, the

scar tissue round his mouth creasing as he fought to control his anger. 'And besides, you were always supposed to be the clever one, brother.'

'I suppose I was.' He turned his head at a knock on the door. 'Enter. Ah, Fiona!'

A pretty and curvaceous blonde in her mid-twenties came in, bearing a small cup of steaming, strong-smelling coffee. She gave Nina a suspicious look before presenting the drink to Osir with a smile.

He returned it, gently stroking her forearm before taking the cup. 'Perfect as always, my dear. Thank you.' Fiona smiled again, then left, Osir unashamedly checking out her butt as she went. He leaned back, smelling the coffee before taking a sip. 'It's strange. I can have any luxury from anywhere in the world . . . but for some reason, to me there is no better coffee than a cup of Egyptian *saada*.'

Shaban made a dismissive sound. 'Of all the things to be nostalgic about, you choose that slop?'

'What can I say? You can't choose the things you enjoy – they choose you. So you may as well enjoy them without guilt.' He sipped it again with a contented expression.

'That doesn't sound like something Osiris would say,' Nina commented.

'The beauty of Osiris is that there are many ways to interpret his story. As you pointed out in Paris.'

'Are you saying you just make things up to suit your needs?'

A sardonic laugh. 'You are as blunt as my brother, Nina! But you may think that; I couldn't possibly comment.'

Shaban didn't share his levity. 'Khalid! She has been working against us from the start, but now she suddenly turns round and abandons her own *husband* to come here? Do you really think she wants to help us? It's a trick.'

'I'd be pretty damn stupid to come here on my own if I wasn't being genuine,' Nina countered. 'Considering that you and your snakeskinned buddy want to kill me.'

'I'm afraid Sebak and his men can be a little . . . overzealous in protecting the Temple's interests,' said Osir. 'I hope you will accept my apologies. I never wanted anyone to get hurt. All I wanted was to get the zodiac out of the Hall of Records before the IHA opened it, so I could find the Pyramid of Osiris without interference.'

'Why *are* you trying to find the pyramid?' she asked. 'What's in it that's so important to you?'

He finished his coffee and stood, holding out a hand to Nina. She hesitated, then took it. 'I will show you.'

'Khalid!' Shaban hissed, a clear warning.

Osir glared at him. 'You may be my brother, but *I* am in charge of the Osirian Temple, Sebak. Remember that!' Shaban's fury was now so great that he was visibly shaking with rage, but he forced himself to remain silent as Osir turned back to Nina. 'Again, I apologise. Do you have a younger brother? Or sister?'

'No,' she said. 'But Eddie – my husband – he's a younger brother.'

'Then you know something about sibling rivalry.'

'You could say that.' She had only met Eddie's sister a few times, but even though the two formerly antagonistic Chases had gone through something of a reconciliation, their relationship still had a spiky edge.

Osir grinned. 'It is the eldest son's job to take charge of his brother, to look after him when he needs support. And sometimes, to fix his mistakes when his temper overcomes him.' This last was pointedly directed at Shaban, whose face again contorted in silent anger. 'But come,' he said, directing Nina to the door. 'See for yourself why I am searching for the Pyramid of Osiris.'

13

With Shaban following, Osir led Nina through the keep to the courtyard. She had passed the black glass pyramid and nearby helipad on the way in, but only now was she able to give the structure her full attention. From its base, its blank, sloping face and converging sides threw off her sense of perspective, making it hard to judge its true size. But it was taller than any of the castle's towers, around eighty feet high.

'A pyramid in Switzerland?' she said as they approached. 'A bit out of place.' To say the least; unlike the glass pyramid at the Louvre, Osir's edifice was grossly out of proportion with its surroundings, dominating the castle.

'I think it fits well with the scenery,' Osir replied. 'One of the many fine things about Switzerland. Though I admit the one which brought me here was the tax system.'

'I thought religions were tax exempt?' She almost said 'cults', but opted not to antagonise him.

'They are, in most places – once they have been accepted as legitimate, which takes a lot of time and effort. I founded the Osirian Temple fifteen years ago, but it's only in the past five that it has truly begun to grow around the world. But I have other interests, which unfortunately are *not* tax exempt . . . not without a headquarters in Switzerland and some very clever and expensive accountants.'

The open area of courtyard before the pyramid, empty when she arrived, was now occupied by some thirty men in black shorts and T-shirts performing callisthenics. Diamondback, for once without his snakeskin jacket, issued commands like a drill instructor. Shaban diverted to exchange brief words with the American, who glowered at Nina; while Shaban spoke, the men all stood to attention.

'Looks like you've got your own little private army,' said Nina.

'Sebak's idea,' Osir replied as his brother re-joined them. 'For protection. The Temple sometimes attracts trouble – as you may have noticed.' He smiled.

They reached the pyramid, glass doors in its face sliding open to reveal a stylish lobby area within. The people inside bowed their heads respectfully as Osir directed Nina to an elevator. Disconcertingly, the front and rear glass walls sloped to match the pyramid's face, the elevator's cross-section a parallelogram with its shaft ascending at the same angle. It was a very inefficient use of space, the cabin able to hold far fewer people than a conventional design, but Nina suspected her host was more interested in form than function.

Shaban followed them into the elevator, watching Nina coldly as they ascended. The glass walls gave her a view of parts of the pyramid's interior as they rose, the most impressive being a huge chamber: a temple. Unlike the room she had seen in Paris, though, the decorative hieroglyphics here were laser-etched on glass panels, the tall statues of Egyptian gods glinting in chrome.

'This is the headquarters of the Osirian Temple,' Osir announced proudly. 'It is also the headquarters of Osiris Investment Group, SA. There are more ordinary offices in Geneva and elsewhere, but they are all run from here.'

'You run a religion and a business from the same building?'

'The two are more alike than you might think,' he said, smiling. 'Customer loyalty, market share, return on investment . . . all crucial.' The high hall dropped out of sight, two floors of offices passing before the elevator stopped.

Nina caught a strong and distinctive scent in the air: yeast. 'Smells like you run a bakery as well.'

Osir laughed. 'Not quite. But bread has been an important part of my life – my father was a baker, you know. I grew up making bread.' He seemed momentarily wistful as they stepped from the elevator. 'He thought I would carry on his business.'

'Yes,' said Shaban sarcastically, his anger having subsided, 'I'm sure you would much rather be kneading dough than living in a Swiss castle.'

'Fate had other plans. This way, please, Nina.'

She followed Osir through a door, the pungent smell of yeast growing stronger. The far wall of the room they entered was reinforced glass, giving her a view of what looked like a cross between a kitchen and a laboratory occupying the pyramid's apex. Several people wearing white overalls and face masks were at work, some at computers and microscopes, others tending to ovens and large gleaming steel vats. 'Okay,' Nina said, lost. 'This is . . . ?'

'This is why I am searching for the Pyramid of Osiris,' said Osir. 'What do you know about telomeres?'

She blinked, surprised by the conversation's total change of direction. 'Uh, apart from them being something to do with cells . . . nothing,' she admitted. 'I'm an archaeologist, not a biologist.'

'Oh, Nina,' he said teasingly, shaking his head. 'You shouldn't put limits on the boundaries of your knowledge. Look at me. I was a baker, who became an actor, who became a businessman and then a religious leader . . . but I've also become, in my own small way, an expert in the study of life extension.'

'Life extension?' Nina said, trying to conceal her doubtfulness.

'Yes. Ultimately, that is what the Osirian Temple is about – avoiding ageing, avoiding death. Becoming as immortal as Osiris. My interest – my obsession – began when I was an actor. A star, rather. I may not have been as famous around the world as the stars of Hollywood,' a smile of false modesty, 'but certainly everyone in Egypt knew my face when I was younger.'

'And you wanted to keep it looking young.'

'Of course! Wouldn't you?'

'I dunno,' said Nina, 'I was . . . kinda chunky when I was twenty. I prefer how I look now I'm older.'

'Then you are a very lucky – and unusual – woman!' Osir laughed. 'But all that means is that you are happy as you are *now*. With every passing moment, you are moving beyond that – and your own body is working against you. Every cell in your body is slowly destroying itself, and there is nothing you can do about it. Unless,' he said, making a sweeping gesture towards the vats, 'you can stop your body's self-destruct – and reverse it.'

'That's what this is?' she asked. 'You're making an . . . immortality drug?'

This time, she couldn't keep the scepticism from her voice. 'I've heard that tone before,' said Osir – not accusingly, but with resignation. 'But yes, that is what I am trying to do. I love my life – and I want to keep on loving it! I started with simple treatments, like diet and exercise plans, then moved on to vitamins, antioxidants, hormones—'

'Which you sell to the Osirian Temple's followers.'

'Yes. Each branch of the Temple buys products from worldwide subsidiaries of OIG, which produce them under licence from the parent company. But,' he went on, eyes twinkling, 'the clever part is, the licence fees are more than the wholesale price at which they sell them to the Temples. So technically, all the subsidiary companies operate at a loss . . .'

'. . . and if they're running at a loss, they don't pay any taxes.'

'Exactly. Meanwhile, the Temples make a profit on what they sell, but because they are religious organisations, they pay no taxes either. It's all far more complicated than that, of course – as I said, I have some very expensive accountants and lawyers keeping me one step ahead of the taxman! But it is all legal. Well, it's within the *letter* of the law, at least.'

'It's an impressive setup,' said Nina, thinking of other words to describe it: 'crooked' topping her list.

'Thank you.' Osir seemed genuinely pleased. 'But eventually, I realised that such treatments can only go so far, because of a simple genetic fact. Telomeres are a part of the chromosomes in every cell of the body, a sort of cap. Every time the cell replicates, the telomeres become a little shorter. They are a control mechanism – they stop cells from replicating uncontrollably, like cancers, but they also have a fault.'

Nina saw what he meant. 'If they get shorter each time they replicate, eventually they'll be completely used up.'

'That's right. And when that happens, the cell ages . . . and dies. The process is constant, and unstoppable. No matter how healthily a person lives, there is a built-in expiration date on their body. But,' he said, looking into the lab, 'there is a way to change that.'

'With *yeast*?'

'With a very special *kind* of yeast. Did you know that only one per cent of all the different types of yeast have been classified? They are very simple micro-organisms, but also very varied. Some can be used to produce biofuel, others to break down dangerous chemicals, or deliver targeted doses of drugs inside the body – and, of course,' he added with a smile, 'some simply help make bread. It is one of these that I'm looking for.'

Nina regarded him dubiously. 'You want to find the Pyramid of Osiris . . . so you can make *bread*?'

'Ah! You think I am . . . what is the American expression? "Wacko", that's it!' He laughed again. 'Not just any bread, Nina,' he said, becoming more serious, more intense. 'A special bread, a bread reserved for ancient Egyptian kings . . . and gods. The bread of Osiris.'

His words sparked a memory. 'Wait a minute,' said Nina. 'Macy said there was something about the bread of life on the scroll you kept from the IHA.'

He nodded. 'The one that told me about the Pyramid of Osiris – and what it holds. There are treasures, yes, there is the sarcophagus of Osiris himself . . . but the most valuable thing in his tomb is also the simplest. Bread. *Yeast*. The yeast that turned an ordinary man into an immortal legend.'

'You're saying this yeast made him *immortal*?'

Osir shook his head. 'Not in the way we would use the word. Life expectancy in ancient Egypt was, what, forty years? Forty-five at most? Someone who lived to be seventy would be thought of as impossibly old – and if that person was a king, they would be considered immortal.'

'I can accept that,' Nina said, somewhat grudgingly, 'but how would yeast help him live that long?'

'As I said, there are many different kinds of yeast.' He pointed at a bearded scientist working on a computer. 'Dr Kralj and his team are sequencing the genetic code of certain types, looking for what they believe is the ideal sequence. They might find it tomorrow – in which case, I will soon be the richest man in the world. On the other hand, the search may take a hundred years, and by then I'll be dead, no matter how closely I follow my own teachings. So I would rather find the original strain, which is in the Pyramid of Osiris.'

'So you think the yeast used to bake Osiris's own personal Wonder Bread is some kind of . . . I don't know, life-extending mutant strain?'

'Not all yeasts are good. Some are pathogenic organisms whose spores can infect the human body, or are carriers for viruses. But the yeast used to make the bread of Osiris was different. It is a carrier – but not of a virus. It carries an enzyme called telomerase that repairs and replenishes telomeres.'

All the disparate pieces fell into place. 'It tops them up,' Nina said, 'stops them from getting shorter when the cells replicate.' Her eyes widened as she realised the full implications. 'The cells would live for ever. They'd never die.'

'And so would those who ate it.' Osir smiled triumphantly. 'The yeast provided the enzyme that replenished Osiris's cells, and slowed or even stopped his ageing. To his people, he became immortal.'

'And if the rulers knew that eating this bread helped you live longer, they'd keep it to themselves, of course.' A small frown crossed her brow. 'But wouldn't the yeast die during the baking process?'

'My brother and I *do* know a little about baking,' said Shaban with sarcastic disdain.

'The temperatures in the mud brick ovens used in ancient Egypt were unpredictable,' Osir explained. 'Sometimes the yeast would survive in some form. And if the bakers knew the yeast was the key to long life, they would make sure as much survived as possible.' A crooked grin. 'It would not be the best-*tasting* bread, but that's a small price to pay for eternal life.'

'Hardly eternal,' Nina pointed out. 'You could still die from disease, or being run over by a camel. Ancient Egypt was a dangerous place.'

'But a wise king keeps himself away from danger,' said Osir. 'And Osiris was the wisest king of all. He would not have been elevated to godhood otherwise.'

'So you find his tomb, then cultivate a new strain of the yeast?'

'Yes. Yeast spores can survive indefinitely. Even if the priests left no bread in the tomb to sustain Osiris in the afterlife, there should still be remnants in the canopic jars containing his organs. One way or another, I'm certain we will find samples.' He looked into the lab. 'The original strain has been lost in time like so much else, but here we can make it live again. And with a little genetic modification, it will make me as revered as Osiris.'

Nina regarded him suspiciously. 'Genetic modification?'

Shaban's mouth was a hard line. 'I think you have told her *enough*, brother.'

Osir gave him an irritated glance, but this time acquiesced. 'Sebak has a point,' he said to Nina, his smug affability returning. 'Our little trade secrets aren't really relevant. It's enough to say that there will be great rewards for bringing immortality to the world.'

'Yeah, I'm sure you'll be very rich, and very powerful. Only . . .' She gave him a sly smile, hiding her contempt. 'You can't do anything until you find the Pyramid of Osiris. Which brings us back to business. Like I said, I want my cut. Considering what you stand to make, I'm thinking an amount in the millions would be fair. Dollars, that is. Not Egyptian pounds.'

Shaban let out an outraged snort, but Osir nodded. 'If you help me get what I want, you too will be very well rewarded.'

'Glad to hear it,' said Nina. She held out her hand. 'What do you say?'

'Khalid, you can *not* be serious!' protested Shaban. 'She is trying to trick you! Why won't you believe me?'

Osir stared hard at his brother. 'Because I'm willing to take a chance that she is telling the truth. That's your problem, Sebak – you've never been a gambler. You only dare act when you are certain of success. But I take risks – sometimes I lose, but when they pay off . . .' He gestured at the pyramid around them. '*This*, this is the reward! You never accomplish anything without taking chances.'

'It is a big chance to take,' Shaban hissed.

'But I will take it.' Osir faced Nina. 'I'm willing to take you at your word, Nina. Find me the Pyramid of Osiris, and you will get everything you desire.' He extended his hand; Nina was about to take it when he suddenly brought it up, index finger pointing at her heart. 'But try to deceive me . . .' He looked meaningfully towards Shaban.

'I'll find it,' she said, still holding out her hand.

After a moment, he smiled and shook it. 'Then we have a deal. Excellent.' Shaban turned away in disgust.

Nina pulled free. 'Okay, then. If you'll just show me the zodiac . . .'

Osir chuckled. 'It's not here.'

A chill ran through her. 'What?'

'I have business in Monaco, so my people are reassembling the zodiac on my yacht – I want to be right there while its secrets are deciphered. You'll come with me.' Seeing her uncertain expression, he added, 'It's a very nice yacht.'

'There is nobody else you were planning to meet, is there?' asked Shaban with predatory suspicion. 'Like your husband?'

Nina waved a dismissive hand. 'Oh, God, no. The jerk.' She turned back to Osir. 'So. You have a yacht, huh?'

Macy paced back and forth beside the rental car, looking anxiously along the lake at the castle for any signs of activity – or Nina. She saw neither. More pacing – then finally she couldn't take any more and opened the door. 'How can you just *sit* there?'

' 'Cause it's more comfortable than standing?' Eddie offered.

'You know what I mean! It's your *wife* in there! Why aren't you worried about her?'

'I *am* worried about her.'

'You don't look it! What is this, some British stiff upper lip thing?'

'Just get in and sit down.' Sulkily, Macy climbed in and slammed the door.

In truth, though, he *was* worried about Nina. As he'd told her in Paris, meeting Osir in person was like not only walking into the lion's den, but doing so wearing a jacket made of meat and a T-shirt reading *Lions are pussies*.

But she had her own arguments: that letting Osir raid the Pyramid of Osiris would be an archaeological tragedy; that a dangerous cult getting its hands on a vast fortune could only be a bad thing; that after everything Osir and Shaban had put them through, didn't he want the chance for some payback? He couldn't deny that the last had a certain appeal.

Which still didn't mean he liked her plan. But now that it was in progress, all they could do was wait.

'How do you stand it?' Macy said, breaking the silence.

'Stand what?'

'Just . . . *waiting*!'

'There isn't much else I can do, is there? And you backed her up about going in there in the first bloody place. Did you think she was just going to knock on the door, say "Hi, I've come to see your zodiac," then walk right back out?'

'But she's been in there over two hours! Oh, my God, what if something's happened to her? She might be—'

'She's not,' Eddie said firmly, hoping he was being truthful. 'Okay, you want to know how I stand waiting around like this? Because I'm used to it.'

'What do you mean?'

'Being a soldier isn't all running about and shooting at people. Ninety-nine per cent of the time, it's boring as fuck. You go to a place, then you wait for something to happen. Mostly, you eventually get orders to go to some other place, and wait again.'

'So what do you do to keep occupied?'

'Nothing. Know why?' She shook her head, curious. 'Because when you do something to take your mind off the boredom, you also take your mind off what you're supposed to be waiting for.'

'Which is?'

A thin smile. 'Trouble. If you're chatting with your mates, or listening to your iPod or whatever . . . that's when some arsehole with an AK'll pop up and blow your head off – and you won't even see it coming.'

She looked unhappy at the prospect. 'Oh.'

'So yeah, waiting around doing nothing in a combat zone's a pain in the arse. But that's how I stand it, 'cause it means that when something *does* happen, I'm ready for it.'

'I get you. Although I really don't think I'm cut out to be

a soldier.' She cocked her head. 'Wait, so why are you chatting to me now?'

He grinned. ' 'Cause this isn't a combat zone.' A glance towards the castle. 'Yet.'

She wasn't sure how to respond to that, but the trilling of Eddie's phone immediately took both their minds off the subject. He switched it to speaker mode. 'Nina! Are you okay?'

The reply was a hurried whisper. 'Yeah. I think Osir believed me.'

'You *think*?'

'Well, he didn't have me killed on the spot! Look, I can't talk long – I'm in the bathroom and they'll get suspicious.'

'Did you see the zodiac?' Macy asked.

'No – it's not here.'

Eddie looked at Macy in dismay. 'Bugg—'

'Don't even start,' said Nina, cutting him off. 'It's on his yacht in Monaco. That's where we're going. He's got a private jet at Geneva airport.'

'How am I going to find you if you're on a bloody boat?'

'I don't know! Maybe I can – dammit, gotta go! I'll see you soon, I love you, bye!'

'Love you too,' said Eddie, just after the line closed. He looked at Macy, who had put a worried hand to her mouth. 'Well, that's fucking marvellous.'

'You . . . you know how you didn't want her to go in there, and I was all, "No, we have to find the pyramid before he does"?' she said. 'Now thinking: 'kay, might have been wrong.'

'Bit late,' Eddie growled. He banged a fist on the steering wheel. 'Shit. Monaco's over three hundred miles away. It'll take us at least five hours to drive there through the bloody Alps. Probably more with all the grand prix traffic.' A clattering rumble reached him: a helicopter flying up the valley, heading for the castle. 'And they'll be there in less than an hour.'

'What are we going to do?'

'Get there as fast as possible and wait for her to call us,' he said grimly, starting the car. 'Nowt else we *can* do.' He pulled out, and with a crunch of gravel spun the car round to head south.

14

Monaco

Though hardly the only micro-state to dot the map of Europe, the Principality of Monaco is by far the wealthiest, at least in terms of income per head – and also the most glamorous. The tiny country's location on the French Riviera near the Italian border gives it a warm subtropical climate, and its royal family and casinos add an air of expensive mystique . . . to say nothing of its tax haven status, which makes it a magnet for the super-rich.

It is, however, arguably most famous for its annual motor race, million-dollar vehicles screaming through the twisting streets at over 180 miles per hour. From the foredeck of Osir's huge yacht, the *Solar Barque*, moored offshore beyond Monaco's outer breakwater, Nina couldn't see the Saturday qualifying session as the drivers steeled themselves for the Sunday race – but she could hear it, the roaring wail of ultra-high-performance engines echoing off buildings as cars speared along the harbour front before looping back into the city and making the steep ascent to Casino Square.

'Wow,' she said to Osir. 'Must be distracting if you live there and you're trying to watch TV.'

The cult leader was, in fact, trying to watch TV. 'I think anyone who lives in Monaco and doesn't like the noise of racing cars can afford to take a vacation for one week each year,' he said, eyes fixed on a live broadcast of the qualifying session. 'But then, anyone – *no*!' He muttered an Arabic curse.

'Someone else has beaten Virtanen's lap time?' asked Shaban from a nearby lounger with mocking indifference.

Osir glared at him. 'By over a tenth of a second! We'll be lucky to have a car in the front half of the grid at this rate.'

'We shouldn't have any cars at all. It is a huge waste of money.'

'It helps spread the Osirian Temple's name around the world,' said Osir. 'I consider it worth it – and I am not having this discussion again, Sebak.' His brother scowled and stood, retreating inside the yacht.

Nina turned away from the sunlit vista of the city to Osir. 'You know, I wouldn't have thought they'd let religions sponsor cars.'

'Technically, the Osirian Temple is not sponsoring anything,' he said, keeping a close watch on the screen. 'All the money comes from the Osiris Investment Group.' A new set of numbers appeared. 'Ah, that's more like it! That should put us on the third row.'

'Sponsoring racing teams, running this enormous

yacht . . . the Osirian Temple's not really like other religions, is it?'

Osir eyed her over his sunglasses. 'You sound disapproving, Nina.'

She shrugged. 'Not my concern. I'm just sayin'.'

'My clever accountants worked out a way for the *Solar Barque* to cost me absolutely nothing, thanks to some loss-making subsidiaries and carefully crafted leaseback agreements with OIG. Since I can have it, I may as well enjoy it. And you may as well too.' He pushed an intercom button on his lounger's arm. 'Nadia? Two martinis, please.'

'I'm okay,' said Nina, holding up a hand.

'I insist. On a beautiful day like this, you should take the maximum pleasure from every one of your senses.'

'I'd rather be working on the zodiac.'

'When it's ready,' he said, to her disappointment. 'My experts are making sure it is as perfectly reassembled as possible. It will still take them hours, but I don't want the slightest clue to be missed.'

She couldn't stop herself from saying, 'Then maybe you should have left it on the ceiling of the Hall of Records.'

He smirked. 'Now you really *do* disapprove.'

'Moving it wouldn't have been my first choice – especially since your brother and that asshole Diamondback tried to kill me while they were doing it.' She shot a venomous look at the deck above. Diamondback was leaning against the rail, surreptitiously keeping an eye on her. 'But it's done. So I might as well profit from it.'

'And you will, Nina. We both will.' He smiled, then turned as a lithe young Jamaican woman in a bikini arrived with a tray. 'Nadia, thank you.'

Nadia handed the tall glasses, ice clinking, to Nina and Osir. 'Is there anything else you want?' she asked in a suggestive tone.

Osir grinned. 'Always, my dear . . . but not just now. Perhaps after the party at the casino.' He gave her backside something between a brush and a swat as she turned to leave, making her giggle.

'You got a hunky guy in Speedos for me?' Nina asked. She had seen several other young women in similar states of near-undress since boarding – along with numerous green-blazered guards, some armed with silenced MP7 sub-machine guns.

'I'm sure we could arrange one.'

She got the feeling he wasn't joking. 'So, tell me,' she said, wanting both to change the subject and to pass the time until she could legitimately go for another 'bathroom break' – her first attempt to contact Eddie from the yacht had failed because the head she chose had zero cell phone reception, 'how does a guy go from being a baker to founding his own religion? With a spell as a movie star in between, too.'

Osir sat up and muted the flatscreen, pleased at the opportunity to talk about his favourite subject: himself. 'I said in Switzerland that I like to gamble, yes? Well, I became an actor because I took a gamble. I was only fourteen, and a movie was being shot in my town. From the moment I saw the actors, and the crew attending them, I knew I had to be a part of it – somehow. But they were only on location for three days before going back to the studio. So every day I sneaked out of school and hung around the shoot, talking to people between takes – including the lead actor, Fadil. I tried to convince Sebak to come with me – he was twelve – but he was afraid of being caught, and thought our father would be furious.'

'And was he?'

Osir smiled. 'Oh, yes. But I'll come to that. On the last day, they were shooting a scene where the two leads get out of a car and go into a hotel, and they needed some extras in the background. Because one of the people I had befriended was the assistant director, he called me over.'

'And so began a movie career,' said Nina. For all her distrust of Osir, with his rich voice and expressive face she couldn't help warming to him as a storyteller.

'Not quite,' he said. 'Skipping school was only a small gamble. The *big* gamble was when I gave myself a line during the take.'

'Ooh. I bet the director was mad.'

He smiled again, no longer looking at Nina but somewhere off into the sky. 'I can still remember it – Fadil was having trouble getting a big case out of the car. I saw that the director was about to say "Cut", so I stepped forward and said, "Help the gentleman with his case? Only ten piastres," and held out my hand like Oliver Twist!'

'And what happened?'

'The director was so surprised, he forgot to call for a cut,' he said, laughing, 'and Fadil, since he knew me, improvised rather than getting angry. He said, "If you take *all* the lady's cases, I'll give you twenty!" Everyone laughed, and the director decided to keep it in the film. I even got paid! You will never guess how much.'

'Twenty piastres?'

'Out of Fadil's own pocket. So that was my big gamble,

and my first screen appearance. Of course, Sebak was incredibly jealous, so he told my parents what I had done. And yes, my father was furious. But a few days later he got a letter from the director. After he saw the dailies from the location he realised there was a later scene where he could follow up my little joke in a way that helped build Fadil's character. To do that, though, he needed me again . . . so he asked if I would come to Cairo to shoot the new scene.'

'Wow,' Nina said, impressed. 'It really did pay off.'

'More than I could ever have dreamed. My father took a little persuading, but I got my way; there are advantages to being the first-born son! So I went to Cairo, and since I was working at the studio, I needed to sign a contract. My birth name, Khalid Shaban, was the same as another actor's, so they asked me to pick a stage name. I chose Osir – after Osiris, of course. I thought it would bring me luck.'

'And it did.'

'It certainly did. By sixteen, I was in regular work as an actor – small parts at first, but building my skills and making friends on both sides of the camera. By eighteen, I had starred in my first film, which was quite successful by Egyptian standards. The studio wanted more, but I was due to start my three years of national service in the army. So the studio head, who had friends in the government, pulled a few strings.'

Nina sipped her martini. 'And got you out of military service?'

He nodded. 'I would have done it, but I'm glad I didn't have to. I was having too much fun! I was only eighteen, but I was famous, making lots of money, travelling – and meeting many beautiful women.' Osir smiled broadly – a smile which, to Nina's surprise, quickly faded. 'All this only made Sebak even more jealous . . . and then he had his accident.'

'What happened to him? I mean, he obviously got burned, but . . .'

'It happened in the army.' Osir shook his head sadly. 'Unlike me, he was conscripted. So he was already angry about that. Then, only a few weeks into service, he was in a truck that crashed and caught fire. He was in hospital for two months, with one side of his face, and more, burned away . . . then he was made to go straight back into his unit to serve the rest of his three years. He was understandably bitter.'

'I'm not surprised.' The revelation did nothing to make Nina more sympathetic to Shaban, but she could understand his constantly simmering rage at the world.

'When he came out of the army, I did what any elder brother should, and took care of him. I found him work as my assistant, and when I established the Osirian Temple I made him a key part of it.'

'How *did* you establish the Osirian Temple? Setting up a religion isn't exactly something you can buy a Dummies' Guide for.'

Osir chuckled. 'I made a movie called *Osiris and Set*, eighteen years ago. I played Osiris; it was destined, I suppose! It was very successful – it even had a release, a small one, in America, which is very rare for Egyptian films. Because of it, I was for a time the biggest star in Egypt. Everyone knew me, everyone wanted to hear what I had to say . . . it was like being worshipped, just as I had been as Osiris in the movie.' He regarded Nina knowingly, clinking the ice in his glass. 'You've been famous – in a different way, but you know what it's like. And how it is . . . *addictive*.'

'I wouldn't say that, exactly.'

A sly smile. 'Oh, Nina. The first time you saw yourself on television, the first time you saw your own face on a magazine cover . . . wasn't it a thrill? The world was watching *you*, listening to *you*. There is no feeling like it. And no one is immune to its siren song – not even a scientist. You can't tell me that after having experienced those heights, you are happy to fall into obscurity.'

'I wouldn't mind, so long as it's *wealthy* obscurity,' Nina said, playing her role. But she reluctantly had to agree that he had a point.

Osir saw her doubt, and smiled again. 'But as for me, I wanted more. Not just as an actor, or even as a star. I wanted to be loved,' he thumped his heart, '*here*. To have people believe in me, follow me—'

'Worship you?'

'What can I say?' He raised his hands in mock apology. 'Yes, I wanted to be worshipped. So I quit acting, and founded the Osirian Temple – and, more quietly, also founded the company that would become OIG.'

'Another gamble,' said Nina.

'The biggest of my life. I am a Muslim, after all,' Nina noted that he used the present tense, 'and to Islam's more fundamentalist followers, who are unfortunately growing in strength in Egypt, apostasy is a crime that deserves death. I received my share of threats. Which was why I put Sebak in charge of protecting me, and the Osirian Temple as a whole. He is very good at his job.'

'Maybe too good,' Nina said. Shaban was now talking to

Diamondback on the upper deck, a hand on his shoulder.

'Again, I apologise. Events got out of control.' Something on the screen caught his eye, and he jabbed at the button to unmute it. 'Second fastest! We are on the front row!' He looked back at Nina. 'Yet more apologies, but this is extremely good news.'

'That's okay,' she said, putting down the glass. 'I need to take a quick break anyway.' She headed into the ship to find another bathroom.

'Where are you?' Eddie said, answering the phone.

'In Monaco,' came Nina's whispered reply. 'I'm on his boat. Ship. Whatever the dividing line is. Where are you?'

'On an autostrada in Italy.' He was speeding, doing thirty over the 130 kilometre per hour limit, but this being Italy impatient locals were flashing past him.

'*Italy?* What the hell are you doing there?'

'It's the fastest route to Monaco. I always wanted to go to the grand prix there, but this wasn't how I planned . . . What about you? Have you seen the zodiac?'

'Not yet. Osir's people are still reassembling it; they won't be done until tonight.'

'Arse,' he muttered. 'I'd sort of hoped you'd got everything sussed by now.' A thought struck him. 'This boat, is it in the harbour,?'

'No, it's off the coast.'

'Buggeration and fuckery! How're you going to get off?'

'Yeah, I was wondering that myself. But listen, Osir said he was going to a party at a casino this evening. I think he wants to take me along.'

'A party? Do you know which casino?'

'No, but it's connected with his racing team, so it shouldn't be too hard to find. Maybe you could hire a boat and follow us back to his ship. It's called the *Solar Barque* – oh, crap, someone's coming. Bye!'

'Bye,' said Eddie, but again not quickly enough to beat the click of disconnection.

'Is she okay?' Macy asked.

'Yeah, but she's on his bloody yacht, and somehow I don't think there'll be much chance of us finding a boat for hire the night before the biggest event of the year.'

'What was that about a party?'

Eddie chuckled sarcastically. 'You sound a bit keen. Why, you wanting to go?'

'No. Well, I don't know. What sort of party?'

'For his grand prix team.'

Her face brightened. 'Oh! Racing drivers? We should *definitely* go.'

'It's not going to be a social visit,' he reminded her. 'Besides, we're hardly dressed for a flash do at some fancy casino.' He nodded at his jeans, T-shirt and leather jacket, and her travel-crumpled shirt and khaki combat trousers.

She smiled and took out her credit card. 'Dressing for a night in Monte Carlo? Priceless.'

15

For all the resort's glamorous reputation, the majority of Monaco's casinos are surprisingly mundane. While the image from many a movie – and the one the Tourist Office wants to present – is of tuxedos, diamonds, and fortunes won on the turn of a card or the spin of a wheel, for the most part the reality is rank after rank of computerised slot machines. Like Las Vegas, Monaco has found that while high-rollers look attractive on the big screen, much more profit can be made from a steady flow of ordinary tourists with no clue about the intricacies of gambling and a hunger and thirst ready to be sated in the casinos' own pricey restaurants and bars.

The principality's newest establishment, however, had opted to hearken back to the idealised fantasy of the Riviera. The Casino d'Azur was a deliberate throwback to the days when being a member of the jet set was an exotic aspiration and not an everyday drudge of tiny meals and confiscated nail clippers. The slot machines were still present, but relatively discreetly, putting the more traditional gambling pursuits front and centre.

Nina looked round as she and Osir entered one of the casino's main lounges. Though she had little interest in gambling beyond the occasional lotto ticket, she couldn't help but be impressed by the architects' efforts. The d'Azur was a rococo homage to the era when Monaco first became a draw for the rich and risk-inclined, and no expense had been spared in making it as authentic as possible, from the low-hanging crystal chandeliers to the darkly lacquered hardwood of the gaming tables. 'Wow. This place looks amazing.'

'As do you, Nina,' said Osir. Despite herself, she felt her cheeks flush. On the one hand she felt silly and self-conscious, dressed in a blue silk evening gown with her hair styled in an elegant twist. On the other, she *was* being taken for a night out in Monaco, which was undeniably exciting . . . even if the company wasn't to her taste. As well as several burly bodyguards, Osir's entourage included Shaban and Diamondback, the latter having reluctantly donned a tie with his snakeskin jacket to meet the evening's dress code.

'Thank you,' she said. Osir himself made a striking figure in a white tuxedo, the confident way he carried himself ensuring there would be absolutely no chance of his being mistaken for a waiter. He led her through the games to a side exit, a member of the casino staff recognising him and waving them through.

The doors led to a courtyard, one roped-off end opening on to Casino Square and the racing circuit. With qualifying over, the track had been re-opened to the public; part of the crash barrier had been removed to allow access to the casino. Nina glanced at the passing people in the hope of seeing Eddie, but there was no sign of him or Macy.

An earsplitting noise caught everyone's attention. A sleek racing car in the green and gold livery of Team Osiris had just had its engine started, the chiselled young blond man in the cockpit grinning up at Osir as he blipped the throttle.

'Ladies and gentlemen! It seems one of the drivers is impatient to get to the race!' boomed Osir, to laughter from the partygoers. Cameras flashed as he went to the car and shook the driver's hand. 'Mikko Virtanen, everyone – who I am sure will be not only the winner of tomorrow's grand prix, but soon the world champion!'

The guests cheered; the engine note fell to an idling crackle as Osir began a speech in his role as the team's major sponsor. Nina looked back towards Casino Square. Still no Eddie. She turned to Osir again – and found that Diamondback had materialised in front of her, leering. 'Lookin' for someone, li'l lady?' he asked.

'Anyone but you.'

'Aw, now that's unfortunate. 'Cause you're gonna keep on seeing me, since Mr Shaban asked me to stay close to Mr Osir's special guest and make sure she don't get into any . . . mischief.'

'I assure you, I have no intention of getting into any *mischief*,' she said, voice acidic. 'Certainly not with Mr Osir.'

'He'll be real disappointed to hear that.' Diamondback laughed, then re-joined Shaban, who was watching Nina with evident suspicion.

Osir concluded his speech, and after exchanging pleasantries with some of the guests returned to Nina. 'It's a little loud out here,' he said, gesturing at another door. 'The ballroom will be quieter, I think.' She was slightly surprised when he took her hand to escort her across the courtyard, but didn't object. Shaban, Diamondback and the bodyguards followed as they walked away, the car revving behind them.

Even through the noise of a busy evening in Casino Square, Eddie heard the distinctive V8 roar from the Casino d'Azur. 'Sounds like the right place.'

Macy regarded the building nervously as they crossed the road. 'I hope she's still okay.'

'She should be – for now. Osir wouldn't have brought her if she hadn't convinced him she can figure out the zodiac. Problem's going to be getting her out once she does it.'

'So what's the plan?'

'Find her. Then after that . . . I'll tell you as I make it up.'

'That doesn't fill me with confidence.'

Eddie grinned. 'Trust me. I've done this sort of thing before.'

'And how did it turn out?'

'Usually with exploding helicopters.'

Macy giggled, then tailed off. 'That wasn't a joke, was it?'

'Just remember to dive if I tell you.' They reached the casino entrance. 'Okay, got your passport?'

Admission to casinos in Monaco is closely governed; legally, the native Monegasques are forbidden to enter the institutions from which their government derives a large part of its revenue. There was also the dress code to consider, but Eddie and Macy now looked the part. He wore a black tux; she a low-cut minidress in a clinging, colour-shifting metallic fabric. Eddie had wanted her to pick something less conspicuous, but her argument had simply been that she was paying for it and wasn't going to be seen in anything 'sucky'.

She handed him her passport. 'Here. Can you keep hold of it? It barely fits in my purse.'

'Never understood that about women,' Eddie said. 'You cart all this crap around with you, but only have a bag the size of a hamster's scrotum to put it all in.' He idly flipped open the passport to look at her picture – then noticed something else on the page and burst out laughing.

'No, no, don't read that!' Macy shrieked, but too late to stop him seeing her full name.

'*Macarena?*' he cackled. 'That's your real name, Macarena? As in . . .' He hummed a few tuneless notes, then did a quick dance move. 'Ay, Macarena!'

'Shut. *Up!*' Macy snapped. 'I hate that song. It came out when I was a kid, and made my life absolute hell. So I'm just Macy, okay? Don't call me that other thing or I'll kick your ass.' She considered whom she was threatening. 'Okay, *not* going to happen, but I'll still be pissed at you. And don't tell Dr Wilde, either.'

'Wouldn't dream of it,' said Eddie, already trying to think up the funniest way to do exactly that.

He showed their passports to the doormen, then had an idea and asked how to find the Team Osiris party, receiving directions in return. Following them, he and Macy reached the gaming room. He could hear the idling racing car outside even through the closed and curtained high windows; casinos invariably kept gamblers shielded from the cycles of night and day, preferring them to lose track of time while playing.

Two more doormen guarded the courtyard door, politely

but firmly turning them away when they were unable to produce an invitation. Eddie peered past them, seeing no sign of Nina or Osir – though he did notice people going through a doorway into another part of the casino.

Looking past the banks of slot machines along the room's side he saw another exit, a second pair of casino employees in attendance. From their position, he guessed that the doors led into the room people were entering from the courtyard. Music came from the other side as he and Macy passed them.

'Party's probably in there,' he said as they headed for the far end of the gaming room. There was a door in the corner, through which he saw a member of the casino staff enter. No keypad or card lock, just an ordinary Yale, so it didn't lead to any of the secure money-handling areas. 'I'm going to gatecrash it.'

'Oh, I'm an expert at that,' Macy said. 'Right behind you.'

'No, you're not. Osir'll probably have his own security in there,' he explained, seeing that she was about to object, 'and I don't want to give 'em the chance to grab you. If you're in here and anything happens, at least you can kick up a stink. They won't do anything in public.'

'But what if they grab *you*?'

'They'll be sorry. Wait here and keep an eye out for me.'

She was annoyed, but remained where she was as Eddie moved away, pretending to take an interest in a nearby game of blackjack while watching the door in the corner.

It wasn't long before it opened to admit another casino worker. Eddie waited for her to pass, then quickly slipped behind her into the corridor beyond. In one direction lay the casino's kitchens; in the other a similar service door led into the function room.

He opened it and glanced through the crack, seeing at least a hundred people, some playing at more gaming tables, others engaged in conversation. A few couples waltzed round an open area of floor before a string quartet.

He tensed as he spotted Diamondback, his snakeskin jacket unmistakable. If he was there, Shaban probably was too, which also meant . . .

'There you are, you bugger.' Osir was seated at a blackjack table – and Nina was beside him, dressed to the nines.

He made his way past the dancers. Diamondback – and Shaban, he saw – stood several yards from the cult leader, in discussion with another group. There were some suited hulks closer to Osir, bodyguards, but they wouldn't recognise him. Keeping partygoers between himself and Shaban, Eddie headed for the table.

Nina had three cards in her hand, totalling eighteen points; Osir, beside her, was standing on nineteen, while the dealer's visible card was a king. The two other players had bust. She pursed her lips. 'Hmm. Tough choice.'

'The odds are not in your favour,' Osir told her.

'I dunno. I feel lucky tonight.' She tapped the table. 'Hit me.'

The dealer put down another card. A three.

'Twenty-one,' Nina crowed. 'Whaddya know?' The dealer turned over his hole card; a jack. More chips were slid across to Nina's pile.

Osir laughed. 'You are *very* lucky tonight.'

'Ah, not so much. My mom taught me how to play when I was a kid – all the stuff about when to hit and when to stand's coming back. Plus, I'm good at math.'

He gave her a sly smile. 'Are you admitting to card-counting, Nina? The casino won't like that.'

She had been – even with four decks in the shoe, enough cards had been played for her to calculate that the number of remaining low-value cards was relatively high and adjust her strategy accordingly – but decided he didn't need to know about her skill at mental arithmetic. 'I wouldn't dream of it,' she said instead. 'Besides, it's your party – and your money. So you get to make the rules.'

'Some things are true in life as well as in cards.' He gestured to the dealer to set up the next game.

'Ay up,' said a gruff Yorkshire voice behind her. Several fifty-euro notes were tossed on to the table. 'Can anyone play?'

Nina looked round. 'Eddie!' she cried, delighted – before remembering that she ought to be anything but. Hoping her outburst had been taken as surprise, she put on a strident, angry tone. 'What the hell are you doing here, you son of a bitch?'

He blinked, bewildered. 'Eh?'

'After what you said to me in Paris?' She stood, getting in his face. 'You can go to hell, you sanctimonious bastard.'

A look of deep hurt replaced confusion . . . before he finally remembered that Nina's plan required her to play a role, which meant he had to do the same. 'There's, er, there's no way I'm going to let you go. Nobody walks out on me. Nobody!'

A tip of Osir's head told his bodyguards to close in. He stared at Eddie with a look of vague recognition. 'Who is this . . . gentleman, Nina?'

'My husband,' Nina growled. 'My *ex*-husband, before too long.'

'Eddie Chase,' Eddie said to Osir. 'I already know who you are.'

The look crystallised. 'From the Osirian Temple in Paris. Of course.'

Shaban and Diamondback hurried over. 'Khalid!' Shaban hissed, leaning close to his brother. 'I told you we couldn't trust her!'

'I don't want him here any more than you do,' said Nina.

Diamondback advanced. 'Then maybe we should see him offa the premises.'

Osir smiled as he raised a hand. 'No, no. Mr Chase wanted to play blackjack, and I would never deny any man that pleasure.' He gestured to the chair on Nina's other side. The man sitting there quickly stood and moved away. 'Please, take a seat.'

'Khalid, can't you just get rid of him?' Nina complained.

'It would be rude to throw him out after he's come all this way.' As Eddie took the offered seat, Osir watched him closely. 'Besides, I'm very interested in finding out what kind of man can claim your heart.'

'Try anything with her and you'll find out,' said Eddie.

Nina sighed theatrically. 'Eddie, you're just embarrassing yourself. I said I don't want to see you, so why can't you just leave it at that?'

' 'Cause you're my wife, and you're supposed to do what I tell you. Love, honour, *obey*, remember?' She jabbed his ankle with the pointed toe of her shoe; he nudged her to remind her to play along. 'So,' he said as he received his chips, 'we going to play some pontoon, or what?'

'The bet is fifty euros, minimum.' Osir nodded to the dealer, who began passing out cards.

'Actually,' said Eddie, 'this is all a bit James Bondy, innit? Having a game of cards with the mastermind.' He looked up at Shaban and Diamondback. 'Henchmen hanging around . . .'

'My brother is hardly a henchman,' Osir replied amiably, checking his cards. A king and a four; fourteen points. The dealer's visible card was a ten. 'Hit me.' A six. 'Stand.'

Nina had a three and a five. 'Hit me,' she said, repeating the command after getting another five. The fourth card was a seven. 'Stand.'

Now it was Eddie's turn, starting with a jack and a six. 'Hit me.' Another six. 'Oh, cock.'

The remaining player also bust. The dealer turned up his hole card: a seven. Blackjack rules forced him to stand on seventeen, meaning Nina and Osir both won their bets. 'Perhaps blackjack isn't your game, Mr Chase,' Osir said smugly.

'That was just my warm-up round.' Another hand began, Eddie again going bust on his third card. 'Bollocks!'

Osir laughed. 'Not so much James Bond as Austin Powers, hmm?'

'Third time lucky.' Another hand. 'In the name of *arse*!'

'I *really* think you should quit,' Nina said through her teeth, having the awful feeling that a chunk of their rent money was disappearing with each round.

'I'm just getting started.'

'Yeah, at losing!'

Eddie's next two cards were an ace and a queen: blackjack. He grinned. 'I don't think you can lose with twenty-one.'

The dealer also scored a natural blackjack. 'Oi, wait, what?' Eddie objected as his chips were whisked away to one side. 'That was a draw!'

'You should have made an insurance bet,' said Osir, unconcerned about losing the round. 'Now you have a push – your bet carries over to the next hand.'

'I knew that,' Eddie said after an awkward pause. The next round began, only for him to bust again. 'Buggeration and fuckery!' He looked at the empty space where his small pile of chips had been, then at Osir's multiple stacks. 'You couldn't do me a favour, could you?'

'I already have,' Osir said, with meaning. He looked round as the string quartet started a new tune. 'Ah! A tango!' He stood, holding out a hand to Nina. 'Would you join me?'

She froze; not because of Osir's offer itself, but at the memories of social embarrassment it brought back. 'I, ah, I can't dance the tango. I can't dance the anything.'

'No need to worry,' he said firmly. 'I lead; all you have to do is follow.' Before she could protest, he led her to the dance floor.

Eddie got up, only to have two of Osir's goons block his way. 'Hey! I want to talk to you, Nina!'

She got his message, returning one of her own. 'It'll have to wait!'

Despite how ridiculous she knew she was being – there were far weightier matters for her to worry about – Nina became more self-conscious than ever when she saw that the other dancing couples had bailed out. And with Osir being the host of the party, attention would be even more focused on him and his partner. 'Y'know, if they played the conga, I could just about manage that.'

'Trust me,' he said. He brought her to the centre of the floor, one arm tight round her waist while the other held her outstretched hand. 'Just look into my eyes, and your body will follow.'

And with that, they were moving.

Nina barely held in a startled yelp as Osir whisked her across the floor. 'Oh, God,' she gasped, struggling to keep her legs even vaguely in step with his. About the only positive thing was that her long dress concealed the worst of her uncoordinated footwork. 'I can't do this!'

'Such negativity! I'm surprised,' Osir said, eyes fixed on hers. 'After everything you've achieved, you're afraid of a simple dance?'

'No, I'm afraid of making an ass of myself!'

He laughed. 'Why? Is the opinion of these people you don't even know important to you? Could anything they say be worse than what you've endured in the past months?'

'The bloke's got a point,' said Eddie, quick-stepping alongside them. 'And I kept telling you the same thing, so we can't both be wrong.' He slid a hand between Nina and Osir. 'Mind if I cut in?'

'By all means,' said the Egyptian, smoothly releasing Nina and stepping back.

Shaban rushed up beside him. 'They are working together. I *told* you!'

Osir shook his head, his smile infuriating his brother. 'Let's see what happens.'

'Eddie, what are you doing?' Nina whispered as he took hold of her. 'You can't dance!'

'Says who?' He glanced at the quartet before looking back into her eyes. ' "Por Una Cabeza" – a tango. Doddle.'

'What? Since when – aah!' He set off in step with the music, carrying her with him. To her amazement, he seemed to know what he was doing. 'When did you learn how to dance? You can't stand even being in the same room when *Dancing With The Stars* is on!'

'You know those mornings I was with Amy?'

'Amy?' Nina frowned, then tried to push away. 'That cop?'

'Hey, *hey*!' he hissed, holding her. 'She was having dancing lessons, and I went with her.'

'Oh, is "dancing lessons" a euphemism now?'

'No, it's actual dancing lessons! Hold on tight – one front ocho comin' up!'

'One what?' Nina began, before Eddie turned her sharply round, then back again. Her heels clattered frantically over the floor. They ended up pressed face to face. 'Whoa! So when – *why* did you learn to dance? You hate dancing!'

'I wanted to surprise you. At the wedding reception.'

'What wedding reception?'

'The one I was going to sort out when I got some money, so we could actually have our family and friends there instead of just the Justice of the Peace! A bit late, I know, but I wanted to do something nice for you.'

'Oh my God,' said Nina, taken aback. 'You actually learned how to dance, just for me? That's . . . that's so *sweet*.'

'Oi,' he warned. 'Don't smile. We're supposed to hate each other.'

She clamped her mouth shut, trying to scowl rather than grin like a fool. 'But why pick dancing?'

' 'Cause you only own maybe three DVDs, and two of 'em are about dancing. *Dirty Dancing*, *Strictly Ballroom* . . .'

'Eddie, this is very lovely and romantic, but just because I like *watching* dancing doesn't mean I can actually *do* it.'

He was surprised. 'I thought you could!'

'Livin' proof that I can't, right in front of you!' She clumsily followed him as he turned, seeing Osir still watching . . . with growing mistrust. 'Look, the zodiac'll be ready by the time we go back to his yacht. We came into Monaco on a boat, a tender or whatever it's called – it's on pier twelve in the harbour. You can't miss it – it's painted the same colours as his racing cars. If you can follow it to his yacht—'

'No way I'm going to leave you with him – he thinks he's pulled!'

'It's the only way to find the pyramid. You've got to get out of here.' An idea. 'Slap me.'

Eddie was aghast. 'I'm not going to bloody slap you!'

'We've got to convince him we've split up.' She raised her voice from the *sotto* level of their discussion, enough to be heard over the music as she attempted to twist free of his hold. 'You son of a bitch! I was finished with you before, and I'm twice as finished now! *Slap me*,' she added from the corner of her mouth, seeing Osir and Shaban approaching. 'You – you needle-dicked limey asshole!'

Eddie's face contorted in dismayed disbelief – then he slapped her. The blow wasn't hard, but the crack was loud enough to catch everyone's attention. 'Sorry,' he mumbled.

'Sorry!' she replied, just as surreptitiously, before shoving him back. The string quartet stopped mid-note, watching the disturbance.

Osir interposed himself between them. 'I think you should leave, Mr Chase.'

'You know what? You're welcome to her,' he snarled. 'Crap party anyway.'

Shaban and Diamondback hurried over. 'We'll show him out,' announced Shaban. The bodyguards lumbered through the crowd to surround Eddie. 'The back way.'

'Get your fucking hands off me,' Eddie said as a suited goon grabbed his upper arm. He jerked away, only for another man to seize him from the other side.

'You can throw him in the harbour for all I care,' Nina shouted, horribly aware that Shaban undoubtedly planned something much worse. 'Get the hell out of here, Eddie!'

That thought was foremost in Eddie's mind. The first goon regained his hold on his arm, and they frogmarched him to the service door. Shaban and Diamondback followed right behind them, the latter with an expectant grin. If they got him out of sight of the casino's visitors and staff, he would be seriously outnumbered *and* outgunned, as he doubted that Diamondback was the only armed member of Osir's security team.

Twenty feet to the door, ten. It was a natural choke point – if both goons tried to hustle him through at once, their movements would be restricted enough to give him a chance to strike. But if they were halfway competent, they would be expecting it . . .

The door opened just before they reached it. A waiter stepped through, carrying a tray bearing several bottles of expensive wine.

He was quite a big guy, heavy—

With both goons still firmly holding his arms, Eddie suddenly hoisted his feet off the ground and kicked the waiter hard in the stomach.

The unfortunate man flew backwards, bottles falling – but Newton's third law held true, the force of the impact knocking both Eddie's captors back in reaction. They collided with Shaban and Diamondback. All five men tumbled to the floor in an unruly heap . . .

With Eddie on top.

He yanked his arms free, elbowing one man in the groin and rolling to a blackjack table. The service door was his best hope of escape – but before he could run through it swung shut, the lock clicking. No time to search the winded waiter for his key.

'You fucker!' Diamondback spat. The American flailed out from under the convulsing bodyguard, clawing for a revolver—

Eddie snatched a card shuffling machine from the table and fired a stream of cards into his face like angry moths. Diamondback threw up his hand to protect his eyes, the half-drawn revolver clunking to the carpet. Eddie hurled the shuffler at his head, scoring a solid-sounding hit, then ran for the entrance to the main lounge.

He risked a glance at Nina as he barged through the startled partygoers, seeing her quickly suppress an enthusiastic *Go, Eddie!* smile as he reached the doors.

16

The two men outside responded to the commotion as Eddie burst into the casino. He punched one backwards, but his companion lunged to tackle the troublemaker—

He suddenly fell on his face with a bang. Eddie leapt over him into the lounge, finding Macy just outside the door with one foot outstretched where she had tripped the attendant. 'Thanks,' he mouthed. She was about to follow him, but he firmly shook his head, gesturing for her to lose herself in the crowd before anyone realised they were together. Just escaping the casino on his own would be tricky enough.

She reluctantly backed away as Eddie rushed across the room between the startled gamblers. Behind, Shaban was screaming orders, Osir's two other bodyguards thundering in pursuit. The pair of attendants at the courtyard entrance also ran to intercept him, weaving round the gaming tables.

The main doors – but casino security staff crashed through them, walkie-talkies crackling. All the gaming areas were closely monitored by CCTV to watch for cheats, whether punters or employees: the alarm had been raised the moment trouble started.

Boxed in. He needed a distraction—

A woman in the casino's uniform was taking a tray of chips to a roulette table. Eddie ran to her – and kicked the tray. Its contents flew into the air, raining down on the surrounding tables like multicoloured hailstones.

The response was instant chaos.

The chips ranged in value from a few euros to tens of thousands – and everybody immediately lunged to grab the latter. A woman screamed as the man beside her knocked her from her stool, and there was a huge crash of glass as a drinks trolley overturned. A blackjack dealer shrieked as her table toppled to the floor in another cascade of scattering chips. The two bodyguards were caught in the scrum of snatching hands.

The near-riot had also cut the security guards off from Eddie – and him from the exits. He clawed through the crowd, looking for a new escape route.

'Get that bastard!' Diamondback roared, barging into the room with another of Osir's bodyguards. His gun was in his hand, anger overcoming any thought of keeping a low profile.

Eddie ploughed forward. Something solid clunked against his foot. A champagne bottle from the trolley. He bent and snatched it up – a club was better than no weapon at all – then saw a clear route out of the money-crazed mob beneath a roulette table.

He rolled under it, scrambling along on his knees as he tore off the foil and unwound the wire cage holding the cork. Shouted French from behind told him that the security guards had lost track of their target. Emerging from beneath the table, he jumped up.

A man yelled as Osir's bodyguard slammed him out of his path. Diamondback was right behind him as the two men rounded the roulette table, coming for Eddie as he pushed his thumb against the cork—

Pop!

The cork shot from the bottle at the head of a sparking geyser and hit the bodyguard square in one eye. He screeched, clapping a hand to his face as champagne sprayed over him. Diamondback tried to push him aside, arm outstretched over the man's shoulder as he took aim—

Eddie threw the still-gushing bottle. Its blunt end hit the revolver, smacking it from Diamondback's hand on to the roulette table. The gun bounced off the baize and landed on the spinning wheel, the wooden butt extending out over its rim.

Diamondback snarled and shoved the half-blinded bodyguard at Eddie, who staggered as the man collided with him, then dived along the length of the table after his Colt. The gun spun out of his reach. He pushed forward on one elbow, grasping again . . .

Eddie threw the bodyguard aside and flung himself on to the table, smashing an elbow down on the other man's spine. Diamondback howled in pain, his twitching hand just missing the gun as it came round again. Eddie dragged him bodily back down the table before punching his head and making a dive for the gun himself.

His fingers closed on empty air as the revolver continued its circuit.

A fist crashed against his skull, jarring his vision. The

Python cruised past once more. Diamondback delivered another pounding blow to the back of his head, slamming his face against the cloth. Before Eddie could look up again, his opponent twisted and kicked him in the side, rolling him away from the wheel in a shower of betting chips.

Diamondback dug one cowboy boot hard into the baize and thrust himself back up the table. He slapped a hand down on the wheel, jarring it to a stop.

Eddie saw Diamondback's hand finally clamp round the gun. The American had kicked him too far away for him to land an effective punch – he needed a weapon to extend his reach, fast.

The croupier's rake—

He snatched it up and swung it at his adversary.

It snapped in half.

The handle was nothing more than a length of black-painted dowel. Diamondback looked at him mockingly, the blow practically painless. He flipped the gun in his hand, bringing it to bear—

Eddie stabbed the pointed, broken end of the rake into his crotch.

This time, the result was anything *but* painless. Diamondback's eyes bugged wide. Eddie saw his chance, grabbing him by his scaly lapels and slamming a steamhammer headbutt into his face before wrenching the gun from his hand and standing on the table to survey the scene.

The chaos had spread to the rest of the room, some people trying to flee, others rushing in from the corners in the hope of claiming a prize before they were all gone.

Somebody screamed, seeing the gun. He looked round.

More security men were hurrying in. He had to get outside. But all the exits were covered.

That left the windows.

He leapt from the table and ran towards the courtyard entrance. An attendant moved to block him, but the revolver's muzzle swinging towards him quickly changed his mind. Eddie had no intention of shooting, though. Even if he'd had more than a puny six bullets, he wasn't about to blast his way out of a building full of innocent tourists. He rounded a craps table, looking up at the ornate ceiling, the chandeliers hanging from it . . .

Another of Osir's men sprang out from behind a row of slot machines. Eddie jinked sideways just in time to avoid being tackled, but the hulking bodyguard still managed to grip his waist. He bashed at the man's head with his elbow as they ran, but the goon wouldn't let go, intent on ramming him into the nearest solid obstacle.

Which was another slot machine, right in front of them.

Instead of trying to dodge, he hooked his arm tightly round the man's neck and deliberately aimed for the machine. The bodyguard realised too late what he was doing and tried to stop, but now the tables were turned, Eddie pulling him towards a very painful collision—

The machine's video screen shattered as the bodyguard smashed into it head first. Eddie reeled back as sparks exploded from the hole – and a cascade of tokens spewed into the tray, the machine chiming happily.

'You hit the jackpot, mate,' Eddie told the unconscious man. He was about forty feet from the nearest curtained window – and thirty-five from a trio of security guards pounding towards him.

He used the slumped bodyguard as a stepping stone to scramble up on top of the row of slot machines, then charged along it. The guards snatched at his legs as he sprinted past, but too late to stop him from making a flying leap off the last machine and grabbing a chandelier.

With a musical clash of crystal, he swung through the window.

The curtains ripped away and wrapped round him as he fell, a protective shroud against the shattering glass. Unable to see, he hit the ground hard, rolling several times. Sharp shards rained round him.

Eddie threw off the curtains and got painfully to his feet. Shocked partygoers gawped at him. 'Don't mind me,' he grunted. 'Just came to see the . . .'

His gaze landed on the green and gold car at the courtyard's centre, its engine still idling. The driver was half standing as he looked over the rear wing to see what had happened. 'Car,' Eddie concluded.

He ran for the vehicle. The driver – he recognised him as a Finn called Mikko Virtanen – stared at him in confusion.

'Sorry, mate,' said Eddie, shoving him out of the cockpit. He pocketed the gun and jumped into the cramped compartment, sliding to a lying position almost parallel to the ground. 'Good luck with the race!'

The team technicians snapped out of their paralysis at the sight of their star driver being carjacked and ran at him – but Eddie had already pulled the lever to engage the clutch. He squeezed the steering wheel paddle to switch into first . . . and pushed the accelerator.

The result was like nothing he had ever experienced.

Without a helmet or earplugs, the engine's howl was

almost deafening, and the jolt of acceleration smacked his head back against the unpadded roll bar so hard that he saw stars.

People leapt out of Eddie's path as the pointed nose of his new ride speared at them, one of the huge front wheels clipping a table and sending hors d'oeuvres to the four winds. He aimed for the street, closing his eyes as he hit the lightweight barrier—

Osir ran out of the ballroom, Nina behind him, just in time to see the car smash through the cordon into Casino Square. '*Zarba!*' he gasped. 'Stop him, somebody stop him!'

Shaban and the bloodied Diamondback burst from the casino. Diamondback raised his second Colt and pointed it at the car, but a frantic screech of 'No! Not here!' from Osir stayed his trigger finger. 'Get after him! Sebak, go!'

With an angry glare at Nina, Shaban ran after the car, Diamondback and another of Osir's bodyguards following. Casino security staff poured into the courtyard, too late to do anything but mill in confusion. Macy appeared in the doorway, but Nina gestured for her to get back inside.

Osir turned to her. 'Your husband just stole a million dollar racecar!'

'Yeah, that's something else about him that drives me mad,' she said, feigning infuriation, 'his total lack of respect for other people's property!'

He shook his head in dismay. 'At least it's only the demonstration car. And since he's not a professional driver, he won't get far.'

Eddie was quickly discovering that driving a racing car was vastly harder than it looked. The slightest touch of the stiff and heavy accelerator seemed to send several hundred horsepower instantly to the rear wheels, making the back end slither about wildly, and with cold tyres and not enough speed for the wings to generate downforce it felt like driving on an ice rink.

To make matters worse, even though he was now on the racing track, the road was still busy with civilian traffic – coming straight at him. He was going round the circuit the wrong way. What was more, since he was sitting so low to the ground, the oncoming headlights were at eye level, dazzling him.

He swerved, barely avoiding the monolithic nose of a Bentley – only to have one end of the front wing disintegrate into razor splinters of carbon fibre as it scraped against the roadside crash barrier. He battled with the steering wheel, ignoring the battery of furiously flashing warning lights on it as he struggled to stay in a straight line.

Back into two-way traffic as he joined the Avenue d'Ostende and descended the hill towards the harbour, but being able to go with the flow was little help as this road was even busier. The back end of a Range Rover loomed: he braked, sliding forward as the wheels locked up. The engine threatened to stall, and he pushed the accelerator again.

Too hard.

The car lunged, cracking his head another blow. The other side of the front wing shattered against the Range Rover's rear wheel, shards stabbing into the rubber.

Eddie swerved away as the big 4×4's tyre exploded and it crashed down on its alloy wheel rim. 'Sorry!'

But the broken chunks of carbon fibre had also damaged his own tyre, the front wheel shuddering as he steered round another car. He was losing what little control he had.

And he could hear something else over the engine's scream – sirens. The police were coming. It wouldn't exactly be hard for them to pick out his car from the rest of the vehicles.

He had to get to the harbour before they caught him.

The other cars almost blocked his view of the road ahead, but he could see enough to tell that he was coming to the bottom of the hill. Which, he remembered from past races on TV, was the location of the first turn after the start.

A *sharp* turn.

'Oh, shit,' he gasped. Even in first gear, he was doing close to fifty miles an hour as he zigzagged through the traffic towards the Saint Devote corner. And the corner itself was busy, a complex intersection in its everyday guise.

He saw what he hoped was a clear line, aimed for it . . .

With a *whap!* of escaping high-pressure nitrogen, the damaged front tyre sloughed off the wheel rim.

The car spun out, sliding almost sideways before the back wheel bashed against a Ferrari, sending Eddie's vehicle into a mad pirouette through the junction. The world was a blur – but he could make out a crash barrier getting closer with each revolution.

He braced himself—

The car crashed sidelong into the barrier, impact-absorbing sections of bodywork crushing flat. Still spinning, scattering debris, it bounced back out into the junction. Cars swerved to avoid the whirling wreck. A large van skidded, heading straight for Eddie's car . . .

Both vehicles stopped at the same time – with the racing car's nose wedged under the van's front bumper.

Groaning, Eddie sat up. His shoulder felt as though it had taken a hit with a baseball bat where he had been flung against the cockpit's edge. But the car's safety features had done their job: he would be able to walk away from the crash.

Or stagger, at least. Head spinning, he clambered out and got his bearings. The long arc of the start/finish stretch led away to the south. Towards the harbour.

'*C'est James Bond!*' someone called. Eddie realised he had already attracted a crowd – considering that a man in a tuxedo had just wrecked a racing car in the middle of Monaco, that was hardly surprising.

The Ferrari's driver stared in horror at the huge dent in its side. 'Send the bill to Team Osiris!' Eddie called before jogging to the nearest gap in the barriers. He pushed through the gawkers, disappearing into the crowd as the first police car arrived.

'He *crashed* it?' Osir said, appalled. Shaban had just phoned him with a report. 'Did you find him?' The reply was negative. 'Then did the police catch him, at least?' An identical response. 'Well, that's *marvellous*!'

Nina had to fight to conceal her jubilation. 'That man destroys everything he touches,' she sneered instead. 'Relationships, lives . . . racecars . . .'

'I can see why you want to be rid of him,' he muttered, before turning his attention back to the phone. 'I'm going back to the *Solar Barque*. Yes, with Dr Wilde. No, I – Sebak, I do *not* want to hear this again. Get as many people as you can. The police will be looking for him as well, so monitor their radios. I want him found.' He listened to Shaban.

'Only if absolutely necessary – I don't want any more trouble with the authorities, not tonight. Capture him and take him to the yacht.'

'You're not going to kill him?' Nina asked as he ended the call.

Osir gestured at the wreckage of the party. 'This will be hard enough to explain. The last thing I need is to turn on the TV and see a news bulletin about Sebak being arrested for your husband's murder!'

'So what are you going to do with Eddie when you find him?'

'The Mediterranean is very big, and very deep.'

'Ah . . . great. That'll save me having to pay for a divorce lawyer.'

Osir laughed coldly. 'Well, I think the party is over. I don't know if the zodiac will be ready yet, but we may as well find out. Give me a few minutes to say my goodbyes.'

He moved to speak to a group of people nearby, as full of bonhomie as if a switch had been flipped. Nina took the opportunity to go to the doorway. She saw Macy amongst the onlookers and waved her closer.

'Where's Eddie?' Macy asked. 'Is he okay?'

'For now – he got away. In a racecar.'

Macy smiled. 'You know, your husband's a pretty awesome guy.'

'Yeah, I like to think so.' She looked back into the courtyard. Osir was still engaged in conversation. 'Look, this might sound weird, but this is probably the safest place for you to be. Shaban and his buddy are out looking for Eddie, and Osir's about to take me back to the yacht to see the zodiac.'

'That's great, but what am I supposed to do when this place closes? I won't be able to get a hotel room even if there are any left – Eddie's got my passport!'

'That's not exactly my biggest worry right now, Macy.' Another glance back; Osir was looking for her. 'You'll figure something out. I've got to go, though. If Eddie or I can't get in touch with you, there's a hotel across the square – wait in the lobby, and we'll find you.'

Macy was unhappy with the situation, but nodded. 'Good luck, Dr Wilde. Stay safe.'

'You too.' Nina backed into the courtyard and went to Osir. 'Are you ready to go?'

'The car is coming to take us back to the harbour.' He put on a smile for the benefit of his other companions. 'It will have to take the long way round – it seems there has been a traffic incident at Saint Devote!' The joke raised some gallows laughter.

Taking Nina by the arm, he went back into the casino. As the attendants backed away to let them through, Macy slipped into the courtyard, moving hurriedly away from the doors before the casino staff spotted her. The party was winding down now that its main attraction had disappeared in a cloud of tyre smoke.

Macy spotted another attraction, though: a handsome blond man in racing overalls, talking agitatedly to a couple of older guys. Guessing he was the driver, she trotted over. 'What happened?'

Virtanen gave her a brief glance – then did a double-take as he registered that she was a young and beautiful woman who wasn't surgically attached to the arm of a middle-aged team sponsor. 'It was terrible,' he said mournfully. 'I was carjacked – a man with a gun! I tried to stop him, but he got away.' His companions rolled their eyes, but said nothing to contradict the star of the team.

'My God! Are you okay?'

'Just a few bruises. I'll still be able to race tomorrow, for sure. But I think I'll go back to my hotel now. Unless,' a suggestive grin, 'you would like to share a drink with me first?'

Macy gave him a perfect smile. 'I think I would.'

17

In the dark, Monaco's waterfront looked like an extension of the city itself, ranks of expensive yachts lined up like gleaming buildings along the jetties.

Nina looked round anxiously as Osir brought her to the *Solar Barque*'s distinctively painted tender. She had hoped to spy Eddie nearby, waiting for the tender to depart so he could follow it to its mother ship. But there was no familiar stocky figure amongst the people boarding the floating palaces, nobody surreptitiously observing them from a neighbouring pier.

Had the police caught him? Or worse, Shaban?

She dismissed the latter as soon as the awful thought came to her. If Shaban had found Eddie, Osir would have been told. But his absence was still a worry – not least because without him, she would have to improvise her own escape from Osir's yacht. With the *Solar Barque* being over half a mile offshore, swimming was not her preferred option.

They boarded the tender and Osir gave an order to its pilot. With a diesel rumble, the boat set off. Even though the evening was warm, the breeze over the open vessel was cold. Nina rubbed her bare arms.

'Here,' said Osir. He took off his jacket and draped it over her.

'Thank you,' she said automatically, keeping to herself that her chill was not solely down to the wind.

They passed more opulent yachts and made their way between the quays marking the boundary of the inner harbour of Port Hercule. The outer harbour's breakwaters extended ahead, the darkness of the Mediterranean visible beyond them. The tender drifted off course from the exit, the pilot having to adjust for what seemed to be a stronger than expected current, but they soon cleared the long concrete barriers and entered the open sea.

Swimming was now an even less appealing idea, Nina decided. Past the breakwaters, the ocean was choppy, the tender bouncing through the waves with great smacks of spray. An anchor chain rattled against the hull with each impact. She looked back to shore. Monaco was aglow against the surrounding hills. It was a spectacular sight . . . but her worries made it impossible for her to appreciate it.

There were numerous other vessels moored offshore, but the *Solar Barque* stood out as large even by the standards of megayachts. The tender pulled up to its stern, where a mooring platform, big enough also to accommodate a pair of smaller speedboats and several jet skis, had been lowered to water level. A crewman tied up the boat, then Osir took Nina by the hand to help her on to the deck.

'I'd like to thank you for your company,' he said. 'Even though things didn't go quite as I planned.'

'My pleasure,' Nina replied. 'And, ah . . . I apologise for

my husband. I just wish I'd been able to persuade him to see things my way. It would have made things a lot less . . . well, expensive.'

'You don't have to take the blame for his actions,' he assured her. 'And as for the money, none of it will matter when we discover the Pyramid of Osiris.'

'In that case,' said Nina, 'we'd better go see the zodiac, hadn't we?'

They entered the yacht and went to one of the upper decks. Osir led her to a door. 'Please, wait in my cabin,' he said. 'I will see if the zodiac is ready.'

The cabin turned out to be larger than her entire apartment, the adjoining bathroom and walk-in closets making it even bigger. It also boasted a mirrored ceiling above the enormous bed. The decor was every bit as playboyesque as his Swiss home, missing only a tigerskin rug to complete the picture. 'This is – stylish,' she managed.

Osir smiled as he went to another door at the room's far end. 'Make yourself comfortable. I will just be a minute.'

She perched on the end of the bed, kicking off her heels and fidgeting with the long dress as she waited. Before long Osir returned, his smile even wider. He pulled a catch above the door, folding panels back to reveal another large room beyond. 'It is ready.'

Nina crossed the room. She looked past Osir . . .

To see, for the first time, the fully assembled zodiac.

Whoever he had employed to restore it, she had to admit they had done an absolutely exquisite job. The six-foot-diameter disc rested on a low circular stand beneath a thick protective layer of transparent bulletproof Lexan. It wasn't until she stepped right up to it that she could see any trace of the cuts made to remove it from the Hall of Records.

Seen in its entirety, the zodiac was spectacular. Smaller than the one in the Louvre, it made up for it with its vibrant colours. Sealed within the Sphinx, protected from the elements, the paint picking out each constellation from the dark background had remained almost intact. A thick, weaving line of pale blue bisected the sky – the Milky Way, she assumed.

There were other markings: the red dot she had seen in Macy's photo, almost certainly Mars, and circles representing other planets. But her attention immediately went to the yellow triangle near the small figure of Osiris.

A pyramid. *Osiris's* pyramid.

She leaned closer. There was something barely discernible painted beside it, very small characters. Hieroglyphs.

Nina looked excitedly round at Osir. 'Have you seen these?'

'Of course,' he said, going to a large table and picking up a printout from beside a laptop. 'I had them translated when the zodiac was still in pieces. They're directions – the problem is, I don't know the starting point. Nobody does. Which is why I need your insight.'

He handed her the translation. ' "The second eye of Osiris sees the way to the silver canyon," ' she read. ' "One atur towards Mercury beyond its end is the tomb of the immortal god-king." An atur, that's an Egyptian unit of measurement, right?'

'Eleven thousand and twenty-five metres.'

Nina instantly performed the mental arithmetic to convert the figure to imperial measurements: 'Six point eight five miles.' Osir raised an eyebrow. 'Like I said, I'm good at math. So the pyramid is just under seven miles from the end of the silver canyon in the direction of Mercury, which is . . . one of these planets on the zodiac, I guess.'

'Actually, it isn't,' he said. 'The planets on the zodiac are Mars, Venus and Jupiter.' He pointed them out. 'But we used their positions to calculate Mercury's position as well. It would have been . . . here.' He indicated a particular spot to the right of the pyramid.

'So, about seven miles east of the end of the canyon. Except,' she continued, nodding at a wall mirror, 'because the map is mirrored since we're looking at it from above rather than below, it's really seven miles *west*.'

Osir was pleased. 'So all we need to do is find the silver canyon.'

'Which means first, we need to find the second eye of Osiris. Where's his first eye?'

'There are two Osiris figures on the zodiac,' he reminded her. 'Perhaps they point the way together?'

Nina bent low to examine them. Typically for Egyptian art they were in profile, only one eye visible on each, but at the small size of the carvings they were nothing more than dots. She drew an imaginary line between the eyes of the two figures, but it neither ran near the pyramid nor seemed to point to anything in particular.

'The Eye of Osiris is also a symbol, isn't it?' she asked.

Osir nodded. 'A sign of protection. Found in temples, tombs . . . it's supposed to help guide you through the Underworld.'

'So fairly common, then. That won't narrow things

down.' She stared at the zodiac, thinking. 'Could the "silver canyon" be a clue? The ancient Egyptians valued silver above gold – were there any silver mines in the pre-dynastic period?'

'I don't know. You're the historian, not me!'

'Point taken. This'll need more research. We need to check the archaeological databases . . .' She tailed off, realising she was slipping into a state of professional excitement over the chance to crack the puzzle – and forgetting that doing so would help the very person she was trying to stop.

'Are you all right?' Osir asked.

'I'm . . . just tired,' she said. 'It's been a hectic day.'

He smiled. 'My apologies – there's no need to solve this riddle in one night. Besides, the race is tomorrow, and I was hoping you would join me there.'

'Sounds cool,' she said, the idea of watching noisy cars screaming past for a couple of hours anything but.

'Wonderful. Then before that, perhaps you'd join me for a glass of champagne?'

'Ah . . . I really ought to go to bed.' Privacy would give her a chance to try to contact Eddie.

'Just one glass, please,' Osir insisted. 'I have a bottle of Veuve Clicquot in the next room – it would be a shame to drink it alone.'

'What about all your . . .' She almost said 'bimbos', but settled on 'young lady friends?'

'My followers?' A jaded shake of the head. 'They are all lovely, but sometimes I prefer more intellectual company. Someone with stories of her own. Like your discovery of Atlantis.' He smiled again. 'Just one glass.'

★

Three glasses later, Nina was kneeling on Osir's bed, her dress spread out around her in a silken circle. 'So I was stuck on this platform with Excalibur, an' Jack was starting up the generator so he could start up a war . . . when *boom!* Eddie'd rigged up a hand grenade as a booby trap. After that, the whole ship started blowing up like something out of a Bond movie. We had to bail out in this sort of jet-glider thing – almost froze to death before we landed on a trawler. Man, that was a bad smell!'

'Your life has been even more of an adventure than mine,' said Osir, stretched out beside her. 'And fortune is certainly on your side.'

'If I were really that lucky, I wouldn't have gotten shot. Check this out.' She hitched up her skirt to reveal the circular scar of a bullet wound on her right thigh. Osir's eyes widened at the sight of the bare leg just inches from his face. 'I wouldn't have had my life and my career wrecked, either.'

'You don't need to worry about that any more, Nina,' he assured her. 'Once we find the Pyramid of Osiris, your life will be . . . anything you want it to be. And very long, too.'

She drained her glass. 'Do I get a free lifetime supply of Khalid's Longevity Bread?'

'You'll get whatever you want.'

'Glad to hear it.' She frowned slightly, thinking back to the lab at the Swiss castle. 'Is it safe, though? You said it was genetically modified.'

Osir chuckled. 'Of course it will be safe. I'll be eating it myself! No, the genetic modifications to the yeast are to make it into exactly what I want it to be.'

'Which is? Or will your brother shout at you if you tell me?'

Another mocking laugh. 'Sometimes it seems that Sebak thinks *he* is in charge of the Temple, not me! No, my brother was being overcautious, as always. The genetic modifications are partly so that we can obtain international copyrights and patents on the new organism – yeast is very easy to cultivate, after all. I don't want everyone being able to bake their own bread of Osiris – they will have to come to the Osirian Temple for it. And also,' his expression became more conniving, giving his handsome features an unexpectedly wolfish look, 'I don't want it to be *too* good at regenerating the body's cells. People buying it once a year is not enough. They need to buy it once a month, or better still once a week.'

'Sounds like you're trying to get them hooked.'

He shrugged. 'What is a modest amount of money every week in return for immortality? Better that it goes to the Osirian Temple than on cigarettes or drink or drugs. We give a good deal of money to charitable causes, after all.'

No doubt in countries where the Osirian Temple wanted political favours, Nina thought. 'So that's what you want: to choose who gets to be immortal?'

'Fitting, don't you think?' said Osir. 'Osiris decided who received everlasting life. I'm just following in his footsteps. But I think the world will think very highly of the man who brought it immortality.' He finished his drink. 'More champagne?'

Nina regarded her empty glass. 'Oh. That went fast. I shouldn't, really . . .'

'I'll open another bottle.' He took her glass, then slid off the bed.

She lay down and closed her eyes. 'Thank you, Khalid.'

'My pleasure,' he said, his smirk anticipating another kind of pleasure. He took another bottle from a fridge under a marble-topped bar, then crossed to the bathroom. 'Excuse me one moment.'

He closed the door, then admired himself in the mirror before stripping to his silk boxer shorts and donning a dressing gown, also silk. A quick splash of cologne, then he stepped back into the bedroom.

To his delight, the lights had been turned down low, and an inviting shape waited beneath the expensive sheets. He climbed on the end of the bed, slowly moving up it. 'I see you've made yourself comfortable.' He gently pulled back the sheets . . . to see Eddie Chase grinning back at him.

'Pucker up, Romeo,' said Eddie, sticking Diamondback's revolver into his face.

18

Osir cringed away as Eddie sat up. 'How – how did you get in here?' he demanded, outrage and fear battling for supremacy.

'Yeah, I was kinda curious myself,' said Nina from the zodiac room, where Eddie had wordlessly signalled her to hide when he crept into the cabin.

Keeping the gun on Osir, Eddie threw back the sheets and stood, his clothing sodden. 'I looked for his boat where you told me at the harbour. Then I swam under the pier to it and grabbed the anchor chain. Just had to hang on until we got here.'

Osir blasted a glare of betrayal at Nina. 'Then you *are* still with him! Sebak was right!'

'Duh,' Nina said. 'Like I was really going to join up with the fruitloop religious cultist who tried to have me killed?' She looked to Eddie. 'Okay, now what?'

He gestured for Osir to move to the bathroom. 'First thing, we tie him up and keep him quiet. Then we work out where this pyramid is, and then we bugger off and find it. Sound like a plan?' She nodded. 'All right, lover boy,' Eddie said, advancing on Osir, 'in there.'

The Egyptian's eyes were fixed on Nina. 'I really did have no desire to see anyone get hurt,' he snarled. 'But now I'm happy to make exceptions.'

'Shut it, arsehole,' said Eddie. He shoved Osir into the bathroom, toiletries clattering to the floor as the stumbling man's elbow swept them from a shelf. 'On your knees, head in the bog like you're about to puke. *Now!*' He pushed the revolver against Osir's head as he knelt at the toilet bowl, then yanked loose his dressing gown's belt. 'Nina, tie his hands behind the pipe.' He kept the revolver firmly in place as Nina secured the other man's wrists to the waste pipe. 'Then find something to tie his feet with.'

She went back into the cabin, returning with a collection of ties hanging over her arm. 'Pick a colour.'

Eddie twisted one into a ball and pushed it into the protesting Osir's mouth, then secured it with a second. He used a third to fasten his prisoner's ankles together before tying the other end to a pipe beneath the washbasin. 'Now listen, King Tut,' he said, tapping Osir's head with the gun. 'One sound out of you, and I'll flush you back to your ancestors. Got that?' Mouth filled with the makeshift gag, all Osir could manage was an angry gurgle. 'Good.'

He left the bathroom and locked the cabin door, then joined Nina at the zodiac. 'So, you found the pyramid?'

'Not yet,' she admitted.

'Well, how long's it going to take?'

'No idea.'

'Maybe if you'd been working on it instead of getting pissed on Osir's champers . . .'

She gave him an irritable look. 'Don't start, Eddie.'

'And while we're at it, what was going on when I came in? You were stretched out on his bed with your skirt hitched up to your knickers!' Concern crossed his face. 'You're *wearing* knickers, right?'

'Which part of "don't" and "start" is so hard for you?' Nina snapped.

'Well, I think part of him was hard for *you* . . .'

She banged a hand on the Lexan. 'For God's sake, Eddie! I was stringing him along so I could get a look at this thing – so can you at least shut up and let me work?' She indicated the table. 'There are some notes his people made over there; can you get them for me, *please*?'

'You'd better not be walking like an Egyptian tomorrow,' he muttered as he collected them.

The notes revealed a great deal about the zodiac: an estimate of the date it was created based on the positions of the planets (she was amused to note that it had been calculated to the month – October, 3567 BC – and intrigued that it indirectly confirmed Macy's theory that the Sphinx pre-dated the construction of Khufu's pyramid), the names of the various constellations, a chemical analysis of the paints, its dimensions to the millimetre, the type of stone from which it had been carved . . . 'Useless,' she muttered, flicking through more pages.

Eddie had returned to the cabin to keep watch while she read; now he came back in. 'What?'

'These tell me everything about the zodiac – except what I need to know. The hieroglyphs tell you how to reach the Pyramid of Osiris, if you already have certain other facts. Osir's people worked out the position of Mercury, which was one clue – but we don't know the others.'

'What're the clues?'

'A place called the silver canyon, which we have no idea how to find, and the second eye of Osiris. And we don't even know where the first one is, never mind the second.' She walked round the zodiac, hoping it would give her a literal new angle on its secrets. No flashes of insight came to her. 'What am I missing?' she wondered aloud.

'If it's Egyptian stuff, Macy might know.' Eddie reached into his tuxedo jacket. 'Did you see her?'

'Yeah, I told her to wait for us.'

'Hope she found a hotel – that tinfoil dress won't keep her too warm ... oh, bollocks.' He had wrapped the passports and his phone in a plastic bag to protect them from the seawater, but the seal hadn't been as secure as he'd hoped. The passports were damp but would be salvageable if given time to dry; the phone, on the other hand, released a sad little dribble of water from its casing. 'Hope you've still got your phone.'

'Yeah, but it's with my things two decks down. I don't want to go wandering round the ship unless I have to – especially now we've got its owner tied up in the john. If anyone gets suspicious, this'll be the first place they come.'

'Guess you'll have to suss it out without Macy, then.'

Nina fruitlessly re-checked the notes for any clue she had missed, then turned her attention to a shelf of reference books about ancient Egypt, searching the indexes for any mentions of the silver canyon or the eye of Osiris. The former had none; the latter several, but only in the context of Egyptian symbology, nothing tied to a specific real-world location.

'I don't get it,' she sighed after some time, returning to

the zodiac. 'Where's it telling us to go? It's got to be connected to the stars somehow – we've got the constellations, the Milky Way, planets – how do they all tie together? I mean, the pyramid's marked right there, complete with directions, so what's the starting point?'

Eddie shrugged. 'Dunno – all I know about Egypt is what I saw in *The Mummy*.'

'Which was hardly an impeccable source.'

'Maybe not. I'll tell you something, though – that's not the Milky Way on there.'

She looked at the light blue line. 'It's not?'

'No, it's the wrong shape. I know what the Milky Way looks like, and that ain't it.'

'Okay, so if it's not the Milky Way, what is it? What else would they put on a star map?'

An idea occurred to Eddie. 'It's not a star map,' he said, going to the mirror. 'There're stars *on* it, but they're not what it's all about.' He stared at the reflection, a knowing smile spreading across his face. 'Take a look.'

He took an atlas from the shelf and flipped through it as Nina peered at the reflected zodiac. 'What am I supposed to be seeing?' she asked.

'This.' Eddie held the atlas open at a particular map: Egypt. He ran a finger down the page, tracing the course of a river from north to south. 'Remind you of anything?'

She looked at the map, then the reflection in the mirror, the map again . . . 'It's the same shape,' she realised. 'Oh my God, it's the Nile!'

'Put the thing on the ceiling, and it matches the shape of the Nile if you sort of project it upwards,' he said, nodding.

'Make it into a normal map, though, and it gets flipped over.'

Nina hurried back to the zodiac, sweeping the notes aside so she could see the river's path. 'So this is the Nile delta at the north, which means the other end . . . Eddie, bring the map over here.'

'You didn't say the magic word,' he said, but brought the atlas to her anyway, comparing it to the painted line. Even taking the mirroring effect into account, there were differences. 'The delta's not the same – there're more rivers on the old map.'

'The Nile used to have more mouths; some of them silted up,' Nina told him distractedly, fixing on something much further upstream. 'Look, look at this! This big bend in the river, where it goes round the Valley of the Kings . . .' She tapped excitedly on the Lexan. 'This Osiris figure, the one that wasn't on the Dendera zodiac – look where its eye is!'

Eddie mentally flipped the zodiac to match the map. The figure's head corresponded to a point west of the river, near a kink in its otherwise northward course. 'So what's there now? Some place called . . . Al Balyana.'

'That's not all that's there.' She practically skipped back to the table, dress swirling, to pick up a coffee-table book full of lush photography. 'It used to be one of the most important places in Egypt.' The appropriate page found, she rushed back to show him. 'Abydos. The city of Osiris!'

The photographs showed several large ruined structures. 'Looks like they need to get the builders in,' Eddie joked.

'After *we* get in,' said Nina, scanning through the text. 'There must be something pointing the way to this "silver canyon" – once we find it, we're only seven miles from the pyramid.'

'Find what?'

'The second eye of Osiris. I think it's a double clue – there's the eye of the second Osiris here on the zodiac, which tells you to go to Abydos . . . but the hieroglyphics said the second eye "sees the way" to the canyon. The one on the zodiac's just a dot; it doesn't see anything. My guess is that somewhere in Abydos there's the actual symbol of the Eye of Osiris, and the direction it faces is where we're meant to go. I've got no idea where in Abydos, though – Macy might know.'

'Then we'd better get off this boat and find her.' Eddie eyed the zodiac.

Nina knew the look. 'No. Absolutely not.'

'Absolutely not what?'

'You are *not* smashing the zodiac!'

'It'll stop Osir's lot from finding the pyramid.'

'They already have all the clues, they just weren't smart enough to figure them out. If we leave it intact, it can be returned to Egypt.'

'Only if Imhotep back there gets arrested,' he said, jabbing a thumb at the bathroom.

'If we beat him to the pyramid, we can expose him for what he's done.'

'One flap of that dressing gown and he'd have exposed himself, all right.'

'Oh, give it a rest,' Nina huffed. She tugged the grips from her hair and shook out the twist, fashioning it back into a ponytail. 'I still need to get my things.'

He drew the revolver. 'I'll check that your boyfriend's still praying to the great god Armitage Shanks, then we'll go.'

Osir was still where they had left him. Eddie poked the gun into the furious Egyptian's back, then made sure he was firmly tied to the waste pipe. 'Okay,' he said, returning to the bedroom, 'let's—'

Someone knocked on the cabin door.

Eddie whipped up the gun. 'Shit!' Nina whispered, frozen beside him. 'What do we do?'

'Shh!' In the bathroom, Osir made muffled grunts; Eddie rushed back and kicked him. 'You shuddup an' all!'

'Khalid!' said an impatient voice from outside. Shaban. 'Khalid, I know you're in there. Let me in.' The locked door's handle rattled.

Nina stared at it – then dived on to the bed, the mattress springs creaking loudly. Before Eddie could ask what she was doing, she gasped and moaned in simulated ecstasy. 'Oh . . . oh . . . oh, God, yes, come on, yes, harder, oh!'

The handle stopped moving, and with a clearly audible snort of disgust Shaban walked away. Nina continued her Meg Ryan routine until she was sure he was out of earshot, then jumped off the bed.

'Fuck me,' said Eddie, smirking. 'And I mean that literally. I'm all turned on now!'

'Hold that thought until we're back on shore. And in private.' She went to the door and listened. No sounds outside. 'I think we're clear.'

Eddie joined her, opening the door a crack. The passage was empty. 'Which way?'

'Go right, then round the first corner. There are some stairs.'

He darted out, gun at the ready. Nobody was there. To the

left, smoked glass doors opened on to one of the upper decks; he could see the lights of Monaco through them. He went right, and peered round the corner. Still no one; the promised stairs were some thirty feet away. 'Okay, clear.'

Nina followed him, acutely aware in the yacht's insulated quiet that her long dress was rustling with every step. 'This is why I always wear Dockers,' she whispered.

'If you wore miniskirts, like I keep asking . . .' Eddie paused at the stairs. A faint conversation was audible from the deck above, but it soon became clear that the speakers were not approaching. He descended. 'Two decks down, you said?'

They heard music when they reached the correct deck, a pop beat coming from a cabin. They crept past and headed for Nina's room. She had left the door unlocked; they ducked inside.

Nina quickly shed the dress and changed back into her regular clothes, then gathered her few belongings. 'Should I call Macy?' she asked, holding up her phone.

'Let's get off the ship first,' said Eddie.

'How are we going to get back ashore?'

'Nick a boat.' He stepped into the corridor. 'Okay, come on.'

They moved back to the stairs, approaching the cabin where the music was playing. Pass that, up one level, then they would be on the main deck, needing only to keep out of sight to reach the boats. Simple.

Or not.

The door opened, the music jumping in volume as a young blonde woman carrying two empty glasses stepped out – and found the revolver aimed right between her eyes.

She screamed and jumped back, a man shouting in surprise.

Nina and Eddie looked at each other. 'Leg it!' Eddie yelled.

They ran up the stairs. An alarm bell clamoured as they reached the next deck. Nina heard more voices from above. Osir's crew had been caught off guard by the unexpected alert, but it would only take them seconds to respond.

Eddie took the lead as they ran down the passage. Another smoked glass door ahead led to the aft deck. Someone behind them shouted.

No time to stop and open the door. Instead, Eddie fired a single shot through it. Glass shattered, dropping in a dark cascade to the floor. They crunched over the debris and ran out on to the deck.

It was empty. Ahead, more stairs led down to the mooring platform. 'Which boat?' Nina asked as they raced towards it.

'Whichever's got the keys in!' Eddie replied, glancing back. He saw someone emerging from a door on the deck above, and fired another shot to force him back inside.

Nina hurried down the steep stairs as he crouched and took cover at the top. Not liking the look of the small, exposed jet skis, she went to the boats. The speedboats would be faster, but the *Solar Barque*'s tender still had its key in the ignition.

She climbed aboard. 'Eddie, come on!'

Eddie glanced round at the burble of the tender's engines. 'Untie it!' he shouted. His gunshot had made the crew more cautious, nobody wanting to be the first to put himself in harm's way.

That wouldn't last. As soon as Shaban or Diamondback arrived, they would order a rush on the boat dock. And with only four bullets remaining, his chances of holding it off were slim.

He looked back at Nina. She was still unravelling the ropes.

Two men ran on to the upper deck and dived in opposite directions to the floor. Eddie shot at one, but missed. Three bullets left.

'Eddie!' The tender was free; Nina jumped behind its wheel.

'Get going!' he yelled. She shook her head, unwilling to leave him behind. 'I'll jump on, just get the bloody thing moving!'

The engine growl rose to a roar. He turned to leap down the stairs—

Diamondback burst from the broken glass door. Eddie snapped off another shot, but it went wide as the American flung himself headlong into cover. Two bullets.

The black barrel of an MP7 poked over the upper deck's edge, laser sight flicking on. The needle-thin red beam swept towards Eddie – then jittered in a crazy display as he shot the weapon out of the gunman's hands.

One bullet.

'Fucking revolvers!' Eddie spat. Even with its ammo capacity limited by the sheer size of its .50-calibre bullets, his old Wildey handgun had still been able to manage more than a mere six shots. One bullet, and several targets – it was time to go.

He jumped, landing on the dock with a bang. The tender was pulling away, but Nina was still reluctant to gun the throttle until he was aboard. He straightened, turned, launched himself into a sprint to make a running jump—

A searing pain exploded in the side of his head.

The flash of agony was so overwhelming that he fell, crashing down just short of the dock's edge. He clapped a hand to the wound. It stung viciously, and he felt blood on his palm – but not the torn meat and bone of a direct bullet impact against a human skull. The revolver shot had grazed him, slicing a gash just above his left ear.

If he had started his run on the other foot, if he had thrown his weight left rather than right, he would be dead.

And his wife would be a widow. Eyes tight with pain, he saw Nina looking back at him in horror. He waved desperately at her. 'Get out of here! *Go!*'

It took her a moment to fight through her fear for him – a moment too long. A laser spot swept across the boat, zeroing in on her chest.

Very carefully, she moved her hand away from the throttle.

Eddie heard the clip-clop of cowboy boots approaching. He painfully turned his head, seeing that he had dropped the revolver a couple of feet away. A hand reached down to collect it. 'I think this is mine,' said Diamondback.

'You're welcome to the fuckin' thing,' Eddie groaned. 'There's only one bullet left.'

'It's all I need.' A faint clicking as the trigger was pulled back, the cylinder rotating to bring the last bullet under the raised hammer . . .

'No!' someone almost screamed. Osir. 'You idiot, people will see!'

Eddie heard Diamondback mutter 'So? Fuck 'em . . .' but with a soft *clink* the hammer lowered back into place. The *Solar Barque* was not the only expensive craft moored off

Monaco; the sound of gunfire had probably already caught the attention of people on other yachts.

'Get them out of sight. Quickly!' Osir ordered.

Shaban joined his brother. 'We have to kill them. You should have listened to me.'

'I know, I know. We will. But not here. If the Monaco police come to investigate the gunshots, and we have a ship full of corpses . . .'

The boat was quickly secured, and Nina was brought back on to the dock at gunpoint. Osir gave her an especially disgusted look. 'I didn't want to do this, but you've left me no choice. When this ship leaves Monaco tomorrow, after the race . . . you will both die.'

19

'You know, mate,' said Eddie, voice echoing, 'I really don't like your hospitality.'

'Look on the bright side,' Nina said, looking up at Osir. 'At least he flushed first.'

The cult leader had, with mocking irony, opted to tie up Nina and Eddie where they had tied him – his cabin's bathroom. Nina's hands were secured to a pipe beneath the washbasin, while Eddie ended up in the same position as Osir, wrists fastened to the lavatory's waste pipe and his head over the bowl. They were bound with rope rather than neckties; their legs had been left free, but with a guard watching them all night as Osir and his associates studied the zodiac they had been given no opportunity to turn that to their advantage.

'Aren't you comfortable, Chase?' asked Osir. 'Too bad.'

Shaban stood beside him, rubbing his eyes. 'We are getting nowhere with the zodiac, Khalid. We're wasting time.'

'The answer is there,' Osir said. 'She found it – so can we.'

Shaban sneered at Nina. 'A shame you weren't listening when she did. If they know how to find the pyramid, we should have tortured them for the information.' Another sneer, this time directed at Osir. 'If you weren't so worried about getting blood on your silk sheets . . .'

Osir's face flashed with anger. 'Shut up, Sebak! We will find the pyramid ourselves. There's no need for any unnecessary pain.'

'What do *you* know about pain?' said Shaban, moving almost nose to nose with his brother. The scar tissue across his cheek twisted with his snarl.

An uneasy silence hung between the two men before Osir backed away slightly. 'We *will* find the pyramid ourselves,' he insisted. 'These two we'll . . . bury at sea. But we have other business first – the race.'

'You go,' said Shaban dismissively. 'I'll stay here and,' a cruel smile, 'politely discuss the pyramid's location with Dr Wilde.' Nina tensed.

Osir shook his head. 'You're expected there with me.'

'Then tell them I'm ill.'

'Sebak! This is for the Temple – you are coming with me.' He stared at Shaban. This time, it was the younger brother who backed down, though the tendons in his neck were tight. Osir addressed the guard. 'Watch them until we get back.' The guard nodded, and sat down on a chair facing the bathroom doorway as Osir and Shaban left.

'When does the race finish?' Nina asked.

'Four o'clock,' Eddie told her. 'What time is it now?'

She shifted to check her watch. 'Coming up on ten.'

'Hey!' the guard shouted, raising his MP7. 'Keep still. And no talking!'

Nina knelt back down, watching the guard. After a few minutes, his attention began to wander, the gun drifting away from the prisoners as he looked round the opulent cabin.

She used his distraction to glance over her shoulder. In a corner was a pair of nail scissors, one of the items Osir had scattered when Eddie pushed him into the bathroom. She had spotted them when she was first tied up. But with her hands firmly attached to the pipe, the only way to reach them was with her feet – and she couldn't do so without the guard noticing.

Six hours to find a way . . .

An opportunity took close to four uncomfortable hours to arrive.

The guard was also a racing fan. With the start imminent, he had switched on a large plasma TV. Its position on one wall meant he had to move the chair further away to see both the screen and his captives, dividing his attention.

'You okay?' Nina whispered, her voice covered by the noise of the starting grid.

'My knees are fucking killing me,' came the hollow reply. 'One good thing, mind – I'm not thirsty.'

She wrinkled her nose. 'Gross, Eddie.' A look at the guard; he glanced into the bathroom, but was clearly more interested in the race. 'Listen, there's a pair of scissors here. I'll try to kick them to you when the guy outside isn't looking.'

He turned his head as far as he could. 'If you can get them to my legs, I can try to knock them behind the bog with my knee. But I can't move my hands much. If they end up too far away, we're fucked.'

'Then we'll have to get it right first time, won't we?' She gave him a half-hearted smile; he returned it.

'Do it when the race starts,' he said. 'There's usually a prang in the first corner at Monaco – the crashes are what most blokes are really watching for.'

'I'll only need a few seconds.' Nina watched the guard; bar the occasional glance, he was fixated on the TV. The commentary was in French, but she understood enough to know that the cars were performing their formation lap before the start of the race proper.

Very slowly, she shifted her weight to one knee and slid her other leg out from under her body. Her muscles prickled painfully. The guard looked at her; she froze, afraid that he had seen what she was doing, before exaggeratedly cricking her neck to one side as if relieving stiffness. He frowned, then turned back to the TV.

The commentators became more excited as the cars took their places on the grid. Nina moved her leg out as far as she dared.

'Ready?' she whispered. Eddie raised himself slightly on his toes.

The racers were in position. The guard leaned forward, watching the screen intently. Engines revved as the starting lights came on. '*Un, deux, trois, quatre, cinq . . .*' The commentator paused in anticipation. '*Allez!*'

The engine noise rose to a multi-tonal scream as the cars leapt away from the grid. '*C'est Virtanen, Virtanen!*' the commentator cried. The guard was almost out of his seat with excitement as Team Osiris's star driver took the lead. '*Oh! Oh! Mollard s'est écrasé!*'

Someone had crashed going into the first corner. The

guard jumped up – and Nina jerked her leg, kicking the little scissors.

Even with all the activity on the big TV, the guard couldn't miss the sudden movement in his peripheral vision. He whipped round, gun raised – as Eddie dropped his legs, covering the scissors. Pointing the MP7 at Nina, he rushed into the bathroom. 'I told you not to move!'

'Cramp!' Nina gasped, not lying, as she flexed her leg. 'I've got cramp, it hurts! Don't shoot me, don't shoot!'

'Get back down!' She complied. Pressing the gun against her, the guard bent to check that she was still tied, then leaned down to look at Eddie's bonds. All were still secure. 'Keep still,' he ordered, returning to the cabin. After a few suspicious glares into the bathroom, he turned back to the race.

'Did you get it?' Nina whispered.

Eddie lifted his right leg, revealing the nail scissors under it. Slowly, carefully, he lowered it again and dragged the scissors a few inches forward, then raised his leg and moved it back to its original position before repeating the move. After a minute, the scissors were just in front of his knee.

'This is the tricky bit,' he muttered. He angled his leg out to one side. 'Okay, here we go . . .'

He jerked his knee forward.

The scissors slithered across the polished floor, clacking against the back wall. Eddie winced, but the TV had drowned out the faint noise. He reached for them with his fingertips.

They fell short by mere millimetres.

'Bollocks!' he growled. The rope tying his wrists to the pipe was already pressed against a protruding joint; he couldn't slide his hands any closer. And if he tried to raise his body higher for leverage to push his wrists further through the loops of rope, the guard would see.

He had to take the chance. He levered himself upwards, lifting his backside into the air.

It was undignified, but it worked. The extra weight pushed his wrists little by little through the rope as he wriggled. Hairs were ripped out and friction burned his skin, but his fingers were getting closer to the scissors, closer . . .

'Hey!' The guard ran into the bathroom – just as Eddie's fingertips reached the scissors. The Englishman snatched them up and clenched them in his fist. 'Get back down!'

'Ow, for fuck's sake!' Eddie gasped as the man kicked him. 'I've been like this all day, I'm bursting! I need a piss!'

The guard laughed. 'You're in the right place!' Still chuckling, he checked the ropes again. Satisfied they were still tightly fastened, he went back to his seat.

'Are you okay?' Nina asked quietly.

'He didn't help my backache, but I've got the scissors.' He fumbled them round in his hand, opening the blades as wide as they would go and pressing one against the rope. 'Might take a while, though.'

He began sawing. The small blade and the cramping of his hand made it slow going, but the rope's strands eventually started to fray and split. Ten minutes passed; twenty. The guard remained engrossed in the race, Virtanen involved in a close battle to hold the lead. Half an hour gone. The race was over a quarter done, Osir and Shaban's return drawing closer . . .

Eddie let out a small grunt. 'Eddie?' whispered Nina. 'Did you do it?'

'Yeah,' he replied, keeping the scissors hooked on one finger as he tugged at the rope with his thumb. The severed loop came loose; he slipped his wrist free, then quickly unfastened his other hand. 'Problem is, we're still trapped in a toilet by a man with a gun. Can you get him in here?'

'I'll try.'

Nina lifted her leg again, letting out a strained gasp. The guard stood, annoyed by the interruption. 'I told you to stay still!' he said as he entered the bathroom.

'Please,' she said through a mask of pain, 'my leg hurts so much, I can't stand it any more!'

'You won't have to for much longer,' he said with a sardonic smile, shoving her back into a kneeling position. He examined the ropes round her wrists, then bent to check Eddie's bonds.

They weren't there.

Eddie's hand shot up with savage force and stabbed the scissors point first into his eye.

That the blades were less than an inch long below the hinge didn't matter – the entire length of the scissors disappeared into the guard's skull. The pain and shock froze him in place – long enough for Eddie to roll sideways and grab him by his shirt, yanking him downwards. There was a horrible crack as the man's head struck the flush lever, and he collapsed twitching on to the lavatory.

Eddie pushed the guard face first into the swirling bowl. Collecting the MP7, he quickly untied Nina. 'Flushed with success,' he said, grinning.

She rolled her eyes. 'Is he dead?'

'After all that? I hope so.' The flush cycle ended, the water turning pink round the man's part-submerged head. Eddie watched for several seconds to make sure no bubbles rose from his mouth or nose, then checked the MP7. It was fully loaded: twenty rounds. 'This is more like it – no pissing about with revolvers like we're still in the fucking nineteenth century.'

Nina gratefully stood, rubbing her aching legs. 'What's the plan?'

'Same as last night. Get back to shore, find Macy, find this pyramid. And shoot anybody who gets in our way. Sound okay?'

'I'd prefer it without the shooting part, but otherwise, yeah.' She went into the cabin, retrieved her possessions from the desk where they had been dumped, and was about to go to the door when she changed her mind and instead crossed to the zodiac. Osir and others had been working on it through the night; more notes were scattered about. She picked up a photo of the entire relief and shoved it in a pocket. 'Just in case,' she told Eddie, who had recovered his own belongings and was now waiting impatiently near the door. 'I don't think Osir'll give us another chance to look at it.'

'Still think we should just smash the thing,' he said, checking the corridor. 'Okay, the quickest way down'll be jumping off the balcony to the rear deck. Are you up for that?'

'I'll be okay,' she said, touching his head. The only treatment he had been given after being shot was a large adhesive bandage stuck roughly over the cut; it was now dark with dried blood. That at least meant the bleeding had stopped, but the wound still needed attention. 'What about you?'

'I'll live. Good job it didn't hit my face – it would've ruined my good looks.' A grin creased his battle-worn visage; she smiled back. 'You ready?'

She nodded. Eddie entered the corridor, quickly moving to the glass door. A couple of Osir's bikini-clad girls were sunbathing below, a trio of the yacht's crew with them, watching the race on a flatscreen TV. Two of the men were armed. 'Well, strolling casually to the boats is out.' He raised the gun. 'On three, we both jump. Soon as you land, run for whichever boat's in the water, start it, and *do not stop for anything*. They're going to kill us anyway – if they catch us again we won't get a second chance. All right?'

'All right,' Nina reluctantly agreed. 'I'll tell you something, though.'

'What?'

'I'm not depressed any more.'

'Yeah, nothing like a death threat to pep you up, is there?' They kissed, then Eddie pushed the door open. 'Okay, one, two, three – *go*!'

They burst out into the hot Mediterranean sun and vaulted the railing.

The drop was almost nine feet; Nina's landing was painfully hard, making her fall. Eddie fared better, dropping into a frog-like crouch before springing back up. One of the women shrieked, the other staring at him with dull surprise. The men jumped up, the armed ones fumbling for their guns.

Eddie's MP7 clattered, two silenced bursts stitching lines of bloody holes across the pair's chests.

Noise from behind—

He spun and fired another burst at another man beneath

the balcony, a gun spinning from his hands as he was thrown back against the blood-splattered bulkhead.

Nina got up. 'You okay?' Eddie asked. She nodded. 'Good. Get to the boats.' As she set off, he covered the remaining people. The shrieking woman had progressed to full-blown screams, her companion still regarding him with blank-eyed bewilderment. The unarmed man was eyeing the dead crewmen's guns. 'Can you all swim?'

The responses from the trio were in the affirmative. 'Good. You've got three seconds to start!' He waved his gun at the yacht's side. They got the message and jumped overboard.

He ran after Nina, pointing the gun back at the yacht's superstructure as he reached the stairs to the dock. Another green-jacketed man appeared, pulling the charging handle on his MP7 – only to take a burst from Eddie's gun and crash over a lounger. Knowing his weapon was down to its last few rounds, Eddie dropped it and snatched up one of the dead men's guns as he went past.

Nina checked the boats, not liking what she found. Both speedboats had been winched out of the water, the only floating options for escape being jet skis. 'Eddie, I hope you know how to ride these things, 'cause I don't have a clue!'

'Just start one!' He fired a few shots to force a crewman back into the ship, then jumped down to join Nina. 'I'll drive!'

She started the engine, looking in concern at a prominent warning sticker about the danger from the little craft's powerful underwater jet blast. 'It says we should be wearing wetsuits.'

'Yeah, and we should be wearing life jackets too, but we'll

have to make do!' He vaulted aboard in front of her. 'Take the gun, and don't fall off!'

She clutched the MP7 and gripped his waist tightly as he twisted the throttle, sending the jet ski blasting away from the yacht in a plume of spray.

20

Osir stood at the window of the VIP box, face almost pressed against the glass as the race leaders screamed past – with Mikko Virtanen fronting the pack. 'Yes!' he cried, pumping his fist. It was only OIG's second year as primary sponsor of what had previously been the second-tier Monarch team, but the results already spoke for themselves – and with a win at Monaco, the most prestigious race of all, the publicity boost for the Osirian Temple would be beyond measure.

Shaban was seated behind him, barely paying attention. His phone rang and he listened to the frantic voice on the other end of the line for several seconds before jumping up. 'Khalid!'

'Not now,' said Osir, waving a dismissive hand.

'*Khalid*,' Shaban repeated, the anger in his voice drawing his brother's attention from the race. 'The yacht.'

'What is it?'

Shaban ushered him away from the box's other occupants. 'Wilde and Chase have escaped.'

Osir looked stricken. '*What?*'

'They killed some of our men, then stole a jet ski.'

'When – when did this happen?'

'Seconds ago – they just left.'

Osir tried to devise an authoritative course of action, but all he could manage was, 'We have to stop them.'

'I'll take care of it.' Shaban turned away, raising the phone.

Osir touched his shoulder. 'Discreetly. No trouble. Not here,' he said, almost pleading.

'That depends on them.' He spoke to the *Solar Barque*'s captain. 'Send every man you have after them. Get the tender to intercept them in the harbour. Chase them in the yacht if you have to – they must be stopped. *At any cost.*' He snapped the phone shut, giving Osir a disapproving look before hurrying out.

The open sea off Monaco was choppy enough to make things bouncy for any craft not large enough to ride it out – and for something as small as a jet ski, it was practically a roller coaster. 'Jesus!' yelped Nina as their Kawasaki crested a wave and was airborne for a moment before smacking down heavily in the trough beyond. 'Can't you keep it in the water?'

'Only if you want them to catch us,' Eddie answered. He looked back. A jet ski had already left the *Solar Barque* in pursuit, one of the speedboats had just been dropped into the water to follow them – and the yacht itself was powering up, froth boiling beneath the bow as it used its thrusters to turn round. 'Oh, great! The guy's got his own private navy!'

A wave tossed them skywards again, Eddie battling to keep the jet ski from tipping over as it landed. Another large yacht loomed ahead; he turned sharply round its stern, aiming for the harbour entrance beyond the flotilla of expensive pleasure craft.

Nina glanced round. The pursuing jet ski was gaining fast, and the speedboat was also rapidly closing the gap. 'I think this guy's a better driver than you,' she said as the other jet ski carved cleanly through a swelling wave without losing speed.

'I bloody hate show-offs,' Eddie growled, seeing that the other rider would quickly catch up – and that he was armed.

A flash of fast-moving colour beyond a line of anchored yachts. Even from a momentary glimpse he knew what it was, and turned towards it. 'What're you doing?' Nina asked nervously as the harbour entrance swung away. Their pursuer changed course to intercept them, drawing closer.

'When I say duck, duck. And I mean really, *really* duck!'

They were heading almost straight at the lead yacht's bow. 'You're going to hit it!'

'No, I'm aiming close – but we're gonna be even closer to something else.'

'What do you—' A red and white powerboat shot into view from behind the yacht, thundering along parallel to the line of vessels. 'Holy *shit*!'

The man on the other jet ski raised his gun—

'Duck!' Eddie screamed, dropping as low as he could behind the handlebars. Nina followed suit.

The jet ski zoomed past the yacht, barely missing the powerboat's stern as it crossed behind it – passing *under* the tow-rope hauling a waterskier along in its wake, the line slicing an inch over their heads.

The other rider swerved to follow them past the

powerboat. The tow-line was partly hidden by spray, and by the time he saw it, it was too late—

The line caught him just below the chin. His speeding jet ski kept going as he was snatched from it with a crack of shattering vertebrae, spinning back over the rope to splash into the water. The waterskier hit the corpse, taking off as if hitting a ramp before tumbling to a waterlogged stop.

Eddie turned back towards the harbour entrance. The *Solar Barque*'s speedboat swerved through the anchored boats after them.

Another vessel, green and gold, burst out of the harbour. The yacht's tender, two men aboard. It made a hard turn as it cleared the outer breakwater, coming right at them.

They were cut off.

Eddie made a split-second decision and brought the jet ski back into the millionaires' armada. The larger boats were more powerful, but his Kawasaki had the edge in manoeuvrability. If he could weave through the stationary yachts, he might gain enough of a lead to run for the harbour . . .

Shit!

His plan would fail. The *Solar Barque* was powering for the harbour entrance. If he wasted time trying to escape the two smaller boats, it would block their path.

The speedboat was gaining fast from behind. The tender was also accelerating, smacking hard through the waves.

Every escape route was closed – unless he made a new one.

Nina clung harder to Eddie as he turned the jet ski again and headed straight for the tender. 'Whoa, whoa!' she cried, jabbing a finger at the rapidly approaching boat. 'Bad guys!'

'I know!'

'Then go *away* from them!'

'Trust me!' He jinked from side to side, searching for the perfect wave.

A man in the tender stood up, one hand clutching the windscreen for support as he aimed his gun with the other.

Eddie saw a deep trough in the water ahead, a steep breaking wavecrest beyond it. Right in line with the tender. 'Hang on!'

He swept into the dip, turning the throttle as far as it would go as the jet ski shot up the crest.

And out of the water.

The gunman was about to fire when the jet ski momentarily dipped out of sight beneath his boat's prow – then flew up *over* it, smashing down on the bow.

Gripping the handlebars with all his strength, Eddie leaned over, pulling Nina with him and tipping the jet ski as it skidded sidelong over the decking. The little craft's underside smashed through the windscreen and ground along the tender's side – in the process crushing the driver against his seat back and catching the gunman with a jet blast that struck him like a blow from a baseball bat.

The jet ski flew off the stern and slammed back into the water, only Nina's near death-grip on Eddie keeping her from being flung off. The jet spluttered and coughed before drawing more water into its impeller, sending the Kawasaki surging forward again.

The tender ploughed onwards at full power, the driver dead. The gunman fumbled for the controls, catching the steering wheel and knocking the boat into a turn—

Directly into the speedboat's path as it swung to avoid a head-on collision.

The speedboat ripped through the tender's side, both boats exploding in a storm of shattered wood and fibreglass. Blazing debris rained over the surrounding yachts.

Nina looked back at the cartwheeling wreckage, but Eddie's attention was fixed on what lay ahead. The *Solar Barque* was almost at the harbour entrance. 'Hold on!'

She saw green-jacketed men on the yacht's main deck – all armed. 'They're gonna shoot us!'

He brought the jet ski parallel to the breakwater. 'Shoot them first!'

'I'll never be able to hit them!'

'You don't have to – just keep their heads down so they can't hit *us*!'

Nina pointed the MP7 up at the rapidly approaching ship. 'Oh, God, I'm so not a gun person,' she said, wincing as she pulled the trigger.

The gun bucked in her hand, the bolt's rapid clacking almost as loud as the hissing *thwat* of the suppressor with each shot. Firing one-handed from a bounding vehicle, it was almost impossible for her to aim, but against a target the size of the yacht it didn't matter. Black spots pockmarked the *Solar Barque*'s pristine white superstructure, a window shattering. The men dived to the deck.

'Stop, stop!' said Eddie. 'Save some!' The end of the breakwater was coming up fast. He hauled the jet ski round in a savage left turn, clearing the concrete by inches.

The harbour opened out before them, Monaco shimmering under the sun on three sides. Eddie aimed for the inner harbour; the outer harbour's high quays were built for commercial ships and liners, not tiny pleasure craft. They needed to find a lower pier to get ashore.

Nina looked back. 'Oh, crap!' The *Solar Barque* was right behind them, its prow a giant knife blade slicing through the water. Gaining. 'Faster, faster! Seriously, go faster!'

'It's a jet *ski*, not a jet fighter!' Eddie complained. 'If anyone sticks their head over the side, blow it off!'

Nina awkwardly turned in her seat, pointing the gun up at the looming bow. She saw a man lean over the port side, spotting the jet ski. He hurriedly ducked out of sight as she fired a couple of shots.

They entered the inner harbour, Eddie turning to make landfall at the northwestern corner – and saw a new threat powering towards them. Not from Osir's people; this was a police boat, siren wailing. The chaos outside the harbour had inevitably attracted attention. An officer shouted commands over a megaphone, ordering both vessels to stop. 'Buggeration and fuckery!'

'Any friends in the Monaco police department?' Nina asked hopefully. The absence of an answer was enough. 'Thought not!'

More figures appeared at the bow railing, guns pointing down—

Nina fired first. One man retreated sharply; the other was hit in the shoulder. He spun backwards, finger convulsively tightening on his trigger . . .

Sending a stream of armour-piercing bullets up the front of the superstructure.

The bridge window blew out – and the captain, at the wheel behind it, was hit square in the forehead. He collapsed over the instrument panel, dead. The throttle control was pushed to full beneath him – and with the other crew members all on deck trying to shoot Nina and Eddie, there was nobody to take over . . .

The police boat altered course to cut off the chase. Eddie darted behind it, the jet ski leaping out of the water as it crashed through its wake. He glimpsed an officer in the stern raising a rifle. 'Down!' he warned Nina, looking back to see when the man was going to fire.

He wasn't. Instead, he was leaping desperately out of the boat, his companions diving off the bow.

A moment later, the *Solar Barque* ploughed over the smaller craft, ripping it in half. The smashed boat's fuel tanks exploded, the yacht carving through the fireball as it blindly pursued the jet ski. One of Osir's men flung himself into the harbour as flames rolled across the foredeck.

'Jesus!' Nina cried. 'Are they *insane*?'

Eddie turned again, aiming for a small slipway between the crowded quays. The yacht didn't follow. 'I don't think anyone's driving.'

'What? But I only winged that guy!'

'I'm not complaining!'

The *Solar Barque* surged past behind them, any thoughts amongst its crew of shooting the fugitives replaced by simple survival instinct as they dived overboard. The yacht was powering straight for a clutch of smaller but still hugely expensive vessels in the corner of the harbour, their occupants' attention suddenly diverted from the racing before them to the rapidly approaching behemoth behind. People fled screaming down the gangways.

'Get ready to run,' Eddie told Nina. 'Soon as we hit land,

we leg it, and don't stop until we're half a mile away!'

The jet ski shot up the slipway, keel scraping noisily along the concrete. Crash barriers rose ahead: the racing circuit ran right along the harbourfront. Eddie yanked at the controls, but out of the water there was no way to steer the Kawasaki. It hit the corrugated metal, flinging both passengers painfully against the handlebars.

A race marshal nearby saw the unexpected collision and started to run to them – then froze in shock as the *Solar Barque*, smoke billowing from its scorched bow, rammed into the harbour at close to thirty miles an hour.

The smaller yachts disintegrated into fireballs of multi-million dollar debris as it smashed through them. A larger vessel was flipped on its side – and the megayacht ran up over it to crash down on the quay, its mangled prow ripping apart the crash barriers. The *Solar Barque* skidded across the track like a steel wall, beaching itself in front of a grandstand as it screeched to a stop.

Mikko Virtanen was still in the lead, powering out of the chicane on the harbour's northern side – to find a towering white barrier where he expected to see a corner. The marshals came to their senses and frantically waved warning flags, but it was too late for the Finn.

He stamped on the brakes, his car skidding past Nina and Eddie's position and spinning out before crashing tail first into the hull. Another million dollars of Team Osiris hardware was reduced to shrapnel, what was left of the body whirling back along the track and grinding to a standstill. Again, the car's designers had done their job perfectly; dazed but unharmed, Virtanen shakily opened his visor and blinked up at the people staring at him over the barrier.

Nina nudged Eddie. 'You know you said to run as soon as we got to land?'

'Yeah? Oh, right.' They sprinted away as more marshals hurried to the scene.

'*You* did that?' said Macy in amazement, indicating a helicopter shot of the beached yacht on a TV screen. 'Wow! That must be like a hundred million dollars in trashed boats!'

'I told Osir it'd cost him,' Nina said, looking warily round the hotel lobby. The fences surrounding the circuit were designed to keep spectators *out*; exiting hadn't been hard, but there had been the constant worry that the police were hunting for them as they made their way back to Casino Square. So far, nobody had recognised them – the cameras were focused on the race, not the harbour, until moments before the *Solar Barque* crashed spectacularly ashore – but she still wanted to get out of the principality as soon as possible. At the very least, there would be several angry insurance companies after their heads.

'Sucks for Mikko, though. Poor guy. He really thought he was going to win.'

Eddie gave her a look. 'Wait, you talked to Mikko Virtanen?'

She grinned. 'I did more than just talk to him.' Seeing Nina's and Eddie's expressions of dawning realisation, she went on: 'What? I wasn't going to walk around the streets all night after the casino closed. Where did you think I got this?' She showed off the expensive soft leather jacket in Team Osiris's colours she was wearing over her shimmering dress.

'You didn't nick it off him, did you?' Eddie asked.

'Of course not!' she said, offended. 'It was a gift. You know, he's fast on the track, but in bed—'

'Okay, heard enough,' said Nina hurriedly.

'Nice work in the casino, by the way,' Eddie told Macy. 'That big bugger would've tackled me if you hadn't tripped him.'

Macy smiled. 'I just remembered what you said about always being ready for action – and I figured that with you two, there's always action.'

'Unfortunately,' said Nina, grimacing. 'But never mind that. There are more important things.' She took the photo of the zodiac from her pocket and showed it to Macy. Though crumpled, the picture was still clear enough to show the details of the painted relief. 'I think I figured out where the pyramid is. It's somewhere near Abydos.' She quickly explained her reasoning.

Macy regarded the picture in wonderment. 'That'd make sense. Abydos was supposed to be the site of Osiris's tomb – nobody's ever found it, but the Egyptians definitely believed it was near there. All the First Dynasty pharaohs were buried there so they could be close to Osiris. You think the pyramid's to the west?' Nina nodded. 'That fits, too. The western desert was supposedly where the dead went to enter the Underworld, where the sun went down.'

'What about the "second eye of Osiris"? Does that ring any bells?'

Macy frowned, thinking. 'The *second* eye? I dunno. Unless . . .' Her dark eyes opened wide. 'Unless it's something in the Osireion!'

'The what?' Eddie asked.

'The Osireion – it's a building, it's meant to be a copy of Osiris's tomb.'

'A *second* tomb,' Nina realised. 'A second eye. And if it looks in the direction of the silver canyon . . .'

'. . . we've found the pyramid,' Eddie finished. 'So, back across the Med, then!'

'Rest assured, I will be co-operating with the authorities to find out who was responsible for this catastrophe,' Osir told the news crew. 'It's been a terrible day for the sport, for Team Osiris, for Mikko Virtanen – and for myself personally, as you can imagine.'

'What about the reports of a shootout on your yacht?' asked the newsman, thrilled to have a story more juicy than sports reporting.

Osir needed all his acting skills to keep a neutral face. 'I don't know anything about that, only what the Monaco police have told me. Thank you, and excuse me.' He retreated into the VIP box, the newsman still firing questions as he closed the door.

Shaban and Diamondback were waiting. 'Well?' Osir demanded.

'Wilde and Chase must have got away,' Shaban said grimly. 'The Monaco police haven't caught them, and since it would only take them ten minutes to reach the border I doubt they will.'

'What about the yacht? Did the zodiac survive?'

'Yes, so we still have that, at least. I've arranged for it to be shipped to Switzerland once the police clear the scene.'

'My God,' said Osir, shaking his head as he sat. 'How did they escape?'

'Because you were soft,' Shaban snapped. Osir was startled by the fury in his brother's voice. 'I warned you! You fell for that woman, and she betrayed you. I *told* you to kill her, but you refused – and now look what has happened!'

Osir jumped up again, stabbing a finger at Shaban. 'You do not speak to me like—'

'This is *your fault*!' Shaban roared, making Osir flinch. 'Everything I do, I do to protect the Temple – but this has gone too far for you to tie my hands! If you want to find the Pyramid of Osiris – *and keep it for yourself* – then it will take blood. It has *taken* blood. And because you didn't let me do what needed to be done, the blood is of our own followers instead of our enemies!' His voice softened, slightly, as he put a hand on Osir's shoulder. 'Don't you see, Khalid? If we don't get everything, we will be left with nothing . . . and I will not let that happen. Let me do what needs to be done. We have to find Dr Wilde before she finds the pyramid – and kill her. You know I'm right.'

'Yes,' Osir said reluctantly. 'Yes, you're right. I'm sorry. I should have listened to you, my brother.'

Shaban nodded, satisfaction on his scarred face. 'Then we're agreed. We find them, and kill them, and take the pyramid for ourselves.'

'Agreed,' said Osir.

'Just one minor problem,' Diamondback said, voice heavy with sarcasm. 'We don't know where they're goin', and we don't know where the pyramid is either.'

'We need an expert,' said Shaban. 'Someone who knows the entire history of Egypt.'

'Hamdi?' asked Osir.

Shaban shook his head. 'Hamdi is a glorified librarian. We want someone world-class . . .' He smiled malevolently as an idea came to him. 'And someone with a grudge against Nina Wilde.' Raising his phone, he selected a number: the Osirian Temple's Swiss headquarters. 'This is Sebak Shaban. I need you to contact the International Heritage Agency in New York, and tell them . . . tell them I want to speak to Dr Logan Berkeley.'

21

Egypt

What initially seemed like a simple trip back to Egypt quickly turned into a far more stressful experience. An attempt to book a flight from Nice was stymied when Macy discovered – to her mortification – that her credit card had been cancelled. Her parents had pulled the plug.

An angry phone call home made it clear that her line of credit would be only restored if she agreed to go straight back to Miami. Nina's suggestion that, now they knew Abydos was the key to finding the Pyramid of Osiris, her work was done and she could return to the US did not go down well.

Eddie managed to defuse the tension between the two women by cobbling together an itinerary that was – just – manageable on his and Nina's strained finances, flying from Nice to Athens on a no-frills budget carrier, then on to

Cyprus, and from there a plodding ferry to Egypt's Port Said. Following that was a slow and draining overland journey south by rail to the town of Sohag. Tempers frayed, they traversed the last miles in a rented 4×4, finally reaching their destination three days after leaving Monaco.

If Cairo had been uncomfortably hot, then Abydos, three hundred miles further south on the edge of the Sahara, was almost agonising. The temperature was well over a hundred degrees Fahrenheit, and what breeze there was provided little relief, being laden with gritty, astringent sand. Nina was already on her second bottle of water, and it was still only morning.

As usual, Eddie barely seemed to notice the conditions, still wearing his leather jacket; his only concession to the burning sun was a floppy cloth hat to protect his balding scalp. 'Could be worse, love,' he offered. 'At least it's a dry heat.'

'Hilarious,' Nina snapped. Her pale skin had forced her to cover up, and unlike her husband she was sweltering. 'God, I hate deserts. Why are the best ruins always in such God-awful places?'

But despite her foul mood, she was still impressed by what awaited them. The remains of the ancient city of Abydos sprawled over a wide area, the majesty of the temples in stark contrast to the ugly little village nearby. But when they stood before the structure they had come to see the modern world was figuratively and literally behind them, nothing in sight beyond the partially buried remains of the Osireion except the bleak wastes and distant cliffs of the Western Desert.

They had the place almost to themselves, a coach party

there when they arrived having left for the next destination on its whistle-stop tour of Upper Egypt. A couple of policemen had been lurking nearby – unescorted visits to the ruins were discouraged – but a bribe persuaded them to wander back into the village for a few hours.

'So, what are we looking for?' Nina asked Macy. 'You're the expert.'

'Well, I wouldn't exactly call myself that,' she said, falsely modest.

'You're the nearest we've got,' said Nina dismissively. 'So, what's the deal?'

Macy turned to the much larger, more intact structure behind them. 'That's the Temple of Seti, or Sethos, there,' she said, 'which was built by his son Rameses the Second sometime round 1300 BC. The cool thing about it is that it's totally unique architecturally. All the other Egyptian temples run in a straight line, yeah? You go in through the entrance, and each hall comes one after the other. But this one,' she pointed out a section to their right, 'is kinked.'

'I like a bit of kinkiness,' said Eddie.

Nina shushed him. 'Why's it that shape?'

Macy looked back at the Osireion. 'Supposedly, the Temple of Seti and the Osireion were built at the same time. That's what most of the books say, anyway. So did my professor. But it didn't really make sense to me, and it turns out some archaeologists think so too. I mean, why would you bend your temple in half to avoid another building if they were being built at the same time? It's not like they were short of space to put the second one farther away.' She indicated the empty desert past the ruins.

'So there's another theory?' asked Nina.

She nodded. 'Some people think the Osireion was already here way before 1300 BC. It'd been buried by sand, but Rameses discovered it when the Temple of Seti was being built. Things were too far along for him to stop work on the temple, but he didn't want to knock down the Osireion either . . . so he changed the plans to make the new temple go round a corner.'

'Why'd he want to keep it so much?' said Eddie.

Nina knew. 'Because it was a copy of the tomb of Osiris himself. They'd lost the location of the original tomb centuries earlier, but they realised they had the next best thing.'

'And if we're right,' said Macy, 'somewhere inside it is the Eye of Osiris.'

'Which points the way to his pyramid. So all we have to do . . . is find it.'

They crossed the stony sands to the Osireion. The site was practically a pit, a series of stepped walls leading down to the excavated structure. Compared to the ornate elegance of the Temple of Seti, the exposed ruins were almost brutalist, made of unornamented blocks of pale granite. The hall's floor, some ninety feet long, was hidden beneath a stagnant green pool.

Eddie screwed up his face in distaste. 'I didn't expect to come into the bloody Sahara to go wading. I would've brought my wellies.'

'It's not that deep,' said Nina, descending the steps into the building proper. 'I hope.' She cautiously dipped a boot into the turgid, algae-coated water, finding it was about an inch in depth. 'Ugh. At least we didn't come in the rainy season.' She turned as Macy and Eddie joined her, noticing a dark passage beyond an opening at the northwestern end. 'Where does that go?'

'It's a tunnel that went to the northern entrance,' Macy told her, examining a diagram in her guidebook.

Eddie squinted inside. 'Doesn't go anywhere now – the other end's buried. Hope this eye thing's not in there.' He splashed to the other end of the hall. 'I just thought of something. If this eye's supposed to be looking towards the pyramid, and the pyramid's out to the west somewhere, then it'll be on one of the east walls, right?'

'The man in the funky hat makes a good point,' said Macy, exchanging smiles with him.

Nina unslung her backpack, taking out a flashlight, then waded to an opening in the wall. A ramp rose from the water; the small chamber inside was dry. She entered, blinking as her eyes adjusted to the darkness. Like the hall outside, the walls were plain, unadorned.

Eddie and Macy followed. 'See anything?' Eddie asked.

'Not yet.' Nina carefully scanned the walls for any indications of carvings or markings. Macy, meanwhile, took out a flashlight of her own and conducted a much less methodical examination of the chamber, sweeping the beam around at random. 'Will you cut that out?' Nina demanded. 'You won't find anything just by waving the light about. We need to do a section-by-section search—'

'Ah-ha! Found it!' Macy interrupted. She fixed her torch beam on one particular spot, high on the back wall. 'See? One Eye of Osiris. I rock!'

'That's more like it,' said Eddie, seeing a symbol carved into the stone. 'Archaeology without all the boring farting around.'

Nina's patience finally snapped. 'Will you both goddamn take this seriously!' she shouted, voice echoing round the chamber. 'It wouldn't be boring if you had even the *slightest* interest in what I do,' she said to Eddie, before rounding on Macy. 'And you, if you really want to be an archaeologist, then start acting like one. Or acting like an adult, even!'

Eddie made a sarcastic face. 'Oh, the schoolmistress voice. I love hearing that.'

Macy, on the other hand, was shocked by the attack. 'But – but I still found it,' she said, pointing up at the symbol.

'By sheer fluke!' snapped Nina. 'And because you weren't being methodical, you did exactly what Logan did at the Sphinx, which was rush straight for the obvious prize and completely overlook anything else that might be important.'

Eddie indicated the plain walls surrounding them. 'There isn't anything else.'

'That's not the point!' she protested, before turning back to Macy. 'You're treating this like a high school field trip – and you're acting like one of the cheerleaders giggling on the back seat of the bus with the jocks!'

Macy's dark eyes narrowed angrily. 'I suppose *you* always sat up front with the teachers.'

'Well – yes,' said Nina, taken aback by the challenge, 'but this isn't about me, it's about the work. If we want to find the pyramid, we've got to be professional about it.'

'And you think I'm not, is that it? Excuse *me*, Dr Wilde, but you wouldn't even be here if it wasn't for me. *I* was the one who found out about the other entrance to the Hall of Records, *I* was the one who got us into the Sphinx compound—'

'By flashing your boobs!'

Macy looked offended. 'You think I'm just some bimbo, don't you? Because I'm hot and I don't get straight As in everything, you don't take me seriously!'

'You're not taking *this* seriously!'

Eddie stepped forward, moving between them. ' "This"?'

'All of this!' Nina cried, waving her hands at the ancient structure around them. 'Everything! It's all important, but sometimes I feel like I'm the only person in the world who actually *cares* about it!'

Macy's tone became withering. 'Oh, I see – the entire world of archaeology revolves around you! Dr Berkeley was right, you really *do* have to be the centre of attention all the time.' She pulled out the folded magazine pages and flapped them at Nina. 'You know, when I read this I thought you were so cool and so smart – that you were somebody really special. But you're just like everyone else.' She stalked to the entrance and threw the pages outside. Disappointment overcame her anger. 'Everything's about you.'

'That's not true,' insisted Nina, now on the defensive. 'I don't care about taking the credit.'

'You enjoyed it, though.'

'Of course I did,' she admitted after a moment. 'But that's not why I do what I do. I do it because . . . because I *have* to!'

There was an almost confessional tone to her voice. Eddie raised an eyebrow. 'You *have* to?'

'Yeah. It's . . . it's who I am. My parents spent their lives trying to reveal the truth about the past to the world – not so a few people could profit from it, but for everyone. That's what I do, too.' She paused, almost afraid to confess her feelings. 'And if I can't do it, then what else *can* I do? What else have I got?'

'You've got me,' said Eddie.

'I know. But . . .' For a moment she couldn't face him, before giving him a sad, shameful look. 'But what if that's not enough?'

An awkward silence filled the chamber. Macy stared uncomfortably down at her feet, while Nina again found herself unable to meet Eddie's gaze.

'Well, you know,' he finally said, managing a faint smile, 'I never really did see you as the stay-at-home housewife type.'

'I'm sorry,' Nina said quietly.

He put his arms round her. 'No need.'

'You're not mad at me?'

'Only that you didn't get this out into the open ages ago!' He smiled again, more broadly. 'That's what was wrong all this time? You thought there was nothing else you could do except archaeology?'

Nina nodded. 'Pretty much.'

'Well, that's just fucking daft!' he said, laughing. 'You're the smartest person I know, you could do anything you want. Even dance.' He gave her a pointed look. 'You've just got to *want* to want.'

'I guess . . .'

'So what do you want, right now?'

She didn't answer at first, then one corner of her mouth creased upwards, very slightly. 'I can think of something,' she said, 'but we can't do it in front of Macy.'

He grinned. 'She can join in if she wants – I could handle a threesome!'

'Eddie!' Nina cried, batting his arm. Macy's eyes widened.

He cackled. 'For fuck's sake, you're so easy to wind up. We're married, and you *still* can't tell when I'm taking the piss.'

Nina harrumphed. 'Just for that, we're going to do the other thing I really want to do right now. Which is find the Pyramid of Osiris.' She looked first at the symbol carved on the wall, then to Macy at the entrance. 'But if we're going to do that, we need to be a team again. I'm sorry I blew up at you like that, Macy. I shouldn't have done – *that* was unprofessional. Besides, you were right, we couldn't have done this without you. Any of it.'

Macy still looked sulky, but accepted the apology. 'And maybe I got a bit pissy. So . . . sorry, Dr Wilde.'

'Thanks. And it's Nina,' she added, after a moment. 'Call me Nina.'

The young woman's expression brightened a little. 'Okay. Nina.' She walked back into the chamber.

'So,' said Eddie, 'what've we got?'

At first glance, what Macy had discovered seemed nothing special, a symbol less than two inches high carved into the stone just below the ceiling. It was a stylised eye – the same one featured in the logo of the Osirian Temple.

Eddie checked a compass. 'Okay, so it's looking . . . towards two hundred and ten degrees.' He took out a map and spread it on the stone floor. 'So we're after a canyon on that heading, right?'

'The silver canyon, yeah,' Nina confirmed.

He used the compass to align the map with the real

world. 'There's a fair few canyons out in the desert that way,' he said. 'What did the zodiac say, exactly?'

'Just that the second Eye of Osiris sees the way to the silver canyon. To its start, presumably, because the rest of the hieroglyphs said where to go once you reached its end.'

'Okay, so we want a canyon mouth.' He looked more closely at the contour lines, bunched tightly where streams had cut their way down from the desert's relative highlands. 'Here,' Eddie continued, tapping a spot on the map. 'This canyon leads up to a big open plain, and it starts right in line with where the eye's looking. It opens out here,' another tap, 'so going seven miles west takes you to . . . here.'

Nina leaned closer. The point Eddie indicated on the map contained nothing. Literally nothing; the contours were so widely spaced as to make the region practically flat. 'If that's the right canyon.'

'It's about fifteen miles from here, and the terrain's not too bad. We can drive out there, if we're careful.'

Nina gazed at the expanse of emptiness on the map. It didn't seem likely that an unknown pyramid could possibly be out there, but she had discovered other incredible sites in equally barren environments. 'We'll check out the canyon first – and if it seems to be the right place, we'll follow it and see if it really leads to the Pyramid of Osiris.'

'It must do,' Macy said excitedly, standing up. 'Everything fits. It's *got* to be there!'

'Let's actually find the bloody thing before we start celebrating,' Eddie cautioned.

'We will, I *know* it! Oh, my God! We'll be famous! Okay, you're already famous, but I'll be famous too!' She hurried outside, pausing to collect the scattered pages with a slightly embarrassed look back at Nina. 'If the canyon's only fifteen miles away we'll be there in no time!'

'She's never driven in the desert, has she?' said Eddie as Macy splashed back across the hall. He noticed Nina staring after the younger woman with an expression somewhere between wistful and jealous. 'What?'

'I used to be that enthusiastic once,' she said. 'I kinda miss it.'

'You *are* still that enthusiastic,' he told her, folding the map. 'Christ, once you start on about something I can't shut you up.'

'No, I mean . . .' She sighed again. 'I'm only twelve years older than her, but it feels like a lot more. Where the hell did the time go?'

'You're not going to get all depressed again, are you?' said Eddie, mock-chiding. 'I've had enough of that recently.'

'Yeah, thanks for the sympathy.'

'No, really, if anybody should be getting depressed, it's me. I'll be forty in a couple of years. Forty! That's all old and grown up and stuff.'

'I don't think you'll be growing up any time soon.'

'Tchah!' They followed Macy out of the chamber.

Their battered Land Rover Defender picked its way across the sun-seared desolation. Even with the windows open and the blower on at full blast, the cabin was sickeningly hot, the elderly 4×4 lacking air-con. Eddie, at the wheel of the right-hand-drive vehicle, dealt with the heat with frequent sips from his water bottle, while Nina tried to move as little as possible.

Macy, between them on the centre seat, seemed unaffected by the temperature, almost bouncing with anticipation. 'Are we there yet?' she asked, peering at the GPS unit on the dash.

'Another mile,' said Eddie. 'And if you say that one more time, you're walking the rest of the bloody way.'

Through the shimmering air ahead, something took on form – a cliff stretching from one horizon to the other, cut by Nile floods over millions of years. But as they drew closer, Nina picked out a dark slash gouged into it, something shadowed from the pitiless sun. 'Eddie, you see that? Could be our canyon.'

'Could be,' he agreed, heading for it.

They stopped at the canyon mouth. Nina exited and donned a baseball cap, glad to be out of the draining heat of the Land Rover even if it meant exposing herself to the sun's full fury. Something in the canyon wall caught her eye. 'Take a look at this.' The rockface was a pale yellow-grey, sunlight glaring off the sandstone – but in places the reflected light was brighter still, glinting.

'Is that silver?' Eddie asked, making out very fine threads running through the stone.

Macy lowered her sunglasses for a better view. 'Guess that explains the name. You think there's more of it?'

'There must be,' said Nina. 'It'd justify the effort of coming all the way out here. Egypt's got almost no silver deposits, which is why it was considered so valuable back then. Anyone who found a seam would be *very* rich.'

Eddie looked up the canyon, which rose at a shallow angle. The sandy floor was easily wide enough for the Land Rover, only occasional fallen rocks presenting any likely obstacles. 'Think there might be any left? Maybe we could scrape up enough for a silver egg cup or something.'

Nina grinned at the odd image. 'We can see.'

They returned to the 4×4. Eddie carefully guided the Defender up the canyon, dropping them into shadow. Before long the ascent steepened, the turns becoming tighter.

Nina spotted something to one side and told Eddie to stop. 'I think that's our silver mine.' Several roughly rectangular recesses had been dug into the cliff. 'You'll have to live without your egg cup, though. All the best stuff's been taken.'

'Well, arse. Must be the right place, though.'

'I told you,' said Macy. 'We just have to follow the direction of Mercury from the zodiac and we'll find it.'

'I dunno,' Eddie said, sceptical. 'A temple being buried by sand I can go for, maybe even something the size of the Sphinx . . . but a *pyramid*? They're not exactly hard to miss.'

He started the Land Rover again. The ground became even steeper, the walls closing in. The Defender rounded another turn, and entered a tight channel, beyond which was visible nothing but open sky. They had reached the far end of the ravine.

Eddie stopped as they came out of the canyon, checking his compass and the GPS before pointing. 'That's the way the zodiac said to go. Macy, there're some binocs in my rucksack – can you get them for me?'

Macy handed him the binoculars. 'Can you see the pyramid?'

'I spy, with my little eye, something beginning with . . . S.'

'Syramid?'

'Sand,' was Nina's more realistic guess.

Eddie nodded. 'Shitloads of sand, I was going to say, but near enough. How far away is it meant to be?'

'One atur,' said Nina. 'Six point eight-five miles.'

He checked to each side, still finding nothing. 'There's definitely nothing pointy.' He entered new co-ordinates into the GPS. 'If it's there, this should take us right to it.'

They set off again, the vast empty plain opening out all round them. Nina kept watch on the GPS, its display counting down the distance. Four miles, three, two . . . There was still nothing visible ahead, no lost monument rising from the dunes. She looked at Macy. The eagerness on the young woman's face was visibly fading with almost every foot they travelled.

One mile. Still nothing in sight. Eddie gave Nina another glance, his expression warning of impending disappointment. Half a mile. Less. The landscape ahead was indistinguishable from what they had already covered.

The GPS bleeped. 'This is it,' said Eddie, stopping the Land Rover. 'We're here.'

Macy jumped out, turning to see only endless empty desert. 'I . . . I don't get it,' she said, running to the other side of the 4×4 as if expecting to find a different view. 'We followed all the clues, we found the silver canyon . . . why isn't it here?'

Nina put a sympathetic hand on her shoulder as Eddie clambered on to the Land Rover's roof to survey the surrounding plain. 'Hey, it's okay. There might still be parts of it under the sand.'

'Only *parts* of it?'

'This is what archaeology is usually about – it's very, very rare that a completely new site is found intact.'

'They're intact when *you* find them, though.' To Nina's surprise and dismay, Macy seemed on the verge of tears.

'Hey, hey, what's wrong?' she said. 'We haven't even started checking the area yet. We might still find something.'

'No we won't,' Macy stammered. 'There's nothing here. I've wasted your time – I've wasted *everybody's* time, I almost got you both killed, and for nothing! Oh, my God, I'm sorry!'

'What – why are you sorry?' Nina asked helplessly. 'Macy, why are you so upset?'

'Because . . . because Dr Berkeley was right about me! And so was my professor, and so were my teachers at high school . . . and so were you.'

'Right about what?'

Macy couldn't look at her, tears trickling down her cheeks. 'I'm–I'm–I'm worthless,' she managed to say.

'No, you're not,' said Nina, shocked by the young woman's sudden and total collapse of confidence. 'Why would you say that?'

'Because I *am*. I've never had to work for anything in my entire life. I always got whatever I wanted just because I was rich and pretty and popular, and people did things for me.' She bowed her head miserably. 'And the one time, the *one time*, when I really, really try hard to prove I can achieve something myself . . . I completely fail and let everyone down! I let *you* down.'

'You didn't,' said Nina. 'Really, you didn't. You said it yourself – if it hadn't been for you, Osir would have gotten away with the zodiac and nobody would ever have known. And you *have* achieved things for yourself. You got a place on the dig.'

'Only 'cause my mom called in a favour. Oh, God . . .' She finally raised her head. 'I wanted to be like you because I thought you were cool. I never realised how hard you worked, how much you went through. I thought that if I tried to be like you, everything would just come to me like it always did . . . but I was wrong, and now we're in this *fucking* horrible place with nothing to show for it. *Nothing!*'

Nina couldn't think of anything to say. Instead, she put her arms round the sobbing woman, trying to provide some comfort.

'I'm sorry,' Macy mumbled. 'I really am.'

'You don't have to apologise for anything,' Nina assured her. 'And we should still search the area. Maybe there's something to find.'

'There won't be,' she said miserably.

'Oi!' said Eddie, jumping down from the Land Rover. 'Enough with this fucking defeatism, okay? I just got my wife through one bout of it; I'm not having someone else start.'

Nina was about to berate him for his insensitivity when she realised his attitude had changed; his obnoxiousness was a deliberate setup for something. 'What is it?' she asked instead. 'I know that face – you've got something.'

'Yeah, I've got something. It's not a pyramid, but it's man-made.' He pointed northwest. 'Over there.'

Nina saw nothing except more sand and rocks. 'Where?'

He gave her the binoculars and pointed again. 'Those rocks, the ones in a sort of L-shape?'

'Yeah?'

'They're not rocks.'

The magnified view revealed something new. Two large

stones, one flat on the ground touching the base of another poking up from the sands.

Stones . . . with straight edges. Not rocks.

Blocks.

The same size and colour as the ones used to construct the Osireion.

'My God,' Nina gasped. 'It's a building!'

'What's left of one, anyway,' said Eddie.

Macy looked back and forth between Nina and Eddie, wondering if they were playing some cruel joke, before realising they were not. 'Wait, you – you've found something? There's really something here?'

'We were just a bit off course,' Nina told her, giving her the binoculars and pointing out the ruin. Macy gave a little gasp when she saw it. 'See? I told you not to give up, didn't I?'

Macy wiped her eyes. 'Well – well, what are we waiting for?' she said, her hesitant attempt at a smile quickly becoming genuine. She climbed into the Land Rover. 'Come on, let's go!'

'Wow,' said Nina, amused. 'Wish I could bounce back that quickly.'

Eddie put an arm round her shoulders. 'You do all right.'

The two stones revealed themselves as the remains of a small structure, roughly twelve feet by twelve, the other walls barely protruding above the sand. The thickness of the blocks meant the interior was even smaller. If it had once been a dwelling, it would have made a prison cell seem spacious.

Nina had another theory, though. 'It's a marker. There

aren't any natural landmarks, so they had to build one. But what's it marking?'

Macy examined the blocks for further clues. 'Maybe there's another set of directions here.'

Nina shook her head. 'The zodiac text said that after you come out of the silver canyon, the next stop is the actual pyramid.'

'So where is it?' Eddie asked. 'It can't have been buried, can it? I mean, this thing's still sticking up, so unless it's the world's tiniest pyramid we should be able to see *something*.'

'Unless it was buried deliberately.' But she dismissed the idea. The amount of sand needed to completely bury even a small pyramid would be unimaginable.

It was the right place, though. Finding the canyon required specialised knowledge of the Osireion, which would have been limited to a small number of people, and the astronomical calculations needed to deduce the direction of the journey's final leg were the province of even fewer. The pyramid had to be here.

So why couldn't they see it?

It all came back to the zodiac. Nina took out the stolen photo of the ancient relief.

'Doing a bit of astrology?' said Eddie.

'There must be one more clue on here, I'm sure of it.' Macy hopped down to join her as she perused the image. 'Which way's north?'

Eddie checked his compass and pointed. Nina aligned the zodiac with it . . . then flipped the paper over and held it above her head. 'This is how you were meant to view it,' she said. 'Looking up at it – and facing north. The clue's here, it's on the map, it's . . . here!' She brought the chart sharply down, keeping it oriented so that north, which had been ahead of her, was now at the bottom of the page. 'The pyramid marking! Do you see it?'

'Yeah,' said Eddie, 'but what about it? It's just a triangle.'

'Maybe, but which way is it pointing?'

'Down,' said Macy, the implications sinking in a moment later. 'No way!'

Nina smiled. 'Way.'

Eddie frowned at the map. 'Okay, what am I missing?'

'The pyramid on the zodiac, it's upside down,' she told him. 'Don't you see? It's an *inverted* pyramid – and the people who made the map meant it literally. They were representing what was actually here.'

Macy was also caught up in her excitement. 'Some tomb paintings, like Rameses VI's, show the Egyptian Underworld as a mirror world right underneath ours – like a reflection in the Nile. Maybe they built Osiris's pyramid upside down to be an Underworld version of the real ones . . . no, wait, that doesn't work. If the zodiac inside the Sphinx is older than Khafre, it would have to be older than any of the other pyramids.'

'The Pyramid of Osiris isn't an inverted copy of the other pyramids,' Nina realised, breathless. 'The *other* pyramids are inverted copies of the Pyramid of Osiris – they were built above the surface to imitate Osiris's tomb in the Underworld! That's why they put so much effort into matching the shape.'

'Hang on,' said Eddie. 'You're saying they built this pyramid *upside down*?'

Nina scooped a handful of sand from the ground, leaving a roughly conical depression. 'They dug a hole and built the pyramid inside it, with the point at the bottom and working upwards. Or maybe they dug out each new layer below the one they'd just built and filled in the pyramid's core once the outer walls were in place, I don't know. But it wouldn't be any harder than building the Great Pyramid. It might even have been easier – they didn't need to lift any of the stones up, just lower them down. Gravity was on their side.'

'So we're *standing* on it?'

'One way to find out.' She went back to the Defender and took out three shovels. 'Let's get to work.'

'Where?' Macy asked.

Nina indicated the ruin's interior. 'In there. I don't think it's just a marker – it's an entrance.'

They started digging. It was slow going under the baking sun, requiring frequent breaks for water, but after a while Eddie's spade struck something hard. 'Let me see,' Nina said, sweeping away sand with her bare hands. A flat stone slab was revealed.

'Might just be this building's floor,' Eddie cautioned.

'I don't think so. Come on, let's get the rest of it clear.'

They set back to work, Nina now too eager to take any more breaks. By the time they were done, a space just over six feet to a side had been mostly cleared. Nina brushed away more of the gritty covering, finding a narrow crack about a foot in from the wall. She traced its path with her finger; it formed a square. 'It could be a cover stone for the entrance.'

Macy found something else at the slab's centre. 'Look familiar?' she said, wiping away more sand. Revealed in the stone was a carved symbol.

The Eye of Osiris.

'Guess we're in the right place, then,' said Eddie. 'So what now?' The women looked at him. 'Oh, right,' he sighed. 'I get to lift up a two-ton stone block. Bloody marvellous.' But he climbed out of the newly dug pit and returned to the Land Rover for more equipment. 'You,' he said, pointing at Nina as he jumped back down with a long crowbar, 'drink some water. I'm not having you keeling over, all right?'

'All right,' grumbled Nina, who had all but forgotten the heat. She retrieved her water bottle as Eddie examined the slab's outline.

Finding the widest part of the gap, he inserted the crowbar. Straining, he pushed at it. There was a crunch, and the slab shifted slightly. 'Not as heavy as I thought – it'll only give me a *little* hernia,' he said. 'Nina, there's some metal spikes in the Landie. Bring 'em, will you?'

Nina found them. As Eddie levered the slab open little by little, she pushed the tapered spikes into the gradually opening crack so it couldn't fall back down. Before long, a thin line of darkness appeared beneath its lower edge. Eddie moved the Land Rover closer and used the 4×4's winch to raise the slab higher. It rested on an inner lip of stone; grunting, he pushed it up to its tipping point and let it fall back against the wall with a bang.

'There we go,' he said, theatrically wiping dust from his palms. 'Piece of piss.'

'A bit *too* . . . piss piece-y,' said Macy, looking down the hole. 'The entrances to the other pyramids were all hidden.'

Nina had the same thought. 'Either they reckoned the only people who would ever find it were supposed to be here . . . or that's not the only obstacle.'

'You'd better not be saying what I think you're saying,' Eddie growled.

'Afraid I just might be, hon.'

Macy was confused. 'What do you mean?'

'We'll find out soon enough,' Nina said.

They collected their equipment, then, exchanging wary looks, lowered themselves into the hole . . . to become the first people in over six thousand years to enter the Pyramid of Osiris.

22

The floor of the entrance chamber was about eight feet beneath the hole. Sand had seeped through directly below the opening, but beyond it everything was clean.

Almost too clean. There was a stagnant feel to the air. Nothing had moved here since the tomb was sealed, time standing still – or *pausing*, poised, waiting for someone foolish enough to disturb the eternal silence.

Macy shone a flashlight across the walls, revealing the chamber as somewhat larger than the structure above. 'Hieroglyphics,' she said, stepping closer. 'Huh.'

'What?' Nina asked, joining her. 'Can you read them?'

'Just about, but they're weird-looking. They must be really old.'

'They're beautiful, though.' Nina slowly moved the beam of her own light along the white wall. The hieroglyphs were as clear and colourful as the day they had been painted, figures from Egyptian mythology standing amongst the text. She recognised some of them as gods: Ra, the sun-god, creator of all things; Nut, goddess of the sky, her naked body arched to form a vault over the entire earth.

But there was one god missing. 'No Osiris.' The key figure of ancient Egyptian religion was conspicuous by his absence.

'No Horus, either,' Macy added. 'Or Set, or Isis. Not even Anubis, and since he's the god of tombs, you'd kind of expect him to be here.'

'They were all contemporaries of Osiris, or his children,' Nina reasoned. 'They hadn't been deified yet. Which means this place really does pre-date the Old Kingdom – Osiris and the others were already worshipped as gods by 3000 BC.'

'I was right,' said Macy. 'Yay me!'

Eddie explored another part of the chamber. 'Got a doorway here.' A pair of decorated pillars marked the exit. 'There're some stairs. Pretty steep.'

'Let's hold on – this room might tell us something useful.'

Macy examined the texts. 'Freaky,' she said. 'They're lists of all the trials that newlydeads have to go through in the Underworld. Like the Pyramid Texts and the Coffin Texts.'

'They sound cheerful,' Eddie commented.

'Earlier versions of the Egyptian Book of the Dead,' Nina told him.

'Oh, perfect bedtime reading. By Stephenkingmun, was it?'

Macy giggled, then returned her attention to the walls. 'What I don't get is that in the other texts, all this stuff is basically prayers telling you how to get through each *arit*, each land, of the Underworld. Like instructions – if you haven't sinned and you do what it says in the texts, you'll get through all the trials to meet Osiris. This is written differently, though.'

'How so?' Nina asked.

Macy pointed out one section. 'This is talking about the first *arit* of the House of Osiris. When you go in, you have to face the Lady of Tremblings, one of the guardians of the Underworld. But it only really says that she's bad news, "the Lady of Destruction". In the Book of the Dead it also says that she'll deliver the person going through the Underworld *from* destruction if they're doing things right – I remember it, because I thought the idea of being the Lady of Destruction was neat. Kinda metal.'

Eddie nudged Nina. 'You know all about being the Lady of Destruction, don't you?'

She huffed. 'Only accidentally. But the second part's not in this text?'

'Not that I can see,' Macy said. 'It's more like a warning than a prayer. There's nothing about how to actually get through the *arit*.'

'Oh, man!' Nina complained, looking at Eddie. 'You know what that sounds like, don't you?'

'Booby traps,' they said together.

Nina put a hand to her face. 'Just once, just goddamn *once*,' she moaned, 'I'd like to find an incredible archaeological site that's not filled with Rube Goldberg death machines. Is that too much to ask? No collapsing ceilings, no crushing devices, no frickin' *cherubims* waving swords at me!'

Macy was intrigued. 'Cherubims? As in angels?'

'Long story,' said Eddie. 'Okay, so we've got to get past the Lady of Tremblings. What else?'

Macy spent several minutes searching through the hieroglyphics. 'The Lake of Fire – or Devourer by Fire, it's talking about the same thing,' she reported. 'The Lady of Rainstorms. The Lady of Might, who "tramples on those who should not be here", sheesh. The Goddess of the Loud Voice—'

'Nina, they wrote about you!' Eddie put in.

'Well, yeah, I *am* a goddess.'

'I can just leave, if you like,' Macy said peevishly, before turning back to the ancient text. 'So we've got the Goddess of the Loud Voice, the Hewer-in-Pieces in Blood, and then the last thing before you reach Osiris is the Cutter-off of Heads. Real subtle. They're all mentioned in the Book of the Dead, but these descriptions are a bit hinky.'

'It's the other way round,' said Nina thoughtfully. 'The prayers in the Book of the Dead came *from* these – this was the source. The booby traps built to protect Osiris's tomb eventually became part of the religion.'

'We might need more than prayers to get past something called the Hewer-in-fucking-Pieces,' Eddie said, shining his light down the sloping passage. 'There's nothing helpful?'

'Doesn't look like it,' Macy replied. 'The other text's mostly "Osiris is awesome!" kinda stuff. Lots of curses, too. "Desecrate the tomb of Osiris and suffer a thousand agonising deaths", yadda yadda.'

'I don't want to suffer *one* agonising death,' said Nina, joining Eddie. The passage was also decorated, more Egyptian gods ominously watching anyone who dared traverse it. 'Think we can make it through?'

'Depends what state the traps are in,' Eddie said. 'Doesn't

look like anyone's been here before us, so there's no chance Indy or Lara'll have set them off already – but after this long, they might not still be working.'

'Right, like we're ever that lucky.' Nina looked back at Macy. 'What do you think?'

She seemed surprised to be asked. 'Me? I dunno, it's your decision.'

'It's your life,' Nina countered.

Macy considered it. 'I came this far,' she said. 'And you've both kept me in one piece, so let's do it!' She was about to start down the steps when Eddie grabbed her.

'Just one thing,' he said, pulling her back. 'Stay *behind* us, okay?'

The passage descended into the inverted pyramid, making two ninety-degree turns before a pair of ornate pillars marked the entrance to another chamber. 'It's the first *arit*,' said Macy, nervous.

Eddie directed his torch beam into the darkness. 'It's big,' he said. 'Deep, too.'

'A shaft?' Nina asked.

'Right on.' He cautiously advanced on to a little ledge. The shaft's ceiling was about thirty feet overhead, and below it dropped out of sight beyond the range of his light. Two large pipes made from hand-beaten sheets of oxidised copper ran down the height of the far wall, on which was painted a giant female figure, but he was more interested in another object – a long stone beam, extending across the shaft to another ledge on the far side.

'That doesn't look safe,' said Nina. The beam was less than a foot wide, and precariously perched.

Eddie moved to get a better look at the slab's sides. 'You're not kidding. Look at them.' He illuminated the far end, revealing thick carved protrusions and also mechanisms built into the opposite ledge – two large stone cogwheels.

Metal shone dully in Nina's flashlight beam as she directed it above the cogs. 'They're connected to something up there.' A large cylindrical piece of stone hung on a chain from a pulley.

'Think we found our Lady of Tremblings,' said Eddie. 'The weight drops down on the chain and turns the cogs – and they bang against those lumps on the bridge and make it shake.'

'So what sets it off?' Macy asked.

Nina smiled grimly. 'We do. There must be a trigger on the bridge – too much weight, and there's a whole lotta shakin' going on.'

'How do we get across, then?'

'By holding on really tight,' said Eddie, taking a rope from his pack. 'There's only so much chain, so once the weight gets to the end, it'll stop. If I tie myself to the bridge, I should be okay.'

Nina wasn't so sure. 'And what if the entire bridge falls and takes you with it?'

'Then I'll die like Captain Kirk!' Seeing that she was still unhappy, he went on, 'It's either that or stand here wishing we'd brought a twenty-foot plank.'

'You'd better hold on really, *really* tight, okay?'

Eddie looped the rope's end round the bridge, then tied it to his body. 'Okay, here we go,' he muttered, putting a wary foot on the slab.

Nothing happened. It seemed secure and solid. Kneeling,

he pushed the rope a couple of feet across the span before crawling to catch up, then repeating the process. Nina watched nervously.

Halfway across, three-quarters . . .

The slab shifted.

'Oh, shit,' he gasped, clinging tightly to the stone as the chain rattled—

And stopped, the links chinking before falling silent.

'What happened?' an anxious Nina called.

He raised his head. 'Dunno, but I'm happy about it!' He quickly crossed the last few feet, then untied himself and looked round. A large crack ran up one wall. Several chunks of stone had broken loose, and one had come to rest wedged beneath a cogwheel's tooth, preventing it from turning. He tested the stone to see if it was secure. It moved slightly, but the weight bearing down on it held it in place.

'Crawl across one at a time,' he said. 'And *slowly*.'

Nina crossed first, followed by Macy. 'Earthquake damage?' Nina mused, examining the crack. 'Or maybe it's just structural stress.'

'Egyptian builders,' Eddie joked, helping Macy up.

'As opposed to British builders?' she said indignantly. 'What have you got that's stood up for thousands of years?'

'Stonehenge?'

She pouted. 'Okay, I'll give you that. But it's still not as cool as the pyramids!'

Nina saw another descending passage beyond the exit, this one with a sloping floor rather than steps. 'What was in the next *arit*?'

'The Lake of Fire,' Macy remembered. 'Or the Devourer by Fire.'

'Either way, fire,' said Eddie. 'Great. Just what we want in a confined space.'

'The last trap was broken,' Nina said, indicating the rock jamming the mechanism. 'Maybe we'll get lucky again.'

He groaned as he started down the slope. 'Why'd you have to say that? You've just jinxed it!'

The incline was steep enough to be awkward, slowing their progress. The passage made more ninety-degree turns; Nina realised their descent followed a roughly spiral path, making her wonder if the copper pipes in the shaft were connected to another chamber below. Eventually, more ornate pillars marked another room.

Eddie sniffed the air. 'Funny smell. Not sure what, but I don't like it.'

He illuminated the chamber. It was large and rectangular with another exit at the far end, the walls sloping inwards to the roof about fifteen feet above. There were several holes in the ceiling. One of them was large and chimney-like, but it was the smaller ones that immediately made him suspicious: something was clearly supposed to drop out of them.

Except for a relief of a greyhound-faced god watching from one wall, the only objects in the room were several large globe-shaped copper bowls near the entrance. Directly ahead was a square hole in the dusty floor, about three feet across, which turned out to be a pool of some liquid; there was a matching pool by the far doorway. The rest of the floor between the two pools was fractionally lower than the section where they were standing, the perfectly flat expanse stretching the entire width of the chamber.

'Oh, something is *so* wrong with this picture,' Nina said.

It was obviously another booby trap, but she couldn't see the danger. 'Where's the fire?'

'Maybe it went out,' Macy offered hopefully, advancing for a better look at the snarling god.

'Stay still,' Eddie warned as he crouched by the pool and hesitantly dipped a finger in the liquid. 'Just water.' He shone his torch into it, noticing that the pool was only walled on three sides. 'Four feet deep, maybe. Looks like it connects to the hole at the other end.'

'A tunnel?' said Nina. 'Weird. Why not just walk across?'

'You really think it's going to be that easy?'

'Not even for a second. What's that?' She turned her flashlight to something between the hole and the lowered area, a bow-taut length of fine black twine running from floor to ceiling.

'Something I'm not planning on touching,' said Eddie. He directed his light into the tunnel. 'It's threaded across it. You want to go through, you've got to break it.'

'Which I think would be an extraordinarily bad idea, don't you?' Her attention switched to the expanse at the room's centre, where she noticed more threads reaching up to the ceiling – and an *absence* of something. 'You see what's missing?'

'What?' Macy asked, moving to the edge of the small step.

'Gaps. There aren't any lines marking the edges of different slabs. It's like one giant block of stone.'

Eddie examined the walls. 'Biggest blocks here look about six feet by ten. But that floor's easily thirty feet long. It can't be all one slab, can it?'

'I don't see how.' Nina looked round – to see Macy about to take an experimental step. 'No, wait—'

Macy put her foot down on the floor – and it went *through* it.

She yelped, almost pitching forward before Nina grabbed her. 'What the *hell*?' Macy gasped as she hopped back, glutinous strands stretching from her boot's sole to the sluggishly rippling 'hole' in what a moment ago had looked like solid stone. She tried to scrape the substance off. 'Gross! What *is* this?'

'Oil,' said Eddie, coming over. He dipped his hand into what was now revealed as a large pool, disguised beneath a layer of sand. The same thick goo dripped slowly off his fingers when he lifted them out. 'This crap's floating on top of the water, and then they sprinkled all this sand over it to make it look like part of the floor.'

Nina looked up at the holes in the ceiling. 'And I bet if you break those threads, something up there catches light and drops into the oil. *Whoomph!* Roasted robbers.'

Macy rubbed her sole across the floor, disgusted. 'So how do you get across without setting off the trap?'

'Swim under it,' said Eddie, pointing at the water pool, which was clear of the oil. 'The fire'll only be on the surface.'

'It can't be that easy,' Nina said, regarding the faux floor with suspicion. She looked round at the odd copper bowls, and shone her light into one. 'Ah-ha.'

'What is it?' asked Macy.

'There's something inside.' Nina reached into the globe and gripped a handle fixed to its bottom – or, she realised as she lifted it up, its top. 'Know what I think this is?' She lowered it over her head until it touched her shoulders. 'It's a diving helmet!' she announced, voice echoing.

Eddie knocked on it, drawing a yip of complaint. 'You won't get much air in there.'

She lifted it again. 'You don't need to. Just enough to get across.' She gestured at the pool. 'I don't think the holes are connected by a tunnel – they're just ways to get in and out of the pool without touching the oil. Once the rim of this thing is under the surface there'll be air trapped inside it so you can breathe, and then as long as you don't raise it high enough to let in any oil you won't get burned. Then you go through the tunnel into the water hole at the other end, climb out, and hey! You're across.'

Eddie sceptically examined another globe. 'It's too thin to keep the heat out for long.'

'It's the only way to get across without being fried. I'm pretty sure there'll be something to stop people just swimming straight there under the oil.' She held up the primitive helmet. 'I don't think we have a choice.'

Eddie made an aggrieved noise as he shook his head, but acquiesced. 'Okay. But I'll go first.'

'No, I will,' Nina insisted. 'If there are any obstacles under there and I bang into them, I'll need you to tell me which way to go.'

'Are you sure about this?'

'No,' she admitted, going to the water pool. She hesitantly dipped a foot under the surface, then steeled herself and slipped all the way in. 'Oh, ew. I just realised this water's been sitting here for thousands of years.'

'Just don't drink it,' said Eddie. 'Although you could say that about *any* water in Egypt!'

Nina carefully crouched until her head was just above the surface, then reached up to take the helmet from Eddie, gripping the internal handle firmly.

'Last chance to let me go instead,' Eddie said.

'I'll be fine,' she replied as he gave her the globe. 'Hopefully.' Bringing it down to rest on her shoulders, she submerged.

The helmet took a surprising amount of effort to hold down, wanting to float. The water level rose alarmingly as the air inside was compressed, but stopped just short of her nostrils. Acutely aware of her limited oxygen supply, she dropped as low as she could and shuffled into the tunnel. The helmet scraped against its ceiling.

Something tugged across her chest, a momentary resistance . . . then it was gone.

She had broken the thread.

Eddie and Macy reacted in alarm as a scraping sound echoed from overhead. 'What is it?' Macy asked, trying to pinpoint the source.

'Sounds like a lighter,' Eddie began, before the sound's meaning struck him. 'Shit! Nina, you're going to have a fire any second!'

He stared at the ceiling in horror as the sound spread, ancient rollers grinding against metal, producing sparks . . .

Lights flared in the small holes.

Something dropped from one, a wad of cloth trailing a thin line of grey smoke. Only a small piece of it had caught light, the glow barely more than an ember . . .

But it was enough.

The cloth hit the surface, the dusty oil rippling around it. For a moment nothing happened – then a flame leapt up, rapidly expanding outwards. More pieces of cloth fell. Many were unlit, the sparks not having caught the material, but it only needed a few for the surface of the entire pool to erupt.

A lake of fire, just as the hieroglyphics had warned.

And Nina was in it.

She emerged from the short tunnel. The echo of her breathing and the almost total darkness were unnerving . . . but not nearly so much as the sudden light. The pool's floor lit up in rippling orange as the floating oil ignited – and she almost immediately felt the heat, the handle she was clutching warming with alarming speed.

'Oh, shit. *Big* mistake. Huge,' she gasped. Forced to crouch, the best she could manage was an awkward waddle, the water slowing her movements to a slow-motion nightmare.

But this was no nightmare. It was real.

Eddie watched, appalled, as fire surrounded the slowly moving globe. Oil had stuck to it when Nina surfaced, and that too caught light, turning the helmet into a spherical torch. 'Jesus! Nina, turn round! Get back in the tunnel!'

But she could barely hear him, the crackle of flames consuming all other sounds. Filled with fear, she pressed on. The pool was only thirty feet long. It wouldn't take long to cross.

Would it?

Another step, then another. Water lapped at her nostrils, making her splutter. Glancing through the globe's open bottom, she noticed markings on the floor. Hieroglyphs, the Eye of Osiris among them. They almost certainly served a purpose, but she had no time to think what it might be.

The heat coming through the handle was becoming

uncomfortable. Not painful, yet – but it wouldn't take long—

The helmet clanged against something.

Shocked, Nina almost let go of the globe. She tugged it back down and groped ahead with her other hand, finding a stone block that rose almost to the surface. As she'd feared, the pyramid's builders had ensured that nobody could simply swim straight across below the fire.

She moved crab-like to the left, feeling for the block's edge. Her fingers found nothing but flat stone. Another couple of steps. Still nothing. She forced herself to slow her breathing, trying to conserve her limited air.

Oh, God, what if the Egyptians had built a *maze*? If she went into a dead end . . .

There had to be a way through. If the builders had wanted to stop anyone from ever reaching Osiris's tomb, they could have filled in every tunnel. The 'right' people, the priests who turned a king into a god, would have known the path. She just had to find it.

Quickly. Very quickly.

The hieroglyphs . . .

Holding her breath, she tipped her head down into the water. The markings on the floor shimmered in the hellish light from the surface. She had no idea what they said, but the Eye of Osiris was a repeated symbol, its dark iris staring blankly back at her from each.

Except for one.

That iris looked to the left, along the length of the stone slab.

She followed it, hand still outstretched. The handle was now on the verge of actual pain. She flexed her fingers, trying to stave off the moment when it became too hot to bear.

Her other hand was still rubbing against flat stone, stretching on, and on—

A corner!

She gripped the edge, pulling herself round it. A look down revealed another Eye of Osiris, this time gazing 'up' towards the chamber's far end. She went in that direction, quickening her pace. A second upward-looking eye, then one pointing her back to the right.

The smoke from the burning oil swirled up the chimney, but the room's temperature was rising. Arms raised to shield his face from the heat, Eddie watched the globe slide through the flames on a seemingly random path. It was over halfway across, but there couldn't be much air left.

Nina was now fixated entirely on following the trail of eyes. The air was becoming foul – and hot.

Another eye. Forwards. Pain rose in her fingers. How much further? Her chest felt tighter with every breath, a groggy sensation washing over her.

Still another eye, directing her to the right. Her fingers were burning, her trembling hand shaking the globe. A bubble of air escaped from the rim, water rising to replace it.

The next eye looked up – and she caught a glimpse of shadow ahead.

The other tunnel!

She pulled the globe back below the surface, ducking as low as she could to force herself through the low passage. The helmet clanged like a bell as it bumped against the stone. Just a few more steps . . .

The air in the globe popped it sharply upwards as Nina cleared the tunnel and her burned fingers lost their grip. Stagnant water hit her face. She coughed, trying to stand. Her legs had turned to rubber. She fell against one side of the little pool, hands scrabbling weakly for the edge above.

They found it. She pulled herself up, whooping for breath as she cleared the surface.

'She made it!' Macy cried.

'Thank Christ,' Eddie said. 'Nina! Are you okay?'

She made out his voice over the rumble and snap of fire. 'Super fine,' she croaked, giving him a weak thumbs-up. 'There's a path on the bottom of the pool. The Eyes of Osiris look in the direction you've got to go – just follow them!'

Eddie rubbed an ear. 'Did you get that?'

'Follow the direction the Eyes of Osiris are looking on the pool floor,' Macy paraphrased. 'Couldn't you hear her?'

'My ears are getting a bit dodgy,' he admitted. 'Too many explosions.' He surveyed the pool. Nina's path was clearly visible, a weaving line of disturbed oil. 'I'll go next,' he told Macy, giving her one of the helmets. 'You get in right behind me, and keep hold of my jacket.'

He lowered himself into the pool, took several deep breaths to get more oxygen into his system, then submerged and duck-walked into the short tunnel. Macy hesitated, then slipped in behind him and took hold of his jacket's hem.

Knowing what to look for allowed them to make the crossing more quickly than Nina – though the handle inside Eddie's helmet was still painfully hot by the time he reached the other pool. He stood and tossed the globe aside, breathing deeply as Nina helped him out. 'Ow, bugger,' he said, swishing his scorched fingers in the water. 'And that was my wanking hand, too.'

'Oh, *Eddie*,' Nina chided. 'Anyway, I should be enough for you.'

'Well, we've got a fire, we just need a rug . . .'

Macy burst out of the water. 'Oh, my God!' she gasped, glowering at the lake of flames. The floating oil had now been mostly consumed, the fire dying down. 'What kind of twisted bastard would think up something like that?'

'You have to wonder,' said Nina as she checked that her waterproof flashlight had lived up to its advertising. 'But you know what's really worrying me?'

'What?'

'There are five more *arits* to go.'

'I can't wait,' Eddie said sarcastically, running his hands over his clothes to squeeze out the water. 'So what's next?'

'The Lady of Rainstorms,' said Macy, following his example.

'Great. Like we're not wet enough already.' Dripping, they entered the next sloping passage.

23

The tunnel spiralled deeper into the pyramid. More Egyptian gods adorned the walls, warning of certain death for intruders.

Nina was less concerned about supernatural threats than physical ones. Experience had given her painful first-hand lessons that the more grand and important an ancient edifice, the more sadistically ingenious the traps protecting it.

And the Pyramid of Osiris was *very* grand and important.

Pillars marking the next *arit* appeared in her flashlight beam – but there was no new chamber beyond them, the steep passage continuing. 'I just realised something,' said Eddie. 'This'll take us underneath the room we were just in.'

Nina mentally backtracked through the turns. 'Think it'll be a problem?'

'Well, the next trap's about rainstorms, and we'll have a big pool of water right over our heads.'

'Good point.' She directed her light at the ceiling. Unlike

the painted walls, it was just blocks of plain stone. 'I don't see any holes.'

Eddie performed his own examination. 'Ceiling looks okay . . . but these are new.' He turned his light to the floor. On each side against the wall were recessed channels, about four inches wide and somewhat deeper.

'They look like gutters,' Macy observed.

'Nothing like 'em up there,' said Eddie, looking back past the pillars. 'Yeah, I think we're going to get wet again.'

'But what's it going to do?' Nina asked. 'Turn the place into a giant waterslide of death?'

'Don't give them ideas,' said Macy, with a nervous glance at the watching gods.

'This is the only way down,' said Eddie, 'so we'll find out sooner or later. Unless you want to turn round – ah, who am I kidding? I shouldn't even bother asking.'

'It *would* be a waste to give up after getting this far,' Nina pointed out with a smile. 'Besides, the first trap was broken, and we got through the second one without too much trouble.'

'Oh, yeah,' he snorted, holding up his reddened hand, 'wading through a lake of fire was a doddle!'

'Okay, a *little* trouble. But we've been through worse. So long as we keep our heads, we'll be fine.'

Macy raised a finger. 'You remember that the final trap was called the Cutter-*off* of Heads, right?'

'Then we'll duck!' She shone her flashlight down the slope. The passage continued in a straight line for some distance. 'We'll just be really careful and take things slow, okay?'

Eddie put a hand on her damp shoulder. 'Okay, squishy. But I'm definitely going first, okay?'

'Lead on, squashy,' she replied, clapping a hand to his butt.

'Get a room,' Macy muttered. 'Or get a *tomb*! Ha!' Nina and Eddie both groaned. 'What, he's the only one allowed to make jokes?'

'That's 'cause all mine are good,' said Eddie as he started down the slope.

Nina followed. 'That's a matter of opinion, honey.'

'Tchah.' His expression became more serious as he went on, alternating his torch beam between the floor and the roof. Something caught his eye, and he stopped. 'Ay up,' he said, indicating part of the ceiling. 'The gaps between the blocks are getting bigger.'

Nina ran a fingertip along the joint. Fine dust trickled out. 'The mortar's crumbled.'

Macy bit her lip. 'Just what you want when you've got giant stone blocks right above you, huh?'

'Definitely take it slow,' Nina suggested as Eddie set off again.

He nodded, noticing that the apparent shoddy workmanship continued along the ceiling – and also the floor. 'Whatever this Lady of Rainstorms business is,' he said, 'I think she's about to piss down on us any sec—'

The paving slab beneath his foot dropped slightly.

Everyone froze. From behind the walls came a faint clicking, a domino effect working upwards to knock out a final trigger . . .

A hollow clonk, wood being hit with metal – then an unmistakable rushing noise.

Water.

'Bollocks,' Eddie just had time to say before streams

gushed from the cracks in the ceiling.

The downpour emerged from about a thirty-foot stretch of the roof, growing in strength – but not nearly enough to sweep anybody away down the slope. 'I don't get it,' Nina said. 'This couldn't hurt anyone.'

'This isn't the trap,' Eddie said with alarm. He pointed down the passage. '*That's* the trap!'

She saw the cracks in the floor widening rapidly as the water rushed over them. 'Oh, crap. Forget taking things slow – *run*!'

The substance binding the blocks together wasn't mortar or cement. It was a mixture of sand and finely crushed limestone, just barely strong enough to hold everything in place . . . and now being rapidly eaten away as the limestone dissolved and the sand was washed out by the flowing water. The slabs shifted, clonking against each other as the trio raced over them, sinking—

And falling.

With the fragile binding disappearing, the floor did the same. Slabs dropped away into a deep pit below.

And as each slab plunged, the remainder became even weaker.

Eddie realised the gutters were staying intact, but they were too narrow to traverse – especially at a run. 'Get ahead of me!' he yelled. He was the heaviest of the group – if he went through the floor, they all would.

'I can't!' Nina shouted from behind. 'Just go, *go*!'

With a colossal boom, the entire upper end of the sabotaged floor collapsed into the pit. The flood turned into a waterfall, dropping after it, but the damage had already been done. The remaining stones tumbled one after the other into the void, a ripple gaining rapidly on the running figures.

'There!' Eddie shouted. The water sweeping down the slope had revealed the last line of weakened blocks – and beyond them, the floor was reassuringly solid. 'Just a few more yards, come on!'

He dived as the blocks under him shifted, landing hard just past the corroding section. Nina also made a flying leap, barely staying on her feet as she bounded over her husband.

Behind her, Macy started to jump—

The last slabs fell away under her.

She screamed – then the scream was knocked out of her as she fell short and slammed against the newly exposed edge of the pit.

Her torch rolled down the passage as she clawed at the wet floor, unable to find a foothold on the sheer wall. Her elbows slipped over the brink, wrists—

Eddie grabbed her hand just as she lost her grip. 'Nina!' he gasped as Macy's weight crushed his knuckles against the stone edge. 'Get her other hand!'

Nina scrambled back up the slope, seeing Macy flailing below. She reached out for her other hand. 'Macy! Here!'

The young woman looked up at her, terrified. 'Please don't let me fall!'

'You're not gonna fall,' Nina promised. Their fingers touched – then slipped apart.

Eddie was losing his hold. 'Nina, come on . . .' he begged.

Nina dropped to her knees, leaned out over the abyss – and lunged.

This time, she caught Macy's wrist. Straining, almost overbalancing, she hauled her up – taking just enough pressure off Eddie for him to bring round his other arm. 'Got her!' he barked. 'Pull!'

Leaning back, Nina pulled with all her strength. Eddie forced himself upright and dragged her up. She cleared the edge, and all three fell over, Macy landing on top of Eddie.

Nina sat up. 'You okay?' she asked Macy, who nodded. 'Good. Now get off my husband.'

Macy's chest was on Eddie's face. 'I'm fine with it,' he joked, muffled, before helping her off him.

'Thank you,' she whispered, shaking.

A low, crackling rumble made them all look up. 'Don't thank us yet,' said Nina. She aimed her flashlight at the ceiling, and saw water leaking from more cracks above them. 'Come on!'

They jumped up and ran down the slope—

An entire section of ceiling smashed to the floor where they had just been – and thousands of gallons of water followed, the remaining contents of the pool above bursting out. The deluge exploded down the passage after them.

No way to outrun it—

Macy was scooped off her feet as the churning maelstrom caught her, crashing against Nina and Eddie as they too were swept down the passage. They bounced painfully off the walls and floor, pieces of shattered stone pummelling them.

And there was a new sound audible even over the frothing thunder – a rhythmic pounding, growing louder . . .

Macy's flashlight had been caught by the wave's leading edge, a glowing point spinning ahead of them. Eddie saw movement, something rising up past another set of pillars –

then the light vanished, crushed flat as the object slammed down with a monstrous boom. 'Shit!' he yelled as they were carried inexorably towards it. 'Grab on to me!'

Nina clutched his arm, Macy a leg as he jammed his other heel into a gutter. The force of the torrent was too great for him to stop them, but he could slow them just enough to pass through the pillars while the crusher was moving upwards.

If his brief glimpse had been enough for him to judge its timing . . .

Another echoing slam of impact. He raised his foot—

They whipped between the columns, hitting a flat floor. Something huge plunged at Eddie's head—

The crusher smashed down an inch behind him as the water flung him into the chamber beyond. The room was much wider than the passage, the wavefront quickly spreading out and losing its power. The three unwilling watersliders were deposited on the floor, coughing and flapping like beached fish.

The crusher kept pounding, slowing down. Nina retrieved her flashlight and shone it at the source of the noise. It was a stone block, painted with the figure of a woman raising her feet as if stamping on ants. The gutters had channelled the flood into a pair of water wheels; not large enough to power the crusher itself, but capable of tripping some mechanism. 'I guess that's our Lady of Might,' she said, wiping wet hair off her face. 'She really does try to "trample on those who should not be here".'

'Women with big feet, not my thing,' said Eddie tiredly. The heavy tools in his pack had bashed against his back, bruising him. 'Is everyone okay?'

Macy stood as the crusher juddered to a standstill. 'Not feeling so good,' she admitted. She held up her hands, unable to stop them shaking. 'Oh, God, I think I'm gonna puke.'

Eddie stood in front of her, resting his hands on her upper arms. 'Hey, you're okay. And you're not going to puke. Know why?'

She looked into his eyes, uncertain. 'No?'

' 'Cause you'd puke on me! And then we'd have to have words, and that'd be bad all round. So you're going to be fine.' He smiled. It took a few moments before Macy managed to respond in kind, and then only faintly, but it was at least genuine.

Nina smiled as well. 'It's okay, Macy. We beat this trap – *two* traps, actually.'

'Yeah, but there're another three to come,' she glumly reminded them.

'Four-nil to us, so far,' said Eddie, searching for the next exit. Another passage, this one stepped, led downwards. 'And I bet we can make it seven-nil. This Osiris bloke can shove his traps right up his mummified arse!' A grin broke through on to Macy's face.

'Okay, so the next *arit* was the Goddess of the Loud Voice, right?' Nina asked. Macy nodded. 'Let's see if we can shout her down.'

At the entrance to the inverted pyramid, nothing moved except for sand drifting in the breeze. The Land Rover waited silently for its passengers to return, no sound disturbing the emptiness of the desert.

Then . . . a noise came from the northeast.

Growing louder.

A cloud appeared on the horizon, dust swirling through the shimmering heat haze. But it was not a sandstorm. It was too small – and moving with purpose. Heading directly for the ruins.

Something became visible through the rippling air, a slab-like grey and black shape. The noise increased, a roaring thrum of powerful engines and the rasp of whirling propeller blades.

But this was no aircraft.

Sebak Shaban gazed through the bridge windows of the massive hovercraft, a Zubr class assault vehicle designed to carry tanks and other armoured vehicles over almost any terrain. After observing the abilities of the four Zubrs bought by the Greek navy, the Egyptians had recently decided to follow the example of their friend/rival across the Mediterranean and purchase two of the enormous craft from Russia.

Officially, this Zubr was currently undergoing trials before entering full service. That it was almost one hundred kilometres from the isolated desert range where said trials were supposed to be taking place was down to one of the other men on the bridge. 'I like this a lot,' said Shaban to General Tarik Khaleel. 'When the plan is successful, perhaps you could loan one to the Temple. Though I'm not sure where we would park it.'

'Anywhere you want, my friend!' laughed Khaleel. 'And if anyone complains, it has rocket launchers and Gatling guns.' He nodded at the turrets on the foredeck below. 'It's amazing how quickly people shut up when you point a six-barrelled cannon at them.'

'The threat of death is always persuasive, isn't it?' Both men shared sly, knowing smiles. 'How much further?'

'Just under two kilometres,' said the pilot.

'Good.' Shaban entered the weapons room behind the bridge. 'We are approaching the co-ordinates,' he announced. As well as a member of the Zubr's crew, the room contained Osir, Diamondback, Dr Hamdi . . . and the group's newest addition.

'Dr Berkeley,' Osir asked the IHA archaeologist, 'are you absolutely sure they're correct?'

'As sure as I can be,' said Logan Berkeley, annoyed at being doubted. 'The inverted pyramid on the zodiac, the marking representing the Nile, the symbol in the Osireion, the position of Mercury relative to the end of the canyon – it all fits together.' He indicated his laptop, which in one window displayed a satellite image of the desert overlaid with lines marking distances and directions, a photo of the Eye of Osiris inside the Osireion pulled from the IHA's massive Egyptian database in another. 'Either the Pyramid of Osiris is here, or it's somewhere that'll never be found.'

'I hope it's the former,' said Shaban, with a menacing undercurrent.

Berkeley's annoyance increased. 'I'll do what I'm being paid for,' he snapped, 'so there's no need to threaten me.' He looked at Osir. 'It's funny. If you'd tried to buy me off a week ago, I would never have accepted. Now? I just want to get something out of the whole fiasco at the Sphinx.' His face clenched with anger. 'I should have been on the front page of every newspaper in the world, but that *bitch* Nina Wilde turned me into a joke. At least the money will make up for some of that.'

The weapons officer called Khaleel into the room to point out something on a monitor. Osir raised an eyebrow. 'Funny that you should mention Dr Wilde.'

'Why?'

'Because I think she's beaten you again.' The screen displayed an image from one of the hovercraft's targeting systems; the Land Rover would have been unmissable against the blank plain even without the cursor the weaponry computer had locked on to it.

'What? God *damn* it!' Berkeley glared at the monitor. Diamondback sniggered.

'Who is this Dr Wilde?' Khaleel asked.

'A competitor,' Osir told him. He looked more closely at the ruins. 'But she may have done us a favour. There's nobody there, so she must have found a way in. We won't need to use all those bulldozers and diggers we brought after all!'

He went into the bridge, Khaleel, Shaban and Diamondback joining him. Ahead, the faded yellow void of the desert was broken by the spot of colour that was the Defender. The pilot eased back the throttle to slow the 500-ton hovercraft, the three huge propellers above its stern losing speed. 'Your men,' Osir quietly asked Khaleel. 'Are they totally reliable? If one word of this gets back to the government . . .'

'I will vouch for Tarik,' said Shaban firmly. 'I owe him my life.'

'And I will vouch for my men,' added Khaleel. 'We only have a skeleton crew, but I hand-picked them. They will keep your secret . . . for the price you're paying, certainly.'

'Good.' Osir looked back at the ruins as the Zubr

wallowed to a stop, settling on its huge rubber air cushion in a cloud of billowing sand. 'Let's find Osiris . . . and Nina Wilde.'

24

'Wow,' said Nina, aiming her flashlight upwards and finding no end to the black void above. 'That's *tall*.'

'You know where we are?' Eddie said, indicating the two pipes running down the far wall. 'Right under that bridge. If the trap'd been working and we'd been chucked off, this is where we would have ended up. It's at least a two-hundred-foot drop. Splat.'

Nina tried to picture the whole pyramid in her mind's eye. 'Jeez. This place must be as big as the Great Pyramid. Maybe even bigger.'

'That'd explain why nobody tried to out-do Khufu's pyramid,' said Macy thoughtfully. 'If the Great Pyramid was almost, but not quite, as big as Osiris's, no other pharaoh could make their monument bigger than Khufu's without insulting Osiris. And nobody would dare do that.'

'So the pyramids were really just giant dick-waving exercises?' asked Eddie. 'People haven't changed much over five thousand years, have they?' He turned his attention to the pipes. They were connected, one narrowing considerably at its base before widening out conically below a broad horizontal slot. A woman's face had been painted around it, the opening forming her mouth.

'It's like a church organ,' Nina realised. 'They must blow air through it somehow – and that's where the loud voice comes from.'

'If they dropped something down the other tube, it'd work like a piston.' There was another passage near the pipes, this one blocked by a barred metal gate. 'Let me guess. Try to open the gate, the trap goes off, and the whole room gets as loud as a Led Zep concert.'

'The who?' Macy asked.

'No, Led Zep.' Ignoring her blank look, he moved towards the opening.

'Careful, Eddie,' Nina warned.

'Don't worry, I'm not gonna move it. I just want to find the trigger.'

'No, I meant the gate might not *be* the—'

A slab shifted beneath his foot.

'—trigger,' Nina concluded.

'Get into the other tunnel!' Eddie shouted, turning back the way they had come—

A second gate slammed down inside the entrance, making Macy jump. No sooner had its echo faded than another sound began to rise, a deep, mournful note, quickly becoming louder.

And louder.

Air gusted from the slot, the sound resonating up the pipe's length and bouncing back, amplified. The whole room vibrated, dust dancing from the floor, paint and plaster cracking off the walls.

And the chamber's occupants were also affected. 'Jesus!'

Nina gasped, a nauseating sensation rising in her chest cavity. Her own organs were vibrating in sympathy with the booming bass note. She tried to lift the fallen gate, but it refused to budge.

Eddie had no more luck with the other gate. He turned to the pipes. 'Block it! Shove something in it!'

Nina could barely hear him over the thunderous din, but got the gist. She shrugged off her pack and tipped out its contents, balling up the nylon. Macy followed suit. Eddie was already at the pipe, face screwed up in discomfort as he jammed his jacket and his own empty pack into the slot. The note's pitch changed slightly, the escaping air screeching shrilly as its exit was obstructed.

The women staggered across the trembling floor to him. He grabbed their balled-up packs and stuffed them into the gap. Nina dropped her flashlight and clapped both hands over her ears, but it made no difference; the sound was *inside* her, trying to shake her apart from within.

It was doing the same thing to the pyramid. Pieces of masonry fell down the shaft and shattered on the stone floor – small lumps at first, but the cracks spreading across the walls warned that there would be larger ones coming.

Unable to shield his ears, Eddie was finding the noise agonising – but it eased slightly as he twisted the makeshift bungs to block the gaps. Pipe organs were closed at the top, air only able to escape through the slot. If he could completely seal it . . .

The vibration began to die down. All he had to do was hold everything in place and endure the noise for as long as it took for the machine to run out of air—

A clanging shudder ran up the length of the pipe as the

pressure rose – then rippled back down it. A blast of compressed air hit the mouth like a sledgehammer blow, firing the blockage out of the slot and bowling Eddie to the floor. With a ground-shaking *whump* like the clearing of the world's mightiest throat, the terrifying bass note resumed – at full volume. Plaster splintered from the walls, even the paving cracking.

The noise was so overpowering that Nina could barely think. The beam of her dropped flashlight illuminated the bottom of the pipes. Blocking the mouth had failed, but there had to be another way . . .

Something Eddie had said forced its way through the disorientation.

Two pipes, a piston in one, forcing the air ahead of it as it dropped. The air itself acted as a cushion slowing its fall – there was only one relatively small hole through which it could escape, and the hourglass-shaped pinch at the bottom of the organ pipe restricted it further.

She knew what to do.

She grabbed a mallet from Eddie's discarded gear. With her ears exposed, the sound became unbearable – she screamed, but couldn't even hear it. A piece of falling stone hit her arm. More debris crashed around her, a crack leaping up the wall—

She swung the mallet.

It hit the pinch, tearing the metal. A piercing shriek escaped from the rent. Nina hit it again, and again – and the pipe ripped apart.

Air blasted out, the awful bass note dropping in volume. She whacked the pipe again, trying to close off the section producing the sound. The metal bent across the torn hole.

The note faded.

Head ringing, Nina stepped back. The escaping rush of air was still roaring like a jet engine – and there was another sound, a metallic *clung-clung-clung* rapidly getting louder—

Eddie threw her backwards as the bottom of the other pipe blew apart, something inside it hitting the ground so hard that it smashed a crater into the flagstones. *The piston.* With air now freely able to escape from the pipe, there had been nothing to slow it, and it had plunged downwards as fast as gravity could take it.

A last few fragments from high above hit the floor, then the rain of debris stopped. The quiet and stillness was almost shocking. Nina brushed dust from her face, then looked at Eddie. His mouth moved silently.

Oh, God, she was deaf—

'Just kidding,' he said, grinning.

She hit him. 'You son of a bitch!'

'Hey, we're okay. I think.' Concern crossed his face as he clicked his fingers beside one ear. 'Shit, that doesn't sound right.'

'You're surprised, after that?' She retrieved her flashlight, finding Macy. 'Are you okay?'

Macy slowly took her hands from her ears. 'Jeez. My mom and dad were right – you *can* play music too loud.'

Nina helped Eddie up. 'Let's try those gates.'

He went to the exit and strained to lift the gate. It was heavy, but it moved. When they had recovered their gear, he hauled the gate up high enough for Nina and Macy to get underneath, then they supported it as he slid through. He looked back at the wreckage of the trap. 'Five down, two to go.'

'Yeah, but the last two sound really nasty,' Macy pointed out. 'The Hewer-in-Pieces and the Cutter-off of Heads? Not good.'

'We can beat them,' said Nina, oddly buoyed by their survival. 'And then . . . we'll meet Osiris.' They set off down the next passage.

Over two hundred feet above, Osir led his expedition to the Lady of Tremblings. Dust drifted through the room, stirred up by the sound from the massive pipe. 'I think we've found where that noise came from,' he said, directing a powerful torch beam across the shaft.

The rest of his group followed him on to the ledge. Although there were several men in military-style uniforms, wearing equipment webbing and carrying weapons, they were not soldiers: Khaleel, though accompanying Osir out of curiosity, had chosen to leave his men aboard the hovercraft. The troopers were members of the Osirian Temple, Shaban's personal security force.

Shaban gazed at the long drop below. 'Some sort of trap. Wilde and Chase, and the girl – they must have triggered it.' He smirked malevolently. 'I'm in two minds, brother. It would be amusing if they died setting off a trap that we then walked through safely, but I'm also hoping they survive – so I can kill them myself.'

'All that matters is that they can't get out,' said Osir. He turned to Berkeley. 'What do you make of this room?'

'The hieroglyphs in the entrance chamber definitely suggested that each *arit* is booby-trapped.' Berkeley pointed at one of the large cogwheels. 'This would be the Lady of Tremblings, at my guess. Wilde and the others must have activated it when they crossed – and survived.'

'They didn't fall?' asked Hamdi.

'That noise? I think it's safe to assume that was the Goddess of the Loud Voice, which is the fifth *arit*. They got that far, at least.'

'Which means they've cleared the way for us,' said Osir. He stepped on to the bridge.

'Are – are you sure it is safe?' said Hamdi nervously.

Osir took another step. The bridge stood firm. 'Either the trap has been sprung, or it's broken.'

'Lead on, Khalid,' said Shaban as his brother negotiated the crossing. Once he reached the other ledge, he signalled the others to follow.

The cogwheel creaked, the stone jamming it shifting slightly, but nobody noticed.

Another set of columns marked the sixth *arit*.

'Okay,' Nina said, pausing outside. 'Hewer-in-Pieces in Blood, huh? I think we'll need more than a few Band-Aids if this goes badly, so let's figure out how to make it *not* go badly.'

She and Eddie directed their lights through the opening. The level passage ahead was decorated with the now-familiar disapproving Egyptian gods and grim warnings of the fate awaiting intruders . . . but there was also something new.

Something ominous. Set into the walls were numerous horizontal slots, lined top and bottom with rust-red plates of iron.

Eddie aimed his torch into the nearest slot. There was something within, another long piece of metal on a hinge at one end . . . but this was considerably thinner along its edge. 'Okay,' he said. 'Blades inside the holes. I get it. We go down the tunnel and they spring out and chop us into chunks.'

'They're kinda rusty,' said Macy. 'Maybe they won't work.'

'You want to bet your life on that?' Nina asked. Each slot was almost as long as the passage was wide, leaving no room to escape the blades by pressing against the opposite wall – though the sheer number of slots on both sides made finding *any* kind of hiding place almost inconceivable. 'How the hell are you supposed to get through?'

Eddie took out the mallet, crouching with his arm outstretched to tap the floor just past the columns. Nina winced in fearful anticipation of a blade's slicing out from the wall, but nothing happened. He edged closer and tried again, still with no result.

'Trigger's probably somewhere further along,' he said, standing. 'So you're right in the middle when it goes off.' The far wall was a good forty feet away – and even then it only marked a corner rather than the end, the tunnel continuing to one side.

'There's got to be some way through without setting it off,' said Nina.

Eddie hefted the mallet. 'Let me try something.' He tossed it through the columns to land a few feet inside the entrance. The blades remained in place. 'Okay, so that far's safe, at least. Probably.' He stepped forward to retrieve it.

'Don't say "probably" and then walk right into it!' Nina yelled as he returned with the heavy hammer. 'And what are you planning to do, throw it a foot farther along each time?

There's no way to guarantee you'll hit the trigger – and unless you've got some mad boomerang skills I don't know about, you can't get it round that corner either.'

'Okay, so what do *you* suggest?' he demanded. 'We can't just walk into the bloody thing and think light thoughts so we don't set it off.'

'We don't walk,' said Macy, looking more closely at the hieroglyphs. 'I think we're supposed to *run*. This text here's another warning that horrible death awaits, yadda yadda, but it finishes with something like "hurry to Osiris". Or "hasten", maybe. "Hasten to Osiris." '

'They left a clue?' Nina said, surprised. 'None of the other *arits* had them.'

'It's only a few extra characters.' Macy pointed them out at the bottom of a block of text. 'Everything else is the same as we've been seeing all the way down. Easy to miss. There might have been others, but we just didn't notice them.'

'So we're meant to peg it down the corridor, then?' Eddie said, illuminating the passage again. 'Bit of a risk – we don't know what's round that corner.'

'The Cutter-off of Heads, probably.'

'Yeah, that's reassuring.' He returned the mallet to his pack, steeling himself. 'All right. So we have to *run* like an Egyptian.' He looked at Nina. 'Ready?'

'Let's do it,' she said.

'If I get chopped into Oxo cubes I'm going to kick your arse in the afterlife. Macy?' Macy nodded at him. 'Okay. Three, two, one . . . *go*!'

They ran across the threshold.

The blades remained stationary.

Nina's light swept along one side of the passage, Eddie's

the other, as they ran with Macy just behind. Ten feet along, twenty, their clattering footsteps echoing. Thirty, the corner coming up fast—

A dusty crunch as a block shifted beneath Nina's foot.

Her heart clenched with fear – but there was still no movement from the walls.

There was a sound behind them, though. A hollow clonking, some mechanism turning and repeatedly knocking metal against metal.

Counting down.

'*Definitely* run,' Eddie gasped, slowing at the corner to let the women get ahead of him. Torch raised, he glanced back—

Kshang!

Ranks of rusty blades shot out from the slots at the entrance, some swinging forward and others back to dice anyone unlucky enough to be caught between them. Corrosion and time had taken their toll, some swords snapping or wrenching themselves from their hinges to clash against the opposite wall – but the result was still as lethal as its creators had intended.

And it was getting closer.

'*Shiiiiit!*' Eddie burst back into a sprint after Nina and Macy as more blades sprang out one after the other, a wave of death chasing them down the tunnel. 'Runrun*run*!'

Nina didn't need to see what was happening to be spurred on; the rapidly approaching sound was terrifying enough. In her torch beam she saw what she at first thought was the end of the passage – before realising the ornate columns marked the entrance to the next *arit*.

The Cutter-off of Heads.

Out of the frying pan—

The advancing blades reached the corner, rounded it, continued after the running trio without pause. Gaining.

Nina saw something on the walls beyond the columns. More slots – but only one on each side, at about neck height.

And they were running straight at them.

She didn't even have time to shout a warning to Eddie and Macy – they were almost at the columns, and the iron wave was upon them—

She swept up her arms to grab the surprised pair round their shoulders – and yanked her feet off the floor. The extra weight made Macy trip, Nina in turn dragging Eddie down as they tumbled through the next entrance – just as two large spinning discs burst from the walls ahead of them, swinging back and barely clearing their heads as they fell.

'Son of a *bitch*!' Nina spluttered, scrambling out from under the whirling serrated blades. 'They weren't kidding about the name!'

Eddie waited for the two discs to grind to a halt before rising and returning to the entrance, experimentally pushing one of the swords. He expected resistance, but it moved freely, if noisily, on its rusted hinge; the force of its release after six millennia had broken the mechanism. 'Least we'll be able to get back out.'

'We made it,' Macy said, panting. 'We got through – that was the last trap!' She hesitated. 'Right?'

'If the hieroglyphics were telling the truth, then yeah,' Nina assured her. Even so, she still stood with a degree of caution. Ahead was another bend, the passage angling downwards.

She looked round the corner. Steps led down a short distance to another set of columns.

But these were not the kind that marked each *arit*. These were something altogether different.

And magnificent.

'Oh, you've got to see this,' she said softly, barely breathing despite her recent exertion.

Macy gasped at the sight, and even Eddie was impressed. 'Pretty flash.'

The columns were carved in the form of an Egyptian god, mirror-images facing each other. But they were not any of the figures that had watched their descent into the heart of the pyramid. This was another, a man in a tall headdress, bearing a crook in one hand and a flail in the other. His body was encased in tight bindings, like those of a mummy, but his face was exposed, skin an oxidised copper-green. Both figures were liberally adorned with gold and silver leaf.

Osiris.

Between the twin statues was the entrance to a dark chamber. Nina raised her flashlight. More gold and silver glinted within, treasures stacked round the walls, but her gaze was fixed on what lay at the centre of the large room: a bulky, rounded-off object, its skin pure silver.

A sarcophagus.

Nina slowly advanced, checking the two figures for any sign of some last, sneaky trap. There was none. They had reached their goal, the final chamber.

'We found it,' she said, looking at Eddie and Macy in wonderment. 'We found the tomb of Osiris.'

25

They entered the chamber, a match to the Osireion in dimensions and form, torch beams flashing over the artefacts and treasures inside. They ranged from the astounding to the prosaic – gleaming statues of pure gold beside simple wooden chairs; a full-sized boat bearing a silver and gold mask of Osiris upon its prow against which had been propped bundles of spears. It was a find to exceed even the tomb of Tutankhamun. The famed pharaoh had been a relatively unimportant ruler of the New Kingdom, less than three and a half thousand years ago, but Osiris was a myth given flesh, a foundation stone of Egyptian civilisation dating back almost twice as far.

And they were the first to reach him.

Nina examined the sarcophagus. The lid was a larger than life representation of the man within. The sculpted silver face gazed serenely at the ceiling, kohl-lined eyes wide.

'The craftsmanship's absolutely incredible,' she whispered. 'All of this is.' She gestured at the objects surrounding them. 'I never imagined the pre-dynastic Egyptians were this advanced.'

'It's just like Atlantis,' said Macy. 'They were really advanced for their time too, but nobody knew about them. Until you found them.'

Nina smiled at her. 'Y'know, this is really more of a joint discovery, Macy.'

Macy beamed. 'Not bad for a C-student, huh?'

Eddie took a closer look at a set of painted wooden figurines, symbolic representations of the servants who would attend their king in the afterlife, then eyed a cruder statuette carved from an odd purple stone before moving to the other side of the sarcophagus. 'All right, so what do we *do* now we've found all this?'

'Normally I'd say photograph, catalogue, then examine,' said Nina, 'but this isn't exactly a normal case. First thing we need to do is secure it. We'll have to contact the Egyptian government, go to Dr Assad at the SCA.'

'So what about this bread Osir was after?' He looked for anything resembling food. On a small wooden table was what might once have been loaves, but they had long been reduced to mouldering dust. 'Don't think he'll get any sarnies out of them. Is there anything else?'

'Look down.' Eddie did, seeing a recess set into the coffin's base, a pottery jar about ten inches high inside it. 'Canopic jars. The Egyptians used them to store the body's vital organs after they were removed during mummification. Osir thinks there'll be yeast spores in his digestive system.'

Macy saw another jar on the floor by Nina, then went to the head of the sarcophagus to find a third. 'There's one here, too – and there should be another down by his feet.' Eddie checked, and nodded. 'One for each compass point.

This one's got a monkey head, a baboon – it's the god Hapi. That means it's got Osiris's lungs in it.' She was about to pick up the jar when she realised what she had just said and flinched away. 'Gross.'

'Which jars are which?' Nina asked.

'Hapi represented the north, so . . .' She worked out the compass directions. 'The one on your side should be a jackal – that's Duamutef.'

Nina shone her light on the jar, revealing that the painted cap was indeed in the long-eared shape of a jackal's head. 'Yep.'

'So that'll be the stomach. The one opposite'll be a falcon, that's Qebehsenuf. Or is it Qebehsunef? That's what you get for having a language with no vowels, I guess. Anyway, that'll have his intestines inside.'

'Lovely,' said Eddie. 'A jar full of guts.'

'And the one at the south end, under his feet, that should look like just some guy because Imseti was a human god. That'll be Osiris's liver.'

He smacked his lips. 'That's more like it. Anyone got any fava beans?'

'It's six thousand years old, Eddie,' Nina warned with a grin. 'And we didn't bring any Pepto-Bismol.'

'I'll give it a miss, then. So if Osir's after these jars, what should we do with them? Smash 'em?'

'I'd really rather you didn't,' said Osir from the entrance.

Nina jumped in shock, and Macy yelped as they spun to see him leaning almost casually against one of the Osiris figures. Beside him, Shaban's stance was anything but casual as he covered them with a gun.

Osir stepped forward, revealing that more people,

Diamondback and Hamdi among them, had crept down the steps. 'It's more incredible than I imagined,' he said, taking in the chamber's contents. 'And now, it all belongs to me.'

'No, it absolutely does *not*,' snapped Nina.

'We were here first,' said Eddie. 'Finders keepers.'

Shaban gestured for them to move away from the sarcophagus. 'I have something else you can keep. A bullet.'

Osir went to the silver coffin, picking up the canopic jar from its foot. 'And the organs of Osiris himself are here. Just as I said, Dr Wilde.'

Nina was about to reply when someone else entered. '*Logan?*' she gasped. 'Oh, you son of a bitch. You're working for these clowns now?'

Berkeley regarded her coldly. 'This is a habit of yours that's starting to piss me off, Nina. I make a big find, but you've beaten me to it. At least this time you're not making me look like a complete jackass on live TV.'

'Oh, boo hoo,' Nina sneered, pretending to wipe away a tear. 'Poor little Logan, someone stole his thunder – so he's going to go against everything I thought he believed in and sell out to a bunch of wack-jobs from some stupid bogus religion.'

Shaban's scarred face twisted angrily and he aimed the gun at Nina, but Osir shook his head. 'Not in here. I don't want the tomb despoiled.' He put down the jar and slowly circled the sarcophagus. 'Four jars – the liver, intestines, lungs . . . and stomach.' Almost reverentially, he raised the jackal-headed jar. 'This holds the key to eternal life, Dr Wilde. In this jar are spores of the yeast used to make the bread of Osiris. All I need is one sample, and the secret will be mine. I will cultivate it, I will own it, and I will *control* it.'

'That's assuming there are actually any spores in there,' said Nina. 'Maybe Osiris hadn't eaten any bread before he died. Maybe it was overcooked and the yeast cells were killed. You might have gone through all this for nothing.'

'Not nothing,' said Osir, shrugging. 'I'll still have the tomb, no matter what. But that's why I brought Dr Kralj.' He waved for a bearded man to join him. It took Nina a moment to identify him: one of the scientists working with the yeast cultures in the Swiss laboratory. 'There are two canopic jars that can say which of us is right, Dr Wilde – the jar of Duamutef,' he held up the jackal-headed container, 'and the jar of Qebehsenuf. I'm willing to sacrifice one to learn what is in the other. Dr Kralj, which would be better for your test? The intestines, or the stomach?'

'Anything in the intestines would have been through the digestive process,' said the Serbian scientist. 'If there are spores present which survived that, there are likely to be more in the stomach. So the intestines, yes.'

'Then do it.'

Kralj collected the falcon-headed jar. 'No, wait,' pleaded Nina. 'That jar's an incredibly valuable artefact. If you open it, you might as well be destroying it.' She looked at Berkeley. 'Logan, you've *got* to have some feelings about this.' She knew she had struck a nerve – he couldn't keep a conflicted expression off his face – but he said nothing. 'Is however much he's paying you worth this?'

'Dr Berkeley knows a good deal when he is offered one,' said Osir, as Kralj set up a small folding table and placed the jar on it, taking more equipment from a case. 'It's a shame you didn't. If you hadn't betrayed me, we would still have been in this room together – only you would be in charge, not a prisoner.'

Shaban kept Nina, Eddie and Macy at gunpoint, two of his troopers joining him with their MP7s raised. Everyone else watched as Kralj worked on the jar. After laying out a line of small bottles containing colourless liquids, some test tubes and a portable microscope, he examined the carved lid, then used a metal pick to peel away the black resin sealing it. Once it was clear, he looked up at Osir, who nodded.

He carefully turned the lid. The two pieces of ancient pottery scraped against each other . . . then, with a faint crackle as the last remnants of the seal broke, they separated.

'Whoa, shit,' said Eddie, as the stench of something awful permeated the chamber. 'Literally. Smells like his last meal was a kebab!'

Nina suppressed her revulsion. 'It means the seal held, though. The contents were preserved for all this time.'

Kralj used a penlight to examine the jar's interior. Something glistened inside. He tipped three of the bottles into it, swilling the mixture round, then used a large pipette to draw out a sample of the resulting dark slurry. He squirted it into a test tube, then added the last bottle's contents.

'This will take several minutes,' he told Osir as he sealed the tube. 'If there are any spores, the test will show them.'

'Then we'll make use of the time,' Osir replied. He signalled to one of the troopers. 'Open the sarcophagus.'

'For God's sake,' said Nina, appalled. 'This just gets worse. What are you going to do, autopsy the mummy?'

'That's what you're most worried about?' Macy said, eyeing the guns.

Like the canopic jars, the coffin had been sealed with a thick black mixture of resin and bitumen. One of Osir's men carried a small circular saw, which he used to slice into the protective layer as he made his way round the sarcophagus. Another man followed, using a power tool with an abrasive head to grind open the seal along the cut.

It took them a few minutes to complete their circuit. 'Open it,' Osir ordered. Another two men came to the sarcophagus, the group assembling jacks on each side and inserting chrome-steel forks into the now exposed gap beneath the lid.

'Ready, sir,' said one man.

Osir gave Nina a satisfied look, then nodded. 'Do it.'

The four men worked the jacks. Metal creaked, the seal cracking and splintering. One of the forks slipped slightly and gouged the metal, making Nina cringe at the damage.

'Come on!' Shaban barked impatiently. 'Harder!'

The men increased their efforts, straining to lift the heavy lid. A deeper grind came from inside the sarcophagus, then with a jolt it opened. Grunting, they raised the silver figure of Osiris to the full height of the jacks . . . revealing another figure inside.

But this was not a sculpture. This was Osiris himself.

Or what was left of him. The body was mummified, tightly wrapped in a discoloured shroud, arms folded over its chest. The head was covered by a death mask, silver and gold shaped to match the face beneath. Unlike the famous burial masks of pharaohs like Tutankhamun and Psusennes, this was surprisingly modest, lacking their elaborate headdresses. If the mask were an accurate representation of the dead ruler, Osiris had possessed a surprisingly youthful appearance for one so powerful and revered.

Everyone leaned closer to look, even Kralj glancing up from his work. The recess in which the body lay had been matched almost perfectly to its shape, less than a centimetre to spare all round it. The lid had its own precisely shaped indentation set into the solid metal.

Osir gazed down at the man from whom he had taken his name. 'Osiris,' he whispered. 'The god-king, granter of eternal life . . .'

'You almost sound like you believe it,' Nina scoffed.

'A month ago, would you have believed Osiris was not just a myth?' he countered. 'Perhaps there's more truth here than either of us thought.'

'Not your version of the truth. You know, the skip-the-awkward-parts one you push on your followers.'

'Who is to say that my interpretation of the story of Osiris is any less valid than another?' said Osir smugly. 'In fact, I'd say that this,' he indicated the mummy, 'makes it *more* valid. I found the tomb of Osiris because I was *destined* to find it. It proves I really do possess the spirit of Osiris. Wouldn't you say?'

'No, and nor would you if you were actually being honest with the dopes who hand you their money.' Osir merely chuckled, but she noticed Shaban's face tensing once more.

Before she could remark on it, Kralj looked up from his microscope. 'Mr Osir!'

Osir went to him. 'What's the result of the test?'

Kralj carefully removed a slide from the microscope. 'The test result,' he said excitedly, 'is . . . *positive*. There are spores of a yeast strain present.'

Osir could barely contain his exultation. 'Oh, yes! *Yes!*' He clenched his fists in glee. 'I was right! The story of the bread of Osiris was true – and it's going to make me *rich*, Sebak, rich beyond belief!' He clasped his hands round his brother's shoulders and shook him. 'Rich!'

Shaban seemed disgusted. 'Money. Is that all that matters to you?'

'Of course not.' Osir grinned and lowered his voice to a fake whisper. 'There is the sex, too!' He cackled.

'You are pathetic,' Shaban said coldly. 'A disgrace to our family, and an insult to the gods. And I am no longer going to let that insult stand.' The gun came up . . . and pointed at his brother's chest.

Osir at first didn't seem to register it, his mind refusing to accept what his eyes were seeing. 'What are you doing, Sebak?' he finally said with a half-laugh, which faded as he looked into Shaban's face and saw nothing there but anger and hatred. 'Sebak? What is this?'

'This is the end, *my brother*,' he spat. 'You have had your pleasures, you have had everything that you never worked for and never deserved!' He pushed Osir back against the sarcophagus.

Fear rose through Osir as he realised his brother was deadly serious. He looked desperately at the troopers. 'Someone – someone take his gun.' The men stared back, stone-faced. 'Help me!'

'They are not your followers,' hissed Shaban with a thin,

sneering smile. 'They are *mine*. All your followers will now worship me – or they will die.'

Berkeley backed away nervously. 'What's – what's going on?'

'What's going on, Dr Berkeley,' said Shaban, 'is that I am taking my rightful place as the head of the Temple. I am taking my birthright!' He glared at the mummy behind Osir – then spat on it. 'Osiris – pah! Set was the stronger brother. Set was the *greater* brother, but he was kept down by Osiris out of fear!' He was shouting now, spittle flying from his mouth. 'That time is over! My time has come! I am taking what is mine!' His voice rose to a demented scream. *'I am Set! I am reborn!'*

Osir stared at him in horror. 'What . . . what's wrong with you?' he gasped. 'You're not Set – I'm not Osiris! We – we are the sons of a *baker*, Sebak! Nobody has been reborn – it's not real! I made it all up! You know that, you were there when I did it!'

'When you invoke a god, you make that god real,' said Shaban, suddenly chillingly calm. 'You make them *all* real. Your followers worship you as Osiris, so you *are* Osiris. I am the brother of Osiris – so I *am* Set. I am the god of darkness, of chaos, of *death* – and it is my time to rule!'

'You've – you've gone mad!' Osir spluttered. 'What's happened to you?'

The rage returned. 'What's happened to me? Only *you* could not know, Khalid! All our lives, you have been given everything, and I got nothing. You were the favourite son, I was the inferior. You tricked your way to fame and fortune, and I was forced into the army. You had money and women, and I was *burned alive*!' He ripped at his shirt, exposing his chest. It was as hideously scarred as his face, the injuries extending down his body. 'If Khaleel hadn't pulled me out, I would have died. And did you even come to see me in hospital? No!'

'Someone's got big brother issues,' Nina whispered to Eddie.

'Someone's got fucking lunatic issues,' he whispered back.

'I was . . . I was on location,' Osir said in panicked apology. 'I couldn't get away.'

'For two months?' Shaban snarled. 'No! I know what you were doing. You were travelling the world, having sex with whores!'

Osir still had some defiance in him. 'Oh, *now* I see. It's not the money or the fame that made you so jealous. It's that the fire left you less of a man!'

The rage that flared inside Shaban was so fierce he couldn't even speak. Instead, he smashed his brother's face with his gun, sending a spurt of blood across the coffin lid. Macy gasped, and even Eddie flinched.

Osir slumped, clutching his head. Shaban forced his emotions back under control. 'Get that out of there,' he said to Diamondback, jabbing a finger at the mummy.

Diamondback and one of the troopers reached into the sarcophagus. Before Nina even had a chance to protest at the desecration, they hauled the body out of its recess and dumped it unceremoniously on the floor. The burial mask was jarred loose, the corpse's wizened, eyeless face exposed.

Shaban aimed the gun at his brother. 'Get in,' he ordered.

Osir stared at him in pained bewilderment. 'What?'

'Into the sarcophagus! Now!'

'Oh, my God,' said Nina, as realisation struck her. 'Khalid, he's playing out the real story of Osiris and Set – how Set tricked Osiris into climbing into a coffin and sealed him in!'

Shaban smiled malevolently at her. 'I'm glad *someone* knows the true story.'

'You going to chop off his knob and feed it to a fish, too?' Eddie asked.

'I won't need to cut him into fourteen pieces this time. My brother has no Isis to resurrect him.' He looked back at Osir. 'Get in.'

Osir stood firm. 'The Osirian Temple won't follow you, Sebak – they worship Osiris, not Set!'

'You're wrong, brother.' Shaban proudly indicated the troopers. 'While you were drinking and gambling and whoring, I was finding the true believers in the Temple, and you never even noticed. I did not need to be a movie star – strength and power brought them to my side. They have pledged themselves to me, and the rest will do the same . . . or pay the price.'

'What price?' Osir demanded.

'Kralj and the other scientists have been working for me, not you. The yeast used to make the bread of Osiris can do more than give eternal life to those I decide are worthy. It can bring death to those who oppose me!'

Nina gave Eddie a worried look. 'The lab, in Switzerland – they were talking about genetically modifying the yeast.'

'That's right, Dr Wilde,' said Shaban. 'The spores will be spread across the world by my followers. They will put them in crops, animal feed, even the water. Anyone who does not eat the bread of Set,' a momentary smile of triumph at the new name, 'anyone who will not worship their new god, will die as their own cells poison them.'

'You're insane,' said Osir quietly. 'And you wonder why Father preferred me?'

The mention of their father spurred Shaban back to anger. 'Get in the coffin! Get in! Get in!' He struck Osir again and again with the gun, then screamed an order. 'Put him in there! *Now!*'

Four men grabbed the struggling Osir, forcing him into the recess. It was a good six inches too short to fit him, and narrower. He tried to pull free, but Shaban hammered the gun brutally down on to his chest. Osir writhed in pain, winded.

'I am Set!' Shaban shrieked. 'And I am taking what is mine!'

He released the jacks.

Osir only managed a gasp of terror before the heavy metal lid fell with a thunderous whump . . . and a horrible crack of bones from his protruding feet and arms. Macy screamed and looked away. Blood gushed from the silver coffin.

Shaban continued to beat at the lid, denting the precious metal with his gun. 'I am Set!' he roared. 'I am the god!'

'No,' said Nina, shocked and disgusted. 'He was right. You *are* insane.'

He whipped round, finger quivering on the trigger as every tendon in his body tensed with fury—

But he didn't fire.

'Nina,' Eddie said urgently, 'if a guy with a gun says he's a god . . . humour him!'

Shaban drew in a shuddering breath, then backed away. 'No,' he said, forcing himself to calm down. 'No, my brother was right. This tomb should not be despoiled. Osiris is back in his coffin where he belongs. But you?' He regarded Nina, Chase and Macy with contempt. 'You don't deserve to die in the tomb of a god.' He moved round the sarcophagus. 'Take them to the surface and shoot them,' he told his men as he picked up the jackal-headed jar. 'Where is the case?'

As Diamondback and the other troopers hustled Macy, Nina and Eddie to the entrance, one man turned to reveal that he was carrying a sturdy case made of impact-resistant composites on his back. He unfastened the harness clip on his chest and shrugged it off, then opened it to reveal a lining of thick yellow polyurethane 'memory foam'. Shaban carefully pressed the jar into the bottom protective layer, then slowly lowered the lid until the catches clicked shut. 'Guard it with your life, Hashem,' he told the trooper. 'Kralj, stay with him. Don't let it out of your sight.' The scientist nodded, waiting as Hashem donned the case and harness like a backpack.

Shaban turned to see Berkeley and Hamdi both still staring at the bloodied sarcophagus. 'Gentlemen,' he said. 'I hope there is nothing wrong.'

'Not at all,' Hamdi bleated. 'You have my full support, as always. I'll make sure the SCA never learns about this place – it will be our secret. *Your* secret,' he hurriedly corrected himself.

'Good. And you, Dr Berkeley?'

'Ah, I, er,' Berkeley mumbled. 'I'm . . . yeah. I'm on board.'

'I'm glad to hear it.' Shaban gave him a menacing smile. 'Now, go back to the hovercraft. Leave this place for the dead.' As Berkeley and Hamdi quickly made their exit, he stood before the sarcophagus. 'Goodbye, my brother,' he whispered, before turning to leave, returning the tomb to its state of eternal silence.

26

'He's completely insane,' said Nina to Khaleel as the Egyptian officer strode up the passage ahead of her. 'You can't seriously believe he's the reincarnation of Set.'

'It doesn't matter what I believe,' Khaleel replied. 'It matters what *he* believes – and he believes a great deal of money will repay the debt he owes me for saving his life. He's also promised me a position of power if his plan succeeds – and if it doesn't, then I am still rich. So I thought: why not?'

'Because he's a psychopath? If his plan works, millions of people will die!'

Khaleel shrugged. 'We are always being warned of the dangers of overpopulation these days.'

The group came to a stop. After making their way back up through the pyramid, traversing the pit left by the Lady of Rainstorms on a rope attached to the ceiling by spring-loaded climbing cams, they had reached the top of the enormous vertical shaft. 'What're we going to do?' Macy whispered with growing panic to Nina. 'We're almost at the surface, and – and they're going to kill us!'

'They're not going to kill us,' said Nina. 'We'll get out of this.' But despite her defiant words, she felt as frightened as Macy inside. They were unarmed, outnumbered . . . and out of options. She looked back to Eddie, hoping to see some hint on his face that he had thought of a plan. But his expression was nothing but grim.

Everyone bunched up at the bottleneck. The trooper bearing the case, Hashem, was first on to the stone bridge. 'Come on, hurry up,' Shaban growled. Kralj gave him an uncertain look, then followed a few steps behind. Diamondback jabbed his gun at Nina and Macy. They hesitantly stepped on to the narrow crossing, the chain rattling with the extra weight. More troopers went after them.

About to step on to the bridge, Eddie stared at the chain – then his gaze snapped down to the cogwheel beside the beam.

And the piece of stone wedged beneath it.

'Nina,' he called, 'remember when we came in?' She looked back at him, as did Macy. 'There's gonna be a whole lotta shakin' going on.'

Her eyes widened. 'Macy, grab on!' she cried—

Eddie kicked away the stone.

Freed at last, the weight of the large cylindrical block pulled the chain through the pulley – and turned the cogwheels.

Nina and Macy wrapped their arms round the bridge as the cogs' teeth bashed at the protrusions on each side of the stone beam, making it jolt violently. Hashem, furthest from the pounding wheel, staggered, then dropped his gun and dived for the far ledge. He caught the edge, scrabbling for grip.

Kralj was not so lucky. Caught completely off guard, he plunged down the shaft with a terrified, echoing scream. Behind Macy, two troopers were thrown into the void, a third man desperately trying to hang on before he too disappeared into the darkness below.

The last man on the bridge managed to throw himself backwards, colliding with Eddie and Diamondback and sending the remainder of the group tumbling down the sloping passage. Eddie shoved the man off him and kicked Diamondback in the stomach. 'Nina!' he yelled as he jumped up. 'Get across, get out!'

She was already edging forwards, Macy following. 'What about you?' Nina shouted back. 'Come on!'

But his end of the bridge was rocking too forcefully for him to get on. Instead, he slammed a boot into the cultist's stomach and looked for his gun. The MP7 had landed near the edge of the ledge. He lunged for it—

Diamondback's revolver boomed. The American's shot was wild – but it was close enough. The bullet ripped a fingertip-sized chunk of flesh out of Eddie's muscular forearm. He roared in pain and clutched the wound, any thought of grabbing the gun forgotten as he wavered on the edge.

'Eddie!' Nina screamed.

'Get out of here!' he shouted. 'Get the jar!'

She looked round, and saw Hashem clinging to the ledge a few feet away. The case was still on his back. She scrambled to solid ground and stood before the trooper. He had managed to pull his shoulders above the shaft's lip, but with the bulky case affecting his centre of gravity he was having trouble finding enough purchase to climb higher.

'Gimme the case and I'll pull you up!' Nina cried. She reached for the container, finding it was firmly attached to his equipment webbing. Thinking he wouldn't be so dumb as to fight her from his precarious position, she pulled at it—

He grabbed her ankle.

'You gotta be *kidding* me!' she said.

He leered up at her and gripped her ankle with his other hand, getting enough leverage to twist her leg out from under her. She stumbled, landing on her backside. He clamped one hand round her calf.

Macy reached the end of the bridge and jumped up to kick at his arms. 'Let her go!'

'No, get the case!' Nina said. She drew back her other foot, her eyes meeting the cultist's. 'Don't make me do this.'

His only reply was a look of angry determination as he hauled himself higher, fingers digging painfully into her leg.

Her expression hardened. 'Your choice.'

She smashed her boot into his face. Hashem's head snapped back, and his hands slipped down her leg – then closed vice-like round her ankle once more, his weight pulling her towards the edge.

Macy grabbed the case, but couldn't get it free of the webbing. She yanked at the straps, trying to release them.

Nina kicked again, the crack as his nose broke loud enough to be heard even over the booby-trap's pounding.

'Get!' she yelled, punctuating each word with another strike. 'Off! Me! You! *Asshole!*'

Even through his pain, Hashem clung with the strength of the fanatical. He kept wrenching at Nina's leg, every tug bringing her closer to the vertiginous shaft.

Another kick, and one hand slipped free – only for him to reach to the webbing on his chest and pull a knife from a sheath, preparing to stab the blade into Nina's leg—

She kicked him again.

Not in the face, but on his other hand.

The pain as her boot heel hit her shin was intense – but it was nothing compared to the snap of a broken finger. The knife clanged to the floor as the cultist finally screamed, whipping away as gravity pulled him over the edge . . . just as Macy released the clip securing the webbing. He slipped through the harness and vanished into the void, shrieking all the way down.

Macy fell on her butt, dropping the case at the edge of the shaft. Heart racing, Nina looked across the bucking bridge. Diamondback held the wounded Eddie at gunpoint as the rest of the group struggled upright.

Shaban would use Eddie as a hostage, she knew, forcing her to surrender the canopic jar in exchange for his life . . . then kill him anyway. The same would happen if she kicked the case into the shaft.

There was only one possible choice she could make. It was the same choice Eddie had made in a similar situation not long after they first met, only with the players reversed. If she wanted to save him . . .

She had to abandon him.

Leaping to her feet, she grabbed the fallen knife and yanked the case off the floor by its harness straps. 'We gotta go!'

Macy stared at her in shock. 'But Eddie—'

'*Run!*' Clutching the case, she sprinted into the passage. Macy gave Eddie a desperate look – then ran after Nina at the sight of guns coming up. Bullets blasted chunks out of the stonework behind her.

Shaban was red with rage. 'Kill them! *Kill them!*' he screamed, grabbing an MP7 from one of his men to unleash the remainder of the magazine himself. But the women were gone. With an incoherent scream of pure fury, he hurled the weapon to the floor so hard that its plastic handgrip cover shattered. Fists balled, he looked up and saw Eddie.

For a moment, the Englishman thought he was going to throw him off the ledge personally, before some semblance of self-control returned. 'Shoot him!' Shaban ordered. Diamondback grinned.

'Sebak, wait!' shouted Khaleel. Diamondback hesitated at the officer's bark of authority as Shaban whipped round to glare at his unexpected challenger. 'You can use him to bargain for the jar. She won't destroy it as long as she thinks she can get him back.'

Shaban took several long, deep breaths, still shaking with volcanic anger. 'You're right,' he finally said. 'Thank you for stopping me, my friend.'

'I always had your best interests in mind. And mine, of course,' he added with a small smile.

'So we're not gonna kill him?' Diamondback sounded disappointed.

'Of course we are,' Shaban growled. 'When we have the jar.'

'I'll live to be a hundred, then,' said Eddie, holding his wounded arm. 'You'll never catch her. She'll get back to Abydos, tell the Egyptian government what's happened . . . and then you, mate, will be fucked.'

'I don't think so.' The faintest hint of amusement creased Shaban's scarred face as the chain finally jolted to a stop. The remaining troopers rushed across the bridge. 'You don't know how we got here, do you?'

'What the hell is *that*?' Macy gasped as she and Nina climbed a ladder out of the pyramid and ran to the Land Rover, squinting in the brightness of the desert sun.

'Bad news.' About a hundred yards away was an enormous military hovercraft, its forward landing ramp lowered and gaping like a huge dull-witted mouth. Khaleel had provided Shaban with more than moral support. 'But if we can get to the canyon, there's no way it'll be able to follow us.' Nina climbed behind the wheel and put the case on the centre seat, shoving the knife back into the sheath on the harness.

Macy got in the other side. 'But what about Eddie?' she protested as Nina started the engine. 'They'll kill him – they might have killed him already!'

She backed away from the ruin, turning east. 'As long as they think they can use him to get the jar back, they'll keep him alive.'

'And how long will they keep thinking that?'

'Hopefully longer than it takes me to figure out how to rescue him!'

Less than happy with the answer, Macy checked the case for damage, then wrapped a seat belt round it to hold it in place. 'Holy crap!' she squeaked, seeing what else was attached to the webbing. 'There are two hand grenades on this thing!'

'Leave them alone,' Nina cautioned.

'But they're jiggling about and banging against each other! What if they blow up?'

'They'll be fine as long as you don't pull out the pins.' She half smiled, remembering a time when Eddie had given her a similar lesson, then focused her attention on the empty plain ahead.

Shaban's team exited the pyramid to find the Zubr's pilot waiting. The man hastily explained the situation to Khaleel in Arabic before pointing eastwards. Eddie saw a dust trail heading into the shimmering distance. 'Told you you wouldn't catch her.'

'My hovercraft can do forty knots over any terrain,' Khaleel told him smugly, nodding towards the giant vehicle. 'Can your truck do that?'

'Maybe not, but can yours fit down a twenty-foot-wide ravine?'

'It won't need to,' Diamondback drawled. 'We got some other toys.'

Shaban gave an order, and the troopers raced for the Zubr. 'We can still catch her,' he told the others, gesturing for them to follow. A cruel, crooked smile for Eddie. 'I'll make sure you have a good view.'

They started towards the hovercraft, Diamondback prodding Eddie along with his revolver. They were about three-quarters of the way there when the roar of engines echoed from inside it. A pair of small vehicles exploded from the Zubr's hold and flew down the ramp, landing in a spray of sand and snarling off in pursuit of the Land Rover. Eddie recognised them as Light Strike Vehicles – militarised dune buggies, little more than an open frame with four wheels, a powerful engine . . . and a machine gun, mounted on a turret above the driver. They weren't attractive, or comfortable – but there was one thing he knew they definitely were, even over desert sand: *fast*.

Much faster than the Defender.

'The chase begins,' Shaban proclaimed. He gave Eddie another nasty smile. 'A shame it won't be a long one.'

They ascended the ramp. The Zubr's hold was stark and utterly utilitarian, a metal box cavernous enough to accommodate three battle tanks or over three hundred fully equipped soldiers. At the moment, it was home to several dirty yellow excavators and earthmovers, as well as another dune buggy and pallets of equipment and supplies for desert operations. Eddie guessed the Osirian Temple had expected to do a lot more digging to find the pyramid.

Khaleel went to a control panel and called the bridge on a telephone handset. He issued a command. A few seconds later, a rising turbine whine echoed through the space as the Zubr's main engines started, followed by louder buzzing rasps from the four massive lift fans behind the hold's long bulkheads. The vessel wallowed as air was pumped into the skirt, lifting the hulking vehicle off the ground amidst a swirling cloud of sand.

Khaleel operated a control to raise the ramp. Hydraulics

skirled, the metal wedge slamming shut with a reverberating bang. The wind died away, but if anything the noise became louder as the engines came to full power.

Diamondback scaled the ladder in the hold's centre, and waited for Eddie to follow him up to the cramped superstructure. At the top, the American shoved him against a wall, pulling his arms behind his back. Eddie grunted at the pain from the bullet wound.

'Shoulda done this in the pyramid,' Diamondback drawled as he fastened his wrists together with a plastic zip-tie. 'You'd have had a hard time gettin' across that rope over the pit, but I woulda loved to watch you try.'

He pushed him towards a door. Eddie surreptitiously tested his restraints. They were too tight for him to slip loose, the plastic teeth digging into his skin. He needed to find another way to get free.

If there was one.

'Uh-oh,' said Macy, looking through the Land Rover's rear window. 'Dune buggy attack!'

Nina checked the mirror and saw two black shapes pounding through the desert after them. It only took a moment to see that they were gaining. Fast. She searched ahead for anything that might help. The desolate plain was devoid of anything but rippling sand dunes, the ravine still miles distant.

She glanced at the equipment webbing on the case. A knife and two grenades. Eddie could probably have MacGyvered some ingenious weapon out of them, but since she doubted the pursuing drivers would let her get within stabbing range, she was just left with throwing the grenades. And if they saw her doing so, to escape they only had to turn away . . .

The idea that came to her was so simple it seemed almost ridiculous. But it was their only hope.

If she could pull it off.

She scanned the desert again, more urgently. She needed a big enough dune—

Macy shrieked and ducked as a line of bullet impacts raked across the sand, kicking up dusty little geysers as they homed in on the Land Rover. Nina slid low in her seat, turning the wheel – but not quickly enough. The rear window shattered and holes ripped open in the Defender's aluminium sides.

Another crackle of gunfire as the second gunner joined in. Burning orange lines of tracer fire streaked past as Nina changed direction again. She knew she couldn't stay out of their sights for long—

More metal shredded as another burst of bullets stabbed through the bodywork. The windscreen cracked, the window beside Nina blowing out as a tracer round seared through the cabin. A couple of inches lower and it would have hit her in the head.

She spun the wheel, the Land Rover almost tipping over as it slewed through the sand. A pair of holes exploded in the back of the centre seat just above the case. Macy screamed.

Nina straightened out, the LSVs turning to follow. She looked ahead. There was a dune, a long, languid zigzag with an angular wind-carved ridge running along it. Perfect – if they could reach it . . .

Mirror. One of the buggies was about two hundred yards

directly behind, following their tracks. 'Take the wheel!' Nina shouted.

Macy stared in disbelief. 'What?'

'Take over, drive!' She gestured for her to slide across.

Macy did so. 'What are you doing?'

Nina jammed her left foot on the accelerator and hoisted herself up to climb over Macy. She saw in the mirror that the nearer LSV was accelerating, closing the gap to get an unmissable shot. The other buggy stopped firing so as not to hit its comrade. 'Just put your foot on the gas and grab the wheel,' she said. Macy complied, awkwardly squeezing under her. 'I've got an idea!'

In the Zubr's weapons room, Eddie looked over the weapons officer's shoulder to watch the chase playing out on the monitor screens.

A chase that was almost over. The Zubr's fire control computers displayed the range, bearing and speed of all three vehicles beside the cursors tracking them, and the distance in metres of the lead LSV was rapidly catching up to that of Nina's Land Rover.

Shaban, beside him, banged a fist on a console as the lead buggy fired again. 'The driver!' he shouted at the weapons officer. 'Tell them to aim for the driver! We can't risk hitting the jar!'

The seated man relayed the order. 'Is the box bullet-proof?' Hamdi asked nervously.

'Against a handgun bullet, it should be,' Khaleel told him. 'A machine gun . . . I don't know.'

'You'll have to check it when we recover it, Hamdi,' said Shaban. A dismissive glance at Berkeley. 'Dr Berkeley's hands are too shaky, I think.'

Eddie looked at Berkeley, who was in a corner, pale and sickened. 'Having second thoughts, are you?' he said coldly. 'Not such a laugh when it's someone you know who's getting shot at. Still, hey, least you're getting paid!'

'Keep your mouth shut,' said Diamondback, shoving him against a console.

On the screen, the Land Rover drove up a dune, the LSV closing with the gunner taking careful aim . . .

Nina climbed into the back of the Land Rover, taking one of the grenades with her. 'Go straight!' she ordered Macy as she scrambled to the rear door. 'Tell me just before we reach the top.'

'What are you *doing*?' Macy demanded, looking back – and seeing the buggy quickly gaining as the Defender slowed on the incline. She planted both feet on the accelerator.

'Just tell me!' Nina peered through the broken rear window. The first LSV was still roaring along in their tracks, less than three hundred feet behind, two fifty . . .

She gripped the door handle for support, her other thumb through the ring attached to the grenade's pin. 'Come on, come on,' she said, watching the dune buggy close the gap. It was near enough for her to make out the driver's and gunner's faces, leering expectantly as they prepared for the kill. 'Come on—'

'We're at the top!' Macy cried.

Nina jerked her thumb, pulling out the pin – and the spring-loaded spoon popped off the grenade, arming its fuse.

She hoped it was the five-second type . . .

The Land Rover lurched, reaching the top of the dune and ploughing through its ridge. The LSV dropped out of sight behind the crest.

Nina reached through the broken window – and dropped the grenade into the Land Rover's tracks.

She rolled down the cargo bed to hit the seat backs as the 4×4 slithered downhill, picking up speed. She didn't know if the rear door would protect her, but it was all she had . . .

The LSV burst over the crest of the dune, engine howling – and landed right on top of the grenade as it exploded.

The buggy was launched back into the air, flipping end over end amid an eruption of grit and razor-sharp shrapnel. It hit the ground upside-down, driving the gun turret and its lacerated occupant into the sand like a tent peg.

Nina uncovered her ears and looked back. The LSV was a burning wreck – but the second buggy was still very much in the game, vaulting over the top of the dune.

And her trick wouldn't work twice.

27

Shaban stared at the pillar of smoke rising on the monitor. 'What happened? What was that?'

'That,' said Eddie, grinning, 'was my wife.'

The Egyptian's face tightened, and he punched Eddie in the stomach. 'Go after them!' he yelled to the pilots in the bridge, before turning back to the weapons officer. 'Tell them to aim *only* at the driver. If they destroy the jar, I'll kill them myself!' The officer, glad that he worked for Khaleel and not Shaban, relayed the instructions.

Everyone lurched as the hovercraft turned to follow the Land Rover. 'Full speed!' Shaban bellowed. 'Catch them!'

Climbing back into the front seats, Nina saw the LSV rapidly gaining, following a parallel course. The buggy had a clear shot – but something was staying the gunner's finger. 'They're not shooting.'

'You make that sound like a bad thing,' Macy complained.

'It will be in a minute,' she realised. 'They're trying to get closer – so they won't just be shooting at the truck, they'll be shooting at *us*!'

'Oh, great! I *love* the personal touch!'

Nina spotted the hovercraft powering after them, but ignored it. There was a much closer threat. The LSV drew level, machine gun at the ready as it angled towards them, narrowing the gap—

The Land Rover and the LSV were side by side on the targeting monitor. The weapons operator nudged a joystick. The cursor over Nina and Macy's vehicle turned red, the radar automatically tracking the 4×4.

Eddie forced himself to look away, at the room's other occupants. Shaban's eyes were fixed on the monitor with eager anticipation, while Diamondback's expression suggested that he was watching a game of American football, waiting for his team's quarterback to break through the lines and score a touchdown. Hamdi appeared pensive, and Berkeley's head was turned, as if he were unwilling to observe the results of his choice of sides. Khaleel and the weapons officer both watched with professional detachment.

Which meant . . . nobody was watching *him*.

With his hands secured behind his back, the others didn't consider him a threat – and the weapons room's cramped confines had forced Diamondback to lower his gun as everyone crowded round the monitors.

He glanced sidelong once more at Diamondback before making his move—

No matter what Macy did, the Land Rover wasn't quick or agile enough to escape the Light Strike Vehicle. The buggy was less than a hundred feet away, still closing, the gunner lining up the M-60 machine gun on the driver . . .

The LSV's gunner was a silhouette against the desert on the screen. He took aim, body language shifting as he prepared to fire—

Eddie clenched his hands together – and shoved himself backwards against Diamondback, slamming his fists into the American's groin.

Before anyone else could react, he smashed a knee into the side of the weapons officer's head, bowling him from his chair. He whipped round and pushed the joystick with his bound hands – then spun back and banged his forehead down on one set of buttons.

The firing controls for the Zubr's AK-630 Gatling guns.

He had switched the targeting cursor from the Land Rover to the LSV when he hit the joystick – and now both the Dalek-like turrets on the broad main deck obediently locked on to their new prey.

And fired.

Even inside the windowless weapons room the noise of the guns was almost painful, an earsplitting chainsaw rasp as both six-barrelled weapons spat out over eighty 30mm explosive shells every second. The storm of metal didn't merely wreck the LSV – it *obliterated* it, the buggy and its occupants shredded as the AK-630s kept blasting, waiting for human confirmation that their target had been destroyed.

It took several seconds to arrive as Eddie kicked and struggled, trying to keep the room in chaos for as long as possible. Diamondback finally flung him against a console, cracking his head on the metal. The guns' piercing buzz stopped as the dazed weapons officer slapped a hand on the controls.

Diamondback pulled Eddie upright, shoving his revolver under his chin – only to jerk it away as Shaban smashed several punches into the defenceless Englishman's face, shrieking with frustrated fury. He delivered a final blow to Eddie's stomach, then threw him through the doorway to collapse on the bridge's deck.

The Egyptian stormed after him, kicking him in the chest before jabbing a hand at the windows. 'Follow them!'

Macy gawped at the blazing wreckage of the LSV. 'What the hell was that?'

'Eddie!' Nina looked back at the hovercraft with a surge of new hope. He was still alive!

That the Zubr's guns hadn't simply been turned on the Land Rover proved that Shaban was determined not to damage the canopic jar. Which gave her a chance to rescue her husband.

A small chance – but she had to take it.

'Turn us around,' she said. Macy looked at her uncomprehendingly. 'Turn round, go for the hovercraft!'

'Are you nuts?' Macy gasped. 'Didn't you see what just happened to that buggy? I've got *thongs* that are bigger than what's left of it!'

'They won't shoot at us.' *I hope*, she didn't add. 'Go on, go back!'

Macy unhappily brought the Land Rover round in a sweeping curve. 'You know how I thought you were really smart? Hope I wasn't wrong.'

Nina ignored her, trying to assemble all the pieces of her makeshift plan of action. She regarded the grenade, the sheathed knife – then unfastened the case's clasps.

'*Now* what're you doing?' Macy demanded.

Nina opened the case to reveal the jar nestling in its bed of memory foam. Without the lid's pressure holding it down, the jar rose as the lower block returned to its original shape. She drew the knife and sawed away one corner of the foam, ending up with a ragged cube four inches to a side, then closed the case. 'Evening the odds.'

'They're coming back at us,' reported the Zubr's pilot.

'What?' Shaban glared through the bridge windows. The Land Rover was indeed heading straight for the hovercraft. 'She's going to *attack* us!'

'With what?' asked Khaleel.

'The grenades she took from Hashem!'

The pilot made a sarcastic sound. 'A grenade won't hurt us. The hull's armoured – the most she could do is tear the skirt, and that's compartmentalised. It would only deflate one section, not the whole thing.'

'Then what is she doing?'

Hamdi leaned through the doorway. 'Perhaps she's seen sense and wants to surrender?' he suggested hopefully.

Shaban looked at Eddie, who was still curled in pain on the floor, flanked by two soldiers Khaleel had summoned. 'If she is anything like her husband, I doubt it. Get him up.' Diamondback hauled Eddie to his feet and shoved him against the aft bulkhead.

Khaleel looked at the approaching 4×4. 'We could shoot out the engine, force them to stop.'

Shaban shook his head. 'We might damage the jar. If she wants to come to us willingly, let's see what she has in mind. If it's a trick, she'll pay for it with her life.' A menacing look at Eddie. 'And his.'

The hovercraft was a slab of black and grey ahead, its superstructure rising above the flat main deck like a submarine's conning tower. Getting larger very quickly. 'Oh, God, what are we doing?' Macy moaned, seeing its guns.

Nina donned the webbing, carrying the case like a backpack. 'Just swerve when I tell you.' She crouched on the passenger seat. 'Get ready . . .'

'That thing's *huge*!' Macy protested. 'What if it runs us over?'

'I'm kinda counting on you to not let that happen.'

'Oh, no pressure!' The Zubr loomed ever larger, more like a building that had somehow torn itself from its foundations than a vehicle. The roar of its propellers shook the air.

Nina drew the knife. The hovercraft was rushing straight at them, artificial sandstorms blasting out from beneath its skirt. 'Ready, ready . . . *now*!'

Macy turned the wheel sharply, swinging the Land Rover past the oncoming Zubr's starboard side. Nina poised, waiting for the right moment.

Shaban watched the Defender veer from its seeming suicide run. 'Turn, follow her!' he shouted as the 4×4 disappeared into the cloud of sand to his right.

Khaleel opened the hatch to the jutting ledge of the starboard wing bridge, gesturing for a soldier to do the same on the port side in case the Land Rover tried to get round behind them. 'I can't see them, they're in the sand!'

'*Find her!*' Shaban yelled. The pilot turned the wheel, the rudders below the three huge propellers at the stern swerving the floating craft hard to the right.

Sand swept in through the broken windows, grit scouring Nina's skin. She held her position, squinting through the swirling cloud.

The hovercraft was a dark mass to the right, swinging to follow them. 'Keep turning!' she shouted. 'Catch up with it!'

Though part blinded by the spraying sand, Macy spun the wheel, bringing the Land Rover in a tight turn towards the Zubr. The 4×4 had a far smaller turning circle than the giant transporter, cutting inside the larger vehicle's arcing course – and drawing alongside.

The noise was appalling, the sandstorm physically painful at such close range. But Nina needed to get even closer. The hovercraft's side skirt loomed, a rippling black wall of reinforced rubber. She shoved open the door, the blast of air pummelling her.

She raised the knife—

Even with his face pressed against the bulkhead, Eddie couldn't hold back a smile at Shaban's rising frustration. 'Where are they?' the cult leader yelled, running from one wing bridge to the other, hunting for his foes.

The din was worse than ever, but partial respite came from the sandblasting effect as the Land Rover drew right alongside the hovercraft, most of the escaping air sweeping below it. Nina had a clear view of the black rubber five feet away, four—

She jumped.

Springing from the Defender, she slammed against the skirt – and stabbed the knife into it.

Air gushed out round the blade with a whistling shriek, but it held firm as Nina dangled from the hilt, the tendons in her arm straining. She kicked at the skirt, which gave just enough for her boots to gain a little traction and let her pull herself up to grip the knife with both hands.

She glanced back. Although she had protested Nina's plan, Macy had done as instructed and retreated into the dust cloud to get as far from the hovercraft as possible.

The ground rushed past below. Even turning, the Zubr was still doing over thirty miles an hour. And only Nina's hold on the knife was keeping her from falling.

She strained to pull herself up, feeling the layers of rubber and fabric warp under her weight. The bottom of the hull was only a couple of feet above her. She was halfway along the hovercraft's length, nearly level with the bridge three decks above. About six feet to one side, metal rungs led up to the narrow side deck.

Gripping the knife tightly with her left hand, Nina stretched up her right arm and tried to reach the lip of the hull. Her fingertips fell six inches short. She dug her feet into the curved rubber for extra grip, clasping both hands round the hilt and forcing herself higher. The knife shifted, its edge cutting through the skirt.

'Shit!' she gasped as the rushing wail of air grew louder. If the hole got much bigger, she wouldn't be able to hold the knife in it – and would fall.

More desperately, she again reached up for the hull – but was still a couple of inches off.

'There!' cried the pilot, pointing. Shaban saw the Land Rover emerge from the cloud and speed east across the desert.

'Go after them,' he ordered. The pilot brought the Zubr on to a pursuit course.

The skirt rippled beneath Nina as the hovercraft turned. The knife jerked again, lengthening the slit. She could feel it slipping.

Straining, she hauled herself up on the hilt and lashed out with her right hand—

Her fingertips found the edge of the hard metal. Gripped it. She released the hilt, reaching up. The knife was blown out of the hole. She clambered sideways towards the ladder. A final stretch, and her hand clamped round the bottom rung.

The co-pilot noticed a flashing warning light. 'Sir! There's a leak in the skirt.'

'Where?' demanded the pilot.

'Starboard side, centre section.'

Khaleel looked down from the wing bridge – to see Nina climbing the ladder to the side deck. 'Wilde's on board!' he shouted, drawing his pistol.

Shaban ran to him. 'Don't shoot!' Khaleel gave him a surprised look. 'She's got the case – if she falls, it might break the jar. Send your crew to catch her.'

Nina reached the top of the ladder, disappearing from view beneath the edge of the main deck. Khaleel cursed, then moved to issue orders over the public address system. Shaban turned to Eddie. 'She actually thinks she can rescue you.'

'She's a smart lass,' Eddie replied.

'She ain't *that* smart,' snorted Diamondback. 'Comin' aboard this thing with no way to get off again? That don't exactly make her look like a rocket scientist.'

'It's not like she's up against MENSA,' said Eddie, a comeback that earned him a kidney punch. But even though he was outwardly confident, his thoughts were worried: Nina was unarmed, and outnumbered. What the hell was she planning?

Nina stood on the side deck, getting her bearings. The narrow walkway ran almost the hovercraft's full length; several hatches led inside, the closest right beside her. Another ladder went up to the Zubr's huge main deck, but the open expanse of metal, almost half the size of a football pitch, would offer her almost no cover, and she wanted to avoid being seen for as long as possible—

A door at the stern swung open and two men emerged from the engine room. They ran towards her.

So much for not being seen!

She darted through the nearest hatch, slamming it shut to find herself in a narrow and very noisy hallway. There was a locking mechanism on the inside of the hatch, Cyrillic instructions stencilled on the painted metal – with a sticker bearing both Arabic text and the English words 'NBC Seal' below. She knew from Eddie that the acronym was not a TV network but an abbreviation of Nuclear, Biological, Chemical – the vessel's interior could be sealed to protect the crew against weapons of mass destruction. She pulled a lever, a heavy bolt sliding into place, then tugged down a smaller, red-painted handle to lock it.

The thunder behind the aft bulkhead told her she was right beside one of the hovercraft's lift fans. She quickly went to the other end of the passage. A door in the forward bulkhead opened into a room full of closely packed bunk beds – crew quarters. Considering the noise it didn't seem like the best place to sleep, but that was far from her greatest concern as she saw another hatch leading to the side deck.

Banging from behind as the crewmen reached the door she had just entered and tried to open it. It would only take them a moment to realise it was locked, then they would move on to the next—

Nina ran across the bunk room and yanked the bolt, slamming down the locking lever just as someone rattled at it from outside.

The nearest unlocked hatch was back by the engine room. She had the time she needed.

Unfastening the webbing, she placed the case on a bed and opened it.

Khaleel listened to a report over the intercom. 'She's in one of the starboard cabins,' he told Shaban. 'She's locked the outer hatches, but there aren't many places she can go.'

Shaban nodded. 'Hamdi, as soon as we have the case, I want you to check the jar for damage.'

Hamdi came into the room. 'I'll need some space.'

There was a small metal plotting table behind the two pilots' stations. Shaban swept the maps off it. 'There.' He turned to Diamondback. 'Go and get her. Don't do anything that might damage the case – just bring her here.' Diamondback didn't appear pleased at the implicit order not to shoot her, but he nodded, handing Eddie over to a soldier and leaving the bridge.

The cult leader picked up the PA system's handset. 'Dr Wilde!'

Carrying the case on her back, Nina cautiously opened a hatch and peered into the hold. Right in front of her was another dune buggy, an unarmed civilian model, secured to rings in the deck between a couple of grimy caterpillar-tracked excavators.

She was about to move out when Shaban's voice boomed from loudspeakers. 'Dr Wilde! I know you can hear me. Give yourself up and hand over the jar. If you do not, I'll kill your husband.'

There was a muffled noise, then Eddie spoke. 'Ay up, love.'

Despite the tense situation, Nina couldn't hold in a brief smile at the sound of his voice. The hope on which she had based her gamble had paid off; Shaban was indeed using him to force her hand.

How much longer he – and she – stayed alive depended entirely on Shaban's anger. If he decided to settle his scores before checking his prize . . .

'Forget about me,' Eddie quickly went on. 'Just smash that fucking pot and—' There was a dull thud, followed by a gruff grunt of pain.

'Bring me the jar, Dr Wilde,' said Shaban. '*Now.*' The PA clicked off.

Nina steeled herself, then entered the hold, stepping out from behind the vehicles and raising her hands as members of the hovercraft's crew burst through a hatch. They ran over and grabbed her roughly.

Cowboy boots clanged down the ladder at the cavernous compartment's centre. Diamondback.

'Well, shit,' he said as he swaggered towards her, 'I was kinda hoping you'd put up a struggle. I always like puttin' bitches in their place.' He leered, then gestured with his gun at the ladder. 'Now move it.'

Flanked by the soldiers, Nina went to the ladder. Diamondback ascended, then waved for her to follow. She scaled the rungs to the next deck. A steep flight of metal stairs rose to another level. At the top, a short windowless passage led to the bridge.

Shaban was waiting there – as was Eddie, a soldier holding him against the rear wall near the open port wing bridge hatch. 'Nina! You – oh, for fuck's sake,' he said, joy at seeing her turning to dismay as he realised she had brought the case containing the canopic jar. 'I told you to smash that thing!'

'I'm trying to save your life, Eddie,' she said. 'Just like when you rescued me from Jack Mitchell's ship.' He looked confused. 'When you came into the hold?' she went on, trying to make her meaning subtle in case her captors picked up on it.

It was *too* subtle. His expression was still one of befuddlement.

Shaban's look was of greed, however. 'Put down the case,

Dr Wilde,' he said, indicating the plotting table. '*Very* carefully. Dr Hamdi!'

Hamdi bustled in, chest swelling with self-importance. He squeezed round the table to stand between the pilots, facing the others as Nina eased the case off her shoulders. 'It doesn't look damaged,' he announced as she put it down.

'Move her back,' said Shaban. Diamondback pushed her across to the starboard bulkhead. She saw Berkeley in the weapons room and glared at him; he looked away, ashamed. 'Now, open the case.'

With great care, Hamdi unfastened one latch, then the other. His audience leaned closer. Nina looked across the bridge at Eddie, hoping to make eye contact and give him a silent hint, but a soldier was in the way.

Hamdi took hold of the lid with a theatrical flourish, then lifted it.

There was a metallic clack. A ragged-edged hunk of memory foam sprang from the case, a curved piece of metal popping out from beneath it to spin to a stop on the table.

Eyes went wide as they recognised the object: the spoon of a hand grenade. The piece of foam had held it in place while Nina carefully removed the pin before fully closing the case – with the pressure gone, the spring had been released.

Activating the five-second fuse.

Four seconds.

The bridge suddenly became a mad whirl of movement. Shaban, closest to the case, spun to find an exit. Diamondback flung him into the weapons room, diving on top of him. Khaleel ducked under the sturdy metal table, clapping his hands over his ears. One soldier ran for the stairwell, the man holding Eddie abandoning his charge and diving to the floor.

Three.

Nina and Eddie shared a millisecond look across the room – then both leapt in opposite directions, through the hatchways on to the wing bridges.

Two.

Hamdi's shocked brain finally registered the true nature of the dull green ovoid where he had expected to see the canopic jar. He whimpered, turning to flee, but found his escape routes blocked by the panicked pilots as they tried to get out of their chairs.

One—

Eddie hit the wing bridge's railing, seeing the broad circular vent and spinning blades of a lift fan almost directly below. Not a good direction to jump. Instead, he rolled over the aft-facing section of barrier. Arms still fastened behind his back by the plastic tie, he had no way to cushion his fall as he slammed painfully down.

On the other side of the bridge, Nina vaulted the railing—

The grenade exploded.

28

The reinforced case channelled the blast upwards and outwards at waist height. The two pilots were killed instantly, torn apart by razor-shards of metal. Hamdi was catapulted backwards, smashing through a window to slam brokenly on the main deck below.

The soldier trying to reach the stairwell only got as far as the door, hit in the back by a swathe of jagged shrapnel. The others in the room escaped the direct force of the blast, but were still left near-deafened and disoriented by the detonation.

The port wing bridge hatch was blown off its hinges. It cartwheeled downwards – and was sucked into the gaping maw of the lift fan.

The jet engine-like vanes shattered as the hatch was chewed up, jagged blades flying in every direction. Eddie rolled to flatten his face against the deck as shards clashed against the superstructure above him. The mangled hatch whirled through the vortex inside the vertical shaft – and then there was a horrific deck-shaking bang as it jammed the fan's driveshaft, the torsional force of machinery going from forty thousand revolutions per minute to zero in a millisecond ripping the entire thing apart.

The damage didn't stop at the fan.

The smashed driveshaft was directly connected to one of the gas turbine power plants in the port-side engine room. The effects rippled back along the hovercraft, tearing more equipment apart and filling the engineering spaces with lethal fragments. The turbine blew up, a fireball blasting hatches open.

A quarter of its lift gone, the Zubr wallowed, nose dipping to port. It began to slide off course.

And with the pilots dead and the controls wrecked, there was nobody to stop it.

Body aching from the fall, Eddie struggled to sit up. He was no longer a prisoner, but his hands were still tied behind his back. He had to get free . . .

There was a pointed hunk of metal nearby, a torn piece of insulation burning at one end. He fumbled for it with his left hand.

He felt his skin burning as he gripped it. The metal was still hot. But he grimaced and fought the pain, pressing the flaming end against the plastic tie.

In the weapons room, Diamondback pushed himself off his boss. Berkeley clutched his ears in a corner. The weapons officer was slumped over his console, a shard of flying debris embedded in a neck wound.

Diamondback retrieved his revolver, then helped Shaban up. 'Are you okay?'

'I think so,' Shaban said dizzily – then his face twisted with fury. 'That bitch tried to *kill* me! Go after her, kill her!'

'What about the jar? She musta—'

'*Kill her!*' Shaban screamed. Diamondback flinched, then hurried back into the bridge.

The room was filled with smoke, the consoles on fire. Coughing, Khaleel crawled out from under the table. It was buckled, but had been sturdy enough to protect him from the blast. The soldier by the port hatch was barely conscious, bleeding from several shrapnel wounds. Khaleel moved to check his injuries, but Diamondback jabbed a finger at the opening. 'Go after Chase – I'll get the woman.'

'But he needs—'

Shaban appeared in the doorway. 'Tarik, I will double your money. Just kill them!'

Khaleel hesitated, then went to the hatch as Diamondback ran to the starboard wing bridge and looked out.

Nina was on the deck below by the lift fan. Just as he snapped up his gun, she saw him and ran. A bullet twanged off the foot-high lip of the circular air intake behind her.

The deck was a blank expanse of metal, the only cover the Gatling gun's turret towards the bow – and she would never reach it before being shot in the back.

Only one way to go . . .

She dived for the railing at the deck's edge as Diamondback fired again. The shot cracked off the floor, spitting paint chips at her face as she rolled under the railing and slammed down on the narrow walkway below. Another bullet zipped past; she pushed herself painfully back into cover.

Diamondback lost sight of her. 'Shit!' he hissed, running for the stairs.

On the port wing bridge, Khaleel looked down at the

gaping vent of the smashed lift fan. He saw Eddie, grabbed for his holstered gun—

Skin blistering, Eddie pressed the metal harder against the tie. He felt it give, the plastic stretching, then snapping. He jumped up – and caught movement in his peripheral vision, someone aiming a weapon on the jutting balcony above.

Instinct and training kicked in. He flung the lump of metal upwards, running for the stern as a startled cry confirmed that he'd scored a hit. If he could round the superstructure before Khaleel recovered, he would be temporarily safe—

Shots!

Bullets spanged from the deck, cutting off his escape route. He dived beside the aft lift fan, scrambling round the intake in a desperate attempt to find cover. But it was too low to shield him. Khaleel lined up his sights on the half-exposed figure, and squeezed the trigger.

The bullet flew at Eddie – then suddenly veered downwards, sucked into the huge fan. Eddie raised his head, feeling the powerful suction of air being pulled into the shaft. As long as the vortex was between the two men, Khaleel had no chance of hitting him.

The general realised it at the same moment. He jumped down to the main deck. Eddie scrambled round to make a run for the superstructure, but Khaleel already had his gun back up, covering the gap as he advanced.

He was trapped.

Groaning at the pain from her hard landing, Nina struggled upright and saw she was close to the hatch through which she had first entered the hovercraft. Someone had unlocked it, the heavy door swinging lazily.

She checked that the passage was empty, then entered. The crew quarters were also unoccupied; she went to the bed where she had hidden the canopic jar after booby-trapping the case. With Eddie free, she now had all the cards – once they were both safely off the Zubr, she could destroy the jar's contents and end any hope Shaban still cherished of carrying out his insane plan.

All she had to do was find Eddie.

Still charging across the desert towards the canyon, Macy looked back at the pursuing hovercraft – and was startled to find it was no longer behind her. It had angled away to one side. Something had gone badly wrong – the massive craft was trailing smoke, on fire near its stern.

Nina and Eddie, she knew. Their kind of chaos.

But there was no sign that they had got off the speeding giant. And, she realised, if the hovercraft stayed on its new course it would miss the canyon and continue across the plain.

To the high cliffs at its far end.

'Oh, crap,' she gasped.

Berkeley staggered on to the bridge, looking in horror at the pilots' shrapnel-torn bodies. 'Jesus! What happened?'

'Never mind,' said Shaban. 'We've got to find Wilde – and the jar.' He had already deduced that she couldn't have rigged the grenade until *after* boarding the hovercraft – the risk of the spoon's being jolted loose when she jumped from the 4×4 would have been too great. Which meant . . . 'She must have hidden it. Come on.'

'I, ah . . .' The archaeologist couldn't tear his gaze from the corpses. 'I don't feel too good.'

Shaban shoved him against the bulkhead. 'If you want to stay alive, you'll do what I tell you,' he snarled, pulling him to the stairwell.

Still hunched behind the lift fan, Eddie glanced over the edge of the deck to look for an escape route. No luck. Wind-whipped flames from the damaged engine room were lashing from a hatch forward of his position, the heat and toxic smoke cutting the walkway off from the rest of the vessel.

Khaleel jogged towards him, automatic raised. In seconds, he would have a clear line of fire. Eddie didn't have many options left – but any action was better than waiting to get shot.

He ran for the stern. The three huge propellers towered above him, blades a buzzing blur inside their circular shrouds. He might find cover behind the pylons supporting the engine nacelles, even a way back inside the ship to search for Nina . . .

Too slow. Khaleel cleared the lift fan, taking aim—

A shrill, ululating siren blasted from the superstructure. Someone had finally decided that the engine room blaze was out of control and sounded the alarm to abandon the hovercraft. The piercing wail made Khaleel flinch as he fired. The bullet seared past Eddie, close enough for him to feel its heat.

The gun's slide locked back. Out of ammo. The Egyptian reached for a fresh magazine, but Eddie was already charging at him. Not enough time to reload—

Instead, his hand went to another weapon.

Eddie jerked to a stop as Khaleel jabbed a knife at his chest. The soldier struck again, slashing at his face. Eddie tried to grab his wrist – but he turned the blade to slice through Eddie's sleeve into his already wounded forearm.

The Englishman pulled away in pain, and took a vicious kick to his stomach. Winded, he stumbled backwards, crashing against something at waist height.

The bottom of the propeller shroud.

Eddie swayed back, his head almost sucked into the giant blades. He shoved himself away – as Khaleel stabbed the knife at his heart—

He grabbed the other man's arm, arresting the attack just before the tip pierced his chest, but the force of Khaleel's charge drove him back against the shroud. The gale whipping round them forced both men to squint, eyes fixed on the knife.

Khaleel forced it towards his opponent's throat, the double wound to Eddie's forearm weakening his hold. He tried to push it away, but the most he could manage was to twist it to one side. The tip dug into his jacket – then cut deeper as Khaleel forced the knife down.

Eddie cried out as the point ground against his collar-bone. Khaleel grinned and pushed even harder, leaning closer—

Eddie whipped his head forward. He wasn't at the right angle to score a solid blow with a headbutt – but instead he clamped his jaws tightly shut on Khaleel's nose.

The general screeched, pulling out the knife as he tried to draw back, but Eddie had too firm a hold. There was a hideous wet scrunch of cartilage as he ground his teeth.

With both nostrils crushed shut, the only place the sudden gush of blood could go was into Khaleel's throat. Choking, he spat blood across Eddie's chest, the knife all but forgotten in his desperation to escape the pain.

Eddie refused to let go, worrying the flesh like a terrier. There was another revolting squish – then Khaleel lurched back, a bloodied hole where the end of his nose had been. Eddie spat the chunk of gristle into his eye, then with a roar shoved the Egyptian's arm over his shoulder.

Into the propeller.

There was a clang as the knife was knocked out of the soldier's hand – followed by a swat as his forefinger was sliced off at the first knuckle, exposing a jagged spike of bone. Khaleel screamed. Eddie slammed two powerful blows into his stomach, following them with an uppercut that sent him reeling.

They were right by the side railing. The quickest way to end the fight would be to toss the Egyptian overboard—

He seized Khaleel – and was almost blinded as the other man unexpectedly struck back, stabbing at Eddie's eye with the end of his severed finger. Sharp bone slashed across his eyebrow as he jerked his head away.

The finger stabbed again, cutting his cheek – and Khaleel's other hand clamped round his throat, tendons tight as metal cables. He spat out more blood and a foul Arabic curse. With one arm wounded, Eddie needed both hands to avoid getting the finger in a horribly literal way, giving Khaleel the chance to push him back towards the propeller.

'I'll kill you!' Khaleel gargled, eyes bulging with demented fury. 'I'll kill you, and my dogs will eat your balls, and then I'll fuck your wife before I—'

Eddie let go with one hand, taking the spear of bone across his temple as Khaleel overpowered his wounded arm – and swept up his good arm between the Egyptian's legs to grab him by the crotch. Khaleel's eyes bulged even wider as, with his own rage-powered burst of strength, Eddie flung him upwards.

The gale-force suction dragged him in. Khaleel's skull was instantly pulped by the rapidly spinning blades, a red mist painting the inside of the metal shroud. The headless body slid back down over Eddie and slumped to the deck.

Eddie lowered himself out of the wind. 'Keep your head, mate – oops, too late,' he wheezed, checking the corpse. The Egyptian had holstered his gun after kicking him; he drew it, taking an extra magazine and reloading the weapon.

Wiping blood from his face, he looked round. Some of the crew were on the deck, but none were interested in him or their late commanding officer; they were instead attempting to get off the runaway hovercraft. One man climbed over the railing, trying to slide down the skirt to the ground – but instead he bounced off it, cartwheeling into the dust storm at a neck-breaking angle. His comrades decided they needed a new plan and hurried back into the ship.

Hefting the gun, Eddie searched for his own way inside.

Macy was just about keeping pace with the hovercraft – but through the heat haze she could now see a distinct line cutting across the landscape ahead.

The cliff.

The Zubr was only minutes from destruction.

She had seen people on the deck, but none was Eddie or Nina. 'Come on,' she said, bringing the Land Rover closer, 'get off that thing!'

Clutching the canopic jar, Nina looked into the hold, and saw to her horror that a fire was spreading from a door at its port-side rear. Several men were in the large space, keeping well away from the flames as one operated a control panel. The front and rear ramps lowered, the gritty rush of wind through the hold sweeping the smoke out of the stern – but also fanning the fire.

One man ran towards the hold's rear. Jumping out of the hovercraft's stern offered more chance of survival – were it not for the blaze. The ramp was narrower than the hold, offset to port, and the growing flames were whipping down it. The crewman shielded his face – then sprinted for the square of daylight.

He mistimed it. A swirling gust of fire swept from the hatchway, setting him alight. The burning figure's limbs flailed as he vanished into the sandstorm.

The remaining men were no happier with the forward escape route. One brave – or foolish – soldier took a running jump off the ramp, trying to reach the skirt and climb along it to the side. The reactions of the others made it clear that he wasn't successful. But faced with a choice between slipping off and being dragged under the enormous vessel or the fire, they opted to take their chances, leaping from the ramp one by one.

The last man gone, Nina entered the hold, moving to the dune buggy to check its restraining straps. If she could untether it, maybe it would be fast enough to drive out of the rear ramp without catching fire . . .

She heard feet clanking down the ladder. No time to return to the hatch. She scrambled underneath the earth-mover behind the buggy, peering out to see Shaban and Berkeley descend into the hold. 'Find the jar,' Shaban ordered, gesturing sternwards.

Berkeley baulked. 'There's a big fire back there.'

'Then don't walk into it! Check the bulldozers, see if she hid it inside one of them. Or underneath.'

'What about you?' Berkeley asked as Shaban went to the dune buggy.

'This is our way off. Go on, search!'

Nina tensed, but to her relief Berkeley went to one of the earthmovers on the other side of the hold. She slithered to the rear of the machine she was hiding under. There was another open hatch not far away – if she could reach it without being seen . . .

The fire was growing, grease and spilled oil on the deck catching light. Berkeley finished his examination of the first bulldozer and moved to the one behind it.

The door was about fifteen feet away. Twisting to look back, she spotted Shaban's feet by the buggy as he released the last strap.

He was facing away from her. She might be able to reach the door if she moved now – and if Berkeley didn't see her.

The archaeologist had climbed up to check the cab, his back to her.

This was her chance.

She slid out, about to dart for the door when Berkeley hopped down – and turned.

He saw her.

Their eyes met across the hold. Nina froze. One word from him would alert the cult leader . . .

The word didn't come.

Berkeley blinked, then his expression became studiously blank. He turned away, searching the bulldozer's cab for a second time.

Nina gave him silent thanks, then got ready to run—

'What is it?' Shaban shouted, making both Nina and Berkeley flinch. He had seen the scientist's moment of indecision.

'I–I'm not sure,' Berkeley stuttered, but Shaban was already striding towards her position.

She jumped up and held the jar above her head. 'Don't move! I'll smash it!'

Shaban stopped, holding out his hands. 'Give it to me, Dr Wilde.'

'I don't think so!' She backed away, looking over her shoulder at the spreading fire. 'How about we bake your bread, huh?'

'No!' He advanced another step, torn between the urge to retrieve the canopic jar and the fear of its being destroyed. 'Give it to me and – and I'll let you live.'

Nina kept retreating. 'What, so you can use it to kill millions of people? No way. This ends here, asshole.'

His eyes flicked away from her to the hold's side wall. 'You're right. It does.'

'Nina!' Berkeley cried in warning – too late.

Diamondback dived from the open hatch, tackling Nina. The jar was jolted from her hands as they hit the deck. He just managed to get his grasping fingertips underneath it to stop it from smashing, but couldn't hold on to it. The jar rolled towards the fire – then clanked to a stop against one of the cargo rings.

Shaban let out a deep breath as he realised the jar was safe. He started for it. 'Kill her,' he snapped.

'My pleasure,' said Diamondback. He pulled Nina's head up by her ponytail, reaching into his snakeskin jacket with his other hand to draw his gun—

Everyone looked round as another door flew open.

Eddie jumped through, Khaleel's weapon in his hands. He immediately locked it on to the biggest threat, Diamondback – but the American yanked Nina higher, making her cry out in pain as he used her as a human shield. Shaban hurriedly took cover behind the nearest earth-mover. Berkeley did the same on the other side of the hold, cowering in one of the lowered scoops.

'Eddie,' Nina gasped, horrified by the amount of blood on his face and clothes. 'Oh, my God . . .'

'Hi, love,' he said, before shifting his gaze to Diamondback. 'You. Puff Adder. You've got to the count of three to let her go.'

Diamondback pressed his revolver against Nina's head. 'And you've got to the count of two to drop that piece.'

'Eddie, shoot the jar!' Nina said. He glanced sideways and spotted the canopic jar. 'If you destroy it, they've got nothing!'

'Do that and she dies, Chase!' shouted Shaban, signalling for his bodyguard to hold his fire – for now. In response, Diamondback pulled Nina to her knees, still crouching behind her as he forced her to shuffle away from Eddie.

Eddie tracked them with the gun, slowly following. It was a stand-off; Diamondback knew that if he killed Nina he would die a second later, but Eddie couldn't take a shot without risking hitting her. All he could do was watch as they backed up until they were close to the open door.

'Sebak!' the American called. 'Are the keys in that bulldozer?'

Shaban immediately understood what he was thinking and moved to the earthmover's cab, keeping low to stay out of Eddie's line of fire. He leaned inside. The starter motor chattered, then the diesel engine rumbled to life.

'Whatever you're doing, fuckin' pack it in,' Eddie warned, but he was unable to do anything to stop them. Diamondback, still holding the gun to Nina's head, fumbled in a pocket for a zip-tie. He threaded it through a cargo ring and loosely pushed the end into the fastener, then grabbed Nina's hand and forced it into the plastic loop before yanking it as tight as it would go.

Nina gasped as the tie's toothed inner face chewed deeply into her wrist. She was firmly secured to the ring, her arm bent back painfully. 'You ain't goin' anywhere,' Diamondback drawled in her ear.

Shaban, meanwhile, had figured out the basics of the earthmover's controls. He pulled a lever to raise the dogtoothed front scoop higher off the deck, then wedged a large spanner from a toolbox against the gas pedal. The engine roared, its exhaust pipe spewing out oily brown smoke, but the machine didn't move. It wasn't in gear.

Yet.

He looked up – and saw something through the open front ramp. The line of the cliff-edge ahead. Less than a mile away.

The Zubr would reach it in under two minutes.

Eddie looked between Diamondback and Shaban, the horrible realisation of their plan dawning. He now had a clear shot at the cult leader – but switching his aim would give Diamondback the moment he needed to whip his gun round and shoot him.

The jar—

It rattled against the ring, about the same distance away as Nina.

Shaban saw him look. 'Which do you choose, Chase? Stop me, or save your wife? You can only do one!'

He jammed the stick into the lowest reverse gear – and jumped clear as the bulldozer lurched backwards.

It moved less than a foot before crashing to a stop as the chains securing it to the deck snapped taut. But the restraints were designed only to keep it in place while the hovercraft was in motion, not to withstand the force of several hundred horsepower. Steel tracks screeching horribly over the floor, the excavator started to tear itself free, the cargo rings creaking and squealing.

Diamondback held his place behind Nina, one eye on the snarling vehicle twelve feet away. 'Well, go ahead!' he shouted to Eddie. 'It's your move.'

Eddie glanced at the jar. Could he kick it into the fire before the bulldozer broke free?

But if it came to a choice, he knew there was only one he could make—

A ring snapped. The extra stress on the remaining restraints was too much, and less than a second later they shattered. The bulldozer ground backwards.

Towards Nina.

Diamondback rolled away from her, throwing himself to

the far side of the bulldozer. Eddie fired, but both shots clanged uselessly off the machine.

He ran to Nina, who was desperately trying to free her arm. The earthmover continued its inexorable advance, five feet away, four. Eddie knew there was no way she could get her hand loose in time – and instead jammed his gun against the metal ring.

He pulled the trigger. The bullet severed the tie, ricocheting off the ring and knocking the gun from his hand. The muzzle flame burned Nina's arm. She screamed, but he had already pulled her back as the earthmover ran over the dented ring.

They rolled clear as the hulking machine rumbled past, but the danger wasn't over. Shaban raced past for the canopic jar. Diamondback was a few paces behind him, gun raised. Eddie looked for his own weapon—

It vanished under the bulldozer's track with a crunch of flattening metal.

He hauled Nina with him round the rear of the crawling machine. Diamondback fired, the shot tearing a chunk from the yellow bodywork. The American was about to run after them when he realised there was a shortcut, and jumped up to climb into the cab—

Eddie was already there.

He made a diving tackle over the seat, and both men crashed to the deck. The revolver clattered across the floor.

Shaban reached the jar and snatched it up, feeling a moment of pure relief as he saw it was undamaged and still sealed. He ran back to the dune buggy. Berkeley looked out from his hiding place; the cult leader scowled at him, making him cringe back.

Eddie punched Diamondback – with his injured arm, causing himself almost as much pain as he delivered. The American realised something was wrong and clawed at his adversary's forearm, fingers digging into the bullet wound. Eddie screamed, jerking back and giving Diamondback the chance to kick him away. The bulldozer rolled past them.

Nina climbed into the machine's cab. She kicked the spanner off the accelerator and shoved the gearstick into neutral, the bulldozer clanking to a stop just short of the spreading fire at the back of the hold. In front of the earthmover she saw Diamondback smash an elbow down on Eddie's chest, beyond them Shaban climbing into the dune buggy – and through the gaping forward ramp . . .

The cliff!

Diamondback hit Eddie in the ribs again, then sprang up to find his gun. It was in front of the bulldozer. He grabbed it and straightened, turning to shoot Eddie—

And froze as the dune buggy peeled away with a screech of tyres. Shaban was at the wheel, clutching the canopic jar to his chest. 'Sebak!' the American yelled, voice lost amongst the roar of wind and machinery. '*Wait!*'

Eddie sat up. Diamondback snapped out of his shock at being abandoned and took aim—

Nina slammed the bulldozer into gear.

It jerked forward – and its scoop hit the American hard in his back. His gun flew from his hand and landed in the steel bucket. He reeled towards Eddie – then lurched backwards as a fist ploughed into his face.

Eddie hit him again and again. Diamondback spat out blood. Eddie wound up and smashed an uppercut into his chin that knocked the other man off his feet against the scoop's edge, the metal teeth ripping through the back of his snakeskin jacket.

Diamondback wasn't finished, though. He saw his gun, groped for it—

And was hauled into the air as Nina raised the scoop.

His weight pulled the jacket tightly over the steel teeth, leaving him hanging helplessly. He tried to shrug off the garment, but couldn't get his arms free.

Eddie drove one last punch into his stomach as the bulldozer stopped, then looked towards the bow.

Shaban drove the dune buggy off the ramp.

The rugged off-roader hit the ground hard, slamming the Egyptian against his seatbelt. He just barely managed to keep the vehicle under control with one hand as he gripped the jar. For a moment the Zubr gained on him, the ramp's jutting edge like a huge shovel blade about to scoop up the buggy . . . then he pulled away, making a hard turn to one side. The hovercraft blasted past him.

Heading straight for the cliff.

Macy saw the dune buggy swing away, and realised who was driving.

If Shaban had escaped, then where were Nina and Eddie? Were they—

No. She refused to accept the possibility. They hadn't given up on her; she wasn't going to give up on them.

Jaw set, she dropped down a gear and pushed the accelerator to its limit. The temperature gauge was in the red, the elderly Land Rover overheating, but it still began to overtake the hovercraft.

★

Nina ran to Eddie. 'Are you okay?' she asked, taking in his multiple injuries.

'Nothing a month in the Maldives won't fix,' he rasped, gripping his arm to stop the bleeding. Ignoring the impotently kicking and swearing Diamondback, he surveyed the hold, seeing the hatch leading to the starboard engineering compartment. 'We've got to stop this thing. Maybe we could chuck something in the engine—'

'There isn't time!' Nina cried, jabbing a finger at the front ramp. 'We're gonna go over a cliff!'

'What? Shit!' His search became more desperate. The fire at the rear ramp was now a swirling inferno, and if they tried to jump off from the bow the hovercraft would mow them down.

No way out—

A crash of metal made them whirl – to see the battered Land Rover lurch backwards up the front ramp. Macy had driven directly in front of the Zubr, then braked hard, to be swallowed up like a minnow by a whale. The 4×4 skidded as she slammed on the brakes, slewing round to face them.

Macy sat up, dazed, then her rattled expression became one of delight as she saw Nina and Eddie. 'Come on!' she shouted. 'Get in!'

They ran for the bullet-pocked Defender. 'Logan!' called Nina. 'Move your ass!' Berkeley emerged from his hiding place and scurried for the Land Rover. They all piled in.

Through the bow, Eddie saw the edge of the cliff for the first time, rushing towards them. Too close for the Land Rover to get clear. 'The rear ramp, go!' he yelled.

'It's on fire!' Berkeley protested.

'Just *go*!'

Macy slammed the Land Rover into gear and drove the 4×4 between the two ranks of heavy equipment. She saw the whipping flames. 'Jesus!'

'Go through it!' cried Eddie. Diamondback was still hanging from the earthmover's scoop, but had twisted round enough to reach his gun. '*Go!*'

Diamondback aimed the revolver at the Land Rover's driver as the vehicle charged towards him—

Fear paralysed his trigger finger. He had been so intent on recovering his gun that he hadn't seen the approaching cliff – until now.

He overcame his shock and fired, but a fraction of a second too late. The bullet punched through the Land Rover's roof above Macy's head. The Defender surged past him.

Nina looked back. 'We're not gonna make it!' The Land Rover was designed for endurance, not acceleration.

'We'll make it,' said Eddie, gripping her tightly. They passed the last earthmover, flames swelling ahead as Macy angled for the ramp. 'Although I think we should duck!'

They dropped as low as they could as the Land Rover drove into the blaze, tongues of fire licking hungrily through the broken windows.

They hit the ramp—

The Zubr reached the cliff.

A huge blast of escaping air swept sand and stones off the rockface as the skirt vented into the void below. Its support gone, the hovercraft's bow dropped, the massive vehicle jolting violently as the bottom of its hull ground against the lip of stone. Still driven onwards by its three huge propellers, it balanced like a see-saw – before tipping over the point of no return. Everything inside it that was not lashed down slid forwards . . .

Including the bulldozer on which Diamondback was pinned.

He screamed as the earthmover screeched down the hold. The machine shot out into the open, plunging at the ground with Diamondback trapped on the scoop like a shrieking hood ornament.

Thirty tons of steel smashed down at the base of the cliff – followed by over five hundred tons of metal as the hovercraft landed on top of it. The Zubr exploded with earth-shaking force, a burning mushroom cloud roiling upwards.

Towards the Land Rover.

The 4×4 hadn't gained enough speed to cancel out the hovercraft's forward momentum as it flew out of the stern, and it skidded backwards to crunch to a halt with its rear wheels over the edge of the cliff. The front wheels spun uselessly, lifted off the ground as the back end dipped . . .

Though half stunned by the hard landing, Nina realised the danger – and threw herself against the dashboard.

The shift of weight was just enough to bring the Defender's front end back down, the tyres finding grip and pulling the vehicle back on to the clifftop with a bone-shaking thump. The fireball boiled upwards behind it, setting one of the wheels alight. Still engulfed in the cloud of sand, the Land Rover got about thirty feet before the burning tyre blew out. Macy brought it to a jolting stop.

The dust gradually settled. Coughing, they climbed out. Berkeley shakily faced Nina. 'Thanks for waiting for me.'

'And thanks for . . . sort of trying to help me. I guess,' Nina replied dubiously.

He looked relieved, holding out his hand. 'No hard feelings?'

To Macy and Eddie's surprise, she shook it, once . . .

Then punched him in the face. He dropped on his ass, stunned. 'Actually, yes! That was for selling out in the first place, you son of a bitch!' Eddie pulled her back before she could take another swing.

'What about Shaban?' Macy asked. She looked into the distance, but the dune buggy was long gone.

'Shit!' said Nina, thoughts returning to larger concerns than Berkeley. 'He's got the jar! How're we going to catch up with him?'

'We're not,' Eddie told her. 'He's got a head start – and I bet he'll be able to get someone to pick him up by chopper. That buggy had a sat phone.'

'So he *wins*?' Macy asked, appalled. 'After all that, he gets away with it?'

'No,' said Nina. 'No way. I'm not going to let that happen.' She stared after the departed Egyptian, thinking. 'We need to get back to Abydos.' Both Eddie and Macy appeared on the verge of making sarcastic comments about the obviousness of her plan. 'Don't even start. I said we needed to contact the authorities. We still do.'

'In that case,' said Eddie, indicating the Land Rover's smoking rear tyre, 'we'd better change that wheel. It's a bloody long walk.'

The Egyptian Mil Mi-8 helicopter approached from the west, silhouetted against the bloated red sun on the horizon. It kicked up a swirling vortex of sand as it touched down near the Osireion at Abydos.

Nina, Eddie and Macy stood by the battered Land Rover, Berkeley sitting sullenly in its rear seat, shielding their eyes from the blowing dust. Hatches opened, six men emerging. Five were soldiers, but their uniforms were not the standard tan of regular Egyptian troops: these were the darker camouflage pattern of a special forces team.

The sixth man was a civilian – Dr Ismail Assad, Secretary General of the Supreme Council of Antiquities. 'Dr Wilde,' he said as he reached the Land Rover.

'Dr Assad,' Nina replied. She looked past the helicopter to the desert from where it had come. 'I'm guessing you checked out the GPS co-ordinates I gave you on the phone before coming here.'

'I did. It was . . . incredible.' He shook his head in near-disbelief. 'And I only had time to examine the entrance chamber. How much more is there?'

'A lot,' said Macy. 'All the way down to Osiris's tomb.'

'Incredible,' Assad repeated. 'I left a team from the Antiquities Special Protection Squad,' he nodded at the soldiers, 'to secure the site – the SCA will send a full expedition as soon as possible.'

'Shaban won't be going back there,' Eddie warned. 'He's got what he wanted from it.'

'Yes, the canopic jar you told me about,' Assad said to Nina. 'Are you serious? You believe Shaban is going to use it to make a biological weapon?'

'*He* certainly believes it,' said Nina. 'And he's got the resources of the Osirian Temple – well, the Setian Temple now, I suppose – to back him up. From what I saw in Switzerland, he might be able to do it.'

Assad frowned. 'Maybe so, but weapons of mass

destruction are a little out of my field. And without proof, I can't persuade higher authorities to take action.'

'There's something that *is* in your field, though,' said Nina. 'The zodiac from the Sphinx. I'm sure Shaban has it – Osir would have shipped it back to Switzerland. He even had a space picked out for it in his Osiris memorabilia collection.'

'If Shaban has the zodiac,' Assad mused, 'that would definitely justify taking action. He's an Egyptian citizen, after all – and our government takes a very dim view of archaeological thieves.'

Eddie regarded the soldiers. 'You'd send this lot in to extradite him?'

'I'm afraid I can't comment on whether the ASPS have ever carried out missions outside the country,' the Egyptian said with a small but meaningful smile.

'And if along the way you also happened to find proof that he was manufacturing biological weapons,' said Nina, 'well, then you'd *have* to do something about it, wouldn't you?'

'I suppose I would. But first I would need proof that he has the zodiac.'

Nina looked at Eddie. 'Which means getting back inside the Osirian Temple's headquarters.'

'How are you going to do that?' Macy asked. 'I mean, we saw the place – it's like a fortress. Because it literally *is* a fortress! They won't let you walk right in this time.'

'Maybe not,' Eddie said thoughtfully, 'but there's someone they might . . .'

29

Switzerland

Soft lights washed across the high stone walls of the castle as the last glow of sunset faded behind the Alpine mountains. The pyramid dominating the courtyard took on new form as blue LEDs along its edges flicked on, the black glass building becoming a neon outline topped by an intense beam shining skywards towards the pole star: a pointer to the ancient Egyptian gods.

More lights approached along the lakeside, turning on to the short spur leading to the castle and stopping at the gatehouse. A sleek black Mercedes S-Class, windows tinted almost as dark as the paint. But it wasn't the chauffeur's window that smoothly lowered to respond to the voice from the intercom; instead, the rear window revealed the single passenger.

'Hi there,' said Grant Thorn, flashing his movie star smile

at the cameras. 'Khalid Osir invited me to visit the Osirian Temple. Well, here I am!'

'What brings you here, Mr Thorn?' said Shaban, bland politeness barely covering his contempt – and suspicion.

Grant made himself comfortable on the leather couch in Osir's lounge. 'I was in Switzerland to meet some of the backers of my next movie – gotta keep the money men sweet, right?' He grinned. 'Since I was here, I thought I'd take Mr Osir up on his offer to watch his old movies together. Is he around?'

'My brother is . . . out of the country,' said Shaban.

'Aw, man! When'll he be back?'

A small, crooked smile. 'Not for some time. But your trip might not be wasted. The Temple is holding a special ceremony tonight – you will attend. If you prove your faith and loyalty, you will be rewarded.'

'Cool,' said Grant. 'But if Mr Osir's not here, who's holding the ceremony?'

'I am in charge.' A larger smile, edged with smugness.

Someone knocked at the door. A large, grey-haired man entered: Lorenz, face still bruised from the fight in the Hall of Records. 'The first bus is coming.'

Shaban nodded, then turned back to Grant. 'I have to prepare for the ceremony. Wait here – someone will come for you.'

'Looking forward to it,' Grant said as the two men left. He waited several seconds, then took a cell phone from his pocket – a phone with an open line. 'Did you get that?'

*

'We got it,' said Nina into her wireless headset.

Half a mile up the valley, a pair of Mitsubishi Shogun 4×4s and a panel van were parked overlooking the castle. The van's boxy cargo area was large enough to contain the six-foot-diameter zodiac, but it was currently serving as an impromptu command post for a team of ten soldiers from the Egyptian government's Antiquities Special Protection Squad.

'What kind of ceremony?' asked Assad, in charge of the unit. Nina could only shrug, and Macy had nothing helpful to offer either. He frowned, turning to one of his men. 'He mentioned a bus. See if there's anything heading for the castle.' The black-clad soldier nodded and jumped out. 'The ASPS are only equipped for a surprise raid. If there are more people there than we expected . . .'

'What do you want me to do?' Grant asked. 'This zodiac dealie, it's in a room full of Egyptian stuff – I saw it on the way in.'

Assad shook his head. 'We can't do anything until we have *visual* proof that Shaban has the zodiac. The minister made that very clear – this operation is on shaky enough diplomatic ground as it is.'

'We should have given Grant the camera,' said Macy.

'I think that might have made them a *teensy* bit suspicious,' Nina pointed out. 'Grant, I think the best thing for now is just stay put. Keep the line open; if there's any trouble, we'll let you know so you can try to get out of there.'

'Escaping from a castle? Hey, I already did that in *Condition: Extreme*,' Grant told her, unruffled.

'Well, you only get one take here, so be careful.'

'Will do.' Grant returned the phone to his pocket.

The soldier climbed back into the van. 'A bus just arrived – they're lowering the drawbridge for it,' he told Assad. 'I checked the road along the lake, and there are more coming.'

'This ceremony must be a big thing,' said Nina, concerned. 'What do we do?'

Assad frowned again, thinking. 'We came here to see if Shaban has the zodiac. Let's get proof first.'

Nina nodded. 'Eddie?'

Grant's Mercedes had parked in a lot to one side of the pyramid, near the courtyard's wall. When Grant was taken to Shaban, his chauffeur had remained in the dark-windowed vehicle.

The chauffeur was Eddie Chase.

'I'm here,' he said, donning his own headset, a clip-on unit similar to a Bluetooth earpiece – with a small video camera protruding from its side. 'What's the situation?'

Nina updated him on what Grant had told her. Eddie looked past the pyramid to the castle's gate, seeing the two halves of the drawbridge lowering. There was a dull bang and a rattle of chains as they met, and then a coach crawled across. From the number of faces Eddie glimpsed through the windows, the large vehicle was full to capacity. The bus stopped at the other end of the parking lot.

'Jeez,' said Nina, seeing the passengers disembark over the video link. 'There's a lot of them – and there are more buses coming. How are you going to get into the keep with all those people around?'

'Piece of piss,' Eddie told her. He had been watching the

guards patrolling the battlements through the car's sunroof – their attention was now focused on the crowd spilling from the bus. He slid across to the front passenger seat, then silently opened the door and slipped out. He had deliberately parked the Merc beside a large SUV; now he hunched in the shadows, keeping perfectly still until he was sure nobody had seen him exit. Satisfied, he moved forward until he could see the whole courtyard.

The pyramid's blank glass flank lay ahead, the bus off to the left. To the right was a small ornamental garden – he could use the bushes and trees as cover to reach the keep's side entrance. 'Okay, I think I can get inside without being seen. Which floor's the zodiac on?'

'The third,' said Nina.

'Is that the American third floor or the British third floor?'

He smiled at her faint sigh; transatlantic terminology differences were a reliable way for him to wind her up. 'American, of course.'

'So, the second floor. Okay.' He crossed the gap to the next car and crouched behind it, checking the battlements, the courtyard—

He froze.

Shaban!

The cult leader emerged from the keep's main entrance, heading for the pyramid in the company of three men. Eddie recognised two of them: Broma and Lorenz, apparently taking over the role of Shaban's personal guard from Diamondback. The third, carrying a cylindrical metal container, was unfamiliar.

Nina knew him, though. 'Eddie – the guy with glasses, he's one of the scientists I saw in the lab.'

Eddie was more interested in the object he was holding. There was a symbol marked on the stainless steel. He narrowed his eyes, trying to make it out as the four men approached the pyramid.

They disappeared from sight behind the structure's blue-edged corner. But he had seen all he needed to see. He recognised the symbol: it had appeared in his SAS training for NBC warfare.

Three sets of curved horns, arranged in a circle. *Biohazard*. The cylinder was a containment flask.

For a biological agent.

He suppressed an involuntary chill. The cylinder's contents weren't an immediate threat: if they were, Shaban and his followers would all be wearing hazmat suits. But considering what the Egyptian had said in the tomb, the potential for enormous harm was there – and for all Eddie knew, the four men had already immunised themselves.

He had stopped one biological attack four years earlier. Now he had to stop another.

'Uh, Eddie, where're you going?' Nina asked as he moved back into the SUV's shadow.

'I'm gonna blow up that lab. Top of the pyramid, right?'

'That – that's not why we're here, Mr Chase!' Assad stammered. 'Our top priority is finding the zodiac.'

'*My* top priority's making sure some fucking nut-job who thinks he's an Egyptian god doesn't start spreading killer spores around the world.' Eddie watched as the cultists headed for the entrance through which Shaban had just gone. He wondered why they weren't using the nearer doors on the side of the pyramid facing the drawbridge, but decided it didn't matter. What did matter was that they would give him a way in.

Assad and Nina both continued to protest, but he ignored them, taking a closer look at the newly arrived cultists. Unlike the mix of ages and sexes at the Osirian Temple's gatherings in New York and Paris, this group was predominantly young men, though still of varied nationalities. Shaban's own personal followers from round the world?

Bent low, he moved to the cover of a car closer to the pyramid, then reached up to his headset. 'Okay, I'll have to go off-mike. Can't exactly stroll in there with a camera strapped to my head.'

'Eddie, don't—' said Nina, but he had already removed the earpiece and clipped it unobtrusively to the bottom of his jacket.

The crowd, around fifty people, filed past, led and tailed by more green-jacketed guards. There was a lot of conversation: the tone was excited, expectant, but also tinged with what Eddie could only think of as *gloating*. Whatever the ceremony was, it already had the feel of a victory rally.

A glance up at the battlements, another at the guards behind, waiting for their view to be partly obscured by the throng – then he stood and smoothly matched pace with the group as if he had just emerged from the car.

He tensed, ready to fight or run. Since he was already inside the castle he doubted the cultists would question his right to be there, but if the trailing goons thought he was out of place . . .

Nobody shouted in alarm. A young man gave him a mildly curious look, but returned to his conversation with another. Relieved, but still alert, Eddie marched with the group into the pyramid.

There was no sign of Shaban or the men with him in the lobby, but there were more guards. 'Everyone will wait in here. The temple will be opened soon,' one called over the hubbub as the cultists filled the space, another repeating the instruction in French, then Arabic. Eddie stayed near the fringes of the crowd, checking the exits. A glass lift rising at an angle, a set of large frosted glass doors that he assumed led to the temple, two more smaller doors to each side. The lift couldn't be the only way to reach the upper floors – there had to be stairs somewhere.

A few minutes later, another group of cultists entered. Then another. The lobby quickly became packed to bursting point. Eddie made sure he was right by one of the side doors as the original group moved to make room for the newcomers. A guard was nearby, but he just needed a brief distraction . . .

It came when the temple doors opened. Everyone instinctively turned to see, pushing closer – and Eddie slipped unseen through the side door.

As he'd hoped, it led to a stairwell, the sloping outer wall forcing each flight to ascend at odd angles like an Escher painting. He donned the headset again as he headed for the pyramid's peak.

'Eddie!' Nina snapped as the monitor finally showed something other than the crotch of her husband's jeans. 'About damn time! What's going on?'

'Shaban's gathering the faithful, by the look of it.'

'Yeah, we saw – three busloads of them. I meant, what's

going on with you? What the hell are you doing?'

'I told you – I'm going to take out that lab.'

'With what? You don't have any explosives – you don't even have a gun!'

'I think I'll manage.'

One of the ASPS standing with Assad flinched at Eddie's insouciant tone. 'What is it?' Assad demanded.

The soldier rushed to one of the equipment cases stacked in the van – and gasped an Arabic obscenity. 'Sir, there are two packs of C-4 missing.'

'C-4?' Macy asked as Assad gaped at him.

'Explosives,' said Nina. Macy edged away from the case.

'Yeah, I borrowed 'em while you were getting set up,' Eddie announced, as casually as if he'd taken a pencil without asking.

'Chase!' Assad shouted. 'Get out of there *immediately*! You can't use explosives in there – it'll be a diplomatic catastrophe!'

'Then why did you bring them in the first place?' said Nina, jumping to Eddie's defence despite sharing the Egyptian's feelings.

Assad looked sheepish. 'As a . . . contingency.'

'Well, this is contingency-y,' said Eddie. 'And diplomacy'll be the last thing to worry about if Shaban's turned that crap into a bioweapon. If I take it out now, problem solved. So I'll go upstairs, plant these charges, get Grant and blow the place up before anyone even knows I was here—'

On the screen, he reached the landing of the upper office level – and a door opened in front of him, a guard freezing in surprise as he came face to face with the Englishman.

⋆

'Or not,' Eddie said as he and the guard stared at each other.

The other man snapped out of his shock and tried to grab him, but Eddie slammed a knuckle punch into his throat and sent him lurching back.

The guard lashed out at Eddie's eyes, but he whipped his head back and smashed his boot into the cultist's groin, then punched him in the face so hard that the back of his head smacked against the door. The guard slithered to the floor, out cold.

Eddie dragged him through the door. The offices were lit only at a low level, the occasional screensaver glowing beyond the glass walls. The employees of both Osiris Investment Group and the Osirian Temple were either done for the day or filing into the temple downstairs.

'Eddie! Are you okay?' Nina asked.

'Yeah, fine.' He pulled the unconscious man out of sight, then examined him. He was roughly Eddie's build, and only marginally taller . . .

'Does Nina know about this side of you, Eddie?' said Macy as the Eddie's-eye view showed him stripping the limp guard of his jacket and trousers.

'Funny girl,' he replied. The image abruptly shifted, the camera pointing up at the ceiling.

'What're you doing?' asked Nina.

'I don't want to scare Macy with what's in my pants.'

Macy had become used enough to his innuendoes to respond only with an eye-rolling sigh. Nina smiled. 'I don't think she has anything to be afraid of.'

'Tchah!'

'It's *you* who's got things to be afraid of,' she continued pointedly. 'If you get caught, they'll kill you.'

The camera aimed ahead once more. Eddie's hand – now holding a gun – filled the screen. 'They can try.'

'They *will* try, Eddie! Don't take any stupid chances.'

'You know me, love.'

'Yes, and I'd like to go on knowing you! Be careful, okay?'

'I will. Mr Assad?'

'Yes?' Assad said.

'Get your boys ready. However this turns out, there'll be trouble – and they'll need more than tear gas and pepperballs to deal with it.'

'I see,' Assad said, unhappy. A nod to the ASPS, and they opened more cases, taking out compact FN-P90 sub-machine guns. 'Another contingency,' he told Nina and Macy. 'I really hope we don't have to use them, Mr Chase.'

'Depends on Shaban, dunnit?' The Eddiecam tipped downwards to show him slipping the gun inside his newly acquired green jacket, then picking up the two C-4 packs and their radio detonator to squeeze them into the tight-fitting garment's outer pockets. 'All right, I'm ready.'

'Good luck,' Nina whispered as he moved out.

Eddie returned to the stairwell. No sounds of activity above or below. He didn't know how long he would have before the guard was missed, so he quickly ascended to the top floor.

There was only one route he could follow, which brought him to the lift. A man was waiting for it; he glanced casually at Eddie as he came through the stairwell door, then did a slight double-take. Eddie concealed his concern – the man didn't seem alarmed, just mildly puzzled by his appearance

– and gave him a polite nod, keeping his head turned to conceal the earpiece. The lift arrived just as he passed it; the man boarded without looking back.

The strong scent of yeast hit his nostrils as he entered the next room. 'Smells like a baker's armpit in here,' he said. The opposite wall was glass, giving him a view of the space beyond. The lab was right under the pyramid's cap, the walls rising to meet almost at a point; above was the spotlight sending its beam towards the pole star.

There was only one person inside the chamber, his back to Eddie as he examined an object on a workbench.

One of many objects, all identical. More stainless steel containment flasks, all bearing the biohazard symbol.

'Shit,' Eddie hissed. 'You seeing this? There must be fifty of the fucking things!'

'Oh, my God,' Nina said quietly. 'Shaban's big event, it's not just a ceremony – it's a *start*. He's brought in all his followers from round the world . . . and he's going to give them the spores to take back with them!'

'So quickly?' asked Assad in disbelief. 'He only left the tomb four days ago!'

Eddie surveyed the lab, taking in the large vats used to culture the yeast, the ovens to dry it and extract the spores. The canopic jar, now open, stood inside a glass cabinet. 'Psycho billionaires never hang about with this kind of stuff, do they?' He noticed that the ovens were fed by large tanks of compressed gas. A good place to start an explosion . . .

If he could get to them. The lab's inner door had a keycard lock, and the windows were designed to contain a biohazard – handgun fire would only scuff them.

'How's he going to get in?' he heard Macy ask, but he was already heading for the door. He reached out—

And knocked.

The triple-glazed window absorbed the sound. He rapped harder, finally catching the scientist's attention.

'Open the door,' Eddie mouthed, gesturing for him to come over.

The scientist frowned, but came to the door. He said something, voice barely audible through the glass. Eddie had basic lip-reading skills, but couldn't make out his words, the scientist presumably speaking in a foreign language. Nevertheless, he smiled and nodded.

The man frowned again, bewildered, and swiped his card through the lock. The door slid open. 'Hi there,' said Eddie.

The scientist switched to English on hearing his voice. His accent was thickly Germanic. 'What did you say?'

'I said, "You're fucked." ' Before the man could do anything more than blink in surprise, Eddie yanked him forward to slam his head against the door jamb. The scientist collapsed.

'Ah . . . are you just going to leave him there?' Nina asked as he dumped the unconscious man behind a lab bench. 'I mean, you're planning to blow the place up.'

'He's making a bioweapon, so fuck him.' Picturing the disapproving expression accompanying his wife's frosty silence, he relented, slightly. 'Okay, I'll drag him downstairs when I go. Happy now?'

'Not until you're out of there in one piece.'

He grinned, then turned his attention to the gas tanks. There was a space between them; he activated the detonation circuit of one cigarette-packet-sized block of C-4, then slid the explosive into the gap. 'Hmm.'

'What?' Nina asked.

'Bit obvious. Hang on.' The large steel ovens beside the tanks were open. He reached to the back of one and felt beneath the perforated gas pipe. It was greasy and sooty, but there seemed to be enough room. The second pack armed, he forced it down out of sight. 'There.'

'So now what?'

'Now,' he said, taking the scientist by his arms, 'I get out of the pyramid, push the button and blow this place to buggery.'

'What about all the people in the temple?' Macy asked. 'Won't they all get crushed?'

'I'm tempted to say fuck 'em too, but there's a couple of floors in between,' he told her as he dragged the man to the door. 'Unless this thing's built of cheese and moonbeams, those C-4 packs aren't big enough to bring the whole place down. The top won't be a nice sharp point any more, though.'

'Just make sure you're not inside,' said Nina. 'And don't forget Grant.'

'Hey, he's still technically a client,' he said, using the scientist's keycard to open the door and hauling him through. 'Wouldn't do my job prospects much good if I lost one, would it?' He backed across the room, bumping open the door with his backside to enter the lobby.

A chime sounded.

The lift.

Eddie dropped the scientist and whirled, pulling out his gun—

Too late.

A pair of guards had come from the stairs, weapons pointed at him, and two more armed men rushed from the lift. Broma and Lorenz.

Knowing he had no chance of surviving a four-way shootout, Eddie froze, dropping the gun. 'Arse.'

'Chase,' said Shaban, stepping out between his two bodyguards. His scarred face clenched with anger – and sadistic pleasure. 'Just in time for our ceremony . . .'

30

Nina stared in horror at the screen as Shaban's hand swelled to fill the camera's field of view – and it went black.

'Shit!' she gasped. 'We've got to get him out of there!'

'I can't,' said Assad, dismayed. 'The ASPS don't have authorisation to act until we know the zodiac's there.'

'Grant said it is,' protested Macy. 'Isn't that enough?'

'No, we need visual proof – which is what your husband was supposed to find!' he snapped at Nina.

'Dammit!' She ran to the truck's open rear door and looked helplessly along the lakeside at the castle – then remembered something and switched her headset's channel to the phone. 'Grant! Can you hear me? Grant!'

A rustle of fabric, then: 'Yeah, I'm here.'

'Grant, they've caught Eddie! You've got to get out of there . . .' An idea. 'Your phone! If you take a picture of the zodiac, the Egyptians can move in.'

'Wait – they've caught Eddie? Shit!' The actor's usual laid-back drawl frayed into near panic.

'Grant, Grant, just listen!' Nina shouted. 'Go into the

relic room and take a photo of the zodiac, and we can rescue you and Eddie!' She glanced at Assad for confirmation that a cell phone picture would be enough; he nodded.

'Okay. Rescue. Good idea.' She heard his footsteps as he crossed the lounge – then a sudden *whumph* of material over the mouthpiece as he shoved the phone back into his pocket. 'Shit, someone's coming!'

The sound of a door opening, then a voice: 'Mr Thorn?'

'Y-yeah?'

'The ceremony is about to begin. Come with us.'

'Come with you three guys?' said Grant. 'Sure. My own personal escort, huh? Cool.'

Nina realised what he was telling her – surrounded by three men, he wouldn't be able to take a picture of the zodiac.

And without one . . . he and Eddie were on their own.

One of the guards hurried out of the lab. 'We found this,' he said, holding up a C-4 pack.

Shaban turned over the radio detonator his men had just taken from Eddie in his hand. 'Explosives? Not subtle. But not surprising, from you.'

'I like to be consistent,' said Eddie, forcing himself not to look back towards the oven. The second pack would be harder to find, and since there was only one detonator, Shaban might also think there was only one charge.

But even if the other bomb wasn't found, it wouldn't make much difference: C-4 was a very stable compound, needing extreme heat *and* a physical shock – the kind provided by the blasting cap inside the pack – before it would explode. He needed the radio detonator to destroy the lab. And Shaban seemed unlikely to give it back.

'How did you know I was here?' he asked, trying to divert the Egyptian's mind from the detonator. As long as he didn't think to destroy it, there might still be a chance . . .

Shaban indicated his ill-fitting green jacket. 'Bad tailoring. I always insisted that the Temple's security forces had their uniforms fitted. Khalid liked it because it made everyone look smart, but it has another advantage – it's easy to tell when somebody doesn't belong.'

'Good thinking, Two-Face.'

Shaban's jaw clenched, but he restrained himself from responding personally, instead nodding at Broma – who clubbed Eddie with his gun, dropping him to his knees. 'Ow! Twat!'

'I would have told him to shoot you, but I have something better in mind.'

Eddie didn't like the sound of that, but kept quiet as he was hauled upright. The other man emerged from the lab. 'I couldn't find anything else,' he reported.

Shaban regarded the block of C-4. 'That would have been enough.' He looked back at the detonator, then tipped out the battery before crushing the device under his heel.

'Shit,' Eddie muttered. The only way now to set off the hidden explosive was manually – which would take him with it. The pack had no timer.

The Egyptian read his expression. 'No backup plan? Too bad.' He smiled coldly. 'You've come a long way to be here for my ceremony. So now . . . you can be part of it.'

★

Hands secured behind his back, Eddie was taken at gunpoint into the temple.

It was vastly more impressive than the auditorium in Paris. The doors through which the arriving cultists had entered led to a glass and steel staircase descending into a huge pit-like arena below floor level, the deep space filled with hundreds of people.

A central aisle had been left clear, green-clad men lining it like an honour guard. At its far end was another, narrower flight of stairs rising to a wide catwalk-like extension from the front of a black marble stage. Four large, gleaming chrome statues of Egyptian gods stood at the protruding section's corners. The walls were frosted glass panels laser-etched with hieroglyphs. The whole place seemed like some demented cross between a rock stadium and an Apple Store.

Shaban, Lorenz and Broma had taken a different route through the pyramid, leaving the guards to hustle Eddie down into the pit, along the aisle and up the unrailed stairs to the stage. Seeing that he was a prisoner, the cultists booed and bellowed for his blood. The sight of what, despite its chrome and glass trappings, looked uncomfortably like a sacrificial altar gave Eddie the nasty feeling that they expected to get it.

His captors took him to one side and waited, giving him a chance to look for possible escape routes. The only choices were back down into the pit, exits on each side of the stage – and a set of double doors at the centre of the back wall. This entrance was flanked by a pair of even larger statues. The bodies were of Osiris, similar to the statues outside the god-king's tomb, but the heads were different, the figures having been recently decapitated and replaced by the visage of some strange beast, a fearsome, elongated cross between jackal and horse.

The face of Set.

Shaban had wasted no time in putting his mark on the temple. Eddie now also realised why the cultists had been made to go to the more distant entrance. The double doors led north, to ancient Egyptians the direction reserved for royalty. Osir had designed that feature of the temple for effect . . . but his brother *believed* it.

Minutes passed, the crowd's anticipation rising. Then the lights dimmed.

'Set! Set! Set!' the cultists chanted, raising their clenched fists high to punch the air. '*Set! Set! Set!*'

The doors opened.

Spotlights tracking him, Shaban stepped on to the stage. When he left Eddie he had been wearing an expensive but understated suit – now, his clothes were anything but subtle. He had donned a set of green and black robes, a modern interpretation of traditional Egyptian royal clothing, and an elaborate headdress, again a stylised version of those traditionally worn by the pharaohs. Broma and Lorenz stood in the half-shadows behind him.

The cultists went berserk, screaming 'Set!' over and over again, stamping their feet so hard that the stage floor trembled. Shaban took in the adulation like his brother had before him, then raised his hands. The tumult quickly died down.

'Servants of Set!' he said, voice booming from loudspeakers; the headdress also contained a microphone. 'Welcome! The day has finally come. The worthless platitudes of Osiris have been swept aside. He is no more. I am at last the true leader! I am Set reborn! And I will show the world the true power of a god!'

The response from the crowd was more frenzied than before. Even the guards surrounding Eddie were caught up in the moment – though not, he quickly found when he tested his bonds, enough to forget why they were on the stage. One jabbed a gun into his back as Shaban again signalled for silence.

The scientist who had crossed the courtyard with the cult leader earlier approached, bearing the containment flask. He bowed and presented it to Shaban, then retreated.

'This,' said Shaban in a low voice, 'is the seed of our power. This is how the Temple of Set will spread my will over the world. In this container,' his voice rose as he held the flask over his head, 'is *death*. Death, to those who oppose us. Death, to the unbelievers. Death, to all those who refuse to bow to the might of Set!'

The crowd chanted and stamped again – though, Eddie realised, fractionally less powerfully than before. Maybe not all of them were one hundred per cent behind the idea of global genocide . . .

Shaban lowered the flask. 'This container is just the first. When you leave, you will take with you many more. Slowly, invisibly, you will spread their contents across the world. By the time our enemies realise what we have done, it will be too late – they will already have consumed this death. There is only one way they can survive – by pledging their total obedience and worship to the Temple of Set! You, my followers, will be safe – the bread of Set will protect you.' His voice rose again, almost a scream. 'But only those I deem worthy will receive it – all others will die! *The reign of Set has begun!*'

Another explosion of approval came from the pit – but this time there were noticeable pockets showing rather less enthusiasm. The cult leader returned the flask to the scientist, then faced the crowd once more . . . though Eddie saw a now-familiar tension in Shaban's face, anger just barely contained beneath the surface.

'I know some of you may be having second thoughts,' he said, his voice almost silky, reassuring. Shaban might not have had his brother's oratorical skills, but he had certainly taken notes. 'If you have doubts, now is the time to make them known.' He gestured to the stairs leading up to the stage. 'Come. Step forward. I will end your fears.'

He smiled, but his eyes were crocodile-cold. 'Don't do it!' Eddie shouted, seeing a few of the cultists moving to the aisle, but the guards pistol-whipped him to his knees. His voice was lost in the murmurs of the crowd, those taking Shaban up on his offer being regarded with suspicion, even hostility, by the others.

About twelve men hesitantly grouped in the aisle. 'There are no more?' Shaban asked, mild tone and empty smile again concealing his emotions. He surveyed the crowd for any more signs of disaffection. Seeing none, his lips curled to reveal his true feelings. 'Then bring them to me!' he barked.

The guards lining the aisle had been prepared for this moment. In a sudden burst of action, they closed in from both sides, crashing together like two green waves. Fists and feet flailing, they beat the dissenters to the floor. When the chaos ebbed, the bloodied dozen were dragged up the stairs by three men each. The rest of the crowd began a horrible baying that grew louder and more animalistic as the moaning victims were brought to the altar.

Shaban glared at the doubters with contempt, then turned back to his followers. 'You have accepted me as your leader – as your god! There is no room for doubt, no room for fear – I give you eternal life, and in return I demand eternal obedience! I am your god! *I am Set!*'

'Set! Set! Set!' screamed the crowd.

He moved behind the altar, picking up a long, wicked blade. A nod to the nearest group of guards, and their prisoner was hauled on to the glass-topped block. His cries for help went unheard beneath the mob's yelling.

Holding the knife up to the spotlights, Shaban began a sinister prayer, his amplified words rolling round the chamber. 'I pay homage to you, O Ra, lord of heaven. I am your champion, the doer of your will within this world. Your light falls upon the great mother Nut, whose hands encompass the sky above us, and the great father Geb, whose body spans the earth beneath us. I am your son, your servant . . . your warrior.'

He raised the blade higher. 'In blood, I show my worth,' he proclaimed. 'In blood, I slay your enemies. In blood, I take my rightful place as the ruler of this world, and the next, for all eternity! Those who do not believe, shall suffer! Those who oppose, shall fall! I am Set, lord of the desert, master of darkness, the god of death! I am Set!'

The masses below began their awful chant once more, fists punching skyward in unison. Eddie spotted Grant, who was watching in horror as he realised the ritual's inevitable end, but was too afraid to fight or flee.

'I am Set!' Shaban repeated. 'I have slain the coward Osiris, and now in blood I take dominion over all things! I am Set! Set! *Set!*'

He plunged the knife downwards.

Blood gouted from the helpless man's chest as Shaban stabbed again and again, the guards holding him down as he writhed and convulsed . . . then fell still. Eddie watched, appalled.

But Shaban wasn't finished. Clothes spattered with trickling red spots, he rushed to the next prisoner, face alight with an insane glee. 'I am the bringer of death!' he cried, slashing the knife across the man's throat and sending a crimson spew down his chest. The other men struggled and screamed, but were held too tightly to escape as the knife plunged into their flesh. 'This is the fate of those who question! Those who follow me shall live for ever – and all others will die!'

'Jesus Christ!' Nina gasped, turning pale as she listened to Shaban's rant via Grant's phone. Macy covered her mouth with both hands, eyes wide. 'He's *killing* them!' She faced Assad. 'Send in your men!'

Sweat beaded on the Egyptian's face. 'I . . . I don't have the authority,' he said desperately. 'I need to – I need to call the minister.'

'There's no time! We've got to – oh, shit . . .' She tailed off as Shaban spoke again.

'Grant Thorn,' said the cult leader, the name echoing round the temple. 'Will Grant Thorn step forward? Mr Thorn!'

'I'm . . . I'm here,' Grant croaked, mouth as dry as dust.

'Good.' Shaban smirked nastily. 'I'm sure you all know Mr Thorn. But,' the smirk darkened, 'he was a follower of my brother. It is time to see if he will pledge himself to his new god.'

'Uh . . . sure!' Grant cleared his throat. 'Sure thing! I – I pledge to worship you, O Set! Totally!'

'I will need more proof than mere words,' said Shaban. 'Come up here.'

Grant hesitated, but was pushed forward by a pair of goons. Shaking, he ascended the stairs. At the top, he looked round at Eddie, the statues, the ceiling – anything to avoid Shaban's cold stare, or the bloodied bodies round the altar.

'I'm giving you a great honour, Mr Thorn,' said Shaban, stepping up to him. He was still holding the dripping knife; Grant cringed back from its point. 'You have all seen the fate of those who do not obey my will. Now . . .' He looked round at Eddie, the sadistic smirk returning. 'Now you will see the fate that awaits the enemies of Set.'

'A blowjob from a supermodel?' Eddie shouted, a display of defiance that earned him a hard blow to the head.

Shaban sneered. 'This man,' he said, pointing, 'has opposed us. Has tried to destroy us. Has tried to deny you everlasting life!' The crowd jeered. 'There can be only one punishment – *death*!' He whirled to face Grant, holding up the knife in front of the actor's face. 'And you, Mr Thorn, will prove your loyalty to the Temple of Set – by killing him.'

Grant's mouth moved silently before his voice fearfully emerged. 'Oh, no, I, ah . . . that's really your kind of honour.'

'I insist,' said Shaban icily. He nudged a corpse with his foot. 'And you know what happens to those who do not obey the will of Set.'

Pushing the knife into the reluctant actor's hands, he quickly stepped back out of arm's reach, then gestured to the guards holding Eddie. 'Bring him to the altar!'

'They're going to kill Eddie!' Nina shouted at Assad. '*Do* something!' The Egyptian was trapped between his urge to act and the restrictions of his orders, fumbling with his phone. '*Fuck!*' Frustrated, angry and afraid, she ran to the van's doors and looked at the castle.

The drawbridge was still lowered.

Macy called after her as she jumped down, but she ignored her and hurried to the nearer of the team's Mitsubishi Shoguns. The big 4×4 was fully kitted out for off-road work with heavy-duty tyres, raised suspension, a winch and a bullbar jutting from the front. Both doors on the driver's side were open, and one of the ASPS was perched on the side of the driving seat with his feet on the ground as he smoked a cigarette, waiting for the call to action.

Nina delivered it in a way he hadn't been expecting. 'Hey!'

He looked up – and she punched him, knocking his head back against the door frame. He was more shocked than hurt, but his confusion was enough to enable Nina to pull him from the vehicle. The other ASPS nearby reacted in surprise.

She jumped into the cab and started the engine, slamming the Mitsubishi into gear.

Macy dived through the open rear door. 'Wait!'

'Get out, Macy!' Nina yelled as she swerved the 4×4

round the van. Assad shouted for her to stop as they passed.

'I'm going with you!'

'No, you're not – you could get killed!'

'I'm getting used to it! Besides . . .' Nina flinched as the barrel of a large gun was poked between the front seats. 'This might be handy.'

'That's not even a proper gun!' The odd-looking weapon was an Arwen 37, a fat-barrelled riot gun loaded with five tear gas cartridges in its bulky rotary magazine.

Macy withdrew the Arwen. 'Well, if you want a different one, you'll have to turn round!'

That wasn't going to happen. The Shogun tore down the lakeside road. Nina could hear what was happening inside the temple through her headset. Eddie was still alive, she could tell from the swearing.

But another voice chilled her to the bone. Shaban.

'I pay homage to you, O Ra . . .'

She pushed the accelerator down harder.

Grant's gaze flicked desperately between Eddie and Shaban as the cult leader continued his murderous prayer. His followers chanted the dark god's name as he spoke, eagerly awaiting the deadly climax.

Most of the guards had returned to the pit, but four still held Eddie on the sacrificial block. 'Oi! Scarface!' he shouted. 'Does all this really make up for having your knob burned off?'

Shaban's only response was a furious twitch, but one guard smashed his elbow down on Eddie's stomach. The Englishman let out a choked gasp of pain.

'In blood, I show my worth . . .'

★

The Mitsubishi reached the spur road, Nina skidding it round the corner in a shower of loose gravel. Macy yelped as she slithered across the bench seat.

'Uh-oh,' said Nina. The gatehouse at the lake's edge lay ahead . . . and the drawbridge had just started to rise. Her approach had been spotted.

Macy sat up. 'We're not gonna make it!'

'We've *got* to make it,' Nina told her grimly. Her foot was back down to the floor as they hurtled along the short road. The drawbridge's two halves parted, rising a foot, two . . .

She heard Shaban's prayer continuing over the growl of the engine and Macy's panicked pleas to stop. 'I am Set, lord of the desert, master of darkness, the god of death!'

Grant's hands shook as he held the knife over Eddie. He tried to back away – and felt a gun held by another guard press against his spine.

Shaban fixed him with a malevolent stare. 'I have slain the coward Osiris, and now in blood I take dominion over all things!'

'We're gonna crash!' Macy squealed.

Nina gripped the steering wheel, eyes fixed on the drawbridge. The nearer section was at a twenty-five degree angle, and still rising.

She didn't slow.

The Mitsubishi hit the drawbridge with a bone-jarring crash – and continued up it. It shot off the end, clearing the widening gap and smashing down on the far side with an impact that shattered two of the side windows. Macy screamed.

The front airbags exploded from their compartments, kicking Nina painfully back into her seat – but she saw the pyramid ahead and aimed straight at it.

Shaban's voice rang in her ears. 'I am Set! Set! *Set!*'

'And *match*!' Nina cried—

The Shogun ploughed through the pyramid's glass wall.

31

Eddie stared up at Grant. He could tell from his eyes that the actor wasn't going to drive the knife into his chest. Which was good.

But it was also bad, because it meant Shaban's followers would kill them both.

And pinned to the table, hands tied behind his back, there was nothing he could do to stop it—

Boom!

Everyone on the stage spun at the noise – and, with a colossal crash of exploding glass, the Mitsubishi careered through the double doors.

Heading straight for the altar.

Lorenz tackled Shaban out of the truck's path. Broma rolled the other way. The guards holding Eddie scattered.

The Shogun skidded, swerving to miss the altar – but it couldn't stop in time to avoid colliding with one of the statues. The chrome-plated figure rocked as the 4×4's hefty bullbar smashed a chunk out of its legs, almost toppling into the pit . . . then tipped back and fell. The marble floor was smashed under its weight – as was the scientist. The canister spun away.

The fallen statue rolled and demolished the altar as Eddie flung himself clear, knocking the stunned Grant with him. It continued over the end of the stage, flattening another guard – then the stairway collapsed beneath it, sending the rest of the men flying. Cultists screamed and scrambled backwards to escape being crushed.

Eddie sat up, expecting to see one of the ASPS inside the battered Shogun – and was startled, but delighted, to find Nina at the wheel instead. 'That's what I call gatecrashing!' he called.

'Eddie, come on!' she shouted back – only for her expression to change to alarm. 'Look out!'

Broma was pointing a gun at him—

A flat *thump* came from the 4×4 – and something streaked across the stage to hit Broma's chest with a crack that broke his sternum. He fell backwards into the pit as the object that had injured him bounced back and clanked across the marble, streaming white smoke.

Only it wasn't just smoke. Eddie felt a stinging, burning sensation in his eyes and nose. Tear gas. He looked back at the Shogun to see Macy hefting an Arwen 37 out of the broken window.

'Hold your breath!' Eddie warned. 'Grant, cut me loose!'

The bewildered Grant remembered he was holding a knife. He sawed at the zip-tie with the bloodied blade until it snapped. Eddie shook off the plastic restraint and stood. The tear gas was swirling across the stage, thick clumps of white mist obscuring his view, but he could make out Shaban and Lorenz still on the floor by one of the statues.

He checked the pit. With the stairs destroyed the cultists couldn't reach the stage directly, but there was another way out—

'Shit!' Some of Shaban's followers had already come to the same conclusion and were heading for the stairs at the temple's opposite end. If they got out, he and the others would be massively outnumbered, and probably torn to pieces by the mob.

He ran to the truck. 'Gimme that,' he said to Macy, snatching the Arwen from her and firing the remaining four canisters across the pit at the other set of stairs. The crowd immediately turned back, coughing and clutching at their faces as they tried to escape the searing vapour.

'Get in!' Nina shouted from the 4×4.

'No, you get out!' he countered. 'That gas won't stop 'em for long – we've got to keep them trapped down there!'

'How?'

'With the truck.'

'But we need it to get out of here!'

'Did they raise the drawbridge?'

'Yes, but—'

'Then we won't have time to lower it before that lot come after us like bloody zombies! Come on, shift! You too, Macy!'

Macy climbed out of his side of the Mitsubishi, Nina the other, as Eddie leaned across the passenger seat. 'This worked for Shaban, hope it works for us,' he muttered as he put the Mitsubishi in Drive – and used the empty riot gun to jam down the accelerator.

The 4×4 roared towards the broken stairs as Eddie rolled backwards out of it. He thumped down painfully on debris from the ruined altar, skidding across the marble—

Grant dived and grabbed his arm just before he slithered into the pit, his legs dangling over the edge.

The cultists scattered screaming as the Mitsubishi smashed down to their level. Through some collective obedience the aisle was still more or less clear, though a couple of green-blazered goons were slammed aside as the truck, its suspension grinding, charged along the pit.

It disappeared into the billowing cloud of tear gas—

Another huge crash of breaking glass and steel echoed round the chamber as the 4×4 hit the other flight of stairs, getting halfway up them and leaping out of the miasma like a whale breaching the ocean surface before they collapsed beneath it.

Eddie scrambled back on to the stage. 'Thanks, mate,' he told Grant. With both staircases destroyed, the cultists were trapped in the pit. 'So how do you like *real* action?'

Grant was still shaken. 'I, uh . . . I prefer the Hollywood version.'

'Let's get you back to it, then. Come on.'

They rounded the broken altar. The tear gas from the first canister was still spreading, forcing Nina to retreat towards them. Eddie looked round in alarm. 'Where's Macy?'

Nina's eyes watered as the stinging vapour attacked her mucous membranes. 'In there,' she gasped, pointing into the wafting mass.

'Macy! Can you hear me?' He heard a feminine cough from somewhere in the cloud. 'Okay, we've got to go through it. Hold your breath, keep your eyes and nose covered, and grab hold of me.' He held out his hands.

Grant was also suffering the effects of the pungent

chemicals, face screwed up in discomfort. 'Aren't you feeling this?' the actor asked Eddie as he and Nina took hold of him.

'Nah, this is pretty weak – the SAS chucks you in rooms full of way worse stuff in training. You get used to it, like vindaloo. Okay, ready?' They both nodded, holding their noses. '*Go!*'

He rushed into the cloud, pulling Nina and Grant behind him. His eyes immediately started streaming, and his exposed skin felt as though it was being jabbed by hot needles – his training had made him more resistant than most to the effects of tear gas, but not immune, and it was several years since he had last undergone the experience. But he kept going until they emerged into clearer air on the other side.

Where was Macy?

The fog's boundary was uneven, clumps still hanging stubbornly despite the light breeze coming through the smashed doors. Another cough, and he spotted a half-shrouded shape. 'Macy! Over here, c'mon!' He shook off Grant and Nina and started towards her.

A blink to clear stinging tears from his eyes—

There were now *two* shapes in the mist.

'*Macy!*'

Too late.

The other figure resolved itself into Shaban. He grabbed Macy from behind, pressing a gun to her head to use her as a human shield – then realised his opponents were unarmed—

Nina pulled Grant behind one of the remaining statues as Eddie dived for the only cover he could reach – the cloud of tear gas. A bullet carved a vortex through the swirling mist just above him as he rolled deeper into the dense fog.

Losing sight of him, Shaban blasted two more shots at Nina and Grant, smacking chunks out of the statue. Then he shoved the gun against Macy's head again, making her scream as the hot metal burned her, and dragged her backwards.

'Lorenz!' he shouted. 'Get the canister!'

Nina risked a quick glance out from behind the statue, and saw the stainless steel container lying on its side across the stage. Lorenz picked it up and looked to Shaban for orders.

'Get to the helicopter!' the Egyptian shouted as he retreated, hauling the struggling Macy with him.

Eddie burst from the cloud to take cover behind the statue nearest Shaban and his lackey. Shaban fired again, the bullet twanging off the chromed figure. 'If you follow, I'll kill her!' he warned as he reached the side exit. Lorenz opened the door, and they backed through.

Eddie let out a hacking cough. 'Jesus!' he wheezed, wiping his eyes. 'They've changed the bloody formula since I last did a gas drill!'

Nina hurried to him, Grant behind her. 'Now what're we gonna do?'

'Get him somewhere safe, for a start,' said Eddie, nodding at the actor. 'Then get that drawbridge down so Assad and his lads can come in.'

'What about you?'

'I'm going to get Macy.' The breeze had wafted the gas far enough down the stage for him to spot something amongst the debris: a gun, dropped by one of the guards. He collected it – then, to Nina's surprise, handed it to her. 'Shoot anything green.'

'Why aren't you taking it?' she asked.

' 'Cause there might still be guards at the gate.'

'I'm not going to the gate – I'm going with you.'

'No, you need to look after Grant.'

Grant looked offended. 'Hey, I can take care of myself, man.'

'You ever fired a real gun?' Eddie demanded.

'Yeah.'

'At a person?'

'No.' His eyebrows shot up. 'Wait, she *has*?'

'Way too often,' said Nina. 'Look, Eddie, you—'

'There isn't time to fucking argue,' Eddie snapped, running after Shaban. 'Just get that bridge down!' He reached the exit and was about to go through when he looked back. 'Oh, and thanks for rescuing me! Now bugger off!'

'Any time,' Nina said with a smile. She turned to Grant. 'Okay, come on.' They ran for the doors.

'You've really shot people?'

'Afraid so. Transfixed a guy with a sword once, too.'

'Wow.' They entered a small lobby, floor littered with broken glass from the Mitsubishi's entrance. Through the gaping hole in the outer wall the drawbridge was visible, still raised. 'Has anyone optioned your life story? It'd make a great movie!'

'Yeah, but who'd play me?' Nina looked outside. Nobody in sight. 'Let's get you out of here – then I can go after my husband!'

*

The side exit led to a corridor along the pyramid's eastern base. Eddie ran down it to the lobby through which he had entered the building.

No sign of Shaban, Lorenz or Macy. Or anyone else – Shaban's followers had been in the temple to hear their godhead's rant, and were still trapped in the pit.

He crossed the lobby. The outer doors slid open as he approached, the sound of a helicopter's engine reaching him. It was nearing takeoff speed. And as soon as the chopper was clear of the castle, Macy would become dead weight – literally.

A quick glance round the doorframe revealed the helicopter, a sleek six-passenger Eurocopter EC130, on the pad in one corner of the courtyard. Lorenz was in the front passenger seat beside the pilot, Shaban and Macy behind them. A glint of metal told Eddie that Lorenz had the gun; his door was ajar so he could shoot at anyone trying to approach.

He needed to get round to the pilot's side to block his aim. If he ran fast enough, he could make it before the aircraft took off – assuming Lorenz wasn't a crack shot.

He took a deep breath . . . and ran.

Nina and Grant reached the gatehouse. Part of the castle's structure had been extended by a booth with mirrored windows: a security station. The drawbridge controls were almost certainly inside.

Nina reached the door first and flung it open – just as the sound of echoing gunfire reached her from the far side of the pyramid. She instinctively looked back. *Eddie—*

A noise inside the booth. Nina whirled to see a guard

drawing a gun. She jumped backwards – and collided with Grant as he tried to follow her inside. He lurched clear, but she stumbled and fell on her back. The gun was jolted from her hand.

The guard ran towards her. She tried to get up, but he was already upon her, pointing his gun down at her head—

A sudden blur of motion, and the automatic flew into the air as Grant leapt up and delivered a high kick to the man's hand. He landed straddling Nina, twisting to slam an elbow into the guard's chest and following it by backhanding him in the face. The man staggered.

Grant grinned at Nina. 'Krav Maga, man! Learned those moves for a movie.'

She wasn't impressed. 'This isn't a movie – and he's not down!'

'Huh?' He looked round – and saw the guard still standing, a hand to his aching nose and an expression of rising anger on his face. 'But that always works on set!'

'Because they're *stuntmen*, idiot – aah!' Nina scrambled out of the way as the enraged guard tackled Grant to the ground and clamped his hands round the actor's throat.

Another shot cracked across the courtyard, one of the pyramid's glass panels shattering behind Eddie as he sprinted to pass in front of the helicopter. Lorenz, already leaning from the cockpit to track him, would in moments be forced either to jump out or shoot through the windscreen to maintain a line of fire – and with the chopper almost at takeoff speed, both options were unlikely.

Which meant he would take one last shot—

Eddie threw himself into a forward roll as the Dutchman

fired again, the bullet kicking up splinters from a flagstone. Without pause he leapt back to his feet and continued running, angling back round to the pilot's side . . .

The helicopter left the ground.

He pushed harder, squinting into the blasting wind. The aircraft ascended at full power, its skids already six feet off the ground in less than a second, rocketing skywards—

Eddie jumped.

One hand fell an inch short – but he clamped the other round the skid as the helicopter turned.

His weight made the aircraft sway, its occupants instantly realising they had another passenger. 'Shake him off!' Shaban ordered.

Eddie pulled himself up to get a grip with his other hand – as the helicopter tipped sharply, trying to jolt him loose.

The guard slammed Grant's head down, squeezing his neck harder. The actor grimaced, eyes bulging. 'Your movies,' the man grunted, 'are *crap*!'

Grant tried to gurgle a riposte as he struck at the guard's head, but he couldn't score a solid blow. The man dug his thumbs deeper into his neck, pushing down on his carotid artery—

'Hey!'

The guard looked round – and Nina kicked him in the face. He rolled off Grant, spitting out blood and broken enamel. But he wasn't out of the fight. He spotted Nina's gun and scrambled for it.

His own pistol had landed further away. Nina dived, landing painfully as she snatched it up and twisted to face her opponent.

He was taking aim—

Nina fired first. A bloody hole burst open in his green blazer as she shot him in the stomach. He screamed, all thoughts of returning fire eradicated by agony.

'Jesus!' Grant gasped. 'You *shot* him!'

'No shit! Get the gun!' As the shocked Grant crawled over and pulled it from the man's shaking hand, Nina rushed into the booth. CCTV screens showed the main gate, the drawbridge and the road on the shore – where she could see the ASPS' van and the other Shogun waiting to cross.

Where were the drawbridge controls? *There* – a panel on one wall. She shoved the lever to the down position and stabbed at a green button. A buzzer rasped, followed by the whine of a motor, then both noises were drowned out by the clank and rattle of chains as the drawbridge descended.

She ran back outside and saw the helicopter rise unsteadily into view from behind the glass pyramid.

Someone was hanging from the skids.

Eddie.

The pilot jerked the cyclic control stick sideways. The helicopter lurched, veering towards one of the castle's towers before he pushed the stick back to counter the sudden move. The passengers jolted hard in their seats, and something banged against the fuselage under the pilot's side window. Macy shrieked.

'Is he gone?' Shaban demanded.

The pilot leaned over to get a better view of the skid—

The door flew open.

A deafening whirlwind blasted into the cabin as the rotor

downwash came through the door – followed by Eddie. He had used the chopper's roll to swing up and hook his legs round the skid, letting him reach the door handle. The startled pilot took a savage punch to the face, and before he could recover Eddie muscled his way inside and put him in a chokehold. 'Land this thing!'

'Shoot him!' Shaban barked.

Lorenz raised the gun – and Eddie hit the struggling pilot again, twisting him into the line of fire. The Dutchman swore, trying to aim round him—

Eddie yanked back the cyclic stick.

The chopper's nose tipped up sharply, throwing everyone backwards. Alarms honked and buzzed: stall warnings. The EC130 was now flying backwards – and descending rapidly, the rotor blades' steep angle not generating enough lift to maintain height.

In the corner of his eye, Eddie saw the pyramid approaching fast—

He released the stick. The pilot slammed it forward and jammed down a rudder pedal in a desperate attempt to regain control before the helicopter smashed into the pyramid. The EC130 pitched forward, spinning. Centrifugal force threw Eddie outwards, only his grip on the pilot keeping him in the aircraft.

He clawed for another handhold – the buckle of the pilot's harness.

His thumb pushed down on the release.

The pilot let out a choked scream of fear as the belts popped free. The only thing now keeping him in his seat was his grip on the controls. The pyramid whirled past, the Eurocopter's tail sweeping barely a foot from the dark glass.

'Take it down!' Eddie roared. '*Now!*'

'Take us up!' Shaban bellowed. He unfastened his own seat belt, leaning across the cabin to pull Eddie's arm off the pilot—

Macy slammed her elbow into the Egyptian's face. He jerked back, headdress flying off.

Lorenz pointed the gun at Macy—

Eddie grabbed the controls again.

Horrified, Nina watched as the helicopter reeled drunkenly back behind the pyramid, losing height. 'Oh, my God!'

Grant stood, rubbing his throat. 'Whoa, I wouldn't want to be in that. Where's Eddie?'

She gave him an anguished look. 'Where do you think?'

The van sped past and skidded to a halt, the Shogun following. Assad jumped out of the latter as his troops deployed, glancing questioningly at the now-unconscious guard. 'Dr Wilde! Where's the zodiac?'

She pointed at the keep. 'Third floor – but listen, the cultists are all trapped in the pyramid! You've got to keep them there until the authorities arrive. If any of them escape with the spores . . .'

Assad was torn, but reluctantly nodded. 'I'll split the ASPS into two teams, one for the zodiac, the other for—' The helicopter wobbled back into view, still spinning. 'What in Allah's name?'

'Shaban's aboard – and so are Eddie and Macy!' The EC130 dropped behind the pyramid once more. Nina stared helplessly after it – then jumped into the empty Shogun.

'Dr Wilde, wait – stop!' Assad cried as the Mitsubishi

peeled away after the helicopter, Nina not even bothering to close the door. 'Not again!'

The Eurocopter was only twenty feet above the courtyard, the pilot unable to increase power as he clung by his fingertips to the collective control lever between the front seats.

Eddie kept his fearsome grip round the man's neck. His grab at the controls had stopped Lorenz from shooting Macy, but the Dutchman was recovering from the dizzying spin.

As was Shaban. Macy tried to hit him again, but he twisted her arm upwards and back. There was a popping crackle from her shoulder, and she screamed. The Egyptian shoved her against the door. She moaned in pain.

Another clack of a seat belt buckle, and Lorenz leaned forward, pointing the gun round the pilot for a clear shot. Eddie grabbed the weapon with his free hand, trying to aim it away from himself.

Both men's hands trembled as they fought to overpower the other, but Lorenz had more leverage. Grunting with effort, Eddie brought one foot up off the skid and into the cabin, forcing himself inside.

The shuddering gun pointed towards the pilot. If Lorenz fired, he would be signing his own death warrant. Eddie pushed harder—

Eyes blazing with hatred, Shaban lunged forward and smashed a fist into his face.

Eddie toppled backwards, losing his grip on the gun . . . and the pilot.

He fell— and slammed painfully against the skid. His

foot was tangled in the seat belt. Dangling upside down, he was less than ten feet above the ground – and the helicopter was still dropping, about to crush him!

Nina slewed the Shogun round the corner of the pyramid – and saw the helicopter ahead, still spinning, losing height—

Coming right at her.

'Shit!' she shrieked, stamping on the brake and diving out of the open door as the EC130 whirled like a sycamore seed at the 4×4—

The gasping pilot sat up – and flinched in shock as he realised how close he was to the ground. Jamming down the other rudder pedal, to counter the spin, he twisted the throttle to increase power.

Eddie's outstretched hands scraped the ground – then the helicopter levelled out. He saw Nina sprawled beside the ASPS' second 4×4 as he was whisked past.

The Shogun—

Nina jumped up. 'Eddie!' she yelled as the chopper steadied, hovering above the courtyard.

'The winch!' he shouted back. 'Chuck it to me!'

'What?'

He jabbed both hands at the Mitsubishi's front end. 'The winch, the *cable*! Throw it!'

The 4×4 had a winch system affixed to its front bumper, a hundred and fifty feet of steel cable with a hook at the end. She ran to it as the EC130 drifted back towards her. Pulling the release lever to let the spool turn freely, she grabbed the hook with one hand and tugged out a length of cable with the other.

'Get us out of here!' Shaban snapped. The pilot applied more power. The helicopter rose again.

Nina looked up at Eddie as he swept past. Their eyes met.

She didn't know if she had pulled out enough cable, but it was the only chance she had to save him.

He stretched out his hands.

She hurled the hook with every fibre of her strength.

The line arced towards him, whipping in the downdraft. He stretched out, grabbed—

Caught.

His forefinger closed round the very tip of the hook. He pulled it up, getting a grip with both hands—

The cable reached the limit of the slack Nina had drawn out. It pulled tight, the spool whining as more line was unwound.

It spun faster. She looked up. The helicopter was ascending ever faster.

Straining, foot twisting in the tangled seat belt, Eddie bent at the waist. He couldn't quite reach the skid. With a roar he pulled harder, crunching his body, but the tension of the cable stopped him short.

The pilot briefly took his hand off the cyclic to close his door, but something obstructed it. Hand back on the stick, he glanced at the straining harness beside his seat. 'He's still here!'

'Lorenz!' Shaban snapped. 'Lean out and shoot him!'

Lorenz looked back uncertainly. 'Lean out?'

'He's hanging from the skid! Shoot under us!' He stabbed an angry finger at the floor. The Dutchman looked more dubious than ever, but obediently turned to take a firm grip on one of his seat belt straps before unlatching his door.

Nina looked frantically between the helicopter and the winch. The cable had almost run out.

Lorenz pushed the door open and leaned out, craning his neck to get a view under the EC130's fuselage. He spotted the flailing figure on the other side of the aircraft and moved out further, taking aim.

Eddie made one final desperate lunge as Lorenz fixed him in his gunsights—

The hook caught on the skid.

A split second later, the cable reached the end of its reel.

Nina leapt back as the Mitsubishi jumped violently. Above, the slamming jolt as the rapidly ascending helicopter came to an abrupt stop flung Shaban and the pilot upwards, the latter smacking his head on the canopy. Macy, strapped in, cried out as she was thrown against her restraints.

For the two men outside the cabin, the effects were more extreme.

Eddie, a moment earlier struggling to reach the skid, was suddenly hurled up against it. On pure instinct, he wrapped his arms round the metal tube, clinging to it.

Lorenz was less lucky, his gun hand catching the edge of the door frame and knocking the pistol back into the cabin as he was thrown upwards—

His head clipped the rotor blades.

Red and grey sprayed across the windscreen, then he fell, the top of his skull missing in a neat line just above his eyes. The tumbling body smashed on the unyielding stone a hundred and fifty feet below.

The dazed pilot slumped against the instrument console, the cyclic stick pushed under him. The helicopter slewed sideways towards the pyramid, trapped on the cable like a hooked marlin leaping from the sea.

Nina yelped and jumped out of the way as the 4×4 followed it. The Eurocopter didn't have enough power to lift the two-and-a-half-ton Shogun – but it could drag it.

Eddie pulled up his free leg and hooked it round the skid. A glance down: the chopper was over the pyramid, heading for the shaft of light stabbing skywards from its summit.

He shook his foot free of the seat belt, then hauled himself on top of the skid. A look through the window revealed the pilot, groggily sitting upright, and Macy behind him. Her face was contorted in pain as she clutched one shoulder.

Shaban was bent over beside her, reaching for something in the footwell. At first Eddie thought he was trying to retrieve the spore canister – then he spotted the steel cylinder on the empty seat next to the Egyptian.

He realised what Shaban was after just as the other man found it and snapped upright, pointing the gun at Eddie—

Macy hit his arm as he pulled the trigger.

The side windows were obscured by a burst of gore as the bullet hit the pilot's head at point-blank range, blowing out half his skull. His body spasmed, kicking down hard on one rudder pedal. The helicopter went into a violent spin.

The pilot's door swung open. Eddie dragged himself inside, climbing over the corpse. Shaban had been thrown over to the cabin's opposite side. Gun still in one hand, he clawed for a handhold with the other.

A blinding light filled the cockpit as the helicopter whirled through the pyramid's beam. Eddie screwed up his eyes, dazzled for the briefest moment.

The flash faded – to reveal Shaban's gun pointing right at his face—

Below, the Mitsubishi crashed through the pyramid's glass side – and the cable snagged on the structure's steel frame. The impact tossed Eddie into the empty front seat and flung Shaban against the door.

It burst open.

The fury in his eyes replaced by fear, Shaban clawed at the door frame. The gun went off in his hand, the shot punching a hole in the rear bulkhead. He dropped the weapon to get a firmer handhold. It spun down to the pyramid below.

Warning buzzers rasped urgently from the console, red lights flashing. Eddie's gaze flicked to them to see one gauge dropping rapidly. Oil pressure. The bullet had damaged the engine.

The EC130 jolted again, straining against the cable. The canister rolled across the rear seats. Eddie and Shaban both looked at it, then each other.

Save it, or destroy it—

Eddie scrambled over the seat as Shaban dragged himself back inside. The cult leader reached the canister first, whipping it up by its handle and catching Eddie a vicious blow on his temple. Another silent explosion of light filled the cabin as the helicopter whirled back through the beam, unable to tear free of its vehicular anchor.

Shaban clutched the cylinder to his chest, kicking at Eddie. 'You are *nothing*!' he screamed. 'You can't beat me! I'm a *god*!'

'If you're a god,' Eddie snarled, seeing the other man gripping the door frame, knuckles white, 'let's see if you can fly!'

He punched Shaban's hand with all his might.

Pain erupted in Eddie's fingers, skin splitting and joints crunching – but it was nothing to what Shaban felt as his hand was crushed against the hard-edged metal. The longest bone of his middle finger snapped. With a scream, he let go – and Eddie drove his bloodied fist into the Egyptian's scarred face.

The Eurocopter swayed back into the dazzling beam . . . and Shaban fell.

Still clutching the canister, he plunged almost seventy feet down the blinding shaft of light – and hit the pyramid's peak with a spine-splintering crack.

Eddie stared down at the splayed figure now blocking the beam, the tip of the summit poking up through his stomach. 'Get the point?' he yelled.

But Shaban wasn't quite dead.

Blood streaming from the massive wound where he was impaled, he still had just enough strength to raise one hand as he tried to open the container – and scatter its deadly contents into the wind.

Eddie was no longer watching – the increasingly noisy warnings from the console had captured his attention. The oil pressure gauge was in the red, dropping rapidly. The engine was about to fail.

Wincing at the pain in his hand, he slid back across the cabin. 'Macy! You okay?'

'He – pulled my damn shoulder out,' she said through clenched teeth. 'Can you land this thing?'

'Nope.'

'What? But – but I thought you were some kick-ass super soldier! You mean you can't fly a helicopter?'

'I keep meaning to learn,' he replied, releasing her harness, then reaching over her to open the door.

She gaped at him. 'What're you doing?'

'We'll have to jump.'

'But we're miles up!'

'Not for long.' The klaxons were overpowered by a grinding from the engine compartment. 'When I tell you to—'

The driveshaft sheared apart. Broken metal clanged against the bulkhead like hailstones.

The helicopter fell.

'Jump! Jump! *Jump!*' Eddie roared. The rotor was still turning, slowing the fall – but with no power and no pilot, the EC130's death plunge would only last a few seconds. He shoved the shrieking Macy out and leapt after her.

They dropped, ten feet, twenty—

And hit the pyramid's sloping side.

The toughened glass cracked – but didn't break. Every nerve on fire from the hard landing, Eddie slithered down the structure, Macy tumbling alongside him.

Shaban turned the lid, needing only one more small movement to open the container . . .

And froze as his pain-dulled eyes saw the helicopter plunging at him.

He screamed—

The EC130 slammed down on top of the pyramid – and continued through it, falling into the laboratory amidst pulverised glass and shredded metal. It hit the floor and exploded, a searing shockwave pounding through the chamber.

Reaching the hidden C-4.

The explosive detonated, ripping apart the gas tank. The

lab was consumed by a colossal wave of fire, the entire top third of the pyramid blowing apart like the eruption of a glass volcano.

Eddie and Macy were already over halfway down. Below, Eddie saw Nina running from the blast, the Mitsubishi half buried in the wall—

'*Jump!*' he cried.

Despite her pain, Macy managed to slam her heels against the glass as Eddie did the same. He went left, she went right, passing on each side of the Shogun—

They hit the ground.

More pain exploded in Eddie's legs as he rolled and bounced across the courtyard. He heard Macy scream again and threw himself at her, shielding her against the rain of glass with his body. More windows shattered as flying debris arced down.

The noise faded.

Bruised and bleeding, Eddie raised his head, wincing at the pain throughout his body. The pyramid's top had gone, swallowed by boiling flames. The deadly spores were destroyed.

'Eddie!' More pain as he looked round, but it was slightly soothed by the sight of Nina running towards him. 'Jesus! Are you okay?'

'I'll tell you when I work out if my legs are still attached,' he rasped. 'Macy, you all right?'

'No,' she said, very quietly. Nina and Eddie shared a worried look. 'But . . . I think I will be. Eventually.'

Eddie tried to laugh, but it turned into a cough. 'Another fucking exploding helicopter. Feels like I'm in one of Grant's movies. Is he okay?'

'Looks like it,' said Nina, seeing the actor rounding the pyramid with Assad and one of the ASPS. She waved, then looked up at the building's burning summit. 'That's one way to take care of a yeast infection. Kind of overkill, but looks like it worked.'

'Bloody well better have,' Eddie grumbled, lifting himself off Macy. 'A pack of C-4 and a chopper blowing up? Anything in there ought to be toast.'

Nina raised her eyebrows. 'Oh . . .'

'What?'

'I just realised. You took out Shaban's spores . . . but you also toasted the bread of Osiris. The source of eternal life.' She pondered that for a moment. 'Still, who wants to live for ever?'

Eddie staggered upright and put his arm round her. 'Depends who you're living with.'

Epilogue

New York City:

Three Weeks Later

Nina gazed up at the dark glass slab of the UN's Secretariat Building as she stepped from the limo. Unlike her last visit, she had no feelings of trepidation. Quite the opposite. This time, she and Eddie were there to be honoured.

The ceremony had come about thanks to the Egyptian government. The discovery of a pyramid in the Western Desert – and the revelation that it contained the tomb of Osiris himself, turning studies of the country's ancient mythology on their head – meant that Egyptology would become the hottest field of archaeology for the next several years. At the very least, the tourist trade was about to see a huge boom.

So the Egyptians had petitioned the UN to recognise Nina and Eddie's achievement in uncovering the Pyramid of Osiris . . . as well as their role in stopping Shaban.

There was a distinct irony, Nina thought, to the fact that her interactions with the IHA had come full circle. The agency had been established in large part to keep the truth about attempted murder on an unimaginable scale from the public; now, the same organisation that had summarily dismissed her eight months earlier was forced to grovel for her co-operation in the investigation of another genocidal scheme.

Despite this, she still hesitated at the entrance. 'You okay?' Eddie asked.

'Yeah. It's just . . . the last two times I came to the UN, I got torn a new one by Maureen Rothschild.'

'The only thing she'll be doing to your arse today is kissing it,' he assured her.

'Good point,' said Nina, grinning. 'Would it be bad manners if I really rubbed it in that I was right and she was wrong?'

'Probably. But I say bollocks to manners!'

Nina kissed him, and then they went inside.

As it turned out, she didn't get the opportunity to say anything to Rothschild, bad-mannered or otherwise. Although Nina recognised several senior IHA staff among the UN representatives and officials in the invited audience, along with Professor Hogarth, the agency's director was conspicuous by her absence.

But she quickly forgot the snub as the Egyptian ambassador to the United Nations, accompanied by Dr Ismail Assad, sang her praises. 'And thanks to Dr Wilde and her husband,' he concluded, 'the most incredible archaeological find in Egypt in a hundred years was not only discovered, but protected.' He nodded at some large photo blow-ups of the tomb's interior; the mummy had been returned to its rightful resting place inside the sarcophagus, and Osir's crushed body removed. 'The tomb of Osiris unfortunately sustained some damage, but its contents remained unlooted. In time, the entire world will be able to see these incredible national treasures. So again, Dr Wilde, Mr Chase – on behalf of the people of Egypt, I thank you.'

Applause rippled through the room as the ambassador shook Nina's and Eddie's hands. 'Thank you,' said Nina as she stood at the microphone. 'Thank you, Mr Ambassador, Dr Assad – and the people of Egypt, of course!' The audience chuckled politely. 'There's somebody else who should be thanked, because without her bravery and determination we would never even have known the Pyramid of Osiris existed. So, Macy,' she said, pointing her out, 'Macy Sharif, can you stand up, please?'

Macy was in the second row, flanked by her parents; the normally shameless young woman blushed at the applause.

'If the IHA's Egyptology department is hiring when she graduates,' Nina went on, 'then she'd certainly get my recommendation, for what that's worth!' As the clapping subsided, Macy sat down with relief. Nina addressed the audience again. 'But what this whole affair shows is how careful we have to be as archaeologists and historians. When we make these amazing discoveries, it's very easy to be affected by the prospect of fame and fortune – and yes, I'll admit to having gone down that road myself. But what happened here was because it became all about money . . . no, not money, about the *prize*. Somebody wanted something so badly, they cut corners to get it. And that nearly led to disaster. So I hope it will act as a warning about what happens when you put money ahead of science.'

The applause was rather more subdued this time, some faces distinctly uncomfortable. Nina hadn't intended to deliver a finger-wagging lecture, but decided what the hell: it needed to be said. She turned to her husband. 'Anything you want to add, Eddie?'

'I'm not much of one for speeches,' he said, shrugging. 'Just glad to have helped – oh, and if someone could pay our travel expenses, that'd be great!' The audience laughed.

'There is one more thing,' said Assad. An assistant handed him a polished wooden box. 'In recognition of the discovery of the Pyramid of Osiris, the Supreme Council of Antiquities has decided to present something to the IHA. A loan, shall we say.'

He opened the box to reveal a small statuette: a crude human figure carved from an unusual purple stone. Nina didn't recognise it, and it took Eddie a moment to realise he'd seen it before – in Osiris's tomb. 'It's a slight embarrassment to admit this, considering my position,' Assad joked, 'but so far we have been unable to identify it – it doesn't match any of the other artefacts in the Pyramid of

Osiris, or anywhere else for that matter. Perhaps the IHA will have better luck!' He handed the box to the bemused Nina as the audience applauded again.

'Ah, you do remember I'm not actually with the IHA any more?' she said from the corner of her mouth.

'But they— Oh.'

The ambassador realised that his compatriot had made a *faux pas* and quickly took the mike to thank everyone for attending, leaving Nina wondering what Assad had been about to say. One of the senior UN officials, an Englishman called Sebastian Penrose, whom Nina had met a few times during the IHA's formation, left his seat and gestured for Nina and Eddie to join him. They did so, and she looked at him suspiciously. 'Okay, what's going on?'

'A slight case of gun-jumping, I'm afraid,' Penrose replied. He signalled to an IHA official, who took the box. 'We meant to discuss this with you after the ceremony.'

'Discuss what?' said Eddie.

'Your returning to the IHA.'

'What?' Nina said in sarcastic disbelief. 'After we got *fired*?'

'Technically, it was a suspension, pending an official inquiry,' Penrose said smoothly. 'I'm, ah, quite confident the final findings will result in reinstatement with full backdated pay and benefits, as well as a compensation package.'

'Yeah, right. I can really see Maureen Rothschild going along with that.'

'Professor Rothschild is no longer with the IHA,' said Penrose.

Nina was surprised. 'Why not?'

'She resigned yesterday. Partly because of the criminal charges the Egyptians are laying against Dr Berkeley – your statement about his change of heart means they're likely to be lenient, but with all the other conspirators dead they still need a scapegoat. Since he was the professor's personal choice to head the Giza dig, that was a huge embarrassment to her, and a sign of poor judgement. Which reflects on her other decisions – such as suspending you.'

'And the other part?' Eddie asked.

'The other part is that you, Dr Wilde, sent her an email describing how the robbery of the Hall of Records would be carried out before it actually happened – and she ignored it. She deleted it, in fact, but it turned out someone else had a copy.'

'Remind me to send Lola a huge thank-you gift,' said Nina. 'So, you want me to come back. What about Eddie?'

'Mr Chase will be reinstated too, of course. And there's another matter: with Professor Rothschild gone, the IHA is currently without a director. You have experience from when you served as Interim Director . . .'

Eddie nudged her. 'Hey, not bad. They don't just want you back – they're offering you a promotion!'

'But do we really want to go back?' she asked him, though her eyes made her answer obvious. He grinned.

'The offer will remain open,' said Penrose. He handed Nina his card. 'For a while, at least. Call me when you make a decision.' He shook their hands and walked away, the official holding the box following.

'Well, bloody hell,' said Eddie. 'They just can't manage without us, can they?'

'Hey, we've gotten pretty good at this kind of thing by now. But you know what's most important? We'll be able to move back to Manhattan!'

He jokingly rolled his eyes. 'Great. Ridiculous rent, crowds, noise, traffic . . .'

'I can't wait!'

'Tchah,' said Eddie, amused. 'There's one good thing, though – I'll be able to afford that wedding reception!'

'*We'll* be able to afford it,' Nina corrected him. 'And maybe I'll join you for some dancing lessons.'

They left the stage to be met by Macy and her parents. 'So what was all that about?' Macy asked once the introductions had been made.

'He was making us an offer,' said Nina.

'Like a *job* offer?' Macy asked excitedly. 'Oh my God, that's awesome! Are you going to take it?'

'Weeeell,' said Eddie, with an exaggerated shrug, 'we haven't quite decided.'

'But,' Nina added, 'you remember that I recommended you for a position at the IHA when you graduate?' Macy nodded. 'I think it's safe to say that if you wanted it it'd be yours.'

The young woman's face lit up. 'Really? Oh, wow! Then I'll try to be interested in more than just Egyptology. Even the Mongolian toothpicks. Thank you!' She embraced Nina.

Eddie watched for a moment. 'So can I join in and finally get my threesome?'

'*Eddie!*' both women shouted, Macy blushing again as she gestured to remind him that her parents were standing three feet away. But then she hugged him too.

'So what are you going to do now?' Macy asked as they separated.

'I'm not sure yet,' said Nina. She smiled. 'But I think we're going to be busy.'

If you enjoyed THE CULT OF OSIRIS turn the page for an exclusive extract of Andy McDermott's explosive new novel

THE SACRED VAULT

Coming soon from Headline

Prologue

Italy

It was a cold, crisp mid-November evening, but part of Giancarlo Mistretta's mind was already on Christmas as he guided his tanker truck along the winding road through the Casentinesi forest. His home would play host to the family's celebrations this year; twenty-three people to cater for, maybe twenty-four if his sister's newest baby arrived earlier than expected. And, of course, everything he did would be under intense scrutiny from both the matriarchs . . .

He pushed his concerns aside as a tight turn appeared in the headlights. Slowing the truck to a near crawl, he checked his watch. Slightly ahead of schedule – there was still one more gas station to supply with fuel before he could return to the depot, but he would be back home in

Florence before seven. Then maybe he and Leany could continue their plan for a baby of their own . . .

He guided the tanker round the corner – then braked. A charcoal grey BMW was slewed across the road, one wheel in the ditch. A woman in a dark blue suit waved for him to stop.

Giancarlo suppressed a sigh. The BMW was blocking the tree-lined road. So much for getting home early. Still, he wouldn't be setting much of an example for any future little Giancarlos if he didn't help a lady in distress.

He stopped ten metres short of the stalled car, taking a closer look at the woman in the headlight beams. Long, glossy black hair, and dark skin – Indian, perhaps? Probably in her late twenties, and quite attractive, in a businesslike way. He could almost hear Leany reprimanding him for that, but married or not, he still had eyes, didn't he?

The woman walked towards the truck. Giancarlo climbed out to meet her. 'Hi,' he called. 'Looks like you could use some help.'

She briefly looked into the woods as she advanced. Giancarlo noticed that her features were marred; only her left eye had moved, the right staring fixedly at him. The pale line of a scar ran from forehead to cheek over the socket. A glass eye. Poor woman!

He glanced at the BMW. 'Are you stuck? I can give you a—'

She whipped out a silenced handgun and shot him three times in the face.

Giancarlo's lifeless body slumped to the tarmac. A man

stepped out of the darkness of the woods. Tall, muscular and dressed entirely in black, Urbano Fernandez regarded the corpse with an expression of mock apology. 'Poor man,' he said. The language was English, but the accent was smoothly Spanish. 'Never any pleasantries with you, are there?' he went on, addressing the woman as she holstered the gun.

'A waste of time,' said Madirakshi Dagdu coldly. As the unfortunate truck driver had guessed, she was Indian, her accent thick and stilted – English was a language in which she had only recently needed proficiency. She indicated Giancarlo's body. 'Dispose of that.'

Fernandez snapped a sarcastic salute. 'Yes, *ma'am*.' He pulled on a pair of black leather gloves, pausing to brush his pencil moustache with his fingertips before dragging the corpse into the undergrowth. 'There was no need for you to be here at all. We don't need to be, what's the word? *Nursemaided*.'

He knew full well what the word was, but took a certain amusement from the frown of deep concentration on the woman's face as she tried to translate it. 'This operation is more expensive than the others,' she said once the meaning came to her. 'My employers want to be sure their money is being used well.'

'It will be worth every dollar,' said Fernandez, dumping the body. There was no point concealing it – the area would be crawling with people soon enough. He went to the tanker. 'Now, go. Meet me down the road.'

Madirakshi returned to the BMW without a word.

Fernandez watched her, thinking it was a shame such an attractive figure was wasted on an ugly personality, then moved to the valves on the tanker's side as the car reversed out of the shallow ditch.

Even after delivering most of the day's supplies, the tanker still contained over two thousand litres of petrol. The Spaniard turned the wheel above one of the gaping stainless steel nozzles. Fuel gushed out. He winced at the sharp smell, backing away to avoid being splashed as he opened the valve wider. The gush became a geyser, spraying into the woods.

He climbed into the cab. The engine was still running, so he released the brake and depressed the heavy clutch to put the truck into gear, slowly following the BMW as it sped away. He checked the mirror to make sure the escaping fuel was still reaching the trees. It was. Satisfied, he increased speed slightly, keeping the truck as close to the edge of the road as he could.

Petrol spewed over Giancarlo Mistretta's corpse as the tanker rumbled into the night.

Half a kilometre down the road, Fernandez saw the waiting BMW, pointing back the way it had come. He pulled over, then hurried to the car.

Madirakshi's only greeting was a cold look. Fernandez ignored it. After tonight, there was only one more job planned, which might not even be necessary if his employers were persuasive enough – and then he would be rid of them and all the freaks they kept as their entourage.

Even before he had fastened his seat belt, the BMW

surged past the tanker, heading back up the road. A smeared pool of blood marked where the driver had been shot; Madirakshi stopped level with it.

Fernandez lowered his window. He took a Zippo lighter from a pocket, and with a single practised move flicked it open and lit it. A moment to regard his flickering reflection in the polished metal, then he tossed the lighter into the trees.

Even before it hit the ground, the results were explosive. The highly flammable vapour rising from the pool of petrol ignited, a fireball boiling upwards into the trees and setting them alight. Giancarlo's fuel-soaked body was consumed by the inferno as easily as the branches. A thick trail of flames raced away down the road

Fernandez shielded his face from the heat with one gloved hand. 'Time we left. *Quickly*.'

Madirakshi needed no further prompting. The BMW sped away. Fernandez looked back as the car reached the corner – to see a huge explosion rip through the forest half a kilometre behind as the tanker blew up, a seething mushroom cloud of blazing orange and yellow rising into the night sky as flaming fuel rained down around it. A moment later, the blast reached him, an earthshaking thump followed by a thunderous roar of air being pulled in to feed the conflagration.

'Perfect,' said Fernandez. 'Now for stage two.'

The BMW raced through the darkened forest, heading for the city of Florence as the trees behind it turned into a wall of fire.

★

The banging of the chair stopped as Braco Zec pointed his gun at the young woman tied to it. 'Cut that out,' he said in fluent Italian. 'I told you, do what we say and you'll live.' He dragged the chair and its gagged occupant away from the wall, then returned to the small apartment's living room. Six other black-clad men and their equipment occupied most of the limited space, but he pushed through them to the window, peeling back his dark balaclava to reveal a weather-worn face, hair shaved down to a grey stubble. Deep creases across his forehead showed that he had witnessed – and endured – far more than most men of his thirty-four years.

The mercenaries had taken over the apartment that afternoon, Zec tricking the woman into letting them in by claiming to be delivering a parcel. The victim had been selected during the operation's lengthy planning phase, being the only single occupant of any of the suitable top-floor apartments on the narrow Via degli Alfani. Considering what was across the street, it was perhaps inevitable that she was an aspiring artist.

He looked out at the eighteenth-century buildings: the museum complex containing the Galleria dell'Accademia. One of Florence's top tourist attractions – and home to one of the world's most famous pieces of art.

Their target.

Zec's phone rang. Fernandez. 'Yes?'

'We're here. Let us in.'

The Bosnian craned his neck for a better look at the street

below. Two figures passed under a streetlight, approaching briskly. Fernandez and the Indian woman. The creases in Zec's forehead deepened. To him, Dagdu's presence was almost insulting, a sign that their employer didn't trust them to carry out the job without supervision. Weren't all their previous successes, including stealing a set of Terracotta Warriors out of their museum in Xi'an, China, and removing one of Islam's holiest relics from Mecca itself, enough to prove their prowess?

He put the thought aside – she was their paymaster's representative, after all – and went back to the hall as the entry buzzer rasped. He pushed the button, then waited with slight anxiety for them to climb the stairs. If any of the other residents chose that moment to leave their apartment, and saw their faces . . .

But there were no such problems. The soft clump of boots outside, then a single sharp rap on the door. Zec opened it, and Fernandez and his companion entered.

The Spaniard shared a brief smile of greeting with his second-in-command. 'Anything to report?'

'You've made the evening news,' Zec told him. 'The fire's spreading – they're calling in fire trucks from every surrounding town. And,' he added meaningfully, 'helicopters.'

'Excellent.' Fernandez dialled a number on his phone. 'Status?'

'Air-traffic control has our flightplan request,' said the voice at the other end of the line. 'We're ready.'

'Then go.' He disconnected. 'Where's the roof access?'

Zec pointed at a skylight. 'Okay, let's get into position.' He moved to address the rest of the team.

Madirakshi, behind him, looked into the bedroom. 'What is this?' she snapped, on seeing the prisoner.

'She won't be a problem,' said Zec. 'She hasn't seen our faces.'

Madirakshi's face was as fixed as her artificial eye. 'No witnesses.' She stepped into the bedroom. The bound woman, facing away from the door, twisted against her restraints, making panicked noises. She didn't need to understand English to recognise the dangerous tone of the new arrival's voice.

'If you shoot her, the neighbours might hear,' Fernandez warned.

'I don't need a gun.' Madirakshi stopped directly behind the other woman, whose muffled cries became more desperate.

'Leave her,' said Zec, coming into the room. 'I promised she would live if she caused no trouble.'

Madirakshi ignored him. She placed her fingers against her right eye socket – and pressed. There was a soft sucking sound, and with a faint plop something dropped into her waiting palm.

Her glass eye, glistening wetly.

Zec had seen many horrific things in his life, but the casual way the woman removed the prosthetic still produced a small shudder of revulsion. Disgust then turned to confusion as she took hold of the eye with both hands . . . and twisted it. There was a click, and it split into two hemispherical halves. What was she doing?

The answer came as she drew her hands apart. Coiled inside the eye was a length of fine steel wire. By the time Zec realised it was a garrotte, Madirakshi had looped it round the defenceless young woman's throat and pulled it tight.

'No!' Zec gasped, but Fernandez put a firm hand on his shoulder to pull him back. The Italian woman couldn't even cry out, her airway crushed by the razor-sharp wire. She convulsed against the ropes. The chair thumped on the floor; Madirakshi pulled harder, sawing the wire through skin and flesh. Blood flowed down the woman's neck. Her fingers clenched and clawed . . . then relaxed. One last bump, and the chair fell still.

Madirakshi unwound the garrotte and turned. For the first time, Zec saw her face as it really was, a sunken hole with the eyelids gaping like a tiny mouth where her right eye should have been. Another shudder of revulsion, accompanied by anger. 'You didn't have to do that!' he said. 'I promised her—'

'No witnesses,' the Indian repeated. She took a cloth from her jacket and ran it down the length of the blood-coated wire. The garrotte clean, she re-coiled it, then fastened the two halves of the eye back into a single sphere. *Snick*. Another practiced move, and with a small but unsettling noise of suction the prosthetic was returned to its home. 'Now. You have a job to do.'

'We do,' said Fernandez before Zec could respond. He leaned closer to his lieutenant, adding in a low voice, 'I think perhaps having a baby has made you go a little soft, Braco. If this is going to be a problem . . .'

'No problem,' said Zec stiffly. 'But I promised her—'

'Never make promises you might not be able to keep,' Fernandez told him, before clicking his fingers. The men in the living room looked round as one, ready for action. 'Let's go.'

Ten minutes later, all eight men were on the apartment's sloping roof.

Fernandez peered over the edge at the Via degli Alfani. Below, Madirakshi left the building. Relieved to be rid of her at last, he backed up and faced his team. 'Ready?'

The responses were all in the affirmative. Each man was now armed, compact MP5K submachine guns fitted with laser sights and suppressors slung on their backs. Other pieces of gear were attached to the harnesses they wore; not mere equipment webbing, but parachute-style straps able to support their bodyweight, and more.

The Spaniard looked at his watch. Five minutes to get everyone across to the roof of the Galleria dell'Accademia, another five to eliminate the guards and secure the room containing their target, five more to prepare it – and themselves – for extraction . . .

Fifteen minutes to carry out the most audacious robbery in history.

Fernandez couldn't hold back a smile. He was already famous – infamous, more accurately – for what he did, but this would take things to an entirely new level. In an odd way, he was almost sad that the general public would never know his true identity. There was a certain romantic appeal to the idea of being Urbano Fernandez, the world's greatest thief . . . but he would much rather remain Urbano Fernandez, wealthy free man. The various nicknames given to him by the international press over his career, which in Italy to his delight included '*il Fantasma*' – 'the Phantom' – would have to do.

First things first: the robbery itself. He gestured to one of his men, Franco, who had already secured one end of a line inside the open skylight. At the other end was a barbed metal spear, currently loaded into a custom-built, gas-powered launcher.

Franco had already selected his target, a squat brick ventilation blockhouse poking up from the Galleria's roof like a periscope. He tilted up the launcher. Fernandez watched him closely. This was a 'wildcard moment', the biggest risk in any operation. If the brickwork was too weak to take the weight, if someone heard the noise of launch or clang of impact and looked up at the wrong moment . . .

At least they could minimise the chances of the last. Franco raised a thumb. Another man, Kristoff, held up a string of firecrackers, lit the fuse – and flung them down the street to the west.

There was a small pedestrianised square at the Galleria's southwestern corner. The fireworks landed at its edge. People jumped at the string of little explosions and flying sparks. Once the initial fright passed, some onlookers were annoyed, others amused by the display . . .

But they were all looking at the ground.

'Now,' said Fernandez.

Franco pulled the trigger.

There was a flat thud as compressed nitrogen gas blasted the spear across the street – and a sharp clang as the spearhead pierced the blockhouse.

All eyes below were on the firecrackers, though.

Franco put down the launcher and tugged on the line, gingerly at first, then harder. The spear held. He pulled a lever on the launcher's side to engage a winch mechanism and quickly drew the line taut.

Fernandez gestured to a third man, Alexander – the smallest and lightest member of the team. He gave the line a tug of his own to reassure himself that it would hold, then clipped his harness to it and carefully lowered himself off the roof.

The others held their breath. If the spear came loose, it was all over.

Suspended below the line, Alexander pulled himself across the street. The cable shuddered, but held firm. Fernandez didn't take his eyes off the spear. The crackle of fireworks had stopped, and now he could hear the crunch of broken bricks shifting against each other . . .

Alexander reached the Galleria's roof.

Mass exhalation. Fernandez realised he was sweating despite the cold. Alexander detached himself from the line, then secured it to the blockhouse.

Thumbs up.

Fernandez hooked himself to the cable and pulled himself across, followed in rapid succession by the others.

He checked his watch as the last man reached the Galleria. They had made it with thirty seconds to spare.

Now for the next stage.

He took out his phone and entered another number. He didn't lift it to his ear as he pushed the final button, though. He was listening for something else.

In a Florentine suburb three kilometres to the southwest, two cars had been parked, one at each end of an unremarkable street.

Each car contained half a kilogram of C-4 explosive, wired to a detonator triggered by a mobile phone. The phones had been cloned; each shared the same number, ringing simultaneously.

An electrical impulse passed through the detonator—

By the time the booms reached the Galleria dell'Accademia eight seconds later, the men on the roof were already moving towards their next objectives.

They raced across the rooftops, splitting into four groups of two men each. Zec and Franco comprised one team, reaching their destination first as the others continued past.

The pair dropped on to a section of flat roof where large, humming air-conditioning units kept the museum's internal temperature constant. There was a small window just below the eaves of the abutting, slightly taller building, the room beyond unlit. Zec shone a penlight inside. An office, as expected. A glance below the frame revealed a thin electrical cable. The window was rigged with an alarm.

He took a black box from his harness, uncoiling wires and digging a sharp-toothed crocodile clip deeply into the cable to bite the copper wire within. A second clip was affixed on the other side of the window. He pushed a button on the box. A green light came on.

Franco took out a pair of wirecutters and with a single snip severed the cable between the clips.

The light stayed green.

Zec touched his throat-mike to key it. 'We're in.'

Inside the museum, the halls and galleries were darkened, lights dimmed to the softest glow. Had it been up to the curators there would have been no light at all, to prevent the artworks from fading, but the security guards' inconvenient human need for illumination had required a compromise.

The Galleria dell'Accademia is not an especially large museum, so the nightwatch usually consists only of six men. Despite the cultural value of the exhibits to the Italian people, this seemingly small staff is not an issue: any kind of alarm would normally result in a rapid and massive police response.

But on this night, the police had other concerns.

Two guards entered one of the upper floor galleries. Familiarity had turned the art treasures into mundane furniture, the monotony of patrolling the halls punctuated only by check-ins with the security office. So the unexpected crackle of one man's walkie-talkie got their attention; the next check wasn't due for twenty minutes. 'What's up?'

'Probably nothing,' came the static-laden reply. 'But the camera in Hall III isn't showing anything. Can you check it?'

'No problem,' said the guard, giving his companion a wry look. That passed as excitement in their job: checking for faulty light bulbs.

They made their way through the gallery to a short flight of steps at its far end. It was immediately clear there was something wrong with the lights in the next room, only darkness visible beyond the entrance. One guard took a torch from his belt, and they advanced into the darkened gallery.

Nothing seemed out of place in the torch beam. The second man shrugged, turning to try the light switches—

A pair of eyes seemed to float in the blackness before him.

Before he could make a sound, he was hit in the heart by two bullets from Zec's MP5K, the suppressor muting the noise of the shots to nothing more than sharp *tchacks*. His partner whirled – and a gloved hand clamped over his mouth, Franco's black-bladed combat knife stabbing deep into his throat.

Both bodies were pulled into the shadows. Zec pulled up his balaclava and picked up the dead guard's walkie-talkie. 'Something's buzzing,' he said in Italian, the low fidelity of the radio disguising his voice 'The camera might have shorted out. Can you check the system?'

'I'll run a diagnostic. Hold on.'

Zec dropped the walkie-talkie. The computer would spend the next thirty seconds checking the various cameras and alarms around the building, eventually coming to the conclusion that the camera in Hall III was no longer working – unsurprising, since he had shot it.

But while the computer was busy, the security systems would be down.

He keyed the throat-mike. 'Two down. Go.'

Fernandez and Alexander were suspended on lines hanging from the roof on the southern side of a courtyard, waiting for Zec's signal: the instant it came, Fernandez kicked open an upper-floor window – the alarm bypassed in the same way as Zec's entry point – and swung inside, unslinging his gun. Alexander jumped down beside him.

He and his team had reconnoitred the Galleria multiple times over the past month, and he knew exactly where he had entered the building – the upper level of the main stairwell. Right now, another team was also entering on the ground floor.

This part of the mission was a hunt – and a race against time. Find the remaining guards . . . and kill them before they could raise the alarm.

Fernandez knew where two of them would be – the security control room. He and Alexander hurried down the staircase. The position of the remaining two guards was another wildcard, which was why he had chosen entry points that would let his team spread out through the museum as quickly as possible. Speed and surprise were everything – it only took one guard to push a panic button . . .

They reached the ground floor. Fifteen seconds before the cameras came back online. Alexander hared off through a doorway to the main entrance hall. Fernandez, meanwhile, shoved through a door marked *Privato* and threaded his way along a narrow corridor.

Another door. Five seconds left. He raised his gun – and kicked open the door.

The guard seated in front of the security monitors looked round in surprise—

Tchack. Tchack. Tchack. The guard crashed off his chair, arms spasming in reflexive response to the three bullets that had just slammed into his skull, splattering blood across the blank monitor screens.

Shit! Where was the other man?

The diagnostic ended, the monitors coming back to life. He spotted one of his men in the Sale Bizantine, another in the Sale Fiorentine. Where were the guards?

There – in the Salone del Colosso. Alexander would be closest to them—

Both guards fell, thrashing in their silent death throes as a burst from Alexander's silenced MP5K cut them down. Confirmation came through his earpiece: 'Two down.'

Just one man left – but where?

The answer was almost comical in its obviousness. Fernandez rushed out of the control room and headed back up the passage to another door marked WC.

He opened it. A small tiled room, two stalls, one closed . . .

The rapid *tchacks* from the gun were louder in here, echoing in the confined space. The stall's wooden door splintered, a startled gasp coming from behind it – along with clanks of shattering porcelain and the dull thud of lead entering flesh. A trickle of water ran out from beneath the door, pinkish rivulets spreading through it.

Six guards dealt with.

Fernandez hurried back into the museum proper, turning left in the entrance hall and looking down the length of the Galleria del David to see his target at the far end.

Michelangelo's David.

Possibly the most famous sculpture in the world, the Renaissance masterpiece towered above its viewers, over five metres tall even without its pedestal. During the day, illuminated mainly by light coming through the glass dome in the ceiling, the marble statue was a soft off-white, almost blending into the blandly painted walls of the semi-circular chamber in which it stood. But at night, lit at an angle by the security lights and with its surroundings in shadow, the naked figure stood out starkly, appearing almost threatening, a faint sneer of disdain visible on the young future king's lips as he prepared to face Goliath in combat.

To Fernandez, the image seemed appropriate. After all, he was about to become the David who defeated the Goliath of the world's combined law enforcement agencies . . .

You haven't done it yet, he warned himself as he marched towards the statue, passing more of Michelangelo's sculptures along the way. Three of his men were already waiting at David's feet, and he heard footsteps behind – Zec and Franco. The last two team members . . .

Were right where they should be. He looked up at the dome, catching a glimpse of movement outside. Everything was on schedule.

'You know what to do,' he announced as he reached the statue. 'Let's make history.'

'Or *take* history,' said Zec. The two men grinned, then everyone moved into action.

One man ran to a control panel on one wall. It was protected by a locked metal cover, but a moment's effort with a small crowbar took care of that. The others went to the statue itself. Fernandez watched as Alexander and Franco climbed on to the plinth, their heads only coming to David's mid-thigh. They took out coiled straps, wider and much thicker than their own harnesses, and carefully secured them round the statue's legs.

Once they were in place, Alexander took out another coil and, keeping hold of the buckle at one end, tossed it upwards. It arced over the statue's shoulder, dropping down on the other side like a streamer. Another man caught the coil and passed it back between David's legs to Franco, who passed it through the buckle, connected it to the leg strap and pulled it tight. The process was repeated with a second strap over the other shoulder.

Alexander quickly used the straps to scale the stone figure's chest, hanging on with one hand as more straps were thrown to him. Fernandez looked on as part of his plan literally took shape before his eyes. The growing web was much like the harnesses he and his men were wearing, designed to spread out the weight of the body over as great an area as possible when it was lifted.

In the case of David, that weight was over six tons – *plus* the pedestal. But that had been planned for.

The Spaniard gestured to the man at the control panel. He pushed a button. A hydraulic rumble came from the floor.

Very slowly, the statue began to rise.

At considerable expense, the Galleria had recently installed a system to protect David from vibrations, whether in the form of earthquakes, city traffic or even the constant footsteps of visitors. Powerful shock absorbers under the pedestal shielded it from tremors – but also allowed it to be elevated for those rare occasions when the statue had to be moved. At full height, there was just enough space for a forklift's blades to slip beneath the base.

That was all the space Fernandez needed.

Zec and the other man at the statue pushed more straps, thicker still and bearing heavy-duty metal D-rings, under the base. Once that was done, they fastened them over the pedestal, then began to secure the harness to them.

Fernandez took out his phone again, dialling the first number he had called earlier. The answer was heavily obscured by noise. 'We're less than two minutes out – but ATC's raised an alarm about us being off course.'

'We're almost ready,' said Fernandez. 'Just follow the plan.' He disconnected, hearing a knocking sound from the dome. Two figures were now visible outside, one of them giving him a thumbs-up.

Zec rounded the statue. 'All set. I just hope the harness holds.'

'It'll hold,' Fernandez assured him. He raised his voice. 'Move back!' He waved for everyone to clear the area beneath the dome.

The men on the roof had also retreated, one of them pushing a button on a control box—

The explosive charges they had placed around the dome detonated as one.

Glass panels shattered into a billion fragments, the severed steel framework plunging down into the gallery and smashing the marble floor. The horrendous noise echoed through the museum's halls – followed by the piercing shriek of sirens as vibration sensors throughout the building were triggered.

The police would be on their way. But with attention diverted by the forest fire to the east and the car bombings to the south, their response time would be slowed, their numbers reduced.

And Fernandez and his men would be gone.

The Spaniard ran back to the statue, looking up at the gaping hole in the ceiling. The two men who had planted the explosives were already rappelling into the museum as the others quickly cleared wreckage out of the way. Even over the alarms he could hear another sound, a thudding bass pounding getting louder and louder . . .

The breeze blowing in through the hole was magnified a hundredfold as a helicopter surged into view overhead, the beat of its rotor blades shaking the air. The massive aircraft was a Sikorsky S-64 Skycrane, the machine's name revealing its purpose: to lift extremely heavy objects.

Like Michelangelo's David.

Cables dropped from the helicopter, heavy hooks on their ends clanging on the cracked marble. Fernandez and his men each took one line and pulled them across to the statue. Six cables were attached to the D-rings on the base, while Alexander and Franco scaled the pedestal again and hooked their lines to the webbing around the great carved figure itself.

Fernandez moved back beneath the hole and looked up. The Skycrane had been painted dark green to match the livery of the Italian Forest Service's fire-fighting S-64s, its radio transceiver hacked to give air traffic control the identification number of one of the real choppers. But where the Italian aircraft had giant water tanks beneath the long dragonfly spine of their fuselages, this had just a bottomless mockup, thin aluminium sheets concealing a powerful winch.

A wave from Fernandez, and the winch began to draw up the cables.

The men took positions on each side of the statue, hands pressed against the pedestal. The cables pulled tight, the straps creaking as they took the strain. The wind grew stronger, the Skycrane's pilot increasing power. Fernandez looked up at the marble figure, hoping his calculations were right. If the harness didn't protect David from the worst stresses of the lift, this would get very messy . . .

The base shifted, stone rasping against the shock

absorbers beneath. Everyone pushed harder to keep it in a straight line as the cables tightened again. They had to get the sculpture directly under the hole before they could escape. This time, the statue moved, grinding across the floor. The cables scraped against the edge of the ruined dome, glass fragments and pieces of broken masonry raining down.

The Skycrane rose more forcefully, the statue jerking up and swinging half a metre before its base crunched against the floor. Fernandez waved angrily at the winch operator looking down from the helicopter's cockpit. Even minor damage to the statue would affect their payment.

The winchman got the message. The statue lifted again, more gently. Another two metres to go before it was in the clear. The men kept pushing, guiding it. One and a half, one . . .

The base thumped down on the broken floor, grinding glass to powder beneath it. Fernandez saw that the cables were more or less dead centre of the circular hole. 'Hook up!' he shouted.

Everyone attached their harnesses to the hooks. Once they were secure, Fernandez gave another signal to the winchman.

The engine noise rose to a scream as the helicopter climbed.

Another jolt as the statue left the floor, this time not coming back down. Fernandez and his team were lifted with it, gripping the cables for support. The noise and downwash from the Skycrane was horrific, but if everything went to plan they wouldn't have to endure it for long . . .

More power. The statue began to twist in the wind as it rose. Fernandez had expected that, but there was no way to prevent it. All he could do was hope the effect didn't get out of control.

Four metres up, five, the ascent getting faster. The Galleria spun around them – and then they cleared the roof. They were out!

He scanned the city as they continued to climb, the Skycrane lethargically tipping into forward flight and turning northwards. Strobe lights flicked through the streets leading to the museum. The police. Fernandez smiled. They were too late.

There was one police vehicle that concerned him, though. Off to the south, he saw a pattern of pulsing lights in the sky. Another helicopter.

Heading towards them.

As he'd expected, it had been called in to provide aerial support for the cops responding to the car explosions – but the Skycrane's deviation from its course and the alarms at the Galleria dell'Accademia had caused someone to put two and two together and realise that the bombs were, like the forest fire, just a diversion.

The Skycrane picked up speed, Florence rolling past below. Not quickly enough. The police chopper would rapidly catch up with the lumbering Sikorsky – and for the plan to succeed, the next stage had to be carried out without witnesses.

Fernandez looked ahead, eyes narrowed against the blasting wind. The city's northern edge was not far away, twinkling lights abruptly replaced by the blackness of woods and fields as the landscape rose into the hills. No roads; only an aircraft could pursue them.

But he had planned for that. Another member of his team was positioned on a rooftop at the city's periphery, directly beneath the Skycrane's course.

The Sikorsky and its strange cargo swept over the urban boundary. The police chopper was gaining fast. Glaring blue-white light pinned the Skycrane from behind as the other aircraft's spotlight flicked on, playing over the green fuselage before tilting down to turn the suspended statue a dazzling white.

The police helicopter closed in—

And suddenly dropped out of the sky in a sheet of flame, spiralling down to smash explosively into the woods beyond the city.

Fernandez's man on the ground had been armed with a Russian SA-18 anti-aircraft missile, the shoulder-fired weapon homing in on the helicopter's exhaust and detonating over a kilogram of high explosive on impact.

The Spaniard smiled. The Italian air force would now be called in to hunt down the helicopter – which was exactly what he wanted them to do. Because a few minutes from now, he and his men would be putting as much distance between themselves and the Skycrane as possible.

More dark forests below as the Sikorsky descended and slowed. They were nearing their destination: an isolated road winding through the hills. He spotted a red light flashing amongst the trees. The last team member, waiting with the truck.

Treetops thrashed in the helicopter's downdraught as it hovered, the statue swinging pendulously for several worrying moments before settling down. The truck's trailer was directly beneath it – a standard twelve-metre container, with an open top. A metal frame of a very specific shape had been welded to its floor, covered with thick foam padding. Beside the trailer, a large object was hidden beneath a tarpaulin.

'Okay, drop!' yelled Fernandez, pulling out a clip on his harness. His support line uncoiled and dropped away. He quickly rappelled down into the truck, the other men following. The moment their boots hit metal, they detached the lines and stood beneath the statue. Fernandez went to the container's front end, switching on a lamp so the winchman had a clear view of the interior, then joined the others.

The statue's base was about three metres above the container's top, slowly turning. Fernandez signalled for it to be lowered. The winch whined, cables shuddering as the statue descended. The men warily reached up. An agonising moment as the pedestal's corner touched the container's edge, steel bending with a screech, then it slipped inside.

Hands gripped the base, eight men straining in unison to turn David in a particular direction as the great figure continued its steady descent. Fernandez gestured for the winchman to slow. The men pushed harder, the statue still at an angle. Less than half a metre. Another push—

The base lined up with a length of metal pole at the end of the frame. Fernandez waved his hands. The winchman responded – and the statue landed with a bang that shook the entire container.

But the Skycrane's job wasn't done. The container was less than two and a half metres tall, the statue standing high above its top. The men moved to each side of the framework as the Sikorsky slowly moved forwards. The cables pulled tight, dragging the statue after the aircraft – but the bar across the container stopped it.

Like a footballer tripped by a sliding tackle, David began to fall.

In slow motion. The cables and the harness took the strain. Little by little, the giant was lowered towards the waiting frame, each section shaped to support a specific part of the statue's body. Lower. Fernandez held his breath. David's sneer now seemed directed at him personally as the head got closer, daring him to have miscalculated . . .

He hadn't. The statue touched down, the foam compressing, steel creaking – but holding.

'Secure it!' he barked. Three of the men lashed the statue down, the others detaching the cables. Fernandez hurried to the open end of the container and jumped out. The Skycrane increased height slightly and edged sideways, hooks banging on the corrugated metal. Inside the container, the team pulled on ropes hanging over its side – pulling up the tarpaulin so the open roof could be covered.

As the grubby blue tarp moved, it revealed the object lying on the ground.

The sight almost made Fernandez laugh out loud at its sheer audacity, even though he had thought of it in the first place.

A replica of David.

It was crude, only nine-tenths life size, made of fibreglass where strength was needed, chicken wire and papier-mâché and cardboard elsewhere. At close range it looked like a joke, a refugee from a school craft fair. But nobody *would* see it at close range. All they would see was what they had been told to expect: a priceless national treasure suspended from a helicopter.

He and the truck driver secured the hooks to the harness round the duplicate's chest, then Fernandez signalled to the Skycrane. The helicopter's engines shrilled as it increased power, pulling the imitation statue upright, then turning away once its new cargo was clear of the truck.

Fernandez watched the helicopter go. That was the final stage of the plan: the ultimate decoy. The pilot would take the Sikorsky up to ten thousand feet, heading northeast, then lock the controls to put it into a slow but steady descent – and he and the winchman would bail out, parachuting down. When military aircraft intercepted the helicopter, they would be unable to take any action for fear of damaging the statue, leaving them impotently following until it eventually smashed down in the hills some fifty kilometres away . . . by which time the *real* statue would be safely on its way to its new owner, and Fernandez and his team would be better off to the tune of fifty million dollars.

Now, he *did* laugh, unable to hold in his delight any longer. They had done it! He really *was* the greatest thief in history. And with the lion's share of the fifty million going into his bank account, he was more than happy to accept being so anonymously. Interpol had been hunting him and his men since he had accepted the 'commission' over eight months earlier, yet the international police agency was no nearer to catching them now than then. He knew how they worked; how they thought. He would always remain one step ahead.

The tarp roof was secure, the rear doors closed. Still smiling, Fernandez climbed into the cab and signalled the driver to head off into the darkness.

The Hunt for Atlantis

Andy McDermott

A LOST CIVILISATION

The hunt for Atlantis has obsessed many minds. No one knows this better than archaeologist Nina Wilde: it dominated her parents' lives, and now it dominates hers.

A DANGEROUS QUEST

Nina believes she knows where Atlantis is: and when reclusive billionaire Kristian Frost offers her the funding to find it, there's nothing to stop her. With the help of Frost's daughter, Kari, and ex-SAS bodyguard Eddie Chase, the hunt begins . . .

A DEADLY SECRET

But Giovanni Qobras, the leader of the shadowy Brotherhood of Selasphorus, will do all he can to stop them. Nina and her team find themselves in a frantic race across the world to find the lost city before Qobras finds them. For contained within Atlantis is a secret that could destroy civilisation for ever . . .

Hurtling along at breakneck speed, THE HUNT FOR ATLANTIS is the most exciting adventure thriller you will read this year.

Praise for Andy McDermott:

'Adventure stories don't get much more epic than this' *Mirror*

978 0 7553 3912 9

headline

The Tomb of Hercules

Andy McDermott

AN ANCIENT WARRIOR

Studies of an ancient text have convinced archaeologist Nina Wilde that a tomb containing the remains of legendary warrior Hercules may actually exist. If she can locate it, it will be the most important historical find ever to be unearthed.

AN INCREDIBLE TREASURE

As Nina and Eddie Chase, her ex-SAS bodyguard, begin their search it's clear that others want to find the tomb – and the unimaginable riches contained within.

A LETHAL ENEMY

Nina and Chase are soon following a violent trail of corruption and conspiracy around the globe. From Switzerland to Shanghai, Botswana to London, it's a race against time to find the Tomb of Hercules before it falls into the most evil of hands . . .

Praise for THE HUNT FOR ATLANTIS:

'Adventure stories don't get much more epic than this' *Mirror*

978 0 7553 3915 0

headline

The Secret of Excalibur

Andy McDermott

A LEGENDARY WEAPON

Said to make whoever holds it unstoppable in battle, the sword Excalibur has been coveted across the ages, and thought lost for over a thousand years. With a cryptic message to archaeologist Nina Wilde, this may be about to change.

A RUTHLESS ASSASSIN

Historian Bernd Rust believes he can locate Excalibur . . . and that the sword is the key to harnessing an incredible source of energy. Nina is sceptical – until she and Rust are attacked by mercenaries determined to steal his research.

A PERILOUS HUNT

Nina and her boyfriend, ex-SAS soldier Eddie Chase, are soon propelled into a deadly race to find Excalibur. From the deserts of Syria to the arctic wastes of Russia, Nina and Chase must battle a merciless enemy who plans to use the sword's powers to plunge the world into a new era of war . . .

Praise for Andy McDermott:

'A writer of rare cinematic talent' *Daily Express*, Scotland

'Adventure stories don't get much more epic than this' *Mirror*

978 0 7553 4550 2

headline

The Covenant of Genesis

Andy McDermott

AN INCREDIBLE DISCOVERY

Archaeologist Nina Wilde has unearthed an amazing find: evidence of a settlement that existed over a hundred thousand years before any previously known culture. Could an undiscovered civilisation have once ruled the earth?

A MERCILESS FOE

But before Nina can consider her findings her proof is stolen. Nina and her fiancé, Eddie Chase, have been targeted by a clandestine religious group, the Covenant of Genesis, who are determined to suppress all such evidence.

A SHOCKING REVELATION

The Covenant, representatives from three of the world's most powerful religions, will stop at nothing to keep Nina's discovery secret. But why? Could it be that they seek to claim for themselves the most valuable archaeological prize of all time?

Praise for Andy McDermott:

'A writer of rare cinematic talent' *Daily Express*, Scotland